CURSE
of the
FALLEN

Also by H.C. Newell

FALLEN LIGHT

MAIN SERIES

Curse of the Fallen
The Forbidden Realms
Shadows of Nyn'Dira*
A Storm of Sorrows*
The Child of Skye*
Ashes of the Fallen*

ADDITIONAL SHORT STORIES

The Banished
The Broken*
The Brave*

*Forthcoming

H. C. NEWELL

CURSE
of the
FALLEN

THE FIRST NOVEL IN
THE FALLEN LIGHT SERIES

Laeroth
Iziazan
Isles of Erasin
Tildra Wood
Bay of Flames
Black Rock Pass
Northern Nyn'di
Peaks of Draak
Aragoth
Reinwald Gorge
Ivasaar
Sandir
Fru'skogmir
Zaos
Elandor
Brynfa
N

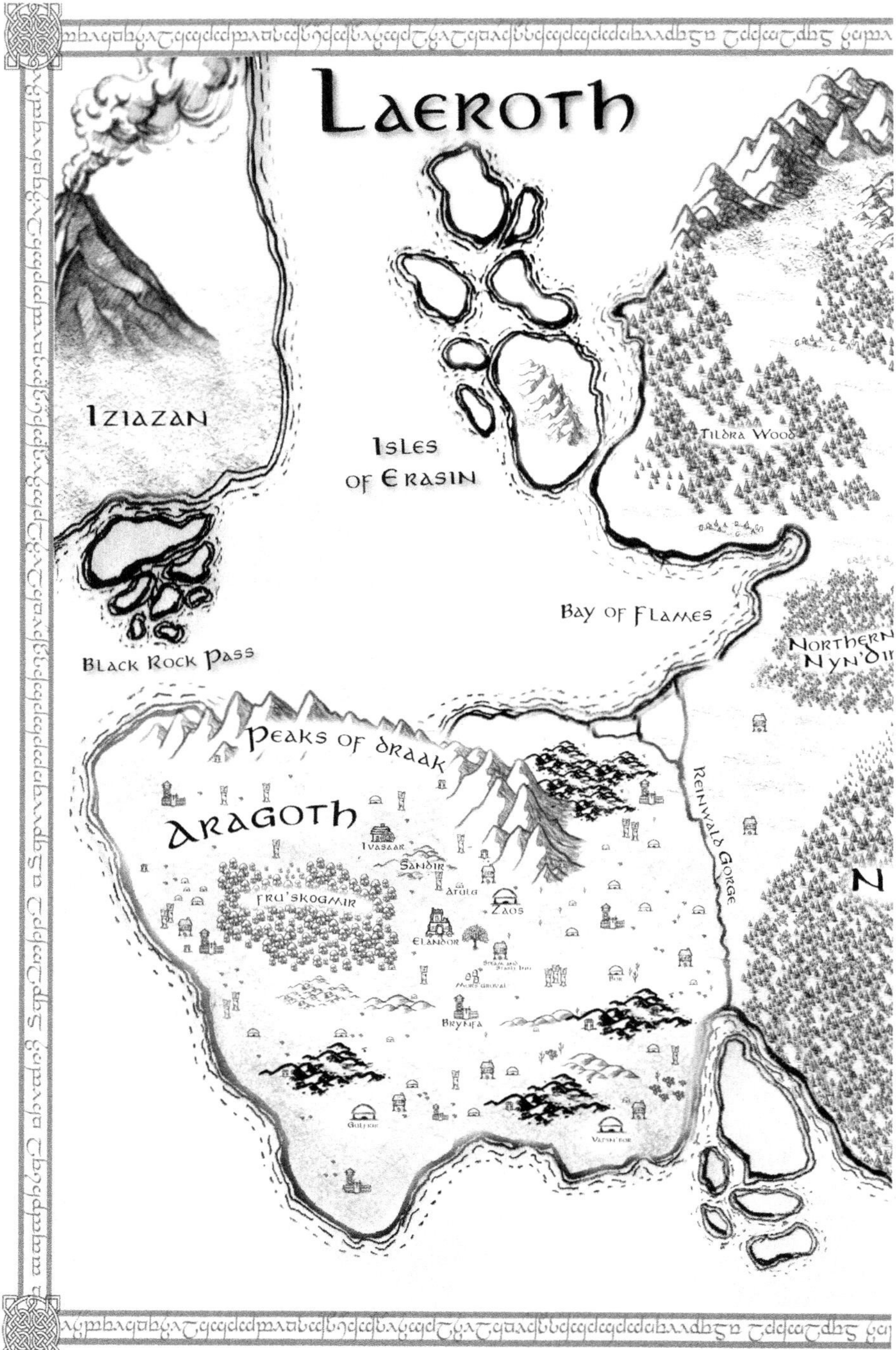

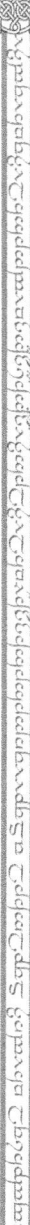

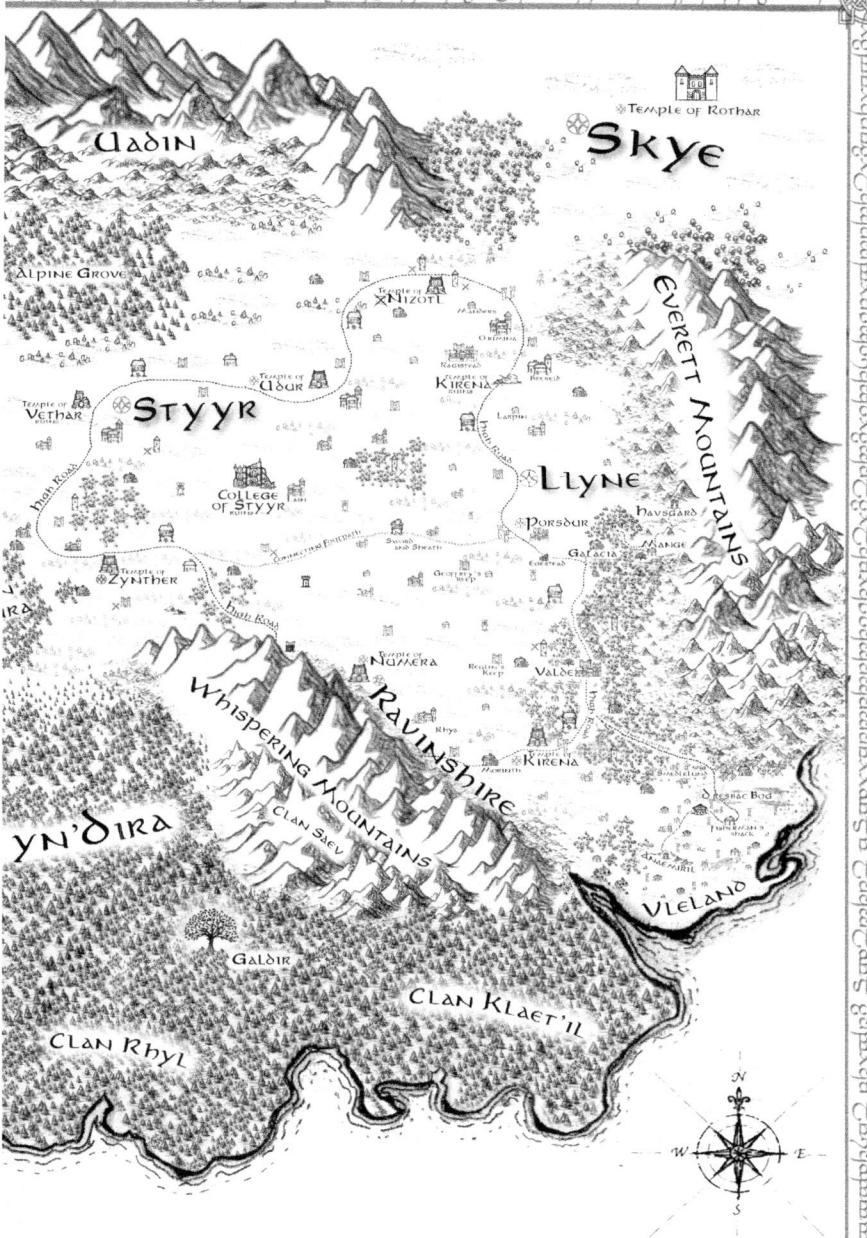

Curse of the Fallen
Copyright © 2022 by H.C. Newell

All rights reserved. Printed in the United States of America. No part of this book may be used or reproduced in any manner whatsoever without written permission except in the case of brief quotations embodied in critical articles or reviews.
This book is a work of fiction. Names, characters, businesses, organizations, places, events and incidents either are the product of the author's imagination or are used fictitiously. Any resemblance to actual persons, living or dead, events, or locales is entirely coincidental.

For information contact:
info@hcnewell.com

Cover Design: Thea Magerand
Map Design: H.C. Newell
Sigil Design: H.C. Newell
Character Art: H.C. Newell
ISBN: 979-8736402403

Second Edition: July 2022
10 9 8 7 6 5 4 3 2

Special Appreciation

To Nikki, for always supporting me.
To Keith, for your obsession with fantasy and reading.
To author Angela Knotts and to Ann, for your help in making the extended edition of this novel even better than I could've imagined.

Dedication

This series is dedicated in its entirety to my husband.

With all my love,
I hope you enjoy *your story*.

Contents

Chapter One	*A Ray of Hope*	1
Chapter Two	*Eye of the Storm*	9
Chapter Three	*Cave of the Ancients*	21
Chapter Four	*In Fate's Hands*	32
Chapter Five	*The Child of Skye*	42
Chapter Six	*Blood and Peace*	48
Chapter Seven	*E'lekgäeh*	55
Chapter Eight	*A fateful Goodbye*	63
Chapter Nine	*Faith in the Unknown*	71
Chapter Ten	*The Letter*	77
Chapter Eleven	*A Journey of no end*	88
Chapter Twelve	*A Fisherman's Tales*	99
Chapter Thirteen	*Wispers and Screams*	107
Chapter Fourteen	*Sword of the Evae*	120
Chapter Fifteen	*Ballads and Bards*	130
Chapter Sixteen	*The Depth of Rage*	142
Chapter Seventeen	*Galacia*	152
Chapter Eighteen	*A Stranger in the Shadows*	160
Chapter Nineteen	*Naik'avel*	169
Chapter Twenty	*The Legends of War*	176
Chapter Twenty-One	*Porsdur*	188
Chapter Twenty-Two	*Echoes of the Past*	198
Chapter Twenty-Three	*Kindness and cruelty*	208

Chapter Twenty-Four	*Pursuit of the Order*	219
Chapter Twenty-Five	*Final Breath*	224
Chapter Twenty-Six	*The Longest Ride*	231
Chapter Twenty-Seven	*Strangers of Mange*	239
Chapter Twenty-Eight	*Purpose and Pain*	247
Chapter Twenty-Nine	*Aerón'dok'fan*	257
Chapter Thirty	*Shadows of Darkness*	263
Chapter Thirty-One	*The Trials of Blood*	275
Chapter Thirty-Two	*Creatures of the deep*	286
Chapter Thirty-Three	*The Futility of Fate*	299
Chapter Thirty-Four	*Reflections of Betrayal*	311
Chapter Thirty-Five	*Reflections of Pain*	320
Chapter Thirty-Six	*Reflections of Regret*	330
Chapter Thirty-Seven	*Reflections of Misery*	337
Chapter Thirty-Eight	*Blood of the First*	349
Chapter One/Epilogue	*Blood and Steel*	

Curse of the Fallen
Pronunciation guide

Broken Order Brotherhood
Nerana (Neer) – NEER-ahna
Loryk (Ebbard) – LORE-ick (EB-BARD)
Gilbrich – Gill-brick
Reiman – RIY-man

Evae
Reiman – RIY-man
Klaud – Cloud
Avelloch – AV-uh-lock
Azae'l – AH-zayl
Nasir – Nah-SEER

Order of Saro
Beinon – BAY-nin; High Priest of the Order of Saro
Nizotl – Nih-ZOL; Divine of Darkness
Numera – New-mare-ah; Divine of Elements

Races
Dreled – DREHL-ed; Theriantrophy halflings
Evae – EE-vay; elves
Nyx – NIX; form of evae who dwell within Vleland
Ahn'clave – ON-CLAVE; dwelled within Anaemiril
Triandal – TREE-ahn-Dahl; race unknown
Klaet'il – klee-uh-TIL; evaesh forest clan
Rhyl – RILL; evaesh forest clan

Curse of the Fallen
Pronunciation guide

Human Territories
Laeroth – LAYR-oth; continent
Llyne – Lin; hold – home to the Broken Order Brotherhood
Porsdur – POHRS-durr; village within Llyne
Valde – VAHL-dee; village within Llyne

Non-Human Territories
Laeroth – LAYR-oth; continent
Vleland – VLEL-and; evaesh territory
Anaemiril – ANN-iy-MEER-ill; ancient cave system
Nhamashel – nah-mah-shell; cave within Anaemiril

Evaesh Words or Phrases
Arun – AH-ROON
Evaesh – Ay-vish
Lanathess – LAHN-ah-THESS
Drimil – DREM-EL
Meena'keen – MEEN-ah-KEEN
Arnemaeus – ARE-nah-MAY-us
Brenavae – BREE-nah-VAY
Travaran – TRAV-are-ahn
Revalor – Rev-ah-lore
Naik'avel – NYE-kah-vell
Haeth'r – HAY-thurr
M'yashk – ME-YASHK
Bael – BAY-ell
Kila – KEY-LAH

The five tenents of the
Order of Saro

1. The Circle of Six must be praised above all else
2. Never dishonor the High Priest
3. Always obey the laws of the Order
4. The impure must be made righteous
5. Magic is the purest form of darkness and those born of its power must be purged

The five tenents of the
Broken Order Brotherhood

1. Abandon your faith in the Circle of Six
2. Never dishonor the Brotherhood
3. Renounce the Order and all its teachings
4. All living beings are born of equality
5. Magic is the purest form of energy and those born of its power shall set us free

"Divine's grace is fleeting and warm. Whosoever challenge it be warned. The love of the Father carries the many. The souls of the wicked be burned aplenty."

- *Prayer to Rothar, overseer of the immortal plane*

CHAPTER ONE

A RAY OF HOPE

"Beware the Child, wicked and torn, who shall carry your soul into the valley of darkness. Seek the Light, O brother, and be cleansed of fury and wrath."
— High Priest Beinon

EBBARD FELL FORWARD WHEN HIS BINDS WERE CUT. Clutching his raw wrists, he crawled to his feet and stepped over a fallen mercenary's body.

"Wonderful," he complained in a trembling voice, "you could've come earlier, y'know?"

His savior pulled down her scarf and stepped into the light, revealing her olive complexion and slender face. Low flickering firelight shone against her bright teal eyes as she looked at the disheveled and beaten man who scolded her.

"Are you hurt?" she asked with a smooth accent indicative of her northern roots. Now she stood hundreds of miles away from her home in the southern reaches of Ravinshire, a region whose outskirts bordered the forbidden and dangerous elvish country of Vleland.

Everyone from here to the furthest reaches of Skye understood that southern Ravinshire was a place meant for the most dangerous of men, or the most foolish of wanderers.

But Ebbard and his savior weren't dangerous, nor were they foolish.

Ebbard tugged on his doublet, proudly straightened his posture, and with forced confidence he said, "I'm just fine, given the near bashed-in skull! What took you so long? I nearly lost my tongue! I'd never sing again!"

"What a shame that would've been," she teased with a smile

H.C. NEWELL

not well hidden.

"Ha. Ha," he mocked. "Get on with it so we can go! I need an apothecary—my 'ead is killin' me!"

She pointed to the door. "Wait there. Gil's coming with herbs and potions."

As Ebbard found himself a chair, the young woman created chaos in the silent night, kicking over empty crates and rummaging through dresser drawers. She wiped her sword clean on her trousers before sheathing the weapon on her belt loop. The dead mercenary's blood stained her clothes as she stepped to his body and dug through his pockets. Parchment crinkled as she retrieved a scroll from his armor.

"Is that it?" Ebbard asked. "All this for a note?"

His savior moved to the fire and quickly read the scribbled parchment. With a deep breath, she crumpled the note into her fist and then tossed it into the flames. The firelight brightened and gave a warm glow to the dark room as the paper burned.

"Was that it?" Ebbard pressed.

She marched away from the hearth and continued her search. "Hardly. That was a bounty. Seems they believe I still have blonde hair and fair skin."

It had been years since she underwent the Change, which permanently altered her appearance to better suit her life of hiding. It was a dangerous procedure that saw most of its patients disfigured or lying in crypts. She was fortunate to have survived with minimal scarring.

"Well, that's a relief," Ebbard said. "What about your eyes?"

Her bright eyes turned to the floor, overcome with anguish. They were unchanged by the procedure and became her most telling feature for those seeking her capture. The door creaked open, and the woman instantly brandished her blade. Her outburst caused Ebbard to nearly fall from his chair. She focused on the door as it gently swung in the breeze, and her gaze shifted to a grey tabby entering the room, its tail whipping through the frosted air.

At the sight of the familiar animal, the woman sheathed her sword with a relieved sigh and then removed a small box and bundle of clothing from her satchel. A warm gust of hot air and

CURSE OF THE FALLEN

bright light quickly filled the dark room where the cat once stood, and she relished in its fleeting warmth. As the light and heat faded, Gil, a pint-sized dreled wearing nothing but his thick body hair, stood in the cat's place.

Gil was a dreled, a shape shifting halfling, able to transform into any animal he saw fit. He often chose the more inconspicuous of creatures, such as a cat, bird, or horse. While the dreleds could transform into great beasts and conquer entire civilizations, they were born with an overabundance of empathy and kindness, leaving them opposed to the ideals of war or greed.

"Gilbrich!" Ebbard sang. "Come to patch me up, 'ave you? Seems Neer 'as got better things to tend to besides the friend who risked 'is life to find 'er little trinket!"

Gil thanked Neer as she passed him his belongings, and he got dressed before pouring herbs into a small mortar. Gil, like all dreleds, stood just three feet tall, was thinly built with defined muscles, and had a raspy soprano voice. Though he was nearly three hundred years old, not a wrinkle creased his smooth skin.

The deep scar along his brow, which he had received many years before during a fight against a Knight of the Order,[°] glowed in the dying firelight. Neer had always admired the scar, as she felt it gave him a fierceness not commonly seen in his kind.

"Toss another'n atop the flames, would ya?" Gil called to Neer. She followed his instructions and stoked the fire while Gil turned to Ebbard. He pulled a wooden crate over and then stood on top of it to bring himself to Ebbard's eye level. "This'll sting a bit," he explained.

Ebbard winced as Gil rubbed paste across his open cuts and swelling bruises. He was held captive for less than an hour's time, but it was enough for the mercenaries to have their fun. Neer was opposed to his idea of being used as bait to lure them into the shack, but he persisted, as he always did, and now saw himself at the wrong end of a bad plan.

---

[*] Taken as infants, by trade or force, the Knights of the Order were genetically modified and brutally trained to be the largest and strongest among humankind. Only males were allowed to join their ranks, and just after acceptance, while still too young to speak, their tongues were sliced from their mouths, forcing them to communicate to only one another through arm and hand gestures.

"Smells terrible!" Ebbard griped.

"It should," Gil said, "'tis a mixture of frog shite and herbs."

Ebbard's eyes widened in shock and disgust. Gil ignored him, wasting no time administering the ointment whose smell grew stronger by the second.

"So, Neer," Gil started, "what'd ya find?"

"The big one had a bounty in his pocket," she explained. "Apparently, I'm worth one hundred gold pieces in any currency."

"Oi!" Ebbard cheered. "That's fifty more than last time!"

"Quiet, you!" Gil smacked his chest. "Keep lookin', lass. The arun must be here somewhere."

"What's with this arun anyway, Neery?" Ebbard asked.

"I've told you a hundred times, Loryk," she started, calling him by his given name, which was a pleasantry only his truest friends were permitted, "I was cursed as a child. If I'm to use my magic"—she grunted while lifting a fallen dresser—"the Order can track my whereabouts."

"So, the arun can lift your curse? Is that why we're lookin' for it?"

"One can hope."

Loryk pondered for a moment. "Why can't you just go on without usin' magic? And why would the Shadow Blades 'ave the arun anyway? They're just mercenaries, after all."

Dust swirled through the room as the dresser dropped back to the floor with a ground-shaking thud. With a sigh, she moved to the bed and tore into the feather mattress with a dagger. "The arun is extremely rare, which makes it even more valuable. And a mage going without their magic is like a delvine[°] breathing out of water. Can they do it? Sure. Is it dreadfully unbearable? Absolutely."

"Them delvine are some fine-looking creatures. 'Ave you seen the paintin's, Gil?" Loryk whistled enthusiastically. "I'd learn to

---

[*] A beautiful, mysterious, and deadly semi-aquatic race that dwell in the waters surrounding the Isles of Erasin.
It is because of their presence that the Isles have been left abandoned and prohibited from visitors. Ghost stories of sinking ships, disappearing islanders, and illnesses that overtook the surrounding lands have engrained within the humans the utmost fear of the dangerous isles to the north.

breathe underwater for them any day!"

Gil scoffed and said, "You're as right to sleep with a delvine as you are that kitchen wench you're always boastin' about!"

"Vaeda was a fine woman!" Loryk argued.

Neer pulled the bed across the floor. "If you have to pay a kitchen wench to lay with you, then you're sure to woo the most beautiful, exotic women to bed," she teased.

"Didn't take much to woo you," he remarked.

She shook her head at his flirting, which she knew was nothing more than a playful tease among friends. While examining the floor, she noticed a thin line against the wooden grain. She pried the wood up with her fingers, only to have it fall back into place. With a frustrated huff, she leaned back and rubbed her face.

"What is it?" Loryk asked.

"A square is cut into the wood. I think it's a hidden door."

"Well, open it!"

"I can't lift it. Each plank is independent."

"Use your dagger, doof."

She rolled her eyes, mostly at herself for not thinking of such an obvious solution, then used the tip of her dagger to carefully lift the planks. With a gasp, she fell back as large spiders raced from beneath the flooring. Loryk leapt atop his chair as the arachnids sprinted across the room to hide in the dark corners.

Neer waited for the creatures to pass, then continued digging into the soil. As her fingers slid across a smooth surface, she dug faster, paying no mind to the scurrying insects or filth beneath her nails. Her heart skipped as she pulled a stone box from its hiding place. She scraped the mud from the lid to reveal foreign symbols engraved along the top.

"This is it...," she whispered. "The arun."

She carefully grasped the lid and took a hesitant breath. Inside the rare and mystical box was energy strong enough to lift her curse. A curse that had followed her since childhood and kept her just within the clutches of the Order of Saro. Once she opened this box, everything would change. All the years of suffering and fear that she had endured would be put to an end. She would no longer have to run or hide or look over her shoulder.

Once she opened this box, she would finally be free.

H.C. NEWELL

With a deep, calming breath, she closed her eyes and removed the lid. Black smoke slowly rose from the arun, followed suddenly by an ear-piercing screech. Gil fell back and landed in the blood of the fallen mercenary. His large, hairy hands covered his ears, and he closed his eyes in agony. Loryk leaned forward atop the chair and gripped his ears while the spiders twitched and shook. Neer, too, gritted her teeth as blood trickled from her ears. She placed the lid into its spot atop the box, and the world fell silent.

The chair creaked beneath Loryk's weight, injecting life back into the quiet room. He gripped the back of the chair and took a shaky breath. "What the 'ells was that?"

Neer explained, her voice hollow and broken, "It's enchanted… I can't obtain the energy inside."

Loryk groaned. "Perfect! This's exactly what we need!"

Gil gripped his forehead in pain. "Quit your whinin'! Let us think for just a second!" he snapped.

Neer clutched the box with a quivering lip, and a single tear glided down her cheek.

"Neer?" Loryk called. He stepped across the room and placed a hand on her shoulder. "It's all right…"

"Four years." She spoke through clenched teeth. "I've been searching for four years. This was my only chance. Nothing else has worked."

"We'll bring this back to Reiman and the scholars. They'll find a way to disenchant it."

She scoffed. Shifting her eyes to the ceiling, another tear fell. She could only imagine the disapproval her father, Reiman, would have at knowing she failed again. To know that she had found what she searched so long to find but wasn't wise or strong enough to understand its power. He warned her about the dangers of this journey and the arun, but she ignored him as she always did.

Her thoughts vanished as Loryk gently wiped her tears away and pulled her into his arms.

Gil stood at the window on his toes and peered over the windowsill. "We've got a problem," he warned.

Loryk rubbed Neer's shoulder. "You all right?" he asked.

CURSE OF THE FALLEN

She nodded with a sniff, and together they stepped to the window. They peered outside to find the village was empty, quiet, and calm. Neer squinted her eyes, hoping to spot what Gil had warned them about, when suddenly, a shadowy figure flew past. Loryk leapt back with a gasp, while the others remained calm.

"Seems that screamin' bit were just an alarm," Gil explained. "It called upon a marq."

"A marq?" Loryk asked with a slight quiver to his voice. "Those aren't real..."

"They're real. Wispy little enchantments, they are. Hard buggers to dispel."

The small cabin shook and splintered as the black smoke enchantment enshrouded the cabin and crept into the cracks along the walls.

"Only magic can destroy a marq," Neer explained.

"Then use it!" Loryk pleaded.

"I'm not strong enough to defeat it! Do you want the entire army at our doorstep once the fight's over? You know the Order can track my magic!"

"Divines..."

"Stop your belly achin'! You're worse than me wife after a long day o' sittin' on her arse!" Gil added.

"I'd gladly trade places with 'er!" Loryk argued. "Neer, what are we goin' to do?"

"I don't know!" she said.

"You've got to teleport us out of here," Gil demanded.

"What? I can't! Teleportation could rip us to pieces!"

"Yeah," Loryk added, "plus they'll follow us right to Llyne. Know exactly where we 'ide out!"

"Better to be followed than dead," Gil said.

"They're one and the same!" Neer argued.

Another jolt violently shook the crumbling cabin, and the group huddled together. The roof collapsed, and wooden planks buckled beneath their feet as the smoke thickened.

"Neer, we've got to flee! If we breathe this in, we're as good as dead," Gil shouted.

"I can't," she argued.

"Do it now!"

H.C. NEWELL

Lightning flashed and winds howled as the dark smoke of the marq seeped further inside. With the arun tucked safely into her leather pack, Neer took Loryk and Gil's hands and gripped them tightly. She closed her eyes, struggling to focus on her magic as the weight of such stress and panic broke her concentration. The stinging warmth of her energy would strengthen in her chest, only to vanish again with another lurch of the walls.

Gil coughed as smoke crawled across the floor. Wrinkles formed along Neer's face as she closed her eyes tighter. Magic surged through her, forming beads of sweat across her temple. A soft glow formed around her, enveloping the trio in warmth, and they disappeared.

Chapter Two

Eye of the Storm

"Let the blood of the unworthy be washed by the Six, for no creature impure shall ascend to Arcae and be marked as an angel of the blessed."

– Rotharion, the Book of Light

RAIN FELL HEAVILY FROM THE dreary morning sky, dripping from the leaves in a small clump of trees. Enormous glowing mushrooms clung to the trunks while shallow puddles formed in the thick grass. Thunder disturbed the quiet morning as it rumbled across the sky.

A wailing shriek jolted Neer into consciousness, and she opened her eyes with a frightened gasp. The sound penetrated her mind before slowly fading into the sound of drizzling rain. Darkness pulled the edges of her vision as she attempted to push herself up but found she was tethered to the ground beneath thick vines.

Her heart skipped as she fought against the vegetation that had coiled around her limbs and slithered across her back. With a hard push, she escaped her binds and crawled to her feet.

Standing in a shallow forest of dead, vine covered trees, she wondered where she was. Her home region of Llyne was to the east of the cabin they fled, and it was there that she wanted her magic to take her. But she was untrained in teleportation, making it unpredictable and dangerous.

She looked over her skin and clothes, checking that her belongings had arrived with her and the magic hadn't left any injuries. Never had she attempted to transport so far, nor had she ever used it on anyone but herself.

Glancing through the trees, she wiped the rain from her eyes to better view her surroundings and found she was alone. Dread washed her of her color as she stepped wearily forward, fearing the worst.

"L... Loryk!" she called, though her voice was weak. With a deep breath, she forced a shout, and the ache in her throat caused her to cough and wheeze. Stumbling back, she leaned against a tree and clutched her chest. Deep breaths escaped her lungs as she fell into a state of misery and panic. They could be anywhere—in Llyne, at the mercenary cabin with the marq, here in the marsh...

Her thoughts sank into despair as she stared at the ground, consumed with grief. Shaking her head to push away the pain, she set her eyes to the shallow woods surrounding her. Sadness wouldn't find them; it wouldn't bring them back.

The magic once filling her was depleted, and she knew with such weakness she'd never make it back to the cabin or to her home of Llyne, where she hoped Loryk and Gil would be. She was lucky to have survived the transportation at all, and she understood that weak magic could be more dangerous than untrained. Should she attempt to teleport, even several yards ahead, she could find herself lying in several bloody pieces across the ground.

"Loryk!" she screamed again, this time with more urgency. "Gilbrich!"

Rain pattered against her skin as she walked to the edge of the tree line and overlooked a canvas of green. The steady downpour blanketed rolling foothills in a constant haze of mist, and she knew she wasn't in Llyne. The landscape was too moist, and the hillsides were too green for the rocky foothills she called home.

She stepped out into the storm and trudged across the murky soil. Mud splashed across her boots as she headed further into the mysterious land, searching for the friends she feared she might never see again.

Still weakened from her teleportation, she leaned against a stone pillar and took several deep breaths. Magic, as she learned in her years of study, was an expression of energy, and any exertion would lead to depletion. The more one trained and strengthened their magic, the more powerful and adept they would become. Neer had never trained with her magic, as doing so would call upon the Order of Saro. But throughout her life, she attained a few spells from accidental incidents.

Her first teleportation was made at just five years old when a knight bolstering the sigil of the Order came for her. In her panic, she closed her eyes and thought of her home. When she reopened them, she found herself there, lying in a confused daze on her bed. Her mother said she was comatose for two days before waking and claimed that her weakness in magic depleted her energy enough to nearly kill her.

Healing was realized at age seven when she found a wounded frog lying by the road after some children had broken its legs for fun. It was her first taste of true anger and sorrow. She conjured all the energy she could muster and pushed it into the small, helpless creature. Its health was replenished, and hers was drained as she gifted the animal with her own energy and life force. Days later, when she skinned her knee, she attempted to heal herself but found the magic only worked if she gifted it to others.

Thunder broke her thoughts, and she glanced through the fog, searching for the others.

"Loryk!" Her voice was drowned by the downpour overtaking the empty land. "Gil!"

She crossed her arms to fight the chill overcoming her and marched through the fog before coming to a narrow river. The gentle current carved through a sloped hill with dead trees and broken trunks outlining the banks.

Moving upstream, she spotted two figures through the mist. They were perched within the grass and slumped against one another in a way one would be in exhaustion or injury. Her heart skipped when Loryk's curly hair came into view, and she sprinted to his side.

"Neer!" he cried. "You're alive!"

Her eyes moved to his body and clothes before she turned to Gil and inhaled a horrified gasp. Thick crimson matted his clothes where his left arm hung by strands of muscle and flesh.

"Gods!" she exclaimed while kneeling at his side. Her hands trembled as they hovered over his opened and bleeding arm. "Gil!" she called, "can you hear me?"

Soft whimpers seeped through his parted lips. Tears swelled in Neer's eyes as she gazed at his injured shoulder, which she knew had been sliced by the teleportation. Her throat tightened as she choked back her emotions and gently touched his arm. Gil unleashed a shriek that echoed over the rainfall, and Neer fell back with a gasp, splashing against the ground.

"Gil!" Loryk called before catching Gil as he fell aside.

Neer shook her head, unable to think beneath the pressure of her guilt and fear. The wound was too deep, her magic too weak. She couldn't save him. He'd bleed out within the hour, and it would be her fault.

She wiped her nose with her wet sleeve and clenched her jaw. Crawling to his side, she took several deep breaths and mustered the courage to heal him. "You're going to be fine!" she exclaimed, though she was convincing herself more than him. "I won't let you die!"

Loryk held Gil tighter as Neer lifted his arm. His body shook, and he unleashed a deep, raw scream. "Hold him!" she demanded as he pulled away. She placed the bones together, closed her eyes, and allowed the hot sting of magic to rip through her as she expelled her energy into him. Magic tore through her, making every breath raw and painful. She grunted through clenched teeth, her body shriveled and ached, but she wouldn't stop until he was healed, even if it meant sacrificing herself.

Gil's loud yelps of pain faded into soft cries and grunts as his muscles fused and his arm was pulled back into place.

"Neer!" Loryk called as she was consumed by her magic. Her olive complexion had faded to light grey while her muscles and skin had shriveled. Deep circles surrounded her dull, half-opened eyes.

The open wound wrapping Gil's arm slowly sealed into a thick scar, and Loryk commanded, "Neer! That's enough!"

Her eyes rolled back, and with a panicked grunt Loryk released Gil to catch Neer as she collapsed forward, weak and barely breathing.

CURSE OF THE FALLEN

Loryk hastily reached into her pack and rummaged through her things. When he found the potion he had been searching for, he quickly popped the cork and placed the vial to her lips. "Drink it!" he ordered, pouring the liquid into her mouth. As it ran dry, he tossed it aside. His thin arms were strong as he held her close and watched the color slowly return to her skin.

The heavy downpour became a light drizzle as Loryk sat alone. Sunlight descended across the horizon, marking nearly an hour's time since Neer had found them.

As Gil softly shuffled from behind, Loryk turned back and watched the dreled sit up, twisting his neck and shoulder.

"Oi," Loryk exclaimed, "You all right there, Gil?"

Gil placed his hand on his forehead and groaned. "I should've turned into a raven and fled. Let you two make the jump yourselves."

Loryk huffed in offense. "She's lyin' 'ere, weak from savin' you! Show some respect."

"Aye...," Gil agreed with a sigh. "But had she not expended such energy, neither of us would be lyin' here at all, now, would we?"

Loryk turned to Neer, who remained motionless in his arms. The fullness had returned to her shriveled face and limbs. "We should've never gone to that mercenary camp," he griped. "Why can't she just live without it? Magic's good for nothin' any'ow. Always causes trouble."

"Quit your belly achin'," Gil said, though it was with less anger than he usually gave. "We're here now. Best to gather what we can and try to find our way home."

"Which way *is* 'ome?"

They glanced through the murky hillsides, and then Gil stood with his hands on his hips, looking around. "Best if I have another vantage point. You going to protect her while I'm gone, lad?"

Loryk sneered and waved an arm in dismissal. "Just get on, you!"

Swirling light engulfed the dreled as he transformed into a falcon and soared from the fading luminance of his magic. Gil disappeared into the mist, and Loryk pulled his dagger from its sheath on his belt. "Don't worry, Neery. We'll get out of 'ere just fine." He glanced at Neer and then returned his gaze to the hillsides.

He sat quietly for what felt like an eternity, the rain shifting from east to west as the sun crept closer to the horizon.

Soon, Neer began to shuffle, and with a slight groan she pushed herself up, clutching her chest as she coughed and wheezed. With a deep inhale, she sat straighter and peered through the mist with tired eyes.

"Neer!" Loryk exclaimed. "Thank the Divines! I thought I'd 'ave to carry you out of 'ere myself!"

"Loryk?" She glanced around in confusion. "Why are we still here? Where is Gil?"

"'E's off lookin' for some place to 'ide! 'Aven't seen 'im in ages."

She groaned while clutching her forehead. "Damn it." Forcing herself to stand, she grabbed Loryk's hand and pulled him to his feet. "Come on. We've got to move."

"What? But Gil—"

"Gil can find us. We can't stay here."

Knowing he'd argue, and feeling too frustrated to care, she walked north, hoping it would lead her to civilization. Her footsteps were clumsy as she slowly woke from her slumber.

"Where're you goin'?" Loryk asked as he caught up to her.

"North."

"What's north?"

Neer stopped and made an inarticulate gesture with her arms. "Look around you, Loryk. *Think*. What other place around southern Ravinshire would have constant rainfall, murky soil, and be devoid of any roads or villages or life?" She watched him for a moment as he placed a finger to his lip in deep thought. When his eyes widened with fear, she gave him a knowing look and continued onward toward Llyne. "We're in Vleland," she said, furthering his look of terror. "If we don't find shelter soon, something else will find *us*."

Humans were banned from all elven territory, and Vleland was home to the nyx, a dangerous race of elves who hunted and fed on the living. The vicious natives would have no trouble giving them a slow and painful death should they be found wandering these lands.

Mist shrouded the rolling hills, and Neer was fearful of what might be lurking in the distance. Her eyes shifted to the sky as thunder rumbled and a strike of lightning jolted the air.

She turned to the east when the flash caught her eye, and she came to a sudden stop.

Loryk, who had been caught in his own petrified ramblings, didn't take notice of her as he walked ahead in his nervousness.

"Those're just tales, Neer!" he said of the nyx. "We can't—"

She quickly stepped forward and covered his mouth while peering through the fog. He was instantly silent as glowing red spots emerged in the distance, and blue felines with red spots and seven long tails came into view. Their long claws sank deep into the soil with every slow step, and Loryk whimpered at the sound of their fiendish snarls.

Neer released her grip on his mouth and pulled her sword from its sheath.

"What the 'ells are those?" Loryk asked, his voice wavering with terror.

"Dren," Neer responded, "they're attracted to blood."

His eyes shifted to her clothes, which were stained in red.

The dren stepped closer, and Neer watched as they circled around. Dren were creatures from ghost stories and legends that were said to stalk their prey before ripping it apart. She never believed the rumors and was haunted by their sudden presence as one crept forward, staring hungrily at Loryk.

"Neer," he whined, "do somethin'!"

Her fingers wrapped tightly around the hilt of her sword as she took a step closer, eying the crouching dren. The creature, with its muscular legs and strong shoulders, slowly turned to her. A deep growl sawed through the air, and its thick paws sank into the sodden grass.

Loryk shuddered, and the dren whipped its head back in his direction. He stumbled back in fear, and the ferocious animal pounced.

Neer lifted her hand, expelling a powerful blast of energy that knocked the dren aside. The animal growled as it tumbled across the wet grass.

As the other felines ran closer, Neer pushed them back with another pulse of invisible energy. A smaller dren leapt forward with its razor-sharp claws aimed at her throat. As it fell closer, Neer sliced her sword deep into its neck. Hot blue blood spilled across her face, and the animal fell from the air, twitching at her feet.

"Neer!" Loryk shouted, and she turned to find the long claws of another dren reaching out for her. As it struck her arm, she sank her sword deep into its side, releasing a pained cry.

She fell to the ground with a grunt and kicked the animal away. Heavy rain soaked into her skin as blood poured from her open wound. The pain was intense, but she couldn't lose focus. Her bright eyes locked onto the four remaining creatures stalking closer.

Thunder shook the ground while lightning flashed across the clouded sky. Neer struggled to hold her stance against the strong winds and heavy rain. Water fell into her eyes, making it difficult to focus on the creatures surrounding her.

With a glance at the oncoming hoard, Neer dropped her sword and lifted her hands in a defensive posture. Beads of sweat formed along her forehead as warm energy filled her chest. As a dren pounced forward, its sharp claws swiping for her chest, she gripped the animal's throats with her magic and squeezed.

She slowly curled her fingers into half fists and the dren fell to the ground, gasping. Mud and grass flung through the air as their strong legs scratched desperately into the soil. Fighting to control her magic, she closed her fists. The crunching of bones filled the air as the dren released their wheezing last breaths. Once the last dren fell, Neer released her hold.

She collapsed to her knees as the weight of magic was lifted from her chest, every deep breath tearing at her aching throat. Bright eyes surveyed the felines lying before her. Blue blood dripped from their opened mouths, and their glowing spots dulled against their lifeless bodies.

Loryk stood nearby, watching as more creatures approached. Neer surveyed the fog and breathed heavily from exhaustion. Along the hillside, she noticed the glowing spots of a dren moving

CURSE OF THE FALLEN

carefully toward Loryk. Before she had the time to react, the creature leapt from beyond the hillside and pummeled him to the ground. He released an agonizing shriek as blood poured from the fresh slash marks across his back.

Neer teleported to the dren and sank her sword deep into its spine. She weakly kicked it aside and stepped to Loryk's aid.

He gasped as she placed her hands on his back, ready to heal his injuries, when hard footsteps splashed nearby. Neer turned with her sword drawn before looking into the familiar hazel eyes of the creature behind. With a relieved sigh, she lowered her weapon, knowing it wasn't a dren that stood before her, but was Gil, who had taken the feline's form.

When more dren appeared, Neer helped Loryk climb onto Gil's back and then settled behind him as they raced away.

The dren quickly followed and struck their tails at the group. Neer desperately pushed them back with a weak blast of energy, and they tumbled down the hill. Her eyes began to cross, and her body was frail as she used her magic far beyond its extent.

"They're going to catch us!" she warned. "What are we going to do?"

Gil ran further from the stampede, crossing over the river and through cemeteries of half-sunken tombstones. The dren were close as he ran further and then leapt into a small cave. His small body tumbled across wet stone as he transformed midleap back into his natural self. Neer and Loryk crashed to the ground, aching from the rough landing.

"Gil?" Neer asked with a groan, surprised by his sudden change.

His feet pattered against the stone as he stood. "Wasn't me, lass... Must be somethin' guardin' this here cave."

Slimy plants and fungi slipped beneath Neer's fingers as she crawled to her knees. Blood drained from a deep slash on her shoulder, saturating the moisture beneath her palms in red. Water dripped from the tall ceiling and pattered against the damp stone ground. Stalagmites and stalactites, covered in orange glowing algae, towered throughout the long, dark corridors.

The angry hissing of the dren echoed from the cave entrance where four felines paced with furious snarls. Neer turned to them with her sword in hand. A large dren, with defined muscles and longer fangs than its companions, crouched in the wet grass. With its hungry eyes on Neer, it pounced into the cave, ready to feast.

Neer held out her weapon, and as the dren leapt through the cave entrance, it faded instantly to ash. She staggered back, perplexed by what she saw. Glancing at the entrance, she noticed the iridescent shimmer of a magical barrier protecting the cavern.

Her thoughts broke at the sound of Loryk's whimpered cry. She rushed to his side and pulled back his torn clothing to reveal a deep gash across his back. He released a loud yelp as she pressed her hands on his skin, expelling her energy into his injuries. His thick blood seeped through her fingers and mixed with the shallow water lining the cave floor.

The edges of his wounds slowly melded together, though not enough to be healed completely, before Neer fell to the ground, heaving. Her skin had gone pale and light-blue veins displayed around her sunken eyes and cheeks. The wound on her shoulder grew larger as her skin began to shrivel.

Gil felt her forehead and snapped his fingers. The sound jolted her awake, but only for a moment. She couldn't focus her rolling eyes on anything. Gil carefully took her arm and guided her across the cave, where she slumped against the wall.

He passed her a canteen. "Slow now," he warned as she drank too quickly, "it's only water. Nothing but time will regain your strength."

Loryk coughed and wheezed as he pushed himself up on shaky arms. Muddy water dripped from his hair as he struggled to catch his breath. The half-healed injuries on his back ached and bled. "What 'appened?" he asked. "Where are we?"

"Careful," Gil urged, "take a seat over here, lad."

Loryk crawled to Neer and sat next to her against the cold wall. His face twisted as he winced and repositioned himself to alleviate the pressure on his wounded back.

"How're you feelin'?" Gil asked.

"Better. What 'appened to 'er?"

"Are you daft, boy? She healed you. Just about killed herself to save your arse!"

CURSE OF THE FALLEN

"What?" He leaned over and looked into her half-opened eyes. "Oh, Neery. Why'd you go an' do somethin' so stupid?"

Her shaky arm struggled to make its way to his face before she took a sharp breath and smacked his cheek. The loud crack echoed through the deep cave.

"What the 'ells!" he exclaimed while clutching his red face. "What was that for!" He turned to Gil, desperate for an answer.

"I reckon she don't like her wits bein' brought into question."

"Well, if she didn't make such unwise decisions, then I wouldn't 'ave to bring 'er wit into question, now would I?"

"Mind your tongue, bard. She just saved your skin."

"Right," he sighed. "Thanks, Neery. I owe you one."

She took a deep breath and softly uttered, "Two."

He laughed through his nose. "So, Gil, where are we any'ow?" he asked.

Gil stepped near the cave entrance and picked up the arun that had fallen from Neer's pack. His stubby fingers wiped the heavy stone object clean, before he tucked it safely back into the bag. "This is Anaemiril," he explained, "the ancient home of the ahn'clave."

"The ahn'clave? I thought they were just legend and myth."

"They were real, child. Very real and very dangerous."

"Great," Loryk griped. "Now what're we to do?"

"We ride out the storm and then break for Llyne at first light. The missus'll have my head if I'm not home come morn."

He peeked outside to find the dark and dreary world had become darker as the sun faded beyond the hillside. Trees blew aside as winds picked up speed, and when lightning struck in the overcast sky, thunder shook the cave.

"Never thought we'd wind up 'ere, did you?" Loryk asked as Gil paced the entrance. "I just 'ope we can make it 'ome. Vleland isn't a place for our kind. If the nyx find us in 'ere, we'll be—"

"Quiet, lad," Gil said with heavy exhaustion. "There's no sense in trudgin' up worries at a time like this. We're alive. Let that be enough for now."

Loryk exhaled a sorrowful sigh. "Yeah, but for 'ow long? I've been runnin' around with Neer for almost a decade now. We never used to care about what trouble we'd get into... but, now...

it feels different. Like we're losin' 'er."

Gil placed his hands on his hips and slowly nodded. "Times are truly changin'. The Order's knockin' on our back door while our only chance of survival is lyin' like a fawn fresh out of the womb."

Loryk ran his fingers through his hair. "She never wanted this, y'know? The magic and responsibility. Just usin' what little she did today just about killed 'er... 'Ow can she ever defeat the Order? Why is it 'er that 'as to do this? She should 'ave a choice in it!"

"We've all got a choice, Ebbard."

"Not Neer! If we don't use 'er magic to take down the Order, we'll never be free from their reign! The 'Igh Priest is too powerful! 'E's got too many enchantments protectin' 'im. It 'as to be 'er... There isn't a choice."

Gil dropped his head. "Some of us are given far worse fates than others. Neer hasn't had an easy life, to be sure, but she's still alive. She's still fightin'. So long as there is breath in her lungs and strength in her bones, we'll fight too."

Loryk nodded, and the conversation fell silent. Lightning flashed through the entrance, brightening the cave. He looked around, examining the walls of their shelter.

"You said the ahn'clave lived 'ere, yeah?" he started. "There must be a way inside, then. Surely, they didn't 'ole up in this small section, watchin' the winds blow rain around."

Gil shook his head. "There's no chance of enterin' the forbidden tombs, lad. We'd wind up dead or worse."

Loryk's face twisted before he glanced at Neer, who was lying unconscious at his side. "What're we to do then?"

"What else, boy?" Stepping over rocks and slippery moss, Gil made his way to Neer, and rested beside her with closed eyes. "We wait."

Chapter Three

Cave of the Ancients

'Saliik nrün 'for vahteil ahn 'clave.'
The blood of the First holds the key.

— First Blood prophecy

NEER SLOWLY WOKE FROM A long and restless sleep. With a tired stretch, she felt the restraint of bandages wrapping her injured shoulder. A stain of light red peeked through the linen where her wound had bled through. She leaned forward with a groan and rubbed her face. Peering at her surroundings, she noticed they were still tucked within the small cave.

Loryk and Gil rested nearby, sleeping soundly with heavy snores that shook the air. Her shoulder ached as she stood and stepped over slippery rocks toward the entry. Outside, the storm raged with rain and lightning. With such an overcast, she couldn't be sure if it was morning or night, though it didn't matter. Until the sun peeked through the clouds in this dreary marshland, they'd be stuck inside the cave. Vleland was too dangerous a place to travel in the shadow of darkness. Even the smallest glimmer of sunlight was the difference between life and death.

Backing away from the entrance, she scanned the damp cavern. Glowing algae clung to the walls, casting a light hue that brightened the cramped space.

She walked back to the others, and a whispered voice cut through the silence, sending chills down her spine as it called, *"Nerana..."*

She turned sharply, her eyes shifting from one direction to the next, never finding its source. Shallow water sloshed beneath her feet as she took a step forward.

"Hello?" she called, her fingers aching as she clutched the hilt of her sword. "Who's there?"

Loryk sniffed as he was awoken by her voice. She turned quickly with her sword drawn, and he leapt from his slumber. "What're you doin'?" he remarked. "'Ave you lost your mind?"

She stepped back and looked around. "Something's here. It spoke to me."

He groaned while climbing to his feet. "This is Anaemiril, Neer. There's magic all around us."

"This was different." She sheathed her sword and stepped to the walls. Her eyes scanned the stone as she hurriedly swiped her hand across the damp, rocky surface.

"What're you doin'?" He ran his fingers through his hair. "God's body, Neer!" With a kick to Gil, he woke the sleeping dreled. "Wake up, you! Neer's gone mad!"

Gil sat up with an exasperated groan. "You ought to know not to wake a man in such a way, boy! I'd be pressed to skin your hide if I weren't so damned exhausted!"

"Look!" Loryk pointed at Neer as she continued searching the walls.

"What in the..." Gil stood and carefully made his way to her side. "What's gotten into you, lass? Why don't you just calm down?"

He reached for her arm, and she pulled away. "Something is here," she remarked. "It's—"

Her words were interrupted by her sudden gasp as she dipped her hand beneath the solid stone. Cold air swirled around her fingers that hovered within the wall. She turned to the others with wide eyes.

"Whoa!" Loryk called. "Did you just... 'Ow did you—"

"It's a mirage," Gil said in a hushed tone of surprise and fear. "I've heard about it in lore but never thought it to be true."

Loryk said, "Well, let's go inside!"

Gil gripped tight to Loryk's trousers and pulled him back with a heave. "You've got a wrong mind if you think I'm going in there

CURSE OF THE FALLEN

while this'n's acting all out of sorts!"

"I'm fine," Neer explained. "And my *mind* is fine." She shot a quick glare to Loryk. "Something spoke to me. It called my name."

"Neer," Gil said, taking her hand and tapping her fingers. "We can't enter these caves. They're too dangerous a place for the likes of us."

"I'm a sorceress. What if—"

"No. We stay out here, and we wait. Then we head home."

She turned back to the mirage where a strong sense of magic beckoned her forward. Shaking her head, she marched across the cave and dug through her belongings for the arun, carefully touching the inscriptions along its top.

"The aruns are too dangerous and mysterious for normal scholars to understand." She turned back to the others. "It isn't a coincidence that we wound up here—in a cave of the ancients! Everyone knows the ahn'clave were magic users! This was their home! Something is calling me inside, and I think it can lead me to the answers. Fate has brought us here. I know it."

Loryk groaned while shaking his head. Fate was something he wasn't too keen to believe, as it was reserved mostly for those who followed the Six,[*] and with his deep hatred for the all-powerful beings also came his refusal to believe in anything that could be of their will or judgement.

Neer wasn't a strong believer in the Divines, either. At least, not in the way the Order had forced the population to be. She understood there were Divines who oversaw the world, but their will and judgement was their own. The Order was just a roadblock to their truth and power.

Fate, on the other hand, was something entirely different. She had seen it in action and understood that, although it couldn't be proven, fate was real, and she would follow it despite the resistance of others.

Her eyes shifted to Gil as he stepped to her side. "Are you sure about this, lass?" he asked.

---

[*] The Circle of Six, or Six, is the collective name for the Divines of the Order of Saro.

23

H.C. NEWELL

She met his gaze, thankful that he, at least, believed in fate too. "I'm sure."

He nodded and then backed away. With a gesture to the mirage, he said with great reluctance, "Then... lead the way."

She tucked the arun safely into her leather pack and stood with Gil and Loryk at the wall. Glancing at them for reassurance, she held her breath and hesitantly stepped inside. Glowing yellow stones lined the walls in swirling patterns that lit the narrow corridors. With a deep inhale, she was surprised to find the faint smell of fresh roses lingering in the air.

Bitter cold filled the damp space as the trio walked silently down the long corridor. Through the empty hall, they came to a large doorway nestled within the stone. Stepping through the arched entrance, they approached another, deeper cavern. Hundreds of tall glowing crystals stood throughout the cave, leaving a soft luminance that brightened the cavern. A large Tree,[*] with thick branches and glowing pastel flowers, stood in the center of the room. Small streams carved through the stone and glowed bright blue as the water crashed over stones and roots.

To the right was an enormous column made entirely of stalactites. Rainwater dripped from the narrow opening in the ceiling and filled the natural moat surrounding the pillar.

Neer and the others stared in wonder as they came to a lonesome doorway across the cavern. The pathway inside was alight with glowing stones along the walls. They passed by several doors and attempted to enter but found each of them were locked.

Gil came to a stop, and Loryk's voice echoed through the empty corridors when he tripped over him. The pint-sized man turned back with a disgruntled and frightening glare.

"Oi, that was on you!" Loryk exclaimed, and Gil turned away with a huff.

The trio stood together at the intersection of several corridors. "Is this... a neighbor'ood?" Loryk asked.

---

[*] Tree is a term used for the large, glowing trees that are found throughout the continent of Laeroth.
The origin of the Trees are unknown, though they are believed to hold powerful magical energy, and even in the harshest of climates, they never lose their glowing flowers or leaves.

CURSE OF THE FALLEN

"This looks safe enough. Seems whatever called you forward knew we'd need a place to rest," Gil stated. "There should be rooms somewhere around here."

"'Ow d'you know so much about this place, Gilly?"

"I've told you near a hundred times!" Gil said before turning around and kicking Loryk, who gripped his shin with a loud cry. "Call me Gilly one more time, boy, and I'll be knockin' on somethin' a little higher up your legs, you hear me?"

"Yes, sir..."

Gil huffed. "I've been alive near three hundred years. Learned much about the ahn'clave and their caverns from the scholars."

"Didn't they vanish a long time ago?" Loryk asked, his voice gruff with pain.

"Do you see any of them around, boy?"

Loryk turned to Neer when she chuckled. "Think this is funny, do you?" he asked angrily.

Neer shrugged with a grin and then turned to Gil. "Being alive for three centuries doesn't mean you'd be a master navigator of these forbidden caves, Gil," she said.

"No," he said, "but I'm sure there are unlocked rooms around here somewhere."

Loryk said, "Are you sure we should be stayin' 'ere, Gil? This place gives me the creeps."

"Scared, Ebbard?" Neer teased.

"You're damned right I am! This place's magic, Neer. We could be led straight into a trap!"

"Best if you wait outside, then, yeah? Keep watch for us." With a sly smile, she stepped forward and wandered down the hall.

Loryk gripped his forehead with a groan. "She's goin' to be the death of me."

Gil huffed with a hidden smile.

They wandered down a long hall and were relieved to find several unlocked doors leading to small bedrooms. Each room had a wooden bed with a feather mattress, a bookshelf, a desk, and a chair. A large crystal hung from each ceiling, glowing bright enough to fill the space with ample light.

"Guess this'll be my room," Gil called. "I wonder if they've got any garments for a dreled or dwarf lyin' about."

"Maybe. We should explore this place a little more," Neer suggested. "Maybe there is food or resources we could—"

"We shouldn't be lurkin' in places we don't belong, Neer," Loryk argued. "We should stick together an' stay where we know it's safe. If we go wanderin' too far, we could get lost or find ourselves in some trap."

"Loryk..."

"Don't give me that tone, Neer. I'm not a child. You've got to start usin' that daft 'ead of yours, or it'll get us all killed!"

"What other chance will we have to be in a place like this?"

"You're jestin', right? You can't be this dense!" He threw his arms up defeatedly. "Just do what you want, Neer. You're goin' to anyway. I'm goin' to bed. See you in the mornin'." He stomped out the door.

She stared in his direction for far too long, wishing for him to return. Her thoughts shifted to Gil when he crawled atop his bed and settled beneath the thick sheepskin blankets.

"He's right, you know," he said.

"What harm is there in looking around?"

"You've always been stubborn as an ox. D'you remember what Master Reiman taught you about that hot head of yours?"

"He also told me to trust my instincts and never let fear guide my actions."

"It's a slippery slope, messing with the unknown. I trust you'll make the right decision."

"You mean your decision?"

"I'm not a survivor. Neither is the lad. You've been doing this your entire life. We're here because we trust you. Just make sure that isn't in vain."

She bade him goodnight and stepped into the hall. Leaning against his door, she held her face in her hands and rethought every decision she made that brought them here: her fight with Master Reiman when he told her she wasn't ready to leave, the agreement with Loryk that he would use himself as bait to lure the mercenaries and obtain the arun, Gil's bravery in tagging along for medical support.

All that she had worked so hard for—freedom, redemption,

CURSE OF THE FALLEN

and honor—could be lost here. This mysterious place was perfect for an ambush. But she knew there was something more. Something she was *meant* to find here. It called out to her, drawing her deeper into the cave and whispering softly through her mind. Never had she been to a place with such magic or power. The chances of her being transported to the doorstep of an ancient, magical cave were too slim to be coincidence.

With a desperate, angry grunt, she marched down the hall and stepped back into the large cave with the enormous stone pillar. Beautiful lights brought life to the dark and dreary cavern. She stepped to the deep moat and admired the glowing water.

Lifting her arms, she examined the dirt and blood covering her skin. While her left shoulder was saturated in her own blood, she knew the remaining crimson belonged to Loryk. Sadness clung to her chest and brought tears to her eyes at the thought of losing him. After the loss of her family, she was reluctant to find another, but Loryk convinced her there was hope, and he had been a constant reminder of her strength and purpose.

Thinking back to their argument, she understood his anger and protectiveness, welcomed it, even. For without his pushiness and long-winded conversations, she would be alone, and of all the things she feared, that was the most of all.

"*Nerana...*"

She turned with a gasp as the voice called to her once more. The faint noise lingered in her mind, though it had long since faded. Her blood ran cold as she glanced around, finding herself entirely alone.

Through several deep breaths, she mustered the courage to speak. "Hello?" she called timidly. With another breath, she regained her composure and spoke with greater authority. "Show yourself!"

A light flickered in the dark hall that led to the rooms where the others rested. She stepped warily to the entrance and unsheathed her sword. As she walked into the hall, the light faded, and a chill ran down her spine.

The caves were lonesome and dark as she stood alone, staring into darkness. Glowing stones that once lined the cave had lost their luminance, leaving her in pitch blackness. Her boots shuffled as she took half a step forward, and she released a terrified gasp when a cold rush of air moved through her, gently nudging her forward. She stumbled and turned with her weapon drawn. "What is this?" she called into the darkness. "Who are you?"

Her hair gently waved when a voice whispered into her ear, *"Trust…"*

A floating orb of light hovered at the end of the hall, and Neer glanced around, petrified with fear. She swallowed the dry lump in her throat and held her sword close. Her eyes were fixed on the shining apparition that waited for her to follow. Her legs trembled as she inched her way closer, checking over her shoulder every few seconds for an intruder.

The light burned her eyes as she timidly approached, and she staggered back when it moved further away. Her eyes darted to her surroundings as she followed it down the pathways, until approaching a single door at the end of a long hall. The light faded as it sank into the door, and Neer was left in the dim glow of the stones that slowly illuminated along the walls.

She looked at her surroundings, being sure she was alone, and then returned her gaze to the door. Her heart throbbed in her chest as she stepped closer and nervously placed her hand on its surface. For a moment, she paused, understanding this could be a trap… a magical apparition left behind by the ahn'clave.

But something bigger drew her here. It called upon her, whispering her name, asking for her trust. She needed to see what was inside, even if it was nothing more than a trick—she had to know why she was led so deep into this ancient, abandoned tomb.

With a deep breath, she pushed through the fear and decided to trust in fate. Her eyes closed tight a she shoved against the door. The old stone shifted before swaying open, and Neer timidly stepped inside.

Hundreds of glowing crystals lined the walls in beautiful patterns, keeping the space well-lit and warm. Neer turned with wide eyes, gazing at the beautiful library of hundreds of tomes and scrolls. A golden globe-shaped chandelier hung from the center of the arched-gable ceiling, and melted candles rested atop old sconces and golden lamp posts.

CURSE OF THE FALLEN

Along the back wall was an enormous hearth with logs stacked neatly within the fireplace. A canopy bed with thick fur blankets sat along the wall to her left with nightstands covered in vials, quills, and parchment.

Neer stepped further into the room, keeping watch for any traps that could be waiting for her arrival. In the center of the room, she approached a large mahogany desk. With another quick glance at her surroundings, she carefully examined the items laid across its surface. Resting beneath piles of scrolls and crumbled ink-stained notes were enchanted prisms and glowing orbs. She fiddled curiously with the items before examining the room once more. Her eyes fixed on a magical object lying between two books on a shelf, and she smiled.

Her feet pattered against the cold stone flooring as she hurried across the room and took the golden object from its place on the crowded shelf. Known to very few, the extremely rare item, a spectromagnificator, was believed to transform natural light into a key for runes and various other enchanted items. She'd only heard of it in old wives' tales and legends; even scholars thought it to be myth.

A shiver trickled down her spine as the cold rush moved through her again. She turned to find the glowing light hovering above a nightstand across the room. Carefully, she approached the bedside table and dug through the drawers. Several leather-bound books, all written in a foreign language, filled the shallow space.

She traced the gold-trimmed symbols marking a blue leather book. With a quick look around the room, she convinced herself the caves were safely protected by enchantments and then focused on her energy.

Magic swirled within her, starting from her chest and expanding outward into her fingers and toes. As quickly as it came, the tingling warmth of her energy faded. The rush of such power was unfamiliar, as she had been forced to withhold her magic since early childhood in an attempt to hide from the Order of Saro. She took a long pause and relished in the feeling of relief, before slowly opening her eyes.

The symbols along the book hadn't changed, but she could

now read them with perfect clarity: *Z'falendel* it read, which she understood to mean "magical runes."

Her loud, excited laughter echoed through the room. "This was what you were leading me to..." she said to the light, which had vanished long ago. She quickly gathered all the books and settled comfortably in front of the hearth. The plush rug was warm and soft beneath her skin, though the chill of the cave had yet to leave her bones.

The logs within the stone fireplace had been perfectly preserved, and she knew without light and warmth she'd soon have to leave the beautiful library. She rummaged the desk for a flint and was happy to find one lying beneath a bundle of untouched parchment. Kneeling in front of the hearth, she flicked the stone, and flames quickly set the logs ablaze.

She warmed herself by the fire before moving back to her stack of books. Opening the cover of *Z'falendel*, she read through several chapters before coming to one of relevance.

The arun, it read, *is a small object which holds immense magical properties... Reciting the spell inscribed along the arun shall dispel the call of the marq. The arun may be activated by way of the triandal or, for the most gifted of mages, the Trials of Blood.*

"The Trials of Blood?" she wondered aloud.

The Trials are a perilous journey through which a magic user must overcome fear, adversity, and strength as they survive the forbidden tombs leading to the hidden cave of Nhamashel. Upon entering the cave, the aforementioned mage must harness the energy flowing through the waters and recite the incantation inscribed along the arun to release the call of the marq... Neer dug the arun from her pocket and examined the beautiful, calligraphic inscription. Focusing on her energy to understand the language, she found herself still unable to read it. Turning back to the book, she continued:

Whosoever shall harness the energy within the arun may use its power once. After which, it shall fade to ash.

Her eyes shifted from the book when she pondered the meaning of a *triandal*. Through all her years of study and training, she had never heard of such a thing. Feeling more confused than ever, she read through the chapter again and focused intensely on the phrase "Trials of Blood." A small section explained the

CURSE OF THE FALLEN

whereabouts of the Trials, which ran along the border of Llyne and Vleland, and she understood the path she must take to rid herself of the curse and finally be free. It was the reason she had been led to this cave, and she wouldn't interfere with her fate.

    She was going to face the Trials of Blood and lift the curse for good.

Chapter Four

In Fate's Hands

"Fate is not determined by the Gods or stars but by those who are willing to seek change."

– Master Reiman

THE NEXT MORNING, NEER AWOKE earlier than the others and found herself back in the library. She'd spent hours searching for anything she could learn about the Trials and arun, but there was no other mention of either in any of the texts.

Exhausting herself with research and reading, she walked to the large chamber and dipped into the moat surrounding the column of stalactites.

Floating on her back, she stared up to the narrow opening at the top of the pillar. Lightning flashed across the dreary sky of Vleland, and she wondered if the storm would ever let up. She knew from her studies that Vleland was a land cursed with rain and clouds. It was meant to keep the nyx from ever leaving, as they couldn't survive without the constant moisture and shade.

Brushing away her thoughts and worries of the weather, Neer dipped beneath the water and scrubbed herself clean. Blood and filth clouded the clear water in shades of dark brown and red. After several seconds, she resurfaced and inhaled a deep breath. The pain in her shoulder had disappeared since her time in the pool, and she curiously unwrapped the bandage to reveal a fresh scar in place of her open wound. She ran a finger along the blemish, confused at how quickly her injury had healed.

Jolted from her trance by a brazen voice, she turned to find Loryk and Gil standing at the edge of the moat. "What do you think you're doin'?" Loryk asked harshly. "We should be gettin' out of 'ere!"

She moved to the water's edge. "I was just waiting for you knuckleheads to wake."

"If you'd 'ave woken me, we could've left before this nasty storm 'it! We can't travel in such a mess!"

Her eyes moved to the ceiling, where the sound of rain pummeled the outside of the cave. A flash of lightning illuminated the narrow opening and created waves of light that glistened against the water trickling down the rock column. "Doesn't it always storm in Vleland?" she asked.

Gil replied, "Not always. Seems we've come at the worst time. Would be smart to wait out such nasty weather."

"It's settled then." She pushed away from the edge. "We wait out the storm and then head home."

"If you say so." Loryk's mood shifted from annoyance to excitement as he stripped off his trousers and jumped into the water.

Neer laughed as he splashed around her.

"You coming, Gil?" she asked.

"Dreleds are no good at swimming," he explained. "We sink like a fresh pile of shite."

"Right...," Loryk started. "But some shit floats, Gilly." He filled his mouth with water and sprayed it like a fountain toward the dreled.

Gil quickly stepped away to avoid the stream. His hand curled into a fist, and a deep scowl crossed his face.

"All right," Neer started with a chuckle, "just sit on the edge, Gil. Don't exclude yourself from the fun."

Gil grumbled as he perched himself on the edge of the moat. Neer gasped when Loryk pulled her beneath the water. He playfully rubbed her head, and she pushed him aside before swimming to the surface. She waited anxiously for him to emerge and then met him with a great splash as he rose to take a breath.

Neer's laughter and smile faded to confusion as Loryk began

wiggling and tugging at his undergarments.

"What's wrong?" she asked.

He twirled around and rubbed his arms and legs. "Why's this water so tingly and warm?"

"What?" Neer moved her arms through the surface and noticed that it gave a warm, tingly feeling. It was a sensation that was normal to her, and she stared curiously at the water. "It feels like magic," she explained.

"Magic?" Loryk said with a scoff. "What're you goin' on about?"

"This is what my magic feels like. When I meditate or prepare to use it, it gets warm and tingly, then it becomes unbearable." She looked at her shoulder and wondered if the magic of the water healed her injury.

"It can't be magic… That's foolish!" Loryk quickly pulled himself onto the dry ledge. "Magic can't be swirlin' in water!"

They turned to Gil as he explained, "It can, actually. Could be enchantments in the cave soakin' into it."

"Or it could be the Divines," Neer said before glancing at Loryk, whose lowered brows expressed his disdain. "It could be!" she argued.

"The Divines aren't real!" he replied. "Don't go spoutin' that nonsense, Nerana! You sound like a right good prude!"

"The Divines are the creators of magic. We know magical energy exists… What's to say the Divines don't exist, too?"

"Because they don't! It's just another way for the Order to keep control of the country! They 'ave us all thinkin' that magic is somethin' evil, and if you're born with it, you're the child of Nizotl° 'imself!" He plopped beside Gil. "Honestly, Neer, I figured least of all you would be followin' the Divines! If anyone in the Brother'ood found out, then Reiman would never 'ear the end of it!"

Gil scolded Loryk as the young man continued his rant. Neer turned away in shame, though she couldn't be angry, as his

---

*The Divine of trickery and deceit.
°Nizotl is the believed giver of magic and darkness. Any human born of magical blood is considered a demon of his creation and is therefore sentenced immediately to death.

CURSE OF THE FALLEN

passion wasn't entirely misplaced. It was part of the mission of the Broken Order Brotherhood to renounce the Divines and dismantle the Order of Saro.

Her adoptive father, Master Reiman, was a founding member of the Brotherhood and highly respected among their people. Should the members of the Brotherhood ever hear of her treacherous beliefs, it could destroy all the honor her father had worked to attain.

"So, child," Gil started, breaking her long and emotional train of thought. "Where were you last night? I heard you sneakin' your way about in the wee hours of morn."

"It wasn't the wee hours of morn."

"What're you goin' on about?" Loryk demanded. "Don't tell me you were explorin' these caves alone, Neer!"

"I found a library," she said excitedly, ignoring his scolding tone, "and I learned something very interesting. Seems the marq enchantment can be lifted from the arun after all! Have you ever heard of a *triandal*?"

"A what now?" Loryk added.

She shrugged. "Gil?"

"Can't say I have."

"If we can't find it, then my only option of dispelling the marq and harnessing the energy in the arun is to go through the Trials of Blood."

"How d'you know that?" Loryk asked.

"I read it in a book about enchanted runes."

"You can read elvish now?"

With a smirk, she said, "There's more to me than meets the eye, Ebbard." Water dripped onto stone as she pulled herself from the water. She shook her brown locks and then wrang them dry.

"Sounds dangerous," Gil started. "I've never heard of such a place."

"There was a map," Neer said as she slipped into her clothes, "to a cave called Nhamashel. It's buried deep within Anaemiril. The entrance is along the wetlands bordering Vleland and Llyne. I'll accompany you two out of Vleland and then head to the cave alone."

"What?" Loryk exclaimed. "Not a chance! We aren't leavin' you be'ind, Neer!"

"It's too dangerous, Loryk. Surviving Vleland is hard enough for a sorceress, and the Trials are even worse."

"You shouldn't go alone!"

"I can't risk your lives. Please. Just this once, don't argue with me."

He turned away with pursed lips. Neer knew he wanted to debate and was glad when he didn't. Looking through the cave, her eyes came to the beautiful Tree, whose wide and tall branches held glowing flowers. Her eyes followed as petals drifted through the air and landed softly on the ground.

"Gil," she started, "is this a Tree? Like the one in Porsdur?"

He examined the large Tree and stroked his beard. "Looks like it. Got the same glowin' flowers and such."

She stepped to the Tree and closed her eyes. Taking a slow breath, she felt the familiar tingle of energy swirling through her. She touched the bark and was filled with warmth and power. With her every inhale, the flowers glowed brighter, and with each exhale they dimmed.

There was only one other Tree of which she knew that held magical energy such as this, and it resided in her village of Porsdur. She would often find herself lying beneath the branches and watching as the petals glowed and dimmed with her every breath, just as they were doing now.

Standing beneath the familiar Tree brought her back to a simpler time, one where she didn't worry about the dangers of the world or the people pursuing her. It wasn't until recently that the Order had begun attacking and raiding innocent villages in her pursuit. The rivers of blood and mass graves of the dead were forever etched in her mind.

Memories of the bodies lying in the open fields after the bloody assault of the Knights of the Order filled her with dread. It was a simple farming village in the heart of Styyr, where a rumor had spread of a sorcerer's whereabouts.

Of *her* whereabouts.

Neer had never visited the village until after the raids... when she and the Brotherhood heard of the massacre and paid their respects.

"What are you doin', boy?" Gil demanded.

Neer turned around as Gil stomped over to Loryk, who was separating dried berries and nuts into three piles.

"What's it look like, imp? I'm rationin' what we 'ave left of our food."

"You've had food this entire time and told no one?"

"Well, I didn't think we'd be stuck in this cave another day!"

Neer closed her eyes with a frustrated huff. If only she had a coin for every time these two bickered, she could've hired a quiet assassin to replace them on this journey. The thought put a bright smile on her face, and she made it a point to remember it for another time, as their argument had grown too heated for such jests.

She stepped to Loryk and said, "We're all hungry. Just give us the damn food, Loryk. All of it."

He dug through a beautiful leather satchel, causing Neer and Gil to share a confused glance.

"What ya got there, lad?" Gil asked.

Loryk pulled the bag closer, though no one had reached for it. "It's a satchel!" he said matter-of-factly.

"We know that," Neer said with a snicker, "but where did you get it?"

"Found it in the chest by the bed! Why?"

Gil rubbed his face with a disgruntled sigh. "You shouldn't go takin' things that don't belong to ya!" he said.

"And who exactly does it belong to? Unless you're sayin' the ahn'clave're gonna rise up from the ashes and demand that I return their fancy wares!"

Gil crossed his arms. "Fine, take what ya will! No one's stoppin' ya anyhow."

"That's right." Loryk snubbed his nose and continued digging through the stolen bag. He retrieved a large handful of dried berries and jerky and promptly split them between the group. "This's all we've got left."

Gil clutched his growling stomach. "I haven't had a good meal since the missus struck down that cow with her bare hands. Ho ho, 'twas a sight to be seen!"

"Like 'ells she did! You're no bigger than my left arm!

H.C. NEWELL

Couldn't've taken down a cow all by 'er lonesome!"

"Aye, but who ever said my lady is a dreled?" he said with a smile. "Close your mouth, child. You look like a trout goin' in for the bait."

Loryk quickly closed his mouth, though his wide eyes remained full of surprise.

"I've got to meet this wife of yours," Neer said snidely.

In all the time she knew Gil, he'd kept his family life a secret from everyone. He understood the dangers that came with his involvement in the Brotherhood and never wanted his family subjected to any acts of revenge or defiance against the movement. Bandit groups and mercenaries would often attack the families of guild members, and Gil decided soon after joining that he'd never introduce his loved ones to anyone associated with the Brotherhood.

Neer fell from her thoughts and gathered what little tinder had fallen from the large Tree before setting up a small campfire. She ate her meal while Gil sparked a flint and then blew the freshly lit flames.

"How long do you think we'll be holed up in this cave, Gil?" she asked.

"Soon as the skies clear, we'll head back to Llyne."

"Do you know where in Vleland this cave is?"

"Haven't a clue. I didn't see the border or signs of civilization." He paused with intent. "Finding this cave was truly a gift. Had we been left out in this storm, we'd have seen our end."

"A gift?" Loryk barked. "From who? The Divines? Don't tell me you still follow the Old Ways,° Gil!"

"Mind your own, lad! I've been alive far longer than you. The Six have been around decades longer than that. You can't argue with the Divine teachings."

"Do you know what the Order 'as done?"

---

* The Old Ways is a belief in the original teachings of the Order of Saro.
Before the reign of High Priest Beinon, who set forth the New Ways, the Order believed highly in the Circle of Seven, that were the seven divines of unity and peace that oversaw and retained the balance of the mortal plane.
Soon after his inauguration, the High Priest bestowed a system of belief that abolished one of the seven Divines and cast another as the purveyor of darkness and evil.

CURSE OF THE FALLEN

"I didn't say I follow the Order, boy! Them pious pieces of filth can choke on a goat's horns!" He spat angrily into the fire. "Damned heathens. Ruining a perfectly good world with their rules and teachin's."

"Come on, Gil...," Neer warned. She knew how he could work himself up.

"Ebbard," Gil started with a huff, "be a good lad and fetch us a cauldron. We could do for some fresh water."

"You want us to drink that magic juice?" He pointed at the moat.

"Are you daft, boy? Take the cauldron and fill it with rainwater! Go on, now!"

Loryk did as he was told without question, which was a rarity for him. The sound of his footsteps dissipated as he made his way through the tunnels and to the bedrooms.

Gil stoked the growing flames, while Neer got comfortable by his side. Sticks popped and hissed as the heat grew. With Loryk gone, the cave was much quieter. Gil and Neer basked in the silence, knowing it wouldn't last for long. They each withheld a groan as only minutes after his departure, Loryk's gleeful voice echoed through the silence, and he stepped back into the large room.

"Looky 'ere!" Loryk said while proudly displaying a foreign instrument. "I found an ocarina! Remember the last one I found, Neer?"

Neer didn't answer as she shook her head, recalling with clarity the enchanted ocarina he found on one of their previous adventures. The magical instrument, which he would use several times a day, compelled those within earshot to dance anytime a note was played. She was far from heartbroken when he woke one morning and found it smashed to pieces.

Gil shook his head. "You shouldn't be rummaging through this stuff, boy! And why're you sittin' around while that cauldron's emptier than my gut after a nice shite?"

"Mind your own, Gil! I'll get to it!"

Neer braced herself as Loryk blew into the instrument and created horrid sounds that pierced the air. Gil swore angrily while Neer covered her ears, thankful she wasn't forced to twirl and jump around.

 With a huff, Loryk set the item aside. "Oh well, it was worth a try." He retrieved a lute hidden behind his back.

 "What's that? You stole another'n?" Gil said with wide eyes.

 "It ain't stealin' if there's no one to own it!"

 "Bah!" Gil cawed. His small arms flew up in defeat.

 The bard tuned the instrument and plucked the strings. Neer smiled as he sang a slow-tempo song. The sound brought her back to simpler, happier times when she first came to the Brotherhood. Back then, Loryk tried teaching her the instrument, but she never had the patience for it. The arguments over her lack of trying and his pushiness nearly ruined their friendship. She chuckled while thinking of their childish behavior.

 His eyes met with hers at the sound of her laughter, and with a wink, he turned back to the lute. Her smile diluted the sharp, daring look she gave.

 "Oh, would you look at that," Gil teased. "I could just smack them googly eyes right outta yer faces!"

 The song abruptly ended when Loryk clutched the neck of the lute. "Listen 'ere you!"

 Neer teased, "Oh, come on, Ebbard. Can't handle a simple jest?"

 "What're you, some kind of... of... queen of the jesters, now?"

 Gil roared with laughter. "Good one, boy! Hoo hoo! If only you were up on stage barkin' this nonsense instead of singin' it!"

 Loryk's eyes narrowed, and his lips pulled together into a tight line. Neer playfully tousled his hair, and he quickly patted his curly auburn locks back into place. He always hated when his hair was a mess, and Neer always took pride in ruffling it up.

 "When're we gettin' out of 'ere anyhow?" Loryk asked grumpily.

 "Soon," Neer stated. "Is there another way out of this cave, Gil? It's a risk to go out the way we came."

 "Haven't a clue," the dreled explained. "It's best not to wander too far. No telling what kind of trouble we could catch ourselves in just by being here."

 "You said this place belonged to the ahn'clave? What

happened to them?"

"No one knows. They just up and disappeared. Left everything behind. Not a trace of them was left except these caves and all the wonders inside."

"Are they still alive, you think?"

"Let's not talk of this, all right?" Loryk interrupted. "It's bad enough we're in this cave in the middle of nyx territory. Last thing we should be thinkin' of are some ancient ghosts comin' to haunt us."

"Scared, Loryk?" Neer teased.

"No! Just... just don't want to talk about it is all! I'm ready to get 'ome!"

As Gil explained his plan to turn himself into a horse and carry them quickly through Vleland, a faint shuffling echoed nearby. Neer turned aside while the others remained in their conversation, unaware of the noise that twitched her ears.

She instinctually clutched the hilt of her sword as she scanned the empty room.

"Neer?" Loryk started. "What're you doin'?"

"Did you hear that?"

"'Ear what? Don't be jestin' at a time like this!"

"Quiet!" she hissed. His eyes widened as she stood with her weapon drawn. She cautiously viewed the room and studied every corner. Her hair stood on end as her heart climbed in her throat.

The familiar shink of a sword being unsheathed sounded from the cave entrance, and Neer twisted her weapon in her hand, falling into a defensive stance. Loryk quivered behind her while Gil transformed instantly into a dren and stepped to her side. A deep growl sawed through his twitching lips.

Neer focused intensely on the entrance as footsteps pattered through the dark halls.

Gripping her weapon tightly, she watched while three shadows emerged from the darkness and the Shadow Blades entered the cave.

.

CHAPTER FIVE

THE CHILD OF SKYE

"No life is more precious than glory and gold."

— Shadow Blade Mercenaries

THE THUD OF HEAVY BOOTS stomped through the corridor where three mercenaries stood at the cave entrance. Rainwater dripped from their soaking armor, forming puddles around their feet.

Neer clutched her sword as her eyes shifted between the strangers. Her heart beat high in her throat, and her knees trembled as the larger of the two men smiled from ear to ear.

"Look who we've found hiding like a rat in a hole," he said arrogantly.

"Finally," the woman at his side said with a snicker, "that bounty will be ours for the taking."

Gil, still in the form of a dren, snarled and whipped his tails.

The woman chuckled. "Is that a dreled? You think a shifter can take on the three of us?"

The larger man's heavy boots clunked when he stepped forward. His dark eyes glared into Neer's. "Turn yourself over, and we'll spare these puppets you call allies," he threatened. The second, much smaller, man nocked an arrow. The larger man continued, "One wrong move, Child, and your friend gets an arrow through the eye."

Neer stiffened as he threatened Loryk. These mercenaries wouldn't leave without her, which gave her no choice but to fight. Energy burned in her chest like a freshly lit fire as she looked into the eyes of the archer.

She disappeared from her place and then reappeared behind him. He exhaled a wheezed gasp as her dagger sliced across his neck. His bow and arrow dropped to the ground as he choked and scratched his bleeding throat. The others turned when their companion fell to his knees. Desperate, gargled breaths bubbled from his lips, and with a final breath, he collapsed in a pool of blood.

A thunderous roar vibrated through the chamber as Gil raced forward to tackle the female mercenary.

The woman leapt aside to dodge his attack. His claws scratched against stone as he slid across the floor.

"Come on, you imp!" she sneered while twisting her weapon.

Gil leapt aside as she swung her sword. His blood sprayed into the air when she sliced into his shoulder. He countered with a hard swipe of his paw, and the woman spun aside, jabbing at his hind leg. His growling echoed against the walls as they continued their battle.

Neer's eyes shifted from Gil to the large man as he stepped closer and shouted, "You think you've won this?"

He swung his battle axe, and she ducked. A rush of air moved past as the weapon grazed over her head. Spinning backward, she put distance between them and held up her sword defensively.

With a snarl, the man swung his axe with a furious cry, and Neer spun aside to evade his deadly attack. As his weapon moved closer to her side, she drew her sword, and their weapons collided with a reverberating clang. Neer looked into his eyes, then pushed herself away. She struck at his throat, and he quickly dodged. With an angry growl, she lunged forward, bringing her blade to his head. He lifted his axe, and her sword collided with its wooden handle.

"So... the *Child of Skye* is nothing more than a woman," he taunted.

His boot knocked the breath from her lungs when he kicked

her stomach, and she rolled across the floor. A fresh cut stung her lip and left the taste of blood lingering on her tongue.

Her eyes lifted to the man above as he stood over her and struck his axe. Sparks flew when the iron blade collided against stone as she rolled aside. He released a vicious growl and swiped his weapon downward again. With another roll, she dodged the second blow and scrambled to her feet.

They stood close, staring into the other's angry, desperate eyes. He was there to retrieve her for a bounty, and the prospect of even the most meager of payments was enough to see him not only into the dangerous land of Vleland, but into the haunted and forbidden caves of Anaemiril.

"How did you find me?" she asked. It was magic that led her to find the hidden entrance to this cave. Had its energy not drawn her to the mirage, she'd have never known of its existence.

The mercenary chuckled with condescending eyes. "High Priest Beinon sends his regards."

His smile faded into a deep scowl as he lifted his axe and struck at her chest. Neer dipped beneath his furious swing and slashed upward across his forearm. Blood sprayed across her face as she sliced through his muscle and struck the bone. He unleashed a powerful scream of rage and pain.

Gil growled in agony, and Neer averted her gaze from the mercenary as the dreled transformed back into himself and collapsed to the ground. A deep gash carved through his leg as he shouted and gripped his wound.

Neer stepped back as the female mercenary approached. Her much larger companion straightened with a furious glare. Blood dripped from his arm and left large spatters across the stone.

"Give up," he said with a growl. "You're outnumbered, demon."

Neer's jaw clenched as her grip tightened on her sword. Energy swirled within her like a raging storm. The cave shifted with a loud creak, sending waves of dust and pebbles falling from the ceiling.

The Tree behind glowed and dimmed with her every breath. Steam formed over the moat and billowed through the large cavern. Loryk looked around in a panic and ran to Gil's side, while

CURSE OF THE FALLEN

Neer focused on her enemies, whose intimidating gazes had dissolved into fear and confusion.

She made a tight fist with her left hand, and the cave shook as large rocks fell from the ceiling. The mercenaries leapt aside as boulders crashed around them. The woman was thrown to the ground and released a hellish scream as her arm was crushed beneath the weight of a heavy stone. Her blood painted the rocks in spatters of red.

Neer jumped back as the man slashed his axe toward her, and then she spun to the left and struck at his side. He smacked her arm away and struck her chin with his fist. She stumbled back in a daze. He sliced his axe across her shoulder, drawing a thick red line, and she fell to the ground with a loud shriek. A deep wound opened her skin and coated her arm in blood. Every heartbeat shook through her body.

The mercenary stood over her and gripped her by the throat. She fought against his strength as he pulled her to her knees. Under such stress, she couldn't focus on her magic. Fighting for a breath that would never come, her lungs started to convulse. Pain burned in her chest as she slowly suffocated.

Her fingernails scratched against his face, leaving thin lines of pain across his cheeks and jaw. She pressed her thumbs to his eyes, but was overpowered by his strength.

Slowly, the world began to fade. The teal of her eyes shined out from the red surrounding them as he choked the life from her body.

As her limbs fell motionless and her body slumped, the man was struck from behind and released a roaring, pained scream. Neer was dropped to the ground and collapsed at his feet. Coughing and wheezing, she caught a glimpse of the mercenary as he gripped a bone protruding from his shin.

He was shrouded in darkness as Loryk stood over him with a bloody iron cauldron in hand. With a desperate cry, Loryk smashed the cauldron over his head. The mercenary's skull split open with a deep crack, and he fell to the floor unmoving. Wide, lifeless eyes stared at Neer before Loryk bashed his head in and his face caved. Loryk screamed and shouted obscenities as blood spattered across his face and arms.

"That's enough!" Gil said, limping over. "That's enough, boy!" He grabbed Loryk's arm to stop him.

Enraged, Loryk took a deep breath. His fair skin was flushed, and his wide eyes were full of hatred. He stared at the man under him, whose head was nothing more than a bloody pulp. Shaking with adrenaline and fear, his gaze shifted to Neer, and he rushed to her side. "Neer!" he called while pulling her into his arms.

She crawled to her knees while rubbing her bruised throat.

"You're all right... You're okay, Neery."

Gil limped over on his slashed leg. "Be a good lad and fetch us some water, would you?" he asked while pointing to the still glowing moat.

Loryk wasted no time filling the cauldron and returning to his friends. Gil gathered the warm water into his hands and poured it over his injured thigh. He winced and grunted as his skin wove back together. Mist rose from the opened wound as his flesh sizzled and popped.

"What's that?" Loryk asked. "It's healin' you?"

"Help her out, would you?" Gil snapped.

Neer recoiled and gritted her teeth as Loryk poured a handful of water over her shoulder. The water evaporated as it touched her bone, and her tissue slowly formed together into a large, puffy scar. Loryk washed the blood away and wiped his filthy hands on his dirty trousers.

They turned when something shuffled from the debris and spotted the woman lying beneath the rocks. She lay in a puddle of blood with her left arm crushed beneath the boulder, pinning her to the ground.

"What're we to do about 'er?" Loryk asked.

Gil sighed and rubbed his face. "We should interrogate her. Find out all she knows." He stepped to the mercenary and asked, "How did you find us?"

Refusing to speak and grunting with agony, she turned away. Muscles tightened in her neck and jaw as she clenched her teeth.

"Come on, now," Gil started, "just tell us what we want to know."

"F... Fu..."

"Don't go getting all snippy on me," he warned. "Tell us what we need, and I'll end this suffering nice and clean."

The woman breathed quickly. Her chin wrinkled and eyes closed tightly. Tears carved trails through the blood on her cheeks. She looked at Gil, then Neer. "Her..." the woman spoke through clenched teeth. "The *Child...*" She stopped to grunt in pain. "He'll find her... This won't end with us."

"How'd you find the cave so quickly?" Gil said, pressing her. "We've been here naught but a day, yet you've trekked your way through enemy lands and into a hidden cavern."

"The stone..." She struggled to speak. "Please! Just kill me!"

"Oi!" Loryk exclaimed. He strode over to the mercenary and stepped on her injured arm. The woman howled in agony. "Tell us what we want to know! You think we want to 'ear your screamin' all night?"

"We're given a stone!" she cried. "It can track her energy! If she's nearby, it'll glow. The closer we are... the brighter it gets!"

"Where is it?"

"Keith had it..." Her voice faded into sobs.

Neer searched the pockets of the man Loryk killed and found several items, including a vial of poison darts, a pipe with herbs, her wanted poster, twenty-seven silver pieces, and a brightly glowing gemstone.

"Is that it?" Gil asked.

The woman nodded. "Please..." she cried.

Gil patted her shoulder in a silent thanks. She whispered a prayer to the Divines as Gil retrieved his dagger and carefully drew it across her throat.

Chapter Six

Blood and Peace

"Lifeless and cold, they hunt in the night, searching for souls to steal. But you'd better beware, for a drop of your blood gives them a great power to wield."

— Tales of the Nyx, human folklore

TWO DAYS PASSED AS THEY rode through the marshy wetlands of Vleland. Horse hooves splashed against wet grass as Gil, transformed now into a stallion, raced across the hillsides with Neer and Loryk on his back.

A hooded cloak, soaked with rain, clung to Neer's shoulders and dripped water across her face and arms. With a shiver, she leaned forward and wrapped tighter around Loryk, hoping for warmth. Pressing her cheek against his back, she eyed the misty hillsides surrounding them. It was a place unlike any she had seen before, with miles of overgrown hills untouched by villages or roads.

Stories of the nyx, the natives of this land, entered her mind, and she recalled the stories of their vicious and repulsive ways. Some tales claimed they could pull the head clean off a full-grown horse, while others warned of their appetites for human flesh. She shuddered at the thought and hoped for their sake that the legends weren't true.

"You all right?" Loryk asked.

"Yeah. Just getting cold," she lied and pulled her cloak tighter around her shoulders. Sharing these stories with Loryk would only lead to his panic and unrest, so she kept the thoughts to herself.

Her attention veered north when shadows of tall trees and weathered homes appeared through the mist as they came closer to a small village. It was the first sign of civilization they'd seen since waking in Vleland, and Neer stiffened as fear caught in her throat.

The scattered homes were empty and appeared abandoned, but the nyx were nocturnal, and these crumbled, isolated homes were the perfect place for them to rest. Glancing at the sky, she took note of the fading sunlight hidden beneath an overcast sky. Night would soon fall and transform the beautiful, desolate marsh into a dangerous feeding ground. The last two days, Neer and her companions were lucky to have found safety within a thicket of trees and behind a half-standing wall.

As if reading her mind, Loryk asked, "Should we stay 'ere?"

"No," she said. "We've traveled this long without encountering any natives. I don't want to find one tucked inside of these houses."

"It'll be dark soon..."

"Stay calm, Lor. We'll find somewhere safe."

Her eyes remained on the homes as they trotted past without incident, and she was relieved they hadn't alerted any possible residents of their presence.

Glowing plants and moss appeared throughout the hills as the day slowly faded into night. Gil treaded carefully as animals woke from their slumber to stalk the empty land.

Neer clutched her sword as a large shadow appeared to the north. Her chest tightened as they came closer, and she exhaled a deep breath at the sight of a large tree standing proudly atop a hillside. Thick limbs hung to the ground, creating a canopy perfect for hiding. She released her weapon, and it slid back into its sheath.

"There," Neer whispered to Gil, "we can make camp beneath that tree."

She glanced at their surroundings as night blanketed the land with a deep shadow of darkness. Gil traveled through the dense fog, trotting closer toward the tree.

Neer studied the shadows of the long, swaying limbs that came into view and twisted her nose when a light breeze moved south, carrying the stench of rotten flesh and decay.

"Divines…" Loryk gagged while covering his nose. "What the 'ells is that?"

"Quiet!" Neer snapped. She peered through the rolling fog and then shifted her gaze to the tree as a low creak came from the branches. Loryk trembled noisily, while Neer was quiet. They withheld violent gags as the pungent odor caught in their throats and brought tears to their eyes.

A shift in the wind parted the fog, and Neer gazed up at the swinging shadows. She gripped the hilt of her sword as the lifeless eyes of several dozen nyx stared back at her.

Skin sloughed from their rotten, sagging faces as they hung upside-down by ropes binding their ankles. Not a sliver of crimson or break in their skin was present across their bodies. They were left to hang until their deaths.

"Neer…" Loryk said with a deep, terrified quiver.

"We need to leave. Now."

Gil moved carefully over the hillside and directly into a village of round, cobblestone homes. Neer stared curiously at the homes. She had always been told that the nyx were reclusive and territorial, living in seclusion and never gathering as a civilized society. Wandering slowly through the village, she now understood the rumors weren't true. The nyx lived just as normally as everyone else.

Low growls overtook the silence as the silhouettes of dogs crept through the fog. The group headed deeper into the settlement, and the heavy stench of death was replaced with the acrid aroma of smoke.

Nearly two dozen houses were clustered together within the shallow valley, leaving them confined to a narrow path that broke through the crumbled, smoldering homes.

Vines wove through the grass, encasing overturned carts and crawling along soot and blood-stained walls. Glowing red eyes belonging to small canine creatures with black, leathered skin

CURSE OF THE FALLEN

and arched, boney backs appeared through the mist as they tore at the burned flesh of the villagers' remains.

Neer gazed upon the ruins of the recently destroyed village and then spotted a familiar symbol burned into the grass. Shifting her eyes to the dogs, which were hungrily devouring the villagers several houses away, she slid from Gil's back and walked carefully through the mud. Ignoring Loryk as he quietly called out to her, she stepped to the symbol. Light tendrils of smoke rose from the freshly carved pattern, and she absently touched the identical branding on her upper arm.

It was a symbol that represented peace and prosperity. Loyalty and faith. But to Neer, it meant something entirely different.

She received the branding at a young age, too young for her to remember, or possibly, the trauma caused her to forget. The old scar was nearly invisible now as age had deprived it of color, but it was there, forever marking her as the property of the Order of Saro.

Hopping back onto Gil's back, Neer settled into place, and the group moved further through the destroyed village, being careful not to make any sound that might alert others of their presence. The tearing of skin and ravenous chewing from the dogs filled the air as they picked through the remains, paying no mind to the intruders passing them by. Loryk closed his eyes and covered his mouth, but Neer couldn't be bothered by the feasting animals. Her mind revolved around the symbols staining the village and why the Order would see fit to attack elvish lands.

The world darkened and grew colder as they moved further through the homes, finding more bodies and canines as they approached the center of town.

"We have to find shelter," Neer explained. "It doesn't look like anyone is here."

"Not a chance, Neer. Uh-uh. We ain't stayin' 'ere!"

"It's too dark to travel. More creatures will come."

"Exactly! This's a feedin' ground! You said not to be caught in a 'ome with the nyx!"

"There isn't a choice! We can't stay out here."

Loryk trembled while gripping tightly to Gil's mane.

"Gil," Neer started with a whisper, "take us to that home

straight ahead."

He followed her command, and while moving through the village, Neer caught a glimpse of a shadow through a break in the homes. The dark figure knelt in the midst of a pack of hungry, growling canines.

"Stop," Neer said, the word spilling from her mouth with fear and urgency. Gil followed her command, and Neer squinted through the darkness. Her heart skipped when the low, pained grunt of a man broke through the vicious growls. She slid from Gil's back. "Stay hidden!" she hissed, before charging between the homes toward the stranger.

Behind the village, four black canines surrounded a bloody and injured man. He knelt atop the grass and swung his sword. A dog leapt at him from behind, clawing his back, and he lurched forward with a pained grunt. He turned around with a twisted face and stabbed the animal through the chest. The dog fell to the ground, twitching as it shriveled and turned to ash.

Neer jabbed to the right as a canine leapt for the stranger. She spun aside to evade its sharp claws and plunged her sword through its ribs. Horrified, she watched as it, too, faded to ash. Her confusion was pushed aside as another dog leapt at her. She struck across its face then stabbed into its chest, and it fell to the ground with a yelp.

Her boots splashed against the wet grass as she scanned the fog, searching for the last canine. Darkness surrounded her as winds swept the mist aside. Suddenly, she was thrust back as a dog leapt from the fog, tackling her to the ground.

She held it back with her arm to its throat, its long claws scratching across her arms and chest. Hot breath shrouded her face with white air as the canine's wide jaws snapped closer to her skin. She turned away with a grunt, pushing harder and fighting against its strength.

The deep growls and vicious biting were interrupted by a sudden yelp, and as the pressure of its attack weakened, its body faded to ash. Neer choked on the particles as they fell over her, clinging to her nose and throat. Rolling over, she crawled to her knees and fought to stay quiet.

The stranger knelt before her with his sword in hand. Neer

struggled to move away and put a safe distance between them as she fought against the raw itch in her throat.

She turned away, red-faced and throat burning, and released several choked breaths. Her eyes shifted to the man as he slumped forward and gripped his bloody side. His white hair was stained in red and clung to his face with moisture. Cuts and bruises painted his fair skin with a mixture of dark purple and bright red. His lack of red eyes and grey skin told Neer he wasn't nyx, but he wasn't elf either. At least, not entirely.

He held the slender, sharp features of their kind, including his inward slanted eyes and pointed ears, though his were smaller and less obvious than a typical forest-dweller. And unlike the others, who had long narrow faces, his was rounder and fuller, making him easy to mistake as a human.

"Who are you?" she asked, her voice hoarse and weak.

His intense, glaring eyes met with hers, and she exhaled a deep breath. It wasn't irrational for him to distrust her. Their races had been feuding for centuries. If not for her adoptive father being an elf, Neer assumed she, too, would hold more hostility toward their kind.

"*Nyn'Dira?*" she asked, referring to the elven forests.

She became curious as his narrow eyes widened before he turned away. Glancing at the fog, she watched as more glowing eyes encroached upon the village, and she glanced at Loryk and Gil, who stood waiting in the street.

"*Come,*" she said in broken elvish, wishing now more than ever she had paid attention during her language lessons. "*Trust.*"

She pulled his arm, and he snatched it away with a vicious groan.

"I..." She struggled to complete her sentence as the dogs grew nearer. Stammering over her words, she settled on a simple phrase she knew he'd understand—"friend." She pointed to herself. "Trust... friend."

He turned away, and Neer clutched her sword as the creatures rustled through the grass. She looked at the stranger with pleading eyes. She didn't want to leave him behind, but she couldn't risk the lives of her friends to save his.

A deep breath escaped his lungs, and with a stiff nod, he

reluctantly agreed to her help. He stood and held the wound on his side. She pulled his arm around her shoulders, ready to help him walk, but he shoved her away. Clutching his opened and bleeding side, he hurriedly limped his way to her companions.

The elf stared at the ground, refusing to meet Loryk's gaze, as they both held the same furious, disgusted expressions.

Neer held her sword outward as glowing red eyes followed her through the mist. Blood curdling hisses and growls converged in a crescendo of hunger and fury as the dogs inched closer. She turned with her weapon drawn, peering at the eyes that stalked forward.

"Go," she demanded of her friends. Her shoulders were square as she prepared to face the influx of ravenous dogs.

The elf looked at her with narrowed eyes, and then turned to the creatures. His lip twitched as he fell into a state of deep, concentrated anger. Unsheathing a second sword from the scabbard across his back, he stood tall and strong next to Neer. She turned to him and noticed the blood spilling from his side.

The light clop of hooves tapping against the ground caught her attention, and she turned sharply to Gil when he became unsettled. "Come on," she grabbed the elf and forced him toward the stallion.

Loryk sneered as he pulled the elf onto Gil's back with a great heave. Neer took Loryk's hand and then glanced at the canines as they lunged forward.

"Come on!" Loryk shrieked while pulling her up. She leapt onto Gil's back and wrapped her arms around the elf's waist as they raced quickly from the dogs that followed.

Chapter Seven

E'LEKGLÄEH

"Lanathess müinoryn varkaad."
The humans shall be our doom.

— Sayings of the evae

MUD AND GRASS TORE FROM the soil as Gil galloped through the village with a sea of red eyes at his back. The shadowy canines snapped at his legs as they drew closer.

"Hurry!" Neer demanded while slicing her blade through a lunging canine's jaw. It fell back and splashed into the mud with a wail before being trampled by the others. "Gil!" she warned.

The dreled moved faster, spraying mud into the air as he fled from the dogs. He came to a stop at a lonesome house along the outskirts of the village, and Neer leapt from his back with the others. She turned to the dogs with her sword drawn, and a flash of light came from Gil as he transformed into a giant mammoth, stomping and swiping his large trunk to keep the dogs away.

"Neer!" Loryk cried as he pushed against the home's heavy stone door.

She raced to his side, and with a heave, the door slid open. They slipped inside with the elf, and Gil transformed into a raven diving in behind them. The dogs charged forward, and with a hard push, Loryk and Neer slammed the door. They jumped back as the dogs raged and clawed from outside, thumping and scratching against the walls.

Neer closed her eyes and caught her breath. Her arms trembled as she held the door closed and fought against the strength of the ravenous animals.

A strong arm hovered next to hers, and she knew it wasn't Loryk who had come to her aid. The room was dark, with not a window or crack in the wall to allow even a sliver of light inside.

"We need something," Neer grunted, hoping for anything that could barricade the door so she could rest.

"Workin' on it, lass!" Gil called from behind, and the walls illuminated with every quick spark of his flint. He paced the small, open room, using the quick flashes of light to search for anything to burn.

"Gil!" Neer begged. Her arms grew tired against the constant thuds.

"Hang on!" Loryk exclaimed, and the light shuffle of leather filled the intense silence as he dug through his stolen satchel. "Got it!" His footsteps pattered against the ground before a light tapping echoed from the floor. The room was illuminated by yellow light when the gemstone in his grasp gleamed with light.

The luminance grew brighter, revealing his upper chest and face. He walked through the small room and came to a thick stone dresser. "Gil!" he called. "Move this, would you?"

Gil transformed into a large boar and pushed the heavy stone dresser in front of the door.

Neer exhaled a deep, relieved sigh as her arms fell to her sides. "Loryk!" she smiled. "You're a genius."

"Guess that thievin' paid off good, then, didn't it? I found this 'ere crystal in the caves with the satchel." He smiled proudly, and gave her knowing look that she knew to mean "*I told you so.*"

With a laugh, she dismissed his gaze and turned away, exhausted.

"Who's this?" Gil asked in his natural form.

Neer glanced at the stranger as he disappeared across the room and sat against the wall. She snatched the gem from Loryk and raced to the elf's side. Through its soft glow, she could see he was leaned back with his head slumped aside and eyes closed.

"I don't know," she said, answering Gil's earlier question, "but

CURSE OF THE FALLEN

he's badly injured."

Gil mixed herbs in a mortar. "He isn't nyx," he said.

"I know. I believe he's from Nyn'Dira."

Loryk added, "Looks a lot like Reiman, don't ya think? Got the same angry look about 'im. Even near death, 'e's just..." He backed away with a shiver. "Never liked that sort. The elves from the forest've always gave me the creeps."

"Piss off, Loryk!" Neer said harshly.

"Sorry, Neery. I know you've got a soft spot for 'em after Reiman raised you an' all."

Gil scooped the green paste from his mortar. "Take his blades, would you?" he instructed.

Neer retrieved the dual short swords from their scabbards on the elf's back. The steel blades were covered in blood and flesh, and the leather-wrapped, twisted handles were faded and unraveling. Even in its worn state, the weapons were more beautiful and well-crafted than any she had ever seen. Her eyes fixed on the purple veins pulsing throughout the length of the weapons, and she slid her finger down the filthy steel, never having seen anything like it before.

"Now, this'll hurt just a bit," Gil explained to the stranger, "but it'll patch you up good as new."

The elf remained silent with closed eyes, and Neer didn't have time to explain that he didn't understand their language before Gil smeared the paste into his deepest wound. With a sharp breath, the stranger opened his eyes as his body tensed in agony, turning his face a deep shade of red. Veins and muscles swelled along his forehead and neck as Gil continued filling the deep gash on his side.

Neer understood the pain of *travaran*, the paste that was currently healing him, as she had been subjected to its agony once before. Watching this stranger struggle without unleashing a hellish scream or fainting from the pain was both admirable and frightening. Most would prefer to endure the torment of their injuries over the torture of travaran, which has been described as molten lava coursing through your veins. Neer could attest to that, as well, though she felt it was an understatement of its affliction.

She took the elf's shoulders and looked into his eyes as he struggled. "You're okay," she said in broken elvish. "Doing good."

His strong muscles tensed as he gripped her forearms, compressing her bones.

As his wound healed beneath the thick ointment, he released his hold and became limp against the wall.

"You did good, lad," Gil explained. "Not many can withstand the pain of travaran. Stuff's got a mightier kick than a buck ready to mate."

"Really, Gil," Loryk said. "Where d'you come up with these sayin's, any'ow?"

Gil gathered his items and said, "Keep them swords hidden. Wouldn't want this fella wakin' in the night and slicin' us to bits."

Loryk trembled. "Great. Enemies outside and in 'ere."

"Quiet, you! The less noise we make the better."

"You two 'ave been talkin' all night!"

Gil scoffed at him. With a sour huff, Loryk folded his arms and sat in a dark corner across the room. While the elf drifted in and out of consciousness, Neer carefully covered his minor scrapes with a gentler ointment. He didn't seem to mind her presence as she brushed back his hair to cover the marks on his face.

He was handsome, with a slender face, narrow eyes, and full lips. She found herself admiring his rugged looks, which still held an air of elegance beneath the anger and blood. His leather armor, that was wet and dirty with blood, made him almost invisible in the shadows.

"That was incredible," Neer said in her common language. She knew he couldn't understand her, but she was sure he wouldn't mind as his eyes struggled to stay open. "Your people are pretty strong, yeah? Some of the bravest and toughest warriors there are. Even the most capable humans struggle to keep up with you in battle." She lifted his arms to cover his injuries. "We don't have to be enemies. I know the world doesn't like what it can't understand, but coexistence isn't always a bad thing." She glanced at him and was shocked to find his angry eyes were glaring at her. Feeling a bit disappointed she turned away and closed

CURSE OF THE FALLEN

her eyes. "*E'lekgläeh*,*" she said in elvish, and shifted her gaze to meet with his, "trust."

His lips pursed together before he turned away. Leaning against the wall, he closed his eyes and twisted his back to get comfortable. Neer exhaled a disheartened sigh, wishing he'd show her a bit of kindness after she risked her life to save him.

She quietly gathered her things, and with another look at the elf, who appeared to be sleeping, she said in his language, "You're welcome."

She carried the light as she walked across the room, and the elf disappeared into the darkness of shadow.

"Shite…" Loryk whined as Neer got comfortable by his side, "we're goin' to be nyx meat, aren't we?"

With a deep breath, Neer removed her boots and leaned against the wall. Gil poured her a handful of nuts and berries before tossing the sack to Loryk, who clumsily dropped it and spilled his dinner across the floor. Gil sighed as Loryk scrambled to pick up his food.

"The plants of Vleland aren't as nice as what we'd find back home, but they'll keep us alive until we reach the border," Gil said, explaining the foul taste of their meal. "I'll be gettin' some rest. One of you should stay up to keep an eye on things. We'll head out come morn."

"Keep that snorin' to a minimum, Gil. I won't 'ave you blastin' a warning signal to everyone around!"

Gil snarled angrily before curling in a corner and closing his eyes. Within seconds, he fell into a deep, rumbling sleep. Neer watched him for a moment before her eyes shifted to the shadow where the stranger lay alone.

"So, found yourself a new friend, did ya?" Loryk said before popping a berry into his mouth. "D'you think 'e's trouble?"

"No," she said.

"Why's 'e 'ere, you think?"

"I don't know. Maybe he was living here or just passing through."

---

* In the language of elves, e'lekgläeh is a term meaning *in the eyes of another*. It's a saying that requests trust and friendship in the form of mercy or understanding.

"Maybe. Good thing you found 'im when you did."

Neer looked at Loryk as he raked his fingers through his messy hair. It was his golden feature, the one all the women talked about—the bard with the curly auburn hair and deep-brown eyes. No one could deny Loryk was good-looking, with his chiseled jawline and high cheekbones. Upon first glance, you'd never expect him to be a bard, with his heavy Southern accent, toned build, and unkept curls, yet many found these a more attractive quality in such an overly handsome man.

"What're you thinkin' about?" he asked.

She blinked her thoughts away. "Nothing important."

"Spill it, you!"

She chuckled. "Just how we met."

"Not important, aye?"

"Do you remember it?"

"'Ow could I forget? I was singin' at the Sword and Sheath while you were waitin' tables."

She turned away, remembering her first nights with Loryk, before she was introduced to the Brotherhood and learned they weren't the rebellious monsters the Order had made them out to be. She was just fourteen when Loryk saved her from Madam Tilly at the Sword and Sheath brothel,[*] where she had been an indentured servant for many years. Many horrible things happened to her at the famed establishment.

Many things that many people would never know about.

Loryk was the first man to treat her with respect since she'd lost her family. But more importantly, he was the first person, other than her parents, to accept her despite her magical blood.

"I watched you every day," he said, breaking her harrowing

---

[*] The Sword and Sheath was a famed, high-class brothel along the border of Llyne and Styyr. Known for its wide selection of the most astute men and women, patrons would visit from all across the country to get a taste of what the "Sheath" had to offer.

Situated in the center of the ever-growing city of Raeg, the brothel was a central hub for travelers, and many believe it was the reason for the creation of the High Road Pass.

Eleven years ago, the prized establishment inexplicably caught fire. And while many residents of Raeg sought the culprit, they were never found. The Sword and Sheath has since been rebuilt under new management, though it's but a shadow of what it once was.

CURSE OF THE FALLEN

thoughts, "cleanin' tables... scrapin' dirty bits from the floor... bein' pulled into rooms you didn't belong in."

"My entire life has been one cesspit after another." She closed her eyes. "I can't keep living this way. Running and hiding. I am so damn tired, Loryk. I just want to feel peace for once before it's all over."

"You can feel peace, Neer. Just give up your magic. Live your life like a normal woman. Settle down. Get married and 'ave a family."

A smile crossed her lips, followed by a sour laugh. "It's every woman's dream, isn't it? To live for her husband and children, never knowing her own worth or how big the world truly is."

"Neer, that's not—"

"That isn't me. I'm not meant to sew linens or raise children."

He sighed. "I know that... It was just... You're my best friend, Neer. I don' want to lose you. We've been through too much. Plus, without you, all my ballads will go to shit. Who else is more excitin' than you?"

"I'll be fine, Loryk. Once I remove this curse, I'll be back to adventuring with you, and you'll be the most famous bard to have ever lived."

For the first time in a long while, he was speechless. His eyes filled with sadness and longing, and a heavy sigh escaped his lips. "I know what this is really about, you know. The reason you're really wantin' to break this curse."

"I don't know what you're talking about."

"You do." His worried eyes bore into hers.

She did know, yet she'd never admit it. Saying it aloud was even more treacherous than being a sorcerer. She'd never say it, yet somehow he knew, and she could see it in his eyes.

"I'm not lettin' you do this alone. What're you goin' to do? Stop me?"

She smiled with sad eyes. "If it keeps you alive, I will."

"You owe me one. I busted you out of that brothel and gave you a 'ome. 'Elped you find that arun there too. Took a right good beatin' for it."

"You really want to come with me? It's dangerous, Loryk. We could both die."

"What's life if you don't got friends to share it with? If you go, then I do too. We're in this together. Always 'ave been."

"If you go, I can't watch over you like before. If you fall behind, it'll be on you to catch up."

"Yes, yes, and I'll wash be'ind my ears and tuck myself in durin' a storm."

"This is serious, Loryk. You can't hold me back. If you go, then you have to understand that. I can't watch over you. You have to keep up."

"I know, Neery. I'll keep up with you. 'Ave been for ten years now."

"Yeah… We should get some rest, Lor. It's a long journey to the Trials."

"All right. Wake me if you need me." He lay against the wall and closed his eyes.

Neer sat awake in her thoughts, worrying over what would come from these mysterious trials and if the path she chose was truly the right one. Gripping the branding on her arm, she worried about the Order and if they'd find her here. If they were the reason behind these vicious attacks that saw so many innocent lives lost, or if the elf across the room knew who was to blame.

Winds battered hard against the home, and she exhaled a deep breath as her heavy thoughts were interrupted. Cold air seeped through the walls while hissing and growling were heard all around. A hard crash shook the farside wall, and Neer gasped quietly. Her body tensed for a moment before she calmed herself and released the grip on her sword. Her eyes moved between the elf and the door as she sat through the long and desperate night, waiting for a morning that never seemed to come.

Chapter Eight

A Fateful Goodbye

"For you are never truly alone if you have faith in the Light."

— Rotharion, the Book of Light

THE SILENCE OF MORNING DRIFTED over the empty village as Neer lay asleep next to Loryk. Her peaceful slumber was interrupted by the sound of stone scraping against wood, and she stretched with a great yawn before turning her attention across the room where the noise came from.

A thread of light brightened the room as the door cracked open, and she could see the elf's silhouette as he pushed against the heavy stone dresser. Neer watched him curiously before turning to Loryk, who was supposed to keep watch after she fell asleep. He snored loudly enough to drown out the sound of the escaping stranger, and Neer shook her head in frustration.

With every push, the elf moved the dresser slightly, until he was able to squeeze through and partially open the front door. Panicked by his departure, Neer jumped to her feet and raced to his side. "Wait!" she begged, pulling him back into the room.

He pushed her against the wall and placed a dagger to her throat.

"What are you doing?" she demanded in her native language, which she knew he couldn't understand. "Who are you? Did you do this to the village?"

His arms were strong and solid as he held the weapon to her neck. Deep creases formed between his brows as he glared at her and spoke too quickly for her to understand.

"Simple. Words." She struggled to pronounce the elvish word.

His eyes narrowed, and the creases deepened. With a growl he explained, "Swords. My swords."

His furious glare would've been enough to frighten even the boldest of men, but Neer found herself oddly relaxed. Somehow, beneath the weight of his anger, she wasn't afraid. Maybe it was his resemblance to her adoptive father, Reiman, or the fact that he had yet to kill her, though he easily could. Even with her years of training, she was no match against an elvish warrior, and she knew it.

"No," she replied while looking into his eyes. "Friend… Enemy?"

She held his angry gaze, not daring to give in as she waited for his response. When he leaned closer, her confidence faltered. The blade cut into her skin with a sharp sting, and warm blood trickled from the shallow incision. "Swords…" he growled, "or death."

She could use her magic to free herself, but doing so would put her and her friends at risk. The Order would've lost her trail by now, and she didn't want to alert them of her whereabouts. Unable to fight him with her strength, she closed her eyes and reluctantly agreed to return his weapons.

With a wary look, the elf stepped aside. Neer touched the cut on her neck and smeared blood across her fingers. The stranger watched with a deadly glare as she moved across the room and retrieved the dual swords from beneath Loryk's lute. Her fingers ran along the elegantly crafted blades as she admired them. They were unlike any she had ever seen, with strong metal and beautifully twisted handles. She offered him the weapons, which she had spent time cleaning as the boredom of keeping watch got the best of her.

He examined the freshly cleaned steel with a curious gaze. The softness of his expression hardened again as he turned to Neer and handed her the dagger he had used against her.

CURSE OF THE FALLEN

Looking down at her empty sheath, she realized the weapon was her own. He must have taken it from her side when he pushed her against the wall. She couldn't decide if she was more frightened or impressed.

She accepted her weapon, which was shoddy compared to his well-crafted blades, and placed it back into the sheath on her belt. Her heart sank when he stepped to the door, and she quickly took his arm, causing him to turn back with a sharp, angry look.

"Stay." Confusion rushed through her as she realized what she had said. Looking into his eyes, she found a familiar gaze, one that reminded her of Reiman. This stranger wasn't like the elves of the stories, who despised humans and killed without mercy. He was different, she could feel it. "Trust... friend."

He turned away with a hard look. His eyes shifted to hers, before he suddenly pulled away from her grasp. "Trust no one." His words stung her heart, and she watched speechlessly as he slipped through the door and disappeared through the village.

Later that morning, Neer waited outside for her friends to wake. While sitting on a fence post, her eyes were set on the horizon where the elf had traveled. She wondered if letting him leave was the right choice or if he could have been with the Order and taken part in the raid on this village. A scoff left her throat. Just the thought of the Order of Saro working together with an elf was absurd. The Order was the reason such hatred existed between the races. The Great War was centuries ago, yet the Order still wouldn't allow their people to forget the genocide caused by the monster race, as they called them. Anyone not born of pure human blood was considered demonic and was to be purged. The worst abominations, however, were sorcerers. Even if they were born of pure human blood, the Order still called for their immediate death.

Neer turned as the fence post shifted, and Loryk made himself comfortable by her side. He sleepily rubbed his eyes and yawned with a great stretch. She playfully ruffled his unkept hair, and he lazily smacked her hand away.

"So," he ventured after several minutes of silence, "you just let 'im go, did ya?"

"Better to do that than leave him alone while we slept." She gave him a knowing look.

"Nothin' you couldn't've 'andled." He stifled a smile. "I figured you'd go easy on 'im. Always been your way. Look strong, but weak as a noodle."

"Still stronger than you."

"A bit cocky there, aren't ya?"

"Cockier than you."

"You jestin' about my cock now?"

"It's the little things."

A large smile brightened his face. He playfully shoved her aside, and she burst into laughter. He watched her with a beaming smile.

"You spriggets ready?" Gil asked. "We should be movin' along."

Gil transformed himself into a stallion, and they took off toward the border of Llyne, where he planned to return to their home of Porsdur. Although her path led her to the Trials, Neer still wanted to see Gil off at the border. It was a destination she intended to go, anyway, as the entrance to the formidable trials rested along the boundary line of Llyne and Vleland.

"Why isn't Gil comin' with us?" Loryk asked as they traveled for miles in silence. "We'd get there must faster if 'e'd run us around on 'orseback!"

"Gil only came to help us get the arun. He's got other things to do besides run us around Vleland."

Gil snorted in agreement, and the conversation came to an end. It wasn't unlike Neer to travel alone, or with Loryk as her only companion. In the years since she had joined the Brotherhood, she traveled throughout Llyne and eastern Styyr without the aid of seasoned warriors such as Gil, and while she longed to have him accompany her through Vleland, she understood his path took him elsewhere.

As the sun set beyond the horizon, they came to the everglades bordering Llyne and Vleland. Tall trees devoid of leaves stood cracked and withered within the deep, stenching waters.

Neer and Loryk dismounted before Gil transformed back into himself. Sodden wood creaked beneath their feet as they stepped

CURSE OF THE FALLEN

onto a long, crooked bridge. Loryk shuddered as alligators and snakes swam through the marsh below.

Gil stopped and turned to the others.

"Guess this is it, then," Neer said. Sadness washed through her like a river. She was afraid for him, though she knew he could take care of himself.

If the Order knew she was here, they'd be waiting on the other side of the long bridge. Surely, Gil would transform into a falcon or another quick moving bird and see himself home in no time, but the Order would be watching, and they'd have no trouble striking down every animal that crossed their path if it brought them closer to finding her.

Gil nodded. "It's all right, child. We'll see each other again." He reached up and took her hand. "Don't go gettin' yourself into trouble. Only use your magic when absolutely necessary, and for the love of all things, start usin' that head o' yours. Think before you react. And you," he turned to Loryk, "stop jabbin' that jaw of yours and actually put your mind and those scrawny pricks you call arms to work. If she winds up dead because of your foolishness, I'll cut off your nuggets and shove 'em up your whiny little arse!"

Loryk stared wide-eyed in fear of the dreled, and with a nervous gulp, he shakily nodded. Although Gil was barely half his size, he could still hold his own, and Loryk knew he never made an empty threat.

"Take care of each other, all right? I'll let Reiman know where you've gone. Make sure you come back home. The both of you."

Neer knelt and pulled Gil into a tight embrace. He was the second person she met in the Brotherhood after Loryk, and she always viewed him as more of a father than a friend. As she stepped away, Loryk and Gil shared a light hug.

With a thoughtful nod, Gil transformed into a falcon and took off into the misty sky. Neer watched him slowly disappear in the growing fog.

"Neer?" Loryk touched her shoulder. With a deep inhale, she looked at her friend, and together they headed back into the dangerous and forbidden land. Heading east in the direction of the Trials entrance, they walked close enough to the border to smell the stench of its marsh yet were far enough away that they weren't in danger of any of its inhabitants.

"Can't believe we're actually goin' back," Loryk remarked. "Seems odd, don't ya think? We were so close to 'ome I could smell it. Feels like we're marchin' to our deaths."

"Don't count us out, yet. We've only just begun."

Neer crossed her arms and eyed the large rolling hills. It was the same scenery throughout the entire country with no trees, roads, or villages. The occasional decrepit structure—crypts or an abandoned home—broke the mundane landscape, but they were few and far between.

"So," Loryk started, "where're we off to again?"

"We need to get to the entrance of the Trials of Blood, where I can use the magic within the cave of Nhamashel to dispel the marq guarding the arun. According to the map, the cave entrance is a few days from here."

"Another cave, huh?"

"This one is far more dangerous."

"'Course it is... Why d'you think the Order were 'ere in Vleland any'ow? Seems a bit odd they'd destroy some village, then be on their way."

"They know I'm here, so I'm guessing they're coming in quiet to send a warning."

"If the elves found out they're killin' off innocents, it'd start a war." He paused. "I think the Order'd like a war. It'll give 'em a reason to kill a bunch of pale faces!"

She twisted her face in anger at his demeaning remark. Though she'd usually say something in the elves' defense, this time she remained quiet. What little energy she had should be saved for a real fight and not some petty squabble.

The grueling day faded into a cold, uncomfortable night as the rain fell steadily from the dreary sky. Neer bundled into her cloak, wishing for warmth and a dry place to rest. Since their venture back into the wetlands, they had yet to pass any structure that could see them safe for the night. Weathered tombstones, broken cobble fences, and stone pillars were the only signs of a former civilization in the forbidden, desolate country.

Loryk wasn't prepared for a journey such as this, and Neer started to wonder if allowing him to come was a mistake. The plumes of his breath turned white as he leaned forward with his hands on his knees, hair clinging to his face from the rain. "I just... I just need a minute to rest," he wheezed.

"Come on, Loryk. We need to stay together."

"Just a minute."

With a frustrated sigh, she pulled him further along. Searching through the fog, was elated to find the shadow of a shack in the distance. A burst of energy caused her to move quicker. She quickly approached the old structure and found it was a half-fallen home covered with thick moss.

"Wait here," she instructed before stepping to the door. She retrieved her dagger and slowly peeked inside. A low whine hissed from the aged hinges. The left side of the home was caved in with beams and molded planks filling the shadows in an avalanche of debris. Moving closer, she peered to the right, where the empty room was covered by a leaking roof. Charred logs rested atop the scorched wooden floor, and a boarded window left the small area dark and musty.

Neer shuffled Loryk inside and secured the door by its latch. As she removed her hood, Loryk stepped to the ashen logs.

"These logs," he started, "they're... dry."

"What?" She moved to his side and touched the remains of the fire. "It's still warm."

"Someone was 'ere."

The color drained from their faces, and with her weapon in hand, she eyed her surroundings. The fallen side was too dense for anyone to hide or slip through, and the open area where they stood left no space for hiding.

"Maybe they were passing through," she said. "It could've been the elf we saved."

"Yeah... O'course. It must've been 'im. The nyx don't use fires to keep warm."

"Right." She exhaled a deep breath, though her nerves never settled. "Come on. We'll freeze if we don't start a fire."

"But it'll draw 'em to us!"

"We have no choice, Loryk. If this is all it takes to frighten you, you should've gone with Gil."

He crossed his arms with a disgruntled huff. Striking a flint, she created a small fire and then leaned against the old wall. Loryk rested beside her, and they combined their dinner of berries and nuts before picking their favorites from the shared pile. Warm flames hissed and popped at their feet and eased the chill in their bones. Neer leaned onto Loryk's shoulder and stared into the tendrils of orange. Her thoughts shifted from one thing to the next, and she was filled with dread, wondering where this journey could take them, and if they would ever see their home again.

Chapter Nine

Faith in the Unknown

"Demons born of darkness and rot plague the night, feasting on the fears of the living. These creatures of strength, agility, power, and guile must never be underestimated. And above all else, they must be destroyed."

— The Art of Darkness: A Tome of Mythos and Legends

Morning sunlight broke through the clouds and gave the world a glimpse of warmth. Neer and Loryk found themselves at a shallow stream, where she filled their canteens while Loryk struggled to catch breakfast. Water splashed as fish swam quickly through the rapids and slid through his wet fingers. He cursed the Divines, the world, the fish, himself, everything he could think of in his frustration.

Neer laughed as she watched him struggle.

"You have to pin it!" she said. "Jab it! Like a spear!"

"What d'you think I am? Made of sharp steel? These're fingers, Neer, not knives!"

"Oh, sorry, my mistake. Then I guess you'll have to grab one!"

He huffed and, with a quick splash, sent water her way. She laughed as it soaked into her clothes. Loryk got back to work, splashing himself as fish swam through his clumsy hands.

While he muttered and splashed through the water, Neer turned to the quiet world around her. Trees, bare of any leaves or blossomed flowers, stood throughout the vast landscape. Rolling hills of moss and grass extended to the horizon while animals scurried around, chasing one another.

In all its depictions and ghost stories, Vleland was never described as being beautiful. Even in its constant dreary and lonesome state, Neer found herself in awe of the crumbled buildings and rolling hills.

"Got it!" Loryk shouted with pride, jolting Neer from her thoughts. He struggled to hold the thrashing fish before it slipped through his fingers and wiggled itself free. He slipped while attempting to catch it and splashed into the shallow water.

"Dammit it all to 'ells!" he cursed. "I give up!"

"Come on." She grabbed her things. "We should get moving. I'm sure we'll find something to snack on along the way."

The sunlight soon vanished behind a veil of mist, and the land was blanketed with a frigid embrace. Wandering through the fog, Neer spotted old, flooded graves and aged crypts standing tall on the hillsides. Vines and shrubs created a natural path through the overgrown gardens that led to the stone entrance of a crumbling tomb. Rain fell softly from the grey sky as strong winds, quick lightning, and roaring thunder swept over the land.

"Loryk!" She grabbed his hand as he fell behind. "Come on!"

Moving slowly through the growing storm, they approached the old cemetery and crypt. Eroded by years of rain, the headstones were nothing more than grey lumps sinking within the soft soil. A stone wall surrounded the small cemetery of twenty tombstones.

Neer and Loryk stepped carefully through the graveyard and approached the small crypt. She pushed hard against the unmoving door. With a huff, she turned aside and called for her friend, "Give me a hand," she said. "Loryk?"

He stood behind her and stared at the cemetery with wide, terrified eyes. She followed his gaze, watching as the ground rippled like waves. The headstones toppled, and the stone walls cracked as the ground shifted and sank beneath them.

A deep rumble shook the ground as mud and grass flung through the air. Neer leaned aside to shield herself from the filth raining over them. Echoing hisses and clicks overlapped from

CURSE OF THE FALLEN

deep within the sinkholes forming across the cemetery. Neer unsheathed her sword as Loryk stepped back with a hard gulp. Somehow, his complexion had gone even paler, and his eyes were nearly bulging from his head.

The clicking became louder as long spider legs, black as slate, emerged from each of the pits. Their bodies rose from the darkness. Large fangs opened as they twitched and blinked their eyes.

The nearest spider reeled its front four legs up toward the sky and then raced across the grass, leading the others. Their legs splashed into the mud as they moved quickly toward the crypt where Neer and Loryk stood.

Neer raised her sword as the first spider climbed the stairs and then leapt in her direction. Its abdomen flexed as it extended a long stinger at her stomach. These weren't ordinary spiders. They were *spindra*, creatures of darkness. She had read about them in her studies during her youth, but she never thought they truly existed.

Remembering her training, which taught her to fight against different types of monsters and creatures of myth, she spun aside to dodge its attack and swiped her blade through its sternum. Her eyes grew wide as the spindra faded to ash, just as the dogs had done in the village with the elf.

Her attention averted quickly to a second spindra as it leapt from the pillar to her left. She jabbed her weapon forward and impaled the creature through its sternum. Ash filled the air as the spindra evaporated. She choked on the particles as they were caught in her throat.

Catching her breath, she was unable to defend herself as another spindra leapt from the pillar and clutched her face. Long legs curled around her head as its body pressed against her cheek. It lifted its two front legs and opened its fangs as Neer pushed against its abdomen.

The pressure of its grasp was lifted as Loryk struck through its back with his dagger, and it fell to the ground. Its wound bled with dark mist as it raced back to the sinkhole from which it came.

"You okay?" Loryk asked and then stumbled forward with a sudden scream. He fell to knees as a spindra clutched to his back,

73

its stinger deep in his skin.

With a desperate cry, Neer plunged her sword into its abdomen and kicked it away. It legs thrashed as it landed on its back. She struck its sternum, and its limbs stiffened in the air before it faded to ash.

"Loryk!" Neer turned back to help and was forced aside as green acid was sprayed in her direction.

A large spindra leapt from above and stung her arm. Intense, burning pain coursed through her veins. She released a raw scream, clutching the swollen, bloody hole left by the stinger.

The spindra's legs clicked as it moved closer, and Neer slashed across its pincers. The spindra reared its legs and emitted a raspy hiss.

Clenching her teeth, Neer fought against the pain and lunged forward. The spindra moved aside and climbed the wall, hovering above her.

Neer blinked her vision into focus and crawled back. The spindra shifted, watching as she moved. Her mind grew weary as its poison moved through her veins. Loryk lay motionless on the steps while Neer fought to stay conscious.

The spindra reared back, ready to make the leap onto her body, when the figure of a man appeared between them. He struck his spear through the arachnid, and it faded to ash at his feet.

Entranced by her sudden hero, Neer was unable to move. A hood kept his face hidden beneath a shadow, and a beautiful evergreen material was draped across his dark chest armor, hanging loosely over his left thigh. Two leather belts, holding several pouches, were secured at his waist.

Long, pale fingers gripped tight to his spear as he stared down at her. He was tall and of average build, though she figured much of his physique was covered by the layers he wore. Her heart sank as he slowly turned to Loryk and then vanished.

She jumped to her feet with her sword in hand. The world spun as she moved too quickly, and she stumbled into a pillar. Her eyes focused on Loryk as the man appeared beside him. Gripping her sword with weakened strength, she stepped to the stranger.

CURSE OF THE FALLEN

"What are you doing?" she demanded. Her sword disappeared from her grasp, and she stumbled forward.

The stranger, who was focused intently on Loryk, gripped her weapon as it appeared in his hand. His gaze never broke from her friend as he tucked it safely into his belt and then retrieved a vial of yellow liquid. As he positioned the elixir above Loryk's swelling, pus-filled wounds, Neer quickly grabbed his wrist. The man turned to her, and she was able to see his long, pale face.

He wasn't nyx, nor was he from the forest. He was a race of elf she had never seen or heard of before—his fair, almost white, complexion looked as though he hadn't seen the sun in years, and his cheekbones were high and long. His long yellow eyes tilted inward toward his narrow nose. Long, pointed ears protruded from beneath his black, loosely pulled-back hair.

"Who are you?" she asked. "What is this?"

The man was as still as a statue. His golden eyes never strayed from hers, and she started to feel threatened.

"Evae?" she asked, using the native word for his kind as opposed to the human variation of *elf*. She hoped for a response but was met with the same expressionless eyes. "Trust?"

His shoulders slowly rose as he inhaled a deep breath and then turned back to Loryk. His quiet voice moved through the air, but he spoke too quickly for her to understand.

"Save him?" she asked in *evaesh*, the language of the elves.

His head fell slightly between his shoulders, and with a deep breath, he said, "Yes."

Tears filled her eyes as she glanced at Loryk. The bard writhed in agony and clenched his fists. The marks on his back swelled even larger and produced orange veins that climbed across his skin like bolts of lightning. She didn't know if she could trust this stranger, who had appeared from nowhere and saved her life, but she knew that without help, Loryk wouldn't make it. Her magic could only do so much, and removing poison wasn't within her abilities.

With a deep breath, Neer released her grip on the stranger's wrist, and he carefully dripped the elixir onto Loryk's back. The potion hissed as it seeped into his wounds.

"Come on, Loryk," Neer cried, "you can't leave me here like

this! Please!"

The stranger spoke calmly, but she hadn't the care to translate or listen. Instead, she stroked Loryk's hair as he slowly fell unconscious. Her chin shook as tears rolled down her cheeks, mixing with the rain falling from her jaw.

The stranger spoke again, this time more urgently, and she broke away from Loryk to focus on him. He reached for her arm, and she instinctually pulled away. Glancing at Loryk, who lay unmoving atop the stone, she feared the potion might have put him to sleep.

The stranger's low voice caught her off guard as he repeated her simple phrase, "*Trust.*"

Taking a moment to consider his offer, she looked at her arm. The swollen injury had doubled in size and oozed with pus. Turning away in disgust, she offered the injured limb to the stranger. He gently took her wrist and dripped the potion over the infected sore. She winced when the elixir hissed and soaked into her skin.

The stranger pulled away and corked the vial. He then motioned to the crypt door. "Open. Inside," he said, and Neer agreed.

Stepping away from Loryk, they walked to the entrance and pushed hard against the heavy door, but the aged stone was stuck in its place. As she leaned away to rest, the elf continued. His face was a deep shade of red as veins swelled in his neck. With a huff, Neer joined him once again, and as the door slowly scraped against the stone flooring, she exhaled a relieved sigh. As she shimmied into the dark and cold room, the stranger gathered Loryk and followed her inside.

Chapter Ten

The Letter

"Vas neemo see'nah"
— Ahn'clave term of endearment

THE ELF CARRIED LORYK INSIDE and laid him carefully on the cracked stone floor. Neer quickly secured the door and rushed to his side. Dull, cloud-covered moonlight illuminated the many cracks along the ceiling, giving just enough light to see his silhouette in the darkness. Through the dim light, she tucked his dirty hair back and examined his face.

"You're all right...," she said. "You're going to be just fine, okay?"

Focused on Loryk, she didn't notice as the elf dug through his pack and retrieved a flint. His face illuminated as he struck the flint and created a small fire atop the stone.

Neer jumped back at the sudden flames. She examined them for a moment, perplexed that they burned without tinder or wood. The elf collected a vial of brown liquid from a pouch on his belt and dripped it over the flames. Shimmering magic rose from the heat like a cloud of iridescent mist. Neer watched in wonderment as the magic formed around them, creating a translucent outline of a dome-shaped barrier.

The trickling sound of water that dripped from the ceiling fell silent as the magic solidified and became invisible. Neer touched the barrier, amazed it could be formed of alchemy, which had been banned in her home country of Laeroth. While she knew of its tricks and creations, she'd never seen it for herself.

Raindrops splashed above her head and glimmered in the firelight as they trickled down the edge of the barrier. Warmth from the fire, which produced no smoke, quickly filled the small space and eased the discomfort in her bones.

The elf leaned against the barrier with his eyes closed. The flickering light reflected against his bright skin, and the pointed tips of his long ears protruded from his wet hair.

"Name?" she asked in broken evaesh.

His eyes slowly opened and met with hers. A curious look tugged at his brows as he answered, "Klaud."

She pointed to herself. "Nerana. Talk… human?"

He was confused by her mispronounced words as she struggled to get them right. After several failed attempts to speak with him, she let out a frustrated huff and decided to use the few words she knew. "Thank you."

He nodded politely.

"You… m-magic?" She half-expected him to deny this and admit he was moving around by the magic of a runestone or alchemy. In all her life and travels, there was one sorcerer she ever knew of, and the loneliness of her existence was crippling.

He responded in perfect evaesh. "Yes."

A large smile brightened her face, and questions raced through her mind. Only alchemists and shamans of the Order were allowed to experiment with magical energy, and even they could only conjure it with potions and runes. To meet a natural magic user—someone born with magic in their blood—was extremely rare.

Her ears twitched when something shuffled against the floor, and she turned to find Loryk slowly waking. Relief overshadowed her excitement as she crawled to his side.

"Loryk?" she cried.

"Neer?" His voice was hoarse and unrecognizable as he coughed and groaned. "Where are we?"

"Take it easy… We're in the crypt."

"Fuck… my 'ead."

CURSE OF THE FALLEN

"You're all right. Here." She handed him a canteen of water. The cold liquid spilled down his neck as he quickly drank his fill. At the last drop, he tossed the container aside and then looked around in a daze. His sleepy eyes widened as they landed on the stranger across the fire. "What's an elf doin' 'ere?"

"He saved us. Gave you a potion that kept you alive."

"A pale face saved us? I don't believe it."

"Well, it's true." She got comfortable by his side. "The other elf didn't harm us either. Seems they aren't as bad as the Order's made them out to be."

"You've always 'ad a soft spot for them creatures." He shook his head. "All right. Well... what's 'is name? I know you know it."

She suppressed a smile and explained, "It's Klaud."

"Cloud? Like the things in the sky?"

"That's what he said."

He sighed. "Elves an' their stupid names. I know a little bit of 'is language if you want me to 'ave a go at 'im."

"You speak elvish?"

"Well, o' course. Every bard does. We gotta learn all the major languages and cultures." He grunted before clearing his throat. "In fact, there was this one time that—"

"Maybe we should save the stories for another time, Lor." She knew all too well how long his stories could last.

"Right." He turned to the elf. Speaking slowly, he communicated with the stranger.

Klaud's eyebrow raised curiously as Loryk's stuttering voice fell quiet, and the silence quickly became awkward as he stared dumbfounded at the bard.

"What did you say?" she asked, unable to translate his horrible excuse of elvish.

"I just asked what 'e wants with us."

"I don't think he wants anything, Loryk."

"Got to be a reason 'e saved us, yeah?"

"Maybe he just didn't want us to die."

He shook his head. "Nope, that's not it. No one risks their own life for a stranger's. Not for no reason, any'ow."

"Okay, but why was he so confused?"

Loryk shrugged.

Neer huffed. "Come on, Loryk. He's a sorcerer! We have to figure out who he is before he leaves!"

Loryk straightened and looked the elf in the eyes. He spoke with great confidence, and if she didn't know any better, Neer would have assumed he was speaking fluently in elvish. But she did know better, and judging by the befuddled look on Klaud's face, she knew that Loryk's proud voice was speaking words he didn't understand.

Loryk fell silent as Neer angrily huffed.

"I'm doin' my best!" he argued. "It's been years since—"

"I'm going to do it."

"Do what?"

"Speak to him."

She stepped to Klaud's side and placed two fingers on his forehead, ready to use her magic to understand and speak his language. He was confused but didn't back away. Instead, he remained unexpectedly calm, looking at Neer with indifference and the hint of intrigue.

She hadn't the time to sort out his expression before Loryk quickly pulled her away.

"Are you mad?" he scolded. "We just fought off the Blades! If they sense you usin' your magic, they'll send more people after us!"

"We have to speak to him!"

"For what? What good'll it do if 'e's a sorcerer? Hmm?"

"He could be the only other magic user alive, Loryk! We can't let him slip away!"

"We can't risk our lives to find out! Look, just let me try again, yeah? You've got to start usin' your 'ead, Neery, or we'll wind up dead."

With a huff, Neer crossed her arms, and Loryk attempted to speak to Klaud. He pointed at the flames, and Klaud responded, though Loryk was now the puzzled one. Neer turned away and closed her eyes as her frustration grew.

The bard handed Neer a vial of clear liquid. "It isn't magic, Neery. It's alchemy."

"No," she argued, "he's a sorcerer. He told me he's magic. I saw him teleporting around!"

"You must've conked your 'ead good durin' that fight. This'n said 'e isn't a magic user."

"You're wrong!" Loryk continued to argue as she approached the elf once again. With a deep sigh, she ignored his pleas and placed two fingers on Klaud's forehead. Hot, tingling energy surged through her. The warmth of her magic traveled from her chest and into her fingers, where it absorbed into his body. His energy swirled with her own as their magic collided. Beads of sweat formed across her forehead as her body tingled and burned. Slowly, the intensity of their energy faded, and chills stood her hair on end as the warmth disappeared. She inhaled a much-needed breath and carefully opened her eyes.

After several deep, nervous breaths, she attempted to communicate. "Can you understand me?" Laughter leapt from her throat when she spoke his language perfectly. She covered her lips with her hands, hoping to quell the excitement that burned inside her.

He was puzzled and intrigued. With a long finger to his chin, he responded. "Yes…"

She bit her lip as another joyous chuckle escaped. "You can understand me?" She couldn't remove the smile from her lips.

"Yes."

"Sorry…" She attempted to compose herself, though the excitement clung to her like metal filings to a magnet. "I'm Nerana. This is Loryk."

The bard gave Klaud a sour look while stiffly waving.

"Why did you save us?" she continued in elvish. "How were you able to teleport? Did you use fire to create this magic?" She shook her head when she realized the mistake in her hurried words. With an embarrassed chuckle, she took a deep, calming breath. "I'm sorry… I'm a sorceress too."

His ears twitched, and a peculiar expression transformed his sullen look into one of confusion and wonder. "You're a sorceress?" he asked.

"Yes! I mean, aside from just using magic to learn your language, I can't really prove it, but I am! Honest. It's why I'm here in Vleland! I'm searching for Nhamashel! I'm to pass a trial that—"

"Neer!" Loryk barked. His disapproving look was enough to keep her quiet. He must've heard her speak the word Nhamashel, as he couldn't have possibly understood everything she said. She turned away, though the embarrassment of speaking so candidly was outweighed by her excitement.

"What's 'e sayin'?" the bard pressed. "Who is 'e?"

"I don't know. I've been talking too much for him to get a word in."

"Well, why don't you stop and let the man speak?" Loryk turned to the elf. "First leaf hits the crib?"

She and the elf shared an equally confused glance as Loryk waited patiently for a response to his outrageous question.

"Loryk...," she started in the common language, "what are you trying to say?"

"I asked what 'e wanted. I thought you could understand their language, Neer. 'Onestly!"

"Just take a rest, all right? I'll keep my head about me."

With a silent huff, he took his place across the fire.

Klaud spoke, while Neer focused on her friend. "You're a sorceress?" he asked.

"Yes," she said and turned back to Klaud.

"And you're human?"

"Of course."

"Peculiar..." He stroked his lip and furrowed his brows.

"What about you?" she pressed. "I saw you teleporting around, and you grabbed my sword from yards away! You're a sorcerer too!"

"No. I'm *eólin*. Magic runs through my veins, but it isn't inherent."

"I don't understand."

"I was not born with magic, yet I possess its power. My energy is limited to apportation and selective teleportation."

"I'm not sure I understand..."

His gaze shifted to Loryk as the bard ate an apple. He bit into the empty air as the fruit disappeared from his grasp. With a surprised gaze, he turned sharply to the others, and his jaw dropped

CURSE OF THE FALLEN

at the sight of his delicious snack in the hand of the elf. Then with a gentle toss, Klaud returned the apple to its rightful owner.

"I can apport loose objects directly into my grip, and my teleportation is limited to small distal jumps." He paused, and at the sight of her eagerness to ask more questions, he quickly interjected. "Why are you in Vleland? This is no place for your kind."

"I could ask the same of you. It's obvious you aren't nyx..."

"I come from the forest but am neither Klaet'il nor Rhyl."

"Those are the two largest forest clans,* right?"

He nodded. "It seems your knowledge of my kind far exceeds that of ordinary humans."

"I was raised by an elf... uhm, evae," she said, quickly correcting herself. Shame befell her as Klaud lowered his brow in disapproval. The term was considered derogatory and impolite, and Neer was ashamed to have used it so casually in his presence. Being from the human country, Neer had grown accustomed to calling the evae by such insulting words, as anything else was viewed by the others as too kind a phrase for the *savages of the south*.

Even Reiman, who himself was an evae, used the slang term as it gained him the trust of the locals who once viewed him as savage and wicked.

"You were raised in the forest?" Klaud asked. His voice dissolved her thoughts and pulled her back into the conversation.

"No. Reiman left the forest about seventy-five years ago. He's been living in Laeroth, in a liberated hold known as Llyne."

He nodded knowingly. "You mentioned Nhamashel?"

Her eyes flickered to Loryk, who was staring intently at them, and she waited for a rebuttal that never came. "Yes," she said, refocusing her attention on Klaud, "I'm to get through the Trials of Blood and gather energy from the caves of Nhamashel to lift a curse."

"A curse?"

"Yes. I have a curse in my blood that tracks my magic.

---

* The elves, or evae, live within the expansive forests of Nyn'Dira in the lower reaches of the continent.
Several clans call the country their home, with the largest being Clan Klaet'il, Clan Rhyl, and Clan Saevrala, respectively.

H.C. NEWELL

Anytime I use it, the High Priest can sense it and find me... He's been following me my entire life."

"The Trials are not to be taken lightly."

Their eyes met, and she grimly explained, "It's the only way."

He turned away with a soft sigh. Firelight glowed on his unnaturally pale skin. Long fingers curled together above his knees as he stared into the flames.

"How do you know about the Trials?" she asked while sitting by his side.

"As it seems, I, too, am headed to Nhamashel." Her eyes glistened as their gaze met. "I have to dispel a curse that's killing someone I love."

Her excitement diminished. Loryk asked what the man was saying, and Neer took a moment before explaining. He scoffed loudly in disbelief.

"You can't believe this, do you Neer? What're the odds that—"

"I have a letter," Klaud interrupted. Though he couldn't understand a word of what Loryk said, it was clear the bard didn't believe him. Klaud retrieved a rolled parchment from a pouch on his belt and passed it to Neer. With a quick glance at Loryk to view his curious reaction, she unrolled the letter. Beautiful elvish calligraphy covered the page. She feared that touching it may destroy its elegance.

Turning to the light, she read aloud for Loryk to hear:

Klaud,

The ingredients which you need shall be found throughout the forest and wetlands. I believe that the Nasir is to blame for my illness as he seeks only to find power, and without my blood it will be easier for him to gain. I can't place the blame on him with indisputable certainty, but I know it was him. Please, Klaud, do not follow in his path. Take the Trials of Blood. It's the only hope of curing my ailments and setting me free. Do this, and we can put an end to his madness.

You must collect:

CURSE OF THE FALLEN

One fisothen from the m'aisha of Vleland
Two nimasar from the caves of Nyn'Dira
Four ounces of spindra ash

Take these ingredients to the waters of Nhamashel, perform the sacred chant, and create the potion that will dispel the illness cast upon me.

Mela'anum, Klaud. Thank you for all you've done for me.
You will always be my light.
Azae'l

Reading further she found a note near the bottom:

Find him, Klaud... bring him home before it's too late.

She read the note four times over before passing it back to its owner. Klaud carefully rolled the parchment and tucked it safely into his cloak. He leaned forward and stared bleakly into the fire. Not even Loryk would break such a heavy silence. Hundreds of questions raced through Neer's mind, but she didn't dare to ask.

Eventually, the silence lifted as Loryk asked her to explain the letter, and she did so with remorse, feeling as if she'd told a secret that was only meant for her to know.

Loryk said, "You don't think he just conjured that up, d'you? 'E is magic, after all. Why would 'e need a letter, any'ow? Couldn't that person've just told 'im what was needed?"

"I don't think so," she remarked. "The words are too meaningful. His look is too... desperate. It felt like more of a farewell than anything. I think it's real."

"Can never tell with you magic users what's real and what isn't. Guess we'll find out in time." He leaned back with his hands behind his head. "Ask if 'e's got any food. I'm starvin'!"

Neer ignored him and instead focused on more important matters. "The Trials," she started in evaesh, "you're to go through them alone?"

"I have no other choice."

"There is no one to help you? Other sorcerers or friends?"

"No... I'm the only one."

"Do you have the ingredients mentioned in the letter?"

His eyes widened, and he sat forward in a sudden panic. The spear apported into his grasp before he shattered the barrier with its sharp tip and then disappeared.

Cold air rushed over Neer like an angry wave as the door of the crypt creaked open and Klaud rushed outside. The enchanted flames never flickered in the breeze that swept through the doorway, carrying a cold chill through the haunting space. Lightning brightened the room while thunder shook the ancient walls.

Neer was silent as she gazed curiously at the door, waiting for Klaud to return. Seconds later, his shadow appeared in the entry before he stepped inside. His bare feet left a trail of mud across the floor as he approached the others. In his hand was a glass vial full of mud.

He placed it into a pouch and collected the potion he used earlier to create the barrier. Neer watched as he dripped a potion over the alchemical flames, and another barrier was formed that trapped the heat inside.

As if he'd forgotten there were others, Klaud undressed and spread his armor and undergarments across the floor. Loryk turned away with an uncomfortable scowl, while Neer watched curiously. Orange light brightened the many scars that extended across his arms, back, and chest. He removed a woven pack and the parchment he so desperately clung to from an inner pocket within his armor. He then spread a few drops of an elixir across his garments before striking a flint and setting them ablaze.

Loryk and Neer jumped back as flames erupted before them. "What the 'ells!" Loryk barked. "'E's mad! Deranged!"

Neer watched in fascination as the fire danced across his clothes. The flames hissed and popped, but not a feather of ash floated through the air. As the fire slowly died, Klaud patted the remaining flames away and revealed his perfectly dried and warm clothing.

He quietly slipped into his outfit and safely tucked away the parchment before passing his woven bag to Neer. He gave a reassuring nod, and she dug through his things. Several dozen vials of varying liquids, a jar of blue capsules, bandages, feathers, flint, and other miscellaneous items made up the contents of the small bag. Digging further, she found objects she didn't recognize, including the wet, dirty vial full of mud.

"Did you just collect this?" she asked, examining the vial. "Is it why you raced outside?"

"Yes. It's the wet ash of a spindra that was just killed." He politely took his bag and items. "I have everything needed to create the elixir to cure her."

"And it's sure to work? I've never known of an elixir that can cure curses. Only the arun can —"

"Neer!" Loryk hissed at her mention of the arun. The object was incredibly rare and dangerously powerful. Telling a stranger, especially one with magic, that they had one was beyond foolish.

"The aruns are rare," Klaud said. Neer's heart sank as she wondered if he caught on that she was carrying the item in her pocket. "Finding one would be next to impossible and using it even more so." His suspicious eyes shifted to her, and he studied her expression as the haunting words slipped from his tongue. "How do you plan to lift your curse?"

His words were expected, but still, she was frozen. He watched her intensely, studying her every movement. With a slight gulp, she explained, "I was told the waters of Nhamashel could give me the strength needed to overcome it." She made up a story she hoped he would believe. "The scholars say the waters of the cave are extremely dangerous but if ingested by a magic user it can strengthen their energy tenfold, allowing them to overcome any ailments that hinder them."

His eyes narrowed with suspicion. "And you believe this? You're willing to sacrifice your life and the life of your friend for this rumor?"

She glared into his eyes, daring him to question her further. "I have to."

With a long, hard look, he turned away. "I will leave for the Trials in the morning. You may accompany me if you wish." His friendly voice turned grim as he gave a deadly warning. "But don't mistake my kindness for friendship. If at any moment you falter or fall, I won't hesitate to leave you behind."

Chapter Eleven

A Journey of No End

"On this day henceforth, there shall be no communion or commerce between evae and humanity. Any entry into foreign soil will be regarded as an immediate act of war."

— Treaty of the Light, post Great War

NEER LAY ASLEEP IN THE crypt, thrashing, and moaning as visions clawed her mind.

She stood alone on a grassy hill, gazing up at the shadowy figure of a man hovering at its peak. Beneath the shadow lay a pile of bodies displaying the pained and broken faces of the people she loved.

The sword in her hand dripped with their blood.

As the shadow flew out of sight, she raced after it, tripping over the bones and blood of the corpses beneath her. Mist obscured her vision as it rolled through the air with a subtle breeze, followed closely by the scent of rain. A flash of lightning struck the ground with a thunderous crack, and Neer fell backward.

Blood spattered beneath her as she collapsed onto a dense, soft surface. She lost her breath as she crawled to her knees and turned to find Loryk's mangled, bloody remains lying beneath her. His cold eyes were unblinking. Purple bruises covered his skin, and a deep slash cut his face from scalp to jaw.

The shadow wisped through the air like liquid black. Neer sat on her knees in quiet sorrow as it hovered before her, bringing itself close enough for her to feel its icy chill. A face was hidden beneath its

CURSE OF THE FALLEN

cloak—one she recognized from years past and hoped to never see again.

As she crawled back, her hand slipped into darkness when the ground vanished and she fell beneath the surface. Her heart raced as she plummeted further before landing with a hard jolt atop an iron table. The coldness of its surface stung her skin as she stared into the darkness surrounding her. Five cloaked men stepped forward and shadowed the dim candlelight flickering in the distance. She was able to see only the glowing outlines of their silhouettes as they stared down at her.

She fought against their unyielding grips as they restrained her ankles and wrists to the table with buckled leather straps. A cold sweat formed over her skin as the orange light from a hot branding iron emerged through the shadow of cloaks. She panicked, screamed, begged for mercy as the heat drew nearer. Her chest shook as her heart throbbed, the fear mounting, until the scorching fire was pressed against her skin, and she was consumed with agony.

With a gasp, she woke from her nightmare. Beads of sweat dripped down her face, and she clutched her racing heart. Looking over her shoulder, she searched for the shadows of her dream, afraid they were close and would find her.

But she was alone, and in her safety, she exhaled a deep breath, sitting forward with her fingers in her hair. The crypt was quiet, and she quickly realized she was alone. The flames of the alchemic fire still burned atop the floor, though the barrier had disappeared. Across the room, Loryk's lute lay on the floor with his belongings.

Shuffling to her feet, she stepped outside and squinted through dull sunlight that was blanketed by an overcast sky. Peering through the dreary morning haze, she looked over the destruction of the graveyard. Her gaze fell to Loryk's blood staining the steps, and sadness weighed her chest at the thought of losing him. He came so close, and the journey had hardly begun. As she doubted herself and the decision to allow him to tag along, her thoughts were interrupted by his loud, boisterous voice echoing from the hillside.

"Again!" he called in evaesh.

Neer followed his sound before finding him standing by a creek with Klaud.

The elf studied the water with a hard look and then hurled his spear. With a great splash, it struck into the stream and then teleported instantly back into his grasp. Water drizzled onto his face from the panicked fish that was skewered by the spearhead.

Klaud removed the fish from the spear and placed it next to two others on a large rock. It was a slimy, awful looking thing, with the smooth, translucent skin of a jellyfish. Neer thought it must be native to this region, as she had never seen anything quite like it.

As she approached, Loryk lifted his gaze and smiled brightly. "Mornin' Neery!"

She smiled politely and came to his side. Her eyes veered to Klaud's spear, and she carefully lifted the weapon into her hands. Twirling it slowly, she noted how lightweight and beautifully crafted it was. Every detail was a piece of art that put human weapons to shame.

She placed the weapon aside as Loryk's offended tone broke the silence.

"What am I s'posed to do with this?"

Before she could ask, she, too, was handed a raw, gutted fish. "What kind of fish is this?" she asked while suppressing a gag.

The gooey green meat sat in her hand like fresh mucus with a smell that was rotten and repugnant. With a horrified gasp, Neer and Loryk watched as green slime slid down Klaud's chin when he took a large bite and feasted on the raw breakfast.

"Oh no..." Loryk covered his mouth before expelling what little contents his stomach held.

Neer turned away and gulped down her nausea. The sound of Klaud chewing while Loryk vomited was far too much for her to handle so early in the day.

"Klaud," she gulped, "why aren't we cooking this?"

"We don't have time to start a fire, and we can't waste the potion," he explained. "It's disgusting, but it'll keep us alive."

"We couldn't have caught anything other than... this?" She extended her palm to hold the fish far from her nose.

"Eat." He wiped his hands together after finishing his meal. "Then we leave."

He washed his hands in the stream while the others struggled with their decision to eat or starve. Neer stared at the translucent membranes and thick veins of her meal before turning her hand over and dumping the fish onto the grass.

Once she and Loryk composed themselves and decided not to eat breakfast, Klaud led them away.

They walked for miles in silence, listening as the winds slowly picked up speed, and waited for the rain to fall. The ruins of cracked moss-covered homes and abandoned graves created a break in the unending green surrounding them. Neer kept her eyes on the weathered headstones, imagining more spindra emerging from the depths.

Crossing her arms to cover the chills that rose across her skin, she turned her attention to Klaud, who led them without a word spoken. She began to wonder why he had come here alone and if the people of the forest were also banished from entering the borders of Vleland, or if it were just humans that had been outlawed.

He walked several paces ahead, and while she was curious for answers, she hadn't the energy to catch up to him for a chat, so instead, she turned to Loryk, who walked alongside her and scribbled into his worn leather notebook.

"What are you writing?" she asked, peeking over his shoulder.

"Oh, nothin'." He quickly closed the book. "Just a story or two."

"You a scribe now, Ebbard?"

"All good bards know their way around words. We're quite a gifted lot."

She snickered. "I still remember that story you told me a long time ago. About some kitchen wench... What was her name again? *Vaeda?*" She suppressed a smile as he glared at her with pursed lips. "She was a charming little thing, yeah?" Neer teased. "With blonde hair and dazzling green eyes."

"That's enough, Neer!" he cried shrilly. "We don' speak of 'er, 'specially in front of strangers."

"Not like he can understand us anyway."

"It don't matter. Keep your 'ead about you! Remember what Gil said? Think before you speak!" Loryk lightly whacked her forehead, and she fell into a fit of laughter while he seethed.

As midday arrived, the sun peeked through parted clouds. It was the first hint of sunlight they'd felt since their arrival to the dreary wetlands, and Neer basked in its fleeting warmth. The rolling hills had transcended into moist plains with large trees and streams carving through the grass. Birds flittered through the air while small animals rummaged the dirt in search of a meal. She inhaled the scent of wet leaves and was startled by the lingering odor of smoke in the air.

"Klaud!" she called to the man walking several paces ahead. He came to a quick stop and turned around, watching as she followed the smell to the top of the hillside. Far below in the wide valley were the remnants of a burned and blackened village. Light grey smoke wisped from the fallen beams and scorched bones that scattered the ground. Neer stood motionless, staring misty-eyed at the village below. The outlined figures of bodies, many of them children, rested in the debris, covered by embers and soot.

"What the 'ells 'appened?" Loryk asked.

Neer couldn't speak. Her mind was elsewhere as she remembered her own village, which was destroyed long ago. She was only ten years old when the Order came and took everything from her, just as they had taken everything from the people below.

"Who were these people?" Neer asked. "Why would they have been attacked like this?"

"They were nyx," Klaud explained. He was stiff as he gazed at the village with sorrowful eyes. Turning away, he exhaled a deep sigh, and said, "Let's go."

"Wait!" she protested. "We should do something! There could be survivors!"

"Do what you must, but I'm not here to help them."

"How can you be so heartless?"

He continued walking without a backward glance, and Neer turned back to the village. She couldn't allow these people to suffer and die, yet she couldn't lose her only hope of surviving the trials. She needed Klaud to get to Nhamashel. Without him, there was no hope of gaining the cure and freeing herself from the

Order's clutches.

She scanned the village and waited desperately for a shift in the ashes or a cry for help, but they never came, and as Klaud disappeared over the hillside, Neer forced herself to step away from the ruins and trail behind him.

"Neer!" Loryk whispered. "Did you notice it?"

"What?" she snapped and instantly regretted speaking so harshly. The guilt of leaving any survivors behind ate away at her.

"The symbol of the Order!" Loryk continued. "It were carved into trees and bodies."

Her heart raced at the mention of the Order. Was this their way of luring her back to Laeroth, where they'd be free to pursue her without the constraints of a potential war with the elves? Coming into Vleland, which was elven land, was strictly forbidden. If the nyx discovered humans were behind these attacks, it would incite a ruthless, bloody war. She angrily clutched her arm, hating to be marked with such a horrid symbol.

As night fell, the group camped beneath a large tree. They secluded themselves beneath a barrier from the heavy winds and dangerous creatures. After being reassured by Klaud that the invisible shield was soundproof, Loryk plucked his lute and wrote a song. As his melodies strummed through the air, Neer closed her eyes and was taken back to her childhood when she and Loryk would run through the fields, chasing the sunlight. As it would dip beyond the horizon, they'd find themselves within Mr. Willard's large wheat field. The old man would've screamed at them for hours if he had ever found them traipsing about in his glorious fields, but the adventurous bard and his boyish friend had always been elusive.

"What're you smilin' about?" Loryk asked with a smile of his own.

"Nothing." Neer turned away to hide the grin she didn't realize she held.

He nodded, knowing it was futile to argue, and instead changed the subject. "Can you ask the pale face 'ow much longer this'll take?"

"His name is Klaud."

The bard scoffed and waved his arms defiantly, reminding her much of Gil. Neer gave a disapproving look before asking Klaud the question.

"We should arrive by midday tomorrow," she translated back to Loryk.

"Do you 'ave a plan?" Loryk asked, and Neer translated again.

"No," Klaud stated, "but I do know that the Trials are said to be extremely dangerous, even for the most gifted of mages. It's unlikely we'll survive."

"Wonderful," Loryk griped.

"It's why I wonder…"—his eyes shifted to Neer's—"why is he here?"

Loryk waited for Neer to translate, but she never did. Instead, she spoke directly to Klaud on Loryk's behalf. "He wants to be."

"You're sending him to his death."

"We both know the risks. Who am I to tell him what to do with his life?"

"If he falls behind—"

"He won't."

"We won't have time to—"

"*He won't.*"

Loryk quietly glanced between them as they glared at one another. Hoping to break the tension, he dug through his stolen jeweled satchel and valiantly displayed the ocarina. Klaud turned away with a grimace as Loryk held the instrument in front of him.

"Almost forgot!" Loryk exclaimed. "Klaud, is it? Play? Can you…" The bard blew into the instrument and created a horrid sound that pierced their ears.

"Give me that!" Neer snatched the ocarina away, and Loryk raised his arms in defense.

With a sneer, Klaud got comfortable and closed his eyes. In time, the others did the same.

The trio lay asleep beneath the safety of their invisible barrier. Alchemical flames cast a soft glow that expanded beyond the reaches of their shelter, creating shadows that danced across the wind-blown grass and puddles. Shadowy animals with glowing eyes and sharp fangs crawled through the darkness, undeterred by the storm that swept the land.

CURSE OF THE FALLEN

A loud crash of lightning brightened the sky, jolting Neer from her slumber. She jumped with a gasp and glanced quickly at Loryk and Klaud, who both sat up with equally tired gazes.

"These damned storms," Loryk griped as he rubbed his face. "'Ow much longer 'til we reach the cave? I'm ready to get out of 'ere."

Neer groaned from the pain in her stiff back as she sat upright. "Careful what you wish for, Loryk. The Trials are far worse than this marshy cesspit."

Her attention moved to Klaud as he sat up and cupped his hands over the fire to warm them. The soft light reflected against his skin, and it was only now that she had taken pause to notice his unique appearance.

The elves of the forest were said to be beautiful, with smooth skin, long faces, and slanted eyes. Klaud had all these traits, but still, he was far less than attractive. His ears were too long, his eyes too narrow, and his skin was sickly white.

She contemplated his looks and wondered if her own imaginings had led her to believe the elves to be far more beautiful than reality would hold. Her adoptive father, Reiman, was an elf, but he looked nothing like Klaud. He *was* handsome, and very much so. Even the other humans, who strongly opposed the elves, couldn't deny he held a physical radiance that was otherworldly.

As Klaud's gaze shifted in Neer's direction, she flinched and quickly turned away, not realizing how lost she had become in her thoughts. Hiding the embarrassment that bloomed across her cheeks, she asked, "Where are you from?"

He was quiet for a moment, and she quickly realized she had asked in her common tongue.

Turning back to meet his gaze, she said in his language, "You said you're from the forest, but you aren't of the larger clans. Is that why you look different from my adoptive father? He's *Rhyl*."

Klaud stared into the flames with distant eyes until he blinked his thoughts away and returned his attention to Neer. "I don't know what I am," he admitted to her surprise. "There are other *eólin* like me. We all carry different magical energy, but our appearances are similar. We do not look like the others, because we are not like the others."

She pulled up her knees and wrapped her arms around them. Loryk had lost interest long ago in their foreign conversation and took to writing fervently in his leather notebook. With a deep exhale, Neer said to Klaud, "*Eólin*... that's being born without magic yet still holding its abilities? It wasn't passed to you through your blood." Klaud nodded in a silent response. She lifted her hands and stared at her palms. "Do you think... that maybe I could be..."

Her words fell silent as the thoughts slipped from her mind like mist from a morning leaf. It was foolish to ponder her existence. She was a sorceress, born of darkness and power. At least, that's what the Order had her believe. It's what they had everyone believe.

"Klaud," she said as another thought entered her mind, "how do you *know* you weren't born of magical energy?"

"A sorcerer may only be born from First Blood lineage, and every First Blood who is born with magic is a full sorcerer."

"What's a full sorcerer? How are they different from you?"

He lifted a hand. "Please. That is enough for now."

Frustrated by her ignorance, she leaned against the barrier with crossed arms. She recognized the phrase First Blood from her studies with Reiman. It was the elvish term for the ahn'clave who vanished long ago. They left behind many secrets and mysteries in the labyrinth of tunnels known as Anaemiril, including the Trials of Blood she was soon to face.

Dawn soon broke, but they never saw it as thick clouds swirled through the sky with heavy rain and strong winds. Neer struggled to push through the cold gusts as she clutched Klaud's arm to keep her footing and not lose track of him.

Streams overflowed, and waterfalls crashed against disturbed waters. The rolling hills had long faded into mountains and foothills that ran along the border of eastern Llyne and the outskirts of the Everett Mountains.°

---

* The rugged mountains hugged the eastern coast of the continent and filled the region of Llyne with its sprawling foothills and densely wooded areas.

CURSE OF THE FALLEN

Neer held tighter to Klaud's arm as they trailed carefully down a winding hillside and came to the edge of a deep pond. A fisherman's shack, covered with mold and cracks, rested along the water's edge to the west with empty barrels, broken fishing nets, and overgrown plants collected along the banks.

The clear water of the pond rippled beneath the impact of heavy rain, and through its surface, Neer could see the murky soil that sloped inward, becoming black at its center.

"This is it!" Klaud's voice was drowned out by the harsh winds.

Lightning struck the ground nearby with a deep crack, and Loryk leapt into the air while clutching Neer's arm. She paid him no mind as she watched Klaud step confidently into the shallow water.

"Klaud!" she called over the sound of wind and rain. "What are you doing?"

Loryk pulled her back as she followed after him. "Are you mad?" he shouted.

"He can't do this alone!"

"'E's deranged, Neer! All them elves're—"

Another crack of lightning vibrated the air, and he pulled her close. Water fell into her eyes as she watched Klaud walk further into the pond. The rippling, waving waters never rose above his waist as he moved closer to its dark, empty center.

He slowly stopped and gazed to the black hole beneath him. Rain soaked through his cloak and clung his dark hair to his shoulders and face. He knelt into the water and pressed against the barrier at his feet. The spear on his back appeared instantly

---

Known for its logging, Llyne was once the central exporter of all lumber in the country of Laeroth, trading their timber for the iron ore of Ravinshire and the fine wares of Styyr.

After the Brotherhood took siege of Llyne sixteen years ago and declared it a free state, the logging region saw a long and harrowing economic depression after it was refused all imports and exports from Styyr and Ravinshire.

Many of its residents lost faith in the Brotherhood and fled from Llyne in a movement known as The Last Stand. After the discovery of iron ore within the mines of the Everett Mountains, however, the Brotherhood saw an increase in residents and profit, and the rebel state of Llyne became the largest producer of steel weaponry and products in the country.

in his grasp as he lifted his hand and then struck the weapon against the barrier. Water splashed across his robes, and his face tightened into an angry, bitter snarl as he jabbed his spear repeatedly into the water.

Several minutes passed before he fell still and silent. Lightning brightened the sky, but he didn't seem to notice as he stared desperately into the water.

His shoulders fell with a heavy, defeated sigh, and he returned to the shore. His long face seemed even longer as he walked past the others without a glance in their direction.

"What's going on?" Neer asked.

"We can't enter," he stated bleakly, before coming to a slow stop. With a grave look, he turned to the others and regretfully revealed, "The cave has been sealed."

CHAPTER TWELVE

A FISHERMAN'S TALES

"The long and winding corridors stretch from border to border, crawling beneath the entirety of the continent, brimming with magic just beneath our feet."

— The Secrets of Anaemiril, evaesh tomes

NEER SAT WITH THE OTHERS at an old, splintered table in a fisherman's shack by the pond. Winds shifted the outer walls and filled the silence with the steady hum of creaking wood.

"What do we do now?" Neer asked. "Is there a way to get inside?"

Klaud leaned forward with a sigh and combed his wet hair away from his face with his fingers. "No, the barrier is too powerful. The First Blood must've sealed it before they vanished, but I believe I know another way. It'll take longer, which is unfortunate, as time is crucial in keeping Azae'l alive."

"Azae'l?"

He turned away and touched his robes where he had tucked the parchment. "She's someone I care for deeply. She is..."—his voice faded—"very important. Losing her would be a great tragedy."

Neer carefully asked, "Why has someone cursed her?"

His eyes moved to the fire in the hearth, and the pull of deep longing came over his face. Unblinking, his gaze shifted to the floor. Warmth from the fire tousled the loose strands of his drying hair as it fell around his shoulders. The green material of his armor moved gently in the light breeze from the flames, and his long shadow stalked the room as he fell into a sad trance.

Loryk continued to play his lute as he eyed the others, never knowing what they said as they spoke too softly and too quickly for him to follow. Distracted, he accidentally plucked a wrong note, creating an unpleasant stroke that ruined the ballad and jolted Klaud from his thoughts.

With a hard blink, the elf straightened his posture and looked into the fire. "What of you?" he asked with forced resolve. "Why have you been cursed?"

Neer wanted to press him for more, to know why he was risking his life, but she decided against it. "I'm a sorceress. The *only* sorceress. That makes me a threat to the Order of Saro."

"The *Order of Saro*?" He spoke a phrase not native to his language.

"They're our leaders. The High Priest supersedes all other priests or high-ranking officials. He's the closest to the Divines that anyone could ever be."

"*Divines*?" Another word that wasn't in his vocabulary.

Neer struggled to find a fitting word but soon shrugged it off, for she didn't have the time, nor the patience, to explain the Divines to him.

"The Order imprisoned me when I was a child," she explained. "The curse was placed in the event that I escaped so they could find me. I suppose they thought I'd be too daft to realize that anytime I used my magic they'd come crawling about." She paused with a somber gaze. "I don't know why they didn't just kill me like all the others. It would've saved me a lifetime of trouble."

"Must be a terrible fate to have to hide who you are or risk certain death."

"It's why I'm risking everything to cure it. I don't even remember what it was like to be normal. To not have this pain built up inside me."

"It's like being under water for a second too long and finding the surface is an inch out of reach," Klaud said sympathetically.

They shared a long, knowing gaze. Never had anyone understood her like this. She turned away and rested her chin on her knees. The silence lifted as Loryk bounded over and stomped his foot against the floor to rid himself of the fish guts he'd so carelessly gotten himself into. Neer gagged at the unbearable stench as he stepped closer.

"What?" he barked. "What else am I to do while you two are off makin' friends and gettin' all googly eyed?"

"Not getting your foot stuck in a jar of entrails would be a start," she scoffed.

He made an inarticulate, sarcastic expression, and with a great thud, he plopped down in a chair beside her.

"So," she said to Klaud, "about this other entrance you mentioned."

The chair creaked as he leaned back. "It's the back entrance of the cave system leading to Nhamashel. I'm certain this is where the Trials will begin, seeing as they've sealed the cave as a diversion to any wanderers."

"A diversion?"

"This sealed cave is the only entrance mentioned in any of their texts, but I know a scholar who studies the First Blood, and he discovered there is a back entrance. Only those worthy enough of knowing its location shall open its doors and enter the Trials."

"Where is it?"

He asked, "Do you have a map?"

"I do, actually."

She dug through her things and retrieved the map she'd found at the library in the caves. Klaud unfolded the parchment, which revealed only the eastern border of Laeroth—Skye, Llyne, and Vleland. He pointed to the thick border of Vleland and Llyne.

"We're here. The cave moves beneath the marshes and under the mountains, coming out here, in Havsgard."

"I know that place!" Loryk beamed. "My father went there for work once! Said they're a ripe old bunch of prudes! Them coal miners once when I was eleven... or was I twelve? No, wait, it wasn't the coal miners, but the diamond diggers. No wait, it were—"

"How in the world are you a famed storyteller?" Neer griped. He choked on his breath and stammered in offense. "How dare you!" he gasped.

Neer ignored his outburst and turned back to the map. "So, the entrance is in Havsgard?"

"Yes," Klaud said, "but it'll be tricky and hard to find."

"Yeah," Loryk added after Neer kindly translated, "I've never 'eard of no cave system bein' in the mines. Surely someone would've found it by now."

"We'll need an object called a *revalor*," Klaud suggested.

"A what?" Neer asked.

"It's an object meant for seeing things which can't be seen."

Her eyes widened. She knew what he spoke of as she had *borrowed* the object many times from Reiman's desk when he wasn't looking. The clear stone was a magical artifact that allowed you to see magically altered objects as you looked through it. Reiman and the warriors would use them to unveil illusions, while Neer and her friends would steal it from his desk and sneak out at night to hunt for a wraith's den, which was said to be hidden behind an illusion of its surroundings. They never found the den, but it never stopped them from searching.

"A glass eye," she explained. "Reiman has one of those! We can get it from his office back home!"

"So what?" Loryk began. "We go 'ome, grab the glass eye, go to 'avsgard and enter the cave?"

"That's right." Her chair creaked as she leaned back. "We just need to wait for this storm to pass."

As the walls continued to sing their creaking, wind-blown songs, Neer tapped gently against the table and glanced around the room. Through a small window, she could see the storm raging outside and knew they'd never be able to leave in such a mess. With an impatient huff, she stood and wandered the shack.

The room was small, with four cracked, unsealed walls that allowed the wind and rain to seep through, leaving the air cold and floor covered with shallow puddles. Hanging on the wall above a molded cot across the room were fishing poles and nets. Empty buckets, cauldrons, and boxes were strewn carelessly around the floor, as if someone had gathered their things and left in a hurry.

Searching for nothing in particular as she sought mostly to the pass the time, she turned to the dresser and slowly pulled open the top drawer. Through the shadowed compartment, a large snake lifted with a violent hiss. With a gasp, Neer slammed the drawer shut and took a quick step back. Rubbing her hands onto her shirt, she gulped down her sudden fear.

"What was that?" Loryk asked.

"A snake," she admitted shakily.

"You go up against giant spiders but can't 'andle a little snake? 'Onestly, Neery, get yourself together." He plucked a string off-key and then quickly scribbled in his notebook.

She ignored his teasing and turned back to the dresser. With a deep exhale, she gained the courage to open the second drawer and peeked inside to find old, stained clothes folded neatly into two separate piles. She dug through the contents and slithered her fingers around a leather coin purse tucked safely into the back corner.

Retrieving the pouch, she pulled the drawstring and overturned the small bag into her palm. Two dozen rusted iron fishhooks spilled into her hand and onto the floor. With a huff, she tossed them on top of the dresser and continued digging through the clothes.

"What're you lookin' for?" Loryk asked.

"Anything," she remarked. "Maybe we can find something useful while we wait."

"This's a forgotten shack. All we'll find're fish guts and the stench of death. May as well just sit down and relax like the rest of us. Right, Klaud?" He glanced at Klaud, who remained silent as he stared back at Loryk without expression. Loryk twisted his face in confusion and then turned to Neer. "Are you sure that's 'is name? It's a bit odd. *Cloud.*"

"I'm sure, Loryk." She ignored his ramblings as he carried on about something she didn't have the care to hear. Searching through the bedding, she found an old leather notebook hidden beneath the pillow. The cot creaked beneath her weight as she sat along its edge and flipped through the weathered pages. She squinted her eyes and brought the journal closer as she read the smudged writing.

God's be good, the journal read. *They've taken everything from me. My home... my girls... even my blasted dog. All for what? Because I chose to stay on the border in my family's land? The Six would never treat a man this cruelly. What have I done to deserve such disgrace?*

She skimmed through several paragraphs when a familiar word caught her eye, and she started reading again.

The Child had better pay for this. For taking my family from me. For bringing them pale faced demons into our lands and causing such strife with the Divines! This is my punishment for forsaking the Order and choosing to stay in Llyne when I should've fled. With that damned elf leading them rebels no one is safe...

Neer reread the paragraph, becoming engrossed in the words as they repeated heavily in her mind. *The Child had better pay for this... For bringing them pale faced demons into our lands.* The Child was a moniker known widely throughout the human country. Short for *Child of Skye*, it was a name given to Neer by the Order of Saro to segregate her existence and strip her of humanity. Whoever wrote this entry believed she led elves into their land to slaughter his family.

A cold sweat dampened her skin as her heart raced. She couldn't breathe. Couldn't think. Nothing but the words, so haunting and dangerous, were present in her mind. Surely, this man was deranged. His mind twisted from living in exile. Neer had never led outsiders into her land, and moreover, she'd never conducted a massacre such as the one inflicted upon this journal's author.

Weighed heavily with guilt and confusion, she nearly jumped from her skin when Loryk's loud voice rang in her ears. The book snapped shut in her hands as she turned to him with a sharp glare.

"What?" she asked, not hearing what he had said.

"I asked what you're readin'."

She tossed the journal onto the bed and then moved to the table. Loryk followed and sat beside her as she explained, "I think the man staying here was fleeing from Llyne."

"Why?"

With hesitation and slight anger, she said, "Because he believes that I've brought elves into our land."

"*What*? Why would—"

"I don't know." She leaned forward with her head in her hands.

He leaned closer, speaking quietly so Klaud wouldn't hear, though the elf couldn't understand him. "There're no elves in Llyne! None except Reiman!"

"He was living in this shack because they destroyed his home, Loryk. You don't forget the faces of the people that killed your family."

"Seven 'ells..." His eyes flashed to Klaud, and then narrowed with suspicion. "What d'you know?" he remarked with sudden fury. "Why're your people comin' into our land!"

Klaud was motionless as Loryk stood and leaned over the table. Neer quickly pulled him back and guided him to the chair with her hands on his shoulders.

"Calm down," she said. "Let me talk to him."

"You're too nice, Neer! If he knows somethin', we need to find out! We can't be runnin' around with the enemy like this!"

She sighed, frustrated that he was right, yet still unwilling to see Klaud as anything but an ally. For now, at least, that's how he would remain. As Loryk crossed his arms in anger, Neer turned to Klaud and asked, "Why are your people invading our country?"

His brows pulled together with genuine confusion. The chair creaked as he repositioned himself and then leaned forward on the table. "They're invading?"

"Yes. Why?"

He pondered for a moment, his eyes moving from one place to the next without ever settling on anything. "I don't know."

"Are you sure?"

Their gazes met, and she could sense his sincerity as his expression washed with fear. "If they're invading, then it's already too late. The cycle has begun."

"Cycle? What are you talking about?"

He jumped to his feet and gathered his things. "We cannot waste any more time. We must leave before it gets worse."

"Hang on! We aren't going anywhere until you tell us what the hells is happening!" She stepped in front of him as he made haste for the door. With her hands in the air, she prepared to stop him, but he disappeared. Sharing a quick glance with Loryk, they snatched their things and chased after him.

"Klaud!" Neer shouted through the wind and rain, but he didn't look back as he marched onward toward the border of Llyne.

Chapter Thirteen

Wispers and Screams

"I bring you my worries, my troubles, my woes, and beg thee to cast them anew. The love of the Mother, graceful and free, please grant peace upon my soul, and shall I give to thee my undying affection, my life, my love."

— Prayer to Kirena, Goddess of the Six

THE WIND AND RAIN SLOWLY faded as Neer and the others crossed the border into Llyne. For now, she had given up on trying to speak with Klaud as he refused to answer any questions, but in her suspicion, she kept him close. If he was going to enter her country, she was going to make sure he didn't do anything foolish.

Pine needles crunched beneath her feet as she moved further from the marsh and deeper into the foothills of the Everett Mountains. Neer looked at the sky as sunlight broke through the clouds, giving her a touch of warmth on the cool autumn day. She gazed at the trees and inhaled the familiar scent of fresh pine air. The tall, rugged mountains were a welcome sight after her long journey through the wetlands of Vleland.

Her attention moved to Loryk as he shook his hair to get rid of the excess moisture in his thick locks. He then tipped his head aside and shook the water from his ear. "Strange, isn't it?" he asked.

"What?" Neer said.

"'Ow just across them murky bridges are never-endin' storms, but 'ere, it's beautiful as can be."

"You've heard the stories," she explained, "Vleland was cursed° long ago, after the nyx took over the continent."

"That isn't 'ow it goes!" he argued, and she let him, knowing it was futile to contend with a storyteller such as himself. Loryk always had a way of romanticizing history, and it suited him well in his profession. "The nyx're wild, fiendish pale-faces, 'ellbent on rage and bloodlust. They lived with the ahn'clave thousands of years ago."

"I don't think it was *thousands* of years, Loryk."

He cut her a sharp look, and she stifled a smile. "Are you tellin' the story?" he barked in defense. She raised her hands in a silent apology, and he continued, "Where was I? Oh, yes, their leader, *Amalgth—*"

Neer chuckled as he made up an odd, elvish sounding name.

"Was said to be the best bard in all the land. Truly a gift sent directly from the Divines to bless all the world with song and story."

"Here we go..."

He ignored her sarcasm as he became lost in his fairytale. "'Is people loved 'is music. They'd dance and sing all 'is songs day and night... but there was one person who never danced. She never sang or tapped 'er foot to the music. And it drove 'im mad. Sick with rage, 'e gave 'er a story she'd never forget and conquered all the land! The only 'ope of stoppin' 'im was—"

---

* The Fall of Vleland is a major story in every history book that tells the triumphs and woes of a people gone mad with power.

Centuries ago, the nyx rose up against the people of Laeroth and began a massacre that lasted two decades and claimed more than ten thousand innocent lives.

The nyx, a nocturnal and bloodthirsty race of elves, slipped through the night like shadows. Their agility and night vision allowed them to move undetected.

After many years of war with the nyx, who made no claims or terms for their uprising, the ahn'clave were successful in forming an airborne curse that altered the biology of the nyx and forced them to require constant moisture to survive. Alongside this, Vleland was also cast with eternal rain and cloud cover that created an organic prison the nyx couldn't survive without.

CURSE OF THE FALLEN

"Quiet!" Klaud hissed from up ahead. He then crouched forward and reached for his spear.

"What's 'e doin'?" Loryk whispered.

Neer swatted incoherently to silence him, and she watched as Klaud snuck further ahead. Hidden within a thicket of shrubs, the elf drew back his spear and then hurled it into the trees. The whimpering cry of a doe soon followed, and Klaud disappeared.

Neer trudged forward and peered through the shrubbery where Klaud reappeared next to an injured doe. He placed his hands on the animal's side and then whispered too low for Neer to understand. As he lifted his hand, the dagger hidden beneath his cloak appeared in his grasp. His voice never faded as he closed his eyes and jabbed deep into the doe's throat. It kicked and released a squeal before falling silent.

"Thank you," he said while stroking the animal's side.

Loryk nudged Neer's arm and whispered, "What's 'e doin'?"

As Klaud wiped his bloody hands onto his cloak, Neer came to his side. He glanced at her before returning his attention to the doe and turning it onto its back. Without speaking, he began cutting the meat and removing the hide.

"Were you speaking to it?" Neer asked.

Klaud removed a handful of innards and dropped them into a pile at his side. He continued carving the animal, and said, "Yes."

"Why?"

"*Daë'vilaahl.* Respect." He leaned back and turned to Neer. "This creature was alive. It was innocent. There is no greater sacrifice than the one it was forced to make. I show honor to that sacrifice."

Turning to the deer, she realized how unaffected she had become to the hunt and was humbled to be in the presence of someone who considered this an honorable sacrifice rather than routine killing. For most, Neer included, animals were nothing more than a meal to be served, and while she'd never want to see one harmed or in peril, the act of ending one's life for her own survival was as natural as breathing.

As Klaud peeled back the hide, Neer turned away and asked, "What did you say to it?"

"*Drétiahl aeloth'mëreen.* It is our wish for peace and comfort as they depart from the living."

"Where do you think they go? Their souls, I mean."

"Everything is made of energy, and when it dies, it is returned to the land and the air."

Neer eyed the leaves as they rustled when a soft breeze swept past. She had never heard of such a belief and admired his willingness to share what had become so dangerous and secretive in the human territories. Faith in anything other than the Order and Circle of Six was punishable by imprisonment or death. Even the mention of such heresy would see the blasphemer and their family in the temple dungeons. Far too often had the rumors flown of children being sent to the gallows for the crimes of their parents. The harsh rulings kept the people fearful and gave unyielding power to the Order.

Her thoughts shifted to Klaud as he separated the meat from bone, and she was surprised at how quickly he had carved such a large animal.

"You should start a fire," he stated. "We can—"

His voice was interrupted by a sudden, horrified scream coming from the distance. Neer stood and unsheathed her sword. Staring in the direction of the sound, she fell silent and still, examining every movement that disturbed the empty wood.

"What was that?" Loryk asked as he inched next to Neer. His dagger shook in his trembling hand as he nervously watched their surroundings. When a woman screamed, he flinched and nearly dropped his weapon.

"*Help us!*" The woman's shrill, panicked voice called from deep in the woods.

Neer stepped forward, waiting for something more, another scream, the patter of footsteps, the clash of swords. But there was silence. With a deep breath, she gripped tightly to her weapon and raced into the woods.

"Neer, wait—!"

Loryk's voice was muffled by the sound of snapping twigs and crunching leaves as Neer ran toward the screams. Low hanging branches scratched her arms and face as she moved through the dense wood and thick underbrush before coming to a shallow pathway covered with pine needles and leaves. She stopped on

CURSE OF THE FALLEN

the trail and searched for the voice that had long since disappeared.

"Hello!" she called. "Can you hear me?"

"Neer...," Loryk said as he came to the path. "What's gotten into you?"

"You didn't hear her?"

He placed his hands to his hips and dropped his head. "We can't go fightin' everyone's battles, Neer. You've got to use that 'ead of yours."

She stepped to him, glaring. "I won't let her die!"

"Who?" Loryk remarked. "It could be a trap! They could be with the Order! Or the Gods-damned *elves*!"

The thought pressed her mind as she wondered if the writings of the fisherman had been truthful, and if the elves were truly to blame for the massacre of his family. If so, they could still be here, watching from the trees or hiding in the underbrush.

They could be with Klaud.

As if the thought had called him forward, the elf appeared along the path nearby with a sack of deer meat slung over his shoulder. The edges of his fingers were still stained with its blood.

Neer stepped forward and closed her eyes, regretting her decision to run so foolishly into the woods and bring herself and Loryk into a potential trap. The Child of Skye was a notorious target, one the Order would pay even the most savage of elves to capture and bring forth to the High Priest.

Surely, Klaud wouldn't travel this far if he had ill intentions. He wouldn't take them into the human country where his people were strictly forbidden. No, she wouldn't believe it. For now, at least, she would trust him, though her confidence waned with every passing moment.

Lost in her indecision, she was startled by the sound of rustling twigs that came from nearby. Broken of her thoughts, she became clear of mind and lifted her sword to better defend herself. With her eyes on the woods, she took a careful step forward, lingering on the edge of the path as she gazed into the endless sea of pine trees and thin grass.

A blood-curdling shriek came from the north, and with a glance at Loryk, Neer followed the harrowing sound. She was sure she could fight her way out of a trap. Her magic was strong enough to save herself and Loryk if she needed it, though she hoped desperately that she wouldn't.

Night fell over the foothills long before the rest of the world as the sun dipped beyond the peaks of the mountains. Moving further into the foothills, the path was cobbled and uneven, and Neer held her sword close as she passed by several cabins nestled deep within the wood. The small homesteads were surrounded by short wooden fences, small vegetable gardens, and clothing lines still hanging with long dried garments. But not a soul walked along the homes as they stood quiet and forgotten.

As Neer moved through the sprawling, abandoned village, a door suddenly burst open, and she came to a startled halt. Wood creaked beneath hard footsteps as a woman marched out onto the porch of the nearest home. She lifted a pickaxe above her head and stared down to the strangers below.

"I'm warning you!" the woman remarked viciously. "Don't step one foot closer!"

"Are you hurt?" Neer asked. "Where are the rest of the villagers?"

The woman spat at her and said, "If you want help, go find it elsewhere! This here's no place for the likes of him!" She pointed at Klaud. "Anyone that walks alongside them demons is a traitor to us all!"

"We heard a woman screaming! She—"

Neer was interrupted by the sound of rustling branches and whimpered cries. Chills crawled across her arms as she found it wasn't the sound of a woman crying for help but was the whimpered cry of the doe Klaud hunted. The animal was carved into pieces, yet its voice echoed through the air like a whisper in the wind.

"What's 'appenin'?" Loryk cried.

"It's a wisper," Klaud said.

Neer's blood ran cold at the mention of the mythical, deadly creature. "What?" she snapped. "Wispers are creatures of darkness! They aren't real!" Her voice wavered between strength and fear as she forced herself to remain calm. Creatures of Darkness were known throughout Laeroth as vicious, twisted creatures full

CURSE OF THE FALLEN

of dark energy and pain. No one knew their origin or reason for existence, and until her recent encounter with the spindra, the large spiders which were creatures of darkness themselves, Neer had always believed them to be tales of fiction.

Klaud's expression transformed from its naturally brooding appearance into one of uncertainty and fear. "We need to leave. We can take residence in one of these abandoned homes!"

As Neer began to argue, the rustling slowly ceased, and the woods were silent once again. Planks creaked beneath the woman's weight as she leaned forward and eyed the woods. "You've called it here! You've brought this plague upon us!"

"No!" Neer explained with a panicked cry. "We thought someone was in trouble!"

"It took them all!" the woman shouted through sadness and pain. "One damned creature got everyone! My Mirabella was ripped to pieces! It mimics her screams at night..."

"My friends and I came to help you," Neer explained. "We're with—"

"The Order!" Loryk interjected harshly, as if the words had been pulled from his lips. His eyes remained on the stranger as Neer gawked at him with confusion and disgust. "We caught this pale-face in the woods last night. Been travelin' to the border to trade 'im off for rations and coin. Posters said they're goin' for fifty silver a 'ead!"

The woman sneered with uncertainty. Her lip twitched and grip tightened on the axe. "I don't want the likes of him around here! We've done lost enough!"

Loryk lifted his arms. "Please, Miss. 'E won't hurt nobody. We even got 'im to fetch us some meat for dinner. You're welcome to supper, should you allow us to stay for the night."

Quick footsteps pattered from inside the home before a young woman stepped onto the porch. Her black hair flowed down to her waist, covering the dirty miner's apron and stained blouse she wore. "Ma, what's—"

"Head inside, Rose," the woman remarked.

As Rose spied the strangers, her eyes widened with glee. "Ma! Do you know who this is?" She raced down the steps, and Neer quickly turned away to hide her eyes, though she didn't need to as Rose fixed her attention on Loryk and smiled, taking his hand. "This is Ebbard of Rhys!"

Loryk straightened his posture and lifted his chin with newfound confidence. With a sly smile he said, "It's nice to meet you, *Rose*." His smile widened as she blushed. "I'd 'ate to trouble two beautiful, strong women such as yourselves, but we 'eard the screamin' and came as fast as we could. Seems it were just a trick from that wisper that's runnin' around."

Rose turned away with sudden sorrow. "It killed them all. My mother and I have survived by keeping quiet and staying indoors. We were set to leave for Smedelund in the morn." She glanced between them, and then turned back to her mother. "We can't let them stay out here. They'll die."

Her mother's angry eyes narrowed, and her grip tightened around the handle of her axe. Loryk squeezed Rose's hand, and she quickly turned to meet his gaze.

"We won't make it much longer like this. I've already been taken by the Blades…" Luckily for the group, Loryk's bruises from his imprisonment in the Shadow Blades cabin still painted his face in various shades of purple and yellow. Shallow cuts covered his arms and clothes, leaving him to look more despondent and wounded than was true. "And the wispers…," he continued, "if we're caught out here, we're good as dead." He glanced at Klaud. "'E's a good one. Will cook up some nice venison with my friend 'ere if you let us stay."

Neer glared as he offered her for servitude. Surely, this tale of woe wouldn't be enough to win over the hearts of such hardy women, but as with most women Loryk came across, they were instantly wooed by his charm and good looks, and Rose wasn't an exception to this as she clutched his hand to her chest, and said, "Come inside. I'll draw a bath and get your wounds patched up good as new. Divines be praised, you found us in time!"

"Thank you. You've truly saved us."

As she turned away and led them up the stairs, Loryk cut Neer a proud, daring look.

"Watch yourself, *Ebbard*," she whispered as they slowly ascended the steps to the porch, "or you'll be the husband of a coal miner."

CURSE OF THE FALLEN

He eyed the beautiful woman who clutched his hand. "I can live with that," he said with a devilish grin.

They were led into the home, and Rose hastily fluffed the pillows on a cushioned bench before Loryk took his place next to her. He exhaled a deep sigh as he sank into the pillows and closed his eyes.

Footsteps descended into the hall as Rose marched from the room to retrieve a cauldron of water. Neer stood by Loryk's side and eyed her surroundings.

"We're with the Order?" she whispered, hoping there was a reason for his lie.

"They're devout," he said of their hosts. "I saw the pendants around their necks. The emblem of Kirena.*"

Neer glanced back to Rose's mother, who stood by the door with a watchful eye on Klaud. Hanging just above her bosom was the iron pendant of a widely blossomed flower. "Good eye," Neer said. "Guess I should go be with Klaud. If we leave him alone too long, they'll get suspicious."

"Keep your eyes covered. If they recognize you, we're done for."

Without response, Neer walked across the room to the table where Rose's mother removed the clutter and instructed Klaud to lay the bloody sack.

"My," the woman said, "guess they was right about you elves. You look strong as an ox. A bit lacking in appearances, though."

Though Klaud couldn't understand, Neer huffed at the insult. Her eyes remained on the woman as she stepped to the counter nearby and began chopping leeks and carrots. Neer glanced to Klaud, and with heavy disdain, she approached the woman's side, collected a knife from the counter, and then grabbed a bushel of carrots for chopping.

---

*One of the six Divines, Kirena is the Goddess of purity, compassion, and health. Her temple resided in northern Llyne before the brotherhood took siege of the land and destroyed all traces of her holy sanctuary.

Rebuilt twelve years ago, the temple of Kirena resides now in eastern Ravinshire and hugs the border of Llyne. All are welcome in her place of worship and praise, though anyone carrying the sigil of the Broken Order Brotherhood are immediately apprehended and thrown into the temple dungeons, never to be seen again.

The woman gave her a cautious glance before wiping her hands onto her apron and stepping aside. "Who are you?" she asked.

"Marie," Neer lied. Being a sorcerer, Neer was always careful to keep her identity hidden, as any ties to her origins could lead to her capture. Even her name was enough to raise suspicion, but her most telling feature was her bright teal eyes. Throughout the years, she had grown used to staring at the ground to avoid recognition.

"I'm Lizbeth. That's my girl, Rose. She's all I've got left." With a sigh, Lizbeth leaned against the counter and stared at the floor with a distant, hollow gaze. "The Child came and set loose wispers in the woods. My Mirabella was taken... sliced up like a pig!" Her face twisted with agony. "The Brotherhood promised peace from the elves, and peace from their resistance with the Order! But look where it's got us! My family...my home... it's all gone. Because of that blasted demon!" She closed her eyes and exhaled a pained breath. "You're truly with the Order? You aren't here to take what little I have left... If so, just leave us be. We're good people. We've done nothing wrong."

"We are," Neer said, keeping her hardened eyes purposely on the vegetables. "Divine's grace is fleeting and warm. Whosoever shall challenge it be warned. The love of the Father carries the many. The souls of the wicked—"

"Be burned aplenty," Lizbeth finished the sacred prayer of Rothar, the overseer of the immortal plane and Divines.

Neer knew each prayer for all six Divines. They were taught to her during her training with the Brotherhood to better conceal her identity and win the trust of those far more devout than herself. And while the words were spoken as nothing more than a manipulation, they still burned her tongue and twisted her stomach.

"How do you know it was the Child?" Neer asked, curious to know where the rumors begun. "Surely, a sorcerer doesn't have the ability to call upon creatures of darkness."

"How else?" Lizbeth wiped her eyes with her apron and blew her nose into a rag. "It's prophecy! Written in the scrolls and passed through the ages by the wicked Nizotl."

CURSE OF THE FALLEN

Neer turned as Rose gasped from across the room. She sat next to Loryk and stared at her mother with her hands over her lips.

"Sorry, Rosie," Lizbeth said. "I know we shouldn't speak of the wicked one. But time's being what they are, there's no need in dancing around the truth."

"The truth?" Neer asked.

"The end is coming. Until we capture that blasted witch, we'll all be suffering."

Neer was silent as Lizbeth bounded across the kitchen and filled a pot with the chopped vegetables and carved meat. "Well, Divines be good," Lizbeth said with a hint of elation to her dreary tone. "You're lucky to have found yourselves here before the wispers got to you." Her red, puffy eyes glanced at Klaud. "I'm going to be keeping my eye on him. He isn't to go nowhere near my girl, you hear me?"

"Of course. You shouldn't have any trouble, though. He's proven useful so far. Seems they make better slaves than they do enemies." Guilt washed through her as the vile, hateful words spilled from her lips. She knew she needed to keep favor with Lizbeth if they were to survive for the night, though doing so filled her with irrevocable shame and disgust.

Lizbeth crossed her arms. "You all look like you've been through hells and back. 'Specially that one." She pointed a thumb to Loryk, who sat on the bench, speaking to Rose.

Neer passed her the chopped vegetables and placed the knife aside. "We have. I haven't seen my home in weeks."

"Yes, well, you three can stay in Mirabella's old room. But for safe measure, I'll be locking you in until morn. I've got a daughter to look after."

"We'd be happy to take residence in another home."

"I want you close. Can't have you snooping about or dragging his kind around here. There's one bed, so you'll have to make do. But after dinner, there's to be silence. The wisper's hunt by sound, you know?"

"Thank you."

"Hmm," she expressed with a stiff nod and then walked across the room to the hearth where she gathered logs to kindle a fire for dinner.

Thankful to be out of Lizbeth's watchful eye, Neer moved to Klaud's side and whispered, "Are your people really here?"

She noticed the hardness of his eyes and tightness in his jaw as he said, "I don't know."

"If they are, then war is inevitable."

"My people don't want war with your kind." He leaned forward onto the table and closed his eyes. "*If* they are here, then they're following a man known as the Nasir. He's a ruthless leader of the klaet'il clan, and he... he's the reason Azae'l is lying on her deathbed."

"Why would he come here?"

"I don't know," Klaud stated while looking into her eyes. "You must believe me. The Nasir and klaet'il have always despised humanity. If the evae have invaded, I know they're with him, but I don't know their plans." He glanced across the room as Lizbeth stoked the fire, and Rose led Loryk down the hall to the bathing room. Returning his attention to Neer, he said, "I can only assume that they're here to reclaim our homeland."

"Why? We've been at peace for centuries."

He scoffed. "Forcing our people into the forest and then hunting us for sport is not peace, *lanathess*. I don't fault the klaet'il for hating your kind, but neither do I condone their killing of the innocent."

Neer gazed at him with confusion and offense as he spoke of the Great War,[*] which saw the humans and elves at war for more than a century. The battle was won in favor of the humans, and immediately thereafter, they banished the elves to Nyn'Dira, where they had since lived in quiet compliance. This exile led to centuries of hatred and resentment from both sides.

Since the war, however, humans had sealed their borders. No one could enter or leave without facing the most severe of punishments. Surely, the humans hadn't entered Nyn'Dira and hunted the elves as he claimed. Such an act of defiance would be

---

[*] 75 years after the integration of humans into the elvish land of Laeroth, the Great War begun. It was a brutal, bloody conflict between the humans and elves that lasted 107 years and claimed nearly a quarter million lives, many of which were non-human.

CURSE OF THE FALLEN

punishable to the highest extent of the law. Neer couldn't believe it, yet she couldn't entirely deny it either. The hatred her kind carried over the other races was strong enough to disobey even the harshest of laws and punishments. And, surely, the Order would see no quarrel with humans killing elves so long as the *demons* of the woods didn't step foot across the border.

"They want war," Neer said of the elves, her voice trailing between anger and denial. "What are they after? To take over Llyne? Kill the High Priest?"

Klaud took pause with his finger to his chin. "The chances of the evae being here are nonexistent. Laying siege to your lands like this is suicide. I imagine your leaders would find it convenient to attack innocent villages and blame my kind to escape responsibility."

Neer nodded in response. She knew she hadn't set loose creatures of darkness in the woods, and it wasn't too off-handed for the Order to place blame on the elves for their own wrongdoings. "You're right," she said defeatedly. "Sorry I doubted you."

"Do not apologize for being cautious. Healthy skepticism will keep you alive."

Neer peered through the room as Lizbeth placed a top onto the cauldron of stewing meat and vegetables. As Klaud leaned against the wall, Neer turned to him and asked, "Why did you trust us so easily?"

He crossed his arms. "I don't."

"You haven't killed us yet."

"There is no reason to kill someone who isn't a threat."

"Hey!" she said with a laugh. "I'm much stronger than you think. And Loryk is... well... he's useful when he needs to be. He got us into this house for the night."

With a silent nod, Klaud turned away, and Neer stood in quiet contemplation. Feeling caged by her thoughts, she stepped to the window and peered out into the woods. A dark, unsettled chill crept into her bones as she imagined the wispers and other creatures of darkness roaming the shadows. And it was then she realized something much more sinister than the elves or Order had come to life, and she feared there might be no way of bringing it to an end.

CHAPTER FOURTEEN

SWORD OF THE EVAE

"We do not seek war, but they leave us no choice. They've condemned us, slaughtered us, and left our corpses in their wake. For that, we will show no mercy."

— Sayings of the evae, clan Klaet'il

MORNING DEW COVERED THE WOODS in a dense and foggy mist. Sunrays peeked through the trees, shining golden light upon a new day as Neer stepped out of Lizbeth's home. Klaud strode close behind while Loryk said his farewell to Rose and her mother.

"Thank you again for all your 'ospitality," he said before kissing Rose's hand. "Divines be praised."

The women bowed with their hands cupped in front of their chests, and Loryk did the same. It was a common gesture of prayer, thanks, greeting, or goodbye used among the richly devout that was rarely seen in Llyne. With another gracious smile to their hosts, Loryk turned and followed Neer and Klaud as they set off toward the High Road.*

Neer rubbed her tired eyes as she followed the uneven

---

* A long stretch of road that travels through each hold in the human territories of Laeroth. The majority of the road is made of loose dirt, while some areas, such as those that travel through the capital hold of Skye, are embellished with packed cobblestones.

footpath. Out of respect for Lizbeth and her late daughter, the trio decided not to sleep in Mirabella's bed, though it was offered to them for the night. Instead, they gathered on the floor to rest. But it wasn't the creaking planks or lack of warmth that kept them far from sleep. It was the screams of the wisper imitating a woman in peril that echoed through the wood until dawn.

Neer gripped her forehead with a slight groan and closed her eyes.

"You good, Neery?" Loryk asked.

"Never better." She stood straighter to make good on her lie, though Loryk could see through it. They'd known each other too long to get away with such falsehoods. Still, he knew better than to press her on it. "You?" she asked.

"Never better," he said, repeating her lie.

She gave a sympathetic grin and then wrapped her arm around his. "Lor...," she started, "do you think we can trust him?"

"Hmm?" He followed her gaze to Klaud, who walked several paces ahead. With a huff, his shoulders fell. "Them elves're tricky bastards, Neer. Always startin' trouble."

"So says the Order."

"A whole nation wouldn't believe the rumors unless there was some truth to it."

She pulled her arm away and shoved her hands into her pockets. "The whole nation believes the rumors about *me*."

He started to speak but closed his mouth without a sound. The rumors of her existence were spread to the furthest reaches of the country; she wouldn't be surprised if the elves believed her to be a demon, as well. Born of magic, she was labeled a child of the vain and deceitful divine, Nizotl, who above all else craved power and dominance. It was part of the teachings to denounce all forms of magic and to purge anyone born of magical blood, and human sorcerers were considered the worst of all. They were ingrates spawned by Nizotl himself to lure mankind to extinction. Every child was tested for magic at birth in the form of a blood sampling. When Neer's came back as magically enhanced, she was immediately sentenced to death. But her parents refused that ruling. They fought back against the Order and went into hiding.

"Where d'you expect we are?" Loryk asked, breaking her of the harrowing thoughts.

She shook her head to clear her mind and then peered at her surroundings. Much of Llyne looked the same—sparse pine and birch trees, rocky soil, and the color brown. It was hard to pinpoint exactly where they could be without a signpost, so she took her best guess. "Close to Valde, according to the map. We can stop there along the way. I hear they have the best ale in all of Llyne; so that's something to look forward to."

"Yeah, just gettin' in there with 'im is the problem." His eyes darted to Klaud.

"It should be all right. Reiman's never had an issue with racism."

"That's because Reiman's the leader of the Brother'ood! 'E's proved 'imself ten times over! These wild pale faces are not welcome in our land!"

She sighed in frustration. "So long as he stays close to us and keeps his head down, he should be all right."

"I don't know, Neer. Our kinds don't mix well. I jus' 'ope no one gives us any trouble."

"Please. Angry villagers are the least of our worries."

The trio stopped as a pained, horrified scream came from the west. Neer pulled her sword from its sheath and looked through the trees.

"D'you think—" Loryk started.

"No," she interrupted. "Wispers are creatures of darkness. They can't survive in the sunlight."

"What about them dogs and spindra in Vleland? They were out in the daytime!"

"The sun was hidden behind the clouds. I suppose it was enough for them to survive."

More terrified shrieks came from the west, and Neer raced forward, leaving the others behind. Loryk called out to her as he trailed behind, falling further back as she moved quickly through the woods.

The trees grew thinner as she approached the logging village of Smedelund. Her heart leapt in her chest, and she ran faster, nearly choosing to teleport herself closer as the acrid smell of

CURSE OF THE FALLEN

smoke and burnt flesh replaced the scent of pine needles and dirt.

The trees emptied into sawed stumps as she neared the tree line, where a cobble fence enclosed two dozen smoldering homes. To the left, the Bursbridge river ran along the western edge of the village where a lumber mill sat full of fresh cut logs. Fires wisped into the air as thick smoke rose from the homes and blackened the sky.

Villagers wailed as they ran through the streets, tripping over the bodies of their fallen loved ones as they fled. Horses whinnied in a stable as they fought to escape.

Neer came to a slow stop as she eyed the symbol of the Order that was painted in blood along the side of the burning stable. She couldn't move. Couldn't breathe as she recalled the destruction of her own village. The taste of soot, the stench of burning flesh... the screams of those she loved falling around her. She was lost, staring at a living memory as a village so familiar to her own was destroyed before her eyes.

Her thoughts vanished when a woman ran from the village gates toward the tree line. Her dress was singed and face was filthy with soot. She panted and cried as she fled from the men and women chasing her. They were unlike any Neer had ever seen, with thick blood painted across their faces and armor made of bones and hide. Black markings were etched along their faces, arms, and chests in sharp tribal designs.

Neer was shaken from her trance when the woman screamed as a sword slashed across her back. Her attackers held sinister smiles as she fell to the ground, unmoving.

They licked her blood from their lips and then stepped away. Consumed with rage, Neer ran at them with her sword drawn. While passing a smoldering home, a fighter stepped in front of her, purposefully blocking the path. Without a break in her stride, Neer sank her blade deep between his ribs.

The man stumbled back, ripping away from the sword lodged in his skin. Neer leapt back as the stranger swiped at her chest with his dagger, and she sliced clean through his wrist. The taste of metal set on her tongue as his blood sprayed through the air, coating her skin with spots of red.

The man dropped to his knees and unleashed a scream that

alerted his comrades. Their devilish eyes narrowed with fury, and they charged forward, their weapons held high and dripping with fresh blood.

Neer returned her gaze to the man at her feet. Blood spilled across his left hand as he gripped his severed wrist. With a twisted snarl, she slashed her sword across his neck, and his echoing screams were silenced as his head fell from his shoulders, landing between her feet.

Her stomach churned with regret and disgust as she stared into his eyes. She had to remind herself that this man was with the others. He destroyed this village and killed innocent people. She couldn't allow her morality to subdue her strength. Forcing her doubt aside, she turned back to the others stalking closer.

Neer stepped forward as a man with a deep scar across his cheek unleashed a war cry and lunged his sword at her throat.

She spun aside to dodge the attack, and a sharp sting grazed her ear as he sliced her skin. Coming to his side, she flung her weapon to his chest, and steel clashed as he lifted his sword to block her attack. With a furious grunt, he kicked her back, and she stumbled aside breathless. A flash of silver cut through the air as he swung at her throat. The glint caught her eye in time for her to lift her sword and block the hit. Neer could smell the sweat and blood dripping down his face as they stood together, pressing against the other's weapon, hoping to gain the upper hand. He smiled with ease as she struggled against his strength.

Her blade scratched against his and she managed to thrust him back before leaping aside. With a spin, she put distance between them and caught sight of a spear being hurled in her direction.

She leapt aside to dodge, but the weapon suddenly vanished from the air. The man who heaved the spear stared wide-eyed in shock. Her hands ached as she gripped her sword tighter, preparing to fight. She examined each of her attackers, noticing the slight limp of the smallest man, the fresh cut across a woman's hand, and the burn mark seared through the armor of another.

As she planned her attack, the man she had pushed back came charging forward. She turned to him, ready for his attack, when he came to a sudden stop. A squealed gasp escaped his lips, and

CURSE OF THE FALLEN

a bloody spear penetrated his chest.

Neer stumbled back when the spear was ripped from his flesh and he collapsed in a puddle of blood. Standing in his place, holding the blood-soaked weapon, was Klaud.

Footsteps sounded from behind as a woman ran toward him, firelight reflecting against her blade as she lifted her sword high into the air. Klaud turned and threw his spear, and the woman was thrust back as it plunged into her chest. Her body hit the ground with a hard thud, and the weapon reappeared in Klaud's grasp. Two men approached Klaud from behind, lifting their swords to strike him, and Klaud turned while twisting his spear to block their attacks.

Neer averted her gaze to another man barreling toward her with fire in his eyes. She ducked beneath his swing and then jabbed toward his middle. The man swiped her blade aside and struck for her neck. As she leapt aside, he followed her movement and drew his sword across her forearm.

With a shriek, she stumbled back. Hot blood soaked into her armor as she held her weapon with a shaky hand, not daring to succumb to her agony in the face of such a threat. In all her years of fighting, she had never witnessed anyone of their skill. They moved like water, flowing and dancing without a break in their stride. It was as if they could predict her movements before she made them.

Suddenly, the man lunged forward and slashed deep into her shoulder. She screamed and dropped her sword. Thick blood flowed down her arm as her flesh was sliced to the bone. The man stood before her with a menacing smile, spewing harsh words in a language she didn't understand. He stepped closer and brought the sharp edge of his sword to her throat. She winced as the blade sliced into her skin and drew a thin line of blood.

He leaned closer and placed a thumb on her cheek. Pulling downward, he widened her eye to reveal its color, and his glowering expression became one of contemplation and shock. Releasing his grip, the man stiffened and pressed lightly against her neck.

"*Nizotl vek'drimil,*" he said with a chilling malice to his voice. "*Mör nuireen'alfaar!*"

H.C. NEWELL

As he tightened his grip and prepared to slice her throat, Neer ignored the danger of using her magic and disappeared.

The stranger staggered back. His eyes darted from one place to the next, never settling on anything as he searched for her. A rift tore through the air with the sound of crackling flames as Neer rolled across the ground several yards away. The magic collapsed in on itself and Neer lay motionless on the ground, blood pooling around her unmoving, injured arm.

The man released a furious growl, his footsteps thudding closer to Neer as his pace quickened. He raised his sword, preparing for a downward strike that would end her life, when Klaud appeared to his left and struck his spear at the man's chest.

Metal clashed as the man lifted his sword to block Klaud's attack. He stepped back as Klaud vanished and reappeared behind him. As the man turned to evade, Klaud followed his movement and plunged his spear deep into his gut.

Neer struggled to lift herself, fighting against the vertigo clouding her mind. Her limbs were numb, and her body was warm as blood poured from her wound. She blinked several times to clear her vision, but her mind was fogged with pain and delirium. The world spun as she crawled to her feet and stumbled into a building.

Klaud stood nearby, dodging the quick sword of a man and woman who fought to kill him. He disappeared as they swung their weapons together in perfect rhythm. The woman ducked as Klaud appeared behind her and slashed his spear. She struck her weapon upward and cut into his forearm.

With a pained groan, he teleported away to put distance between them. He leaned against a post and took several deep breaths. His face was bruised, and his arm was painted in red.

Klaud straightened as the woman ran closer, a sinister grin stretched across her lips and her sword raised. Neer could see his struggle as he fought for the energy to flee, but he had depleted himself. As the woman inched closer, Klaud raised his spear, ready to defend himself. His stance was weaker, and his swollen eyes were heavy with exhaustion.

Blood dripped down the edge of Neer's dagger as she drew back her weapon and threw it. The blade spun through the air, plunging into the woman's back.

She stumbled forward and crashed to the ground at Klaud's feet. He sank his spear into her back, and blood spattered across the shaft of his weapon.

His gaze shifted to the man charging forward. As the stranger raised his sword, Klaud lifted his spear to block the attack. The man struck hard against the shaft of Klaud's weapon and knocked it from his grasp.

Klaud stumbled and reached for the spear he was unable to apport. The man lunged, slipping the edge of his sword into Klaud's side. With a deep grunt, Klaud kicked him back and then fell to the ground with an exhausted yelp.

Neer wiped away the blood dripping down her hand and tightened her grip on her sword. The pain of her injury caused fire to burn through her muscles. Every pulse of her heart throbbed through her arm.

The man pressed his boot against Klaud's back and slowly pushed him into the dirt. Klaud struggled against his weight. His lack of energy depleted his strength, rendering him unable to fight back. With a kick to his side, Klaud groaned in agony and rolled onto his back. The man knelt over him, pulling him up by his collar. His fist collided with Klaud's face, sending blood streaking down his nose and lips. With two more hits, the man dropped him to the dirt.

Klaud lay still as blood poured from the opened wounds on his cheek. The stranger tossed his sword aside and pulled a dagger from its sheath on his hip. A smile split his face as he spoke an intimidating foreign phrase and then struck his weapon at Klaud's chest.

A hair's breadth away, ready to make the final blow, the weapon disappeared, and the man smacked his empty fist hard against Klaud's chest. He turned to find where his weapon had gone, and Neer teleported behind, plunging his dagger deep into his spine.

The man gasped as he fell back. Neer stepped away, leaving the weapon lodged in his flesh as he lay on his side, unable to move. She stood over him, examining the markings and blood that painted his face. "Who are you?" she demanded. With her

H.C. NEWELL

vision still clouded and mind unclear, she hoped her words were as menacing as she intended. "Tell me!"

The man struggled to breathe; his eyes widened with pain. Klaud stood and stabbed his spear through the man's throat, killing him instantly. Neer turned to him, noticing the bruises and blood that covered his skin.

As he stepped away, Neer exhaled a deep, pained breath and clutched her bleeding arm. Loryk slipped from his hiding place behind a shed and came to her side with a yellow vial in hand.

"This'll take the edge off," he explained, shoving the vial to her lips, "'til we can get you patched up."

She gulped the potion and sighed with relief as the pain slowly vanished. The weight of gravity crushed her, and Loryk pulled her close as her legs lost their strength. He helped her lean against a nearby cart and then tossed an identical potion to Klaud, who quickly drank its contents.

Neer leaned back and closed her eyes while Loryk carefully inspected her arm. With a nervous sigh, he removed his tunic and cut it into strips. "This might 'urt a bit," he warned and then wrapped the material tightly around her injury. "You're lucky 'e didn't take off your arm! What were you thinkin', Neer? Goin' after fighters like that! And usin' your magic!"

"I couldn't let them get away with this," she said weakly.

"Yeah. You really showed 'em." He wrapped twine around the blood-soaked strips to hold them in place. "We need to find 'elp fast before an infection spreads."

"My magic will help it heal."

"Right. Sure." He turned to Klaud, who was leaning against a post with his eyes closed. Blood dripped from his fingers as it poured from the injury across his chest. Loryk carefully approached him and then looked at the enemies he killed. "Who were they?" Loryk asked in the common language. "D'you know their language?"

Klaud looked at the men Loryk pointed at. He spoke in elvish, and Loryk was forced to ask Neer to translate.

"They're warriors with someone called the Nasir," she struggled to speak.

Loryk asked, "The who?"

CURSE OF THE FALLEN

Klaud sighed and closed his eyes as Neer translated to elvish. "He's the man that cursed Azae'l," he explained.

Neer's jaw dropped, and she slumped back in disbelief. She turned to the men, noticing their distinct foreign features. How could she have been so blind to it before? Their fighting style, their ruthlessness... it was all exactly as described by the priests of the Order.

"Neer?" Loryk asked. "What's 'appenin'?"

His concerned expression faded into shock as she revealed the truth of the attacks. "These people attacked the villages in Vleland, but they aren't with the Order..." Her terror-stricken eyes met with his. "They're elves."

CHAPTER FIFTEEN

BALLADS AND BARDS

"Of all the things I've loved, I've loved you the most."

— Loryk to Vaeda

NEER WALKED ALONGSIDE LORYK AS the group made their way down the desolate High Road. Being so close to the border left the roads empty, which she was thankful for, as anyone passing by might recognize her or give them trouble for having an elf in their company.

Her gaze veered to Klaud as she imagined the destruction of Smedelund and the subsequent war with his people. The Brotherhood would never stand for an elvish invasion. That, along with the sudden appearance of creatures of darkness, left Neer with an uncertainty about the future of their land.

"I can't believe it," Loryk said as he walked alongside her. "Elves… in Laeroth! The Order's goin' to be knockin' on our doors soon enough with you usin' your magic and the elves runnin' around!"

"If I hadn't used it, we would be dead. I couldn't defeat those warriors without it."

"Elves're superior fighters, Neer. It was foolish runnin' in there alone any'ow!"

Neer stiffened with anger. She knew he was right, though she

CURSE OF THE FALLEN

refused to admit it. Even in the face of defeat, she couldn't allow the innocent to suffer. Too often had she witnessed the wrath of those with power and vengeance destroying the lives of people too weak to defend themselves.

Her thoughts shifted to her injured arm as a strike of pain coursed through her limb. In the long hours since their fight, dark bruises and razor thin scabs had formed across her arms and face.

"You good there, Neery?" Loryk asked. He'd been much more attentive to her lately, mostly because she had never shown a sign of weakness like she did now, and watching her writhe in agony over her sliced shoulder made him more concerned than usual.

She didn't mind it, though. It felt nice to have someone care so deeply for her well-being. Rarely did she have someone make her feel less of a fighter and more of a person. During her training in the Brotherhood, Reiman often ignored her pleas for a break or cries of mercy when the bruises and welts became unbearable. Instead, he'd force her to fight and train for hours on end in the rain, snow, or sun. She couldn't say she minded it now, though. All the harsh lessons he taught made her into a strong and capable fighter, but still, she wondered what could have become of her life had she been given a gentler, more nurtured approach.

"Neer?"

Loryk's soft voice pulled her from her thoughts, and she shook her head with a hard blink. "What?" she asked, before quickly realizing what he had asked, as he asked it near a hundred times since the fight. "Yeah, I'm good."

"It's been two days since we passed the border, and we still aren't there yet," Loryk complained. "Should be gettin' close, yeah?"

"Not too much longer. I'm sure by nightfall we'll make it to Valde." She spoke of the nearest settlement along the High Road. It was a larger community with tall buildings, a newly cobbled road, and some of the best ale in all of Laeroth. Many members of the Brotherhood lived near the bustling town, which undoubtedly contributed to its exponential growth.

Loryk said, "I just hope no one gives us any trouble with 'im. What kind of magic can 'e do any'ow, besides teleportin'

around?"
　Neer shrugged with her good arm. "Why don't you ask him?"
　"I've got somethin' better I need to ask."
　"And what's that?"
　"You'll see. I've been practicin' my elvish all mornin'."
　"Let's hear it then."
　"All right!" He cleared his throat, and with a proud look, he announced, "Glue's on fire. Friends sit the brick."
　Her bright eyes were wide with amusement and pity. She wanted to tell him the truth, to keep him from embarrassing himself, but when Klaud turned to them, she couldn't pass on the chance to tease her friend.
　"Better ask him!" She said as Klaud approached.
　Loryk bowed to him unnecessarily, and Neer choked back a laugh as Klaud became even more confused. Deep wrinkles settled between his brows as Loryk repeated the witless phrase.
　Klaud glanced at Neer, hoping for an explanation, and she shrugged with a glowing smile. "You heard the man."
　"Did I?" he asked quizzically. "What is he saying to me?"
　"Isn't it obvious?"
　Klaud's disdain deepened as Loryk smiled stupidly, waiting for a response. With an unamused sigh, Klaud excused himself from the unpleasant mind game. "No." He walked away, indifferent to the bard's feelings or true intentions.
　"What? Why not?" Loryk barked in his native language. "Neer, 'elp me out 'ere!"
　"Sorry"—she giggled softly—"nothing I can do."
　"Bollocks. The whole lot of you!"
　Neer chuckled and linked her arm with his. She leaned onto his shoulder and held him close as he shook his head in disappointment.
　"My legs're killin' me," he said after minutes of silence. "Wish we 'ad a 'orse or could teleport from place to place."
　"Would be nice, huh?" Neer commented.
　"Ask if 'e can do it."
　Neer straightened and, with a huff, reluctantly asked, "Klaud, are you able to teleport with others?"
　"No," he responded without a backward glance. "I can only

CURSE OF THE FALLEN

move in small jumps, and only the objects attached to my clothes or in my grasp may teleport with me."

Neer translated for Loryk, and he griped noisily.

"We should rest for the evening," Klaud explained. "I'll hunt. You two set up camp."

"But—" Loryk raised his hand, and the elf disappeared before he could get another word in. "Great," he griped.

"Come on, Lor," Neer chuckled. "Best not to anger him."

"Scared 'e'll show 'is true colors?"

"No. I just don't want him to leave us behind. We need him to get through the Trials of Blood. No offense, but you aren't exactly the sword-wielding-heroic type."

He playfully pushed her head. "Sure got your buns out of the fire back in Manders when we were neck-deep in Blades territory, and again in Reglin's Keep when we were ambushed by those giant cave crickets! And again when—"

"You've made your point!" She stifled a smile. "Guess you're stronger than I give you credit for."

"I ain't much of a fighter, but I can protect my own when I need to."

"We've been through a lot, haven't we?"

"O' course! Can't write good ballads if I don't got good stories to tell."

"So I'm just source content, is that it?"

"You know it!"

She cut him a glare, though her scrunched smile was more than enough to show her true emotions. Loryk chuckled with a beaming smile as they continued gathering materials to create a small campfire and then settled far enough from the High Road to keep themselves hidden. If the Order, bandits, or Blades were to pass through, they'd surely come to greet the trio camping by the roadside, and the group didn't want another altercation.

As the sun began to set, they settled around the flames and feasted on a roasted elk. Neer wiped her lips with her sleeve, while Loryk sucked the marrow from his meal. Klaud stared longingly at the note in his hand. His expression was sorrowful as he read the page for the hundredth time. Neer was still curious as to who Azae'l was, but she would never dare to ask. It was clear Klaud was deeply tied to her, and Neer didn't want to upset him further by prying.

The light shuffling of leaves broke the silence, and Neer turned sharply to investigate the sound. Her heart pounded as she imagined more creatures of darkness trudging through the trees in search of a meal. The monsters that once belonged to fairytales and ghost stories had come to life, and Neer was panicked at the thought of being hunted by the dangerous, bloodthirsty creatures of lore.

"'Ey Neer," Loryk started in a nervous whisper. "It weren't really wispers that got that village, was it? Surely, them creatures don't exist!"

She stared further into the darkening trees before turning away. "You saw the spindra. Those are creatures of darkness too."

"But those're normal ones. Giant spiders and mutated canines! Wispers're somethin' else entirely! They're *monsters*."

"Enough Loryk," she hissed. The reality of their presence was enough. She didn't need his words to add to her growing terror. "Just keep your eyes open and don't make a lot of noise."

He quivered while peering through the woods. "Maybe we should take our chances on the Road. It's got to be safer than this!"

"Getting caught by the Order or killed by the Blades isn't any better."

His eyes moved to the sky as bright orange light broke through the canopy in glistening columns. "The couriers are sure to be comin' through soon. I'll bet I can talk 'em into lettin' us ride to Valde. Your arm needs lookin' at any'ow."

Neer huffed, tired of arguing and wishing for silence. Before she had time to speak, Loryk raised his hands in defense.

"I've got a plan, if you'll 'ear it."

With a quick glare, she made an inarticulate gesture with her hand, motioning for him to speak.

With a nod, he leaned closer. "Couriers and merchants always travel until nightfall, and Valde is a big place. If we wait by the Road until one travels by, I can make up some sob story about gettin' robbed and needin' a lift into town. You and that one can

CURSE OF THE FALLEN

sneak into the cart while I'm causin' a scene."

"Loryk," she said with a bit of elation, "that's actually a good idea."

He smiled proudly. "Why're you actin' so surprised? I've gotten your 'ide out of 'ot water a time or two with this 'ere wit." He knocked on his head. "Some say I'm even smarter than *you*."

She chuckled. "Who? The people in your storybooks?"

With a laugh, he shook his head and gathered his things. Neer explained the plan to Klaud, and together they snuffed out the fire before making their way to the roadside. While Loryk peered stealthily through the shrubs, Neer and Klaud hid in the shadows. As the sun slipped beyond the reaches of the horizon, the world was shrouded in darkness.

They waited for nearly an hour before the sound of horse hooves and the creak of a carriage echoed through the quiet woods. "'Ere it comes," Loryk whispered, staring through the brush. "Be ready!"

As the noises grew closer, a man with a heavy southern accent called out, "C'mon now, Truffles, don't go startin' that again." A horse sighed. "There you go. That's a good lass."

Neer's eyes widened at the sound of the accent, which was a rarity to hear anywhere but Ravinshire. Peeking through the trees, she spotted an old man sitting on the bench of a brightly colored merchant cart. He wore a bright green tunic and feathered hat. His two horses trotted proudly across the packed dirt road, though one was giving him trouble as she shook her head and snorted. The man, with his heavy accent that mimicked Loryk's almost identically, patted the horse's hip while begging her to calm.

Loryk took a deep breath, and with a quick nod to Neer, he leapt from the bushes. The horses reared with a loud squeal as the dirty, bruised bard stumbled from the brush and into their path.

The merchant cried out, "Whoa there! Whoa there, lassies!"

"Sorry!" Loryk exclaimed. He spoke with a slight groan as he gripped his side and hobbled closer. "Name's Ebbard. Didn't mean to frighten' your mares."

The merchant grumbled as his suspicious eyes moved from

Loryk to the woods. "Where'd you come from, aye? Why're you out in the woods all by your lonesome?"

"I'm a bard!" Loryk tapped the lute on his back. "Been travelin' for days but lost my way after the Blades came trudgin' through." Another wince. Although she knew he was faking it, Neer started to wonder if he had truly hurt himself. "Said they're on some official Order business, then demanded all my coin!"

With his nose high in the air, the merchant gave a stiff nod. "No funny business. I've got a whip, and I ain't afraid to use it."

"Many thanks. I'm not pullin' anythin' over on you. I know how damning these journeys can be."

"You're tellin' me. Times are tough nowadays, what with the Order bargin' into our lands."

As Loryk climbed onto the bench, the wagon shifted, and he slipped. His eyes darted to the covered cart, which Neer and Klaud had just snuck into.

"You all right there?" the merchant asked.

"Yeah, just caught me off guard with that one." Loryk climbed onto the seat next to the driver. "I'd no idea the Order was steppin' into Llyne."

"Oh yeah, it's big news! Took out most of Orimina and Brereid. Fuckin' daffodils. I'd give 'em a piece of my mind if I 'ad the stomach for a fight. I guess that's why I'm sellin' tapestries instead of swingin' weapons around, aye?"

"What brought you out this way? It's a rare thing to see a southern man out of Ravinshire."

The merchant lightly snapped the reins, and his two horses walked down the dark, desolate road. Bordering the dusty path were thick woods with heavy underbrush. Loryk peered to the trees, glad to be out of the wilderness and closer to civilization.

"Things're changin'," the merchant said. "I saw Priest Ealdir strike down a small girl just for bein' accused of sorcery. I knew 'er since she was just a tiny babe, but them priests and shamans don't care. Neither did the people of the village. Even 'er own two parents bowed down to the priest when their only daughter was cut down before 'em." The man turned away sadly. "I'll never trust in a thing like that again. If that's what the Divine're after — strikin' down children for bein' born different — then they can find faith in someone else."

Loryk nodded sadly. He knew the stories as the Brotherhood often reminded its members of the horrors inflicted by the Order and their followers. He was no stranger to it, having had trouble with his own family and their pious beliefs. It was the reason he abandoned his home and found himself on the doorstep of the rebel movement just over a decade ago.

With a deep breath, the merchant straightened, and forced a smile. "Anyway, enough about that. My name's Timmy," he said. "This 'ere's Annie, and that rascal is Truffles."

"Nice meetin' you," Loryk said.

"So, you're a bard, aye?"

Their conversation was muffled by the rumbling within the cart where Neer crouched beneath baskets of wares and furs. Her hard eyes stared out of the backing, and she watched as the cart moved slowly down the High Road closer to the village. Flashes of her time hiding in a carriage similar to this one were present with every slow lurch of the wheels. She had just escaped from the Order's clutches when she snuck her way onto a passing merchant's wagon. When the merchant found her hiding in his wares, she was immediately sold to the Sword and Sheath brothel. She was only ten years of age when Madam Tilly, the owner of the famed establishment, bought her as a kitchen wench, and only twelve when she was no longer allowed to refuse the advances of the hungry and desperate patrons.

Klaud's foot slipped as they hit a bump, and Neer jumped from her trance with a quick gasp. Their eyes met, and she quickly turned away. With a slow exhale, she released her sword, which she had pulled slightly from its sheath. Klaud's worried look went unnoticed as she stared out the back of the opening with distant eyes.

The lonely woods were soon replaced by bustling streets as they neared the town of Valde. Wooden fences lined the cobblestone roads, while the smell of manure and freshly baked bread filled the air. Lanterns hung on posts bordering the Road and brightening their path with warm pockets of firelight. Neer readied herself as the cart passed by a wheat field and then quickly leapt from the wagon into the grain. She rolled through the dirt, before coming to a stop at Klaud's feet as he teleported himself to her side. He extended his hand and helped her to her feet.

She brushed herself off before peeking through the stalks to the town's entrance. With a disgruntled sigh, she backed away to hide herself as a stranger walked by. The plump young woman, with wavy red hair and short stature, walked tiredly by with an older gentlemen several paces ahead. Her apron and dress were filthy with goat hair and dirt. Neer watched them through the tall wheat as they scurried along the road with seven bleating goats.

"Da!" the young woman called as their goats roamed around in a small herd. "My feet hurt!"

The man turned with a reassuring gaze. He placed a hand on her shoulder and said, "Such is the life of a farmer, Nicolette."

With a slight huff, the woman gathered the goats and followed her father as he walked further up the Road and then disappeared over the hillside.

When the path was clear, Neer motioned for Klaud to follow, and they cautiously stepped onto the Road. Just ahead, the cart moved to the side of the road, where the merchant would set up camp at the entrance of the village. Tall lamp posts and creaking wooden beams lined the street as Neer and Klaud entered the growing village of Valde. They wandered into the bustling streets, passing by tall cobblestone and wood buildings that towered over smaller homesteads. Klaud pulled up his hood to better hide his face, while Neer stared in wonder at the beautiful two-story homes and shoppes.

She looked back as Loryk casually approached from behind. He gripped his neck and complained of the uncomfortable ride. With a disgruntled huff, Neer punched his arm, and he fell silent.

Firelight glistened out of the villagers' windows and opened doors, brightening the streets. The chatter of women calling their children inside while their husbands washed up for dinner filled the evening air. Neer smiled as a young boy raced into his father's arms. He was scooped up, and she watched with longing as their shadows faded into a home full of laughter and voices.

As the door closed, her gaze fell away. She listened to the many conversations of all the families who gathered around their

CURSE OF THE FALLEN

dining tables and longed for the familiarity of having a home. So much of her past was shrouded in anguish and misery. Not many good memories were left to comfort her.

Wandering further into the village, Neer spotted three men enter a building bustling with light and chatter. Rusted hinges whined from a sign swinging above the door that read: Hillebough's Moonshine and Inn.

"Guess this's it," Loryk said.

"You wouldn't have any coin, would you?" Neer asked.

"Knowin' I'd be steppin' into the Blade's den so you could gather that little trinket of yours, I didn't think to fill my pockets," he said, referring to their previous agreement where he was used as bait while Neer went to find the arun. Of course, the mercenaries stole the little money he carried. With a sigh she leaned against a signpost.

"Klaud," she started, "you can make things appear in your grasp, right?"

He lifted his hand to reveal Loryk's lute. The bard spun in circles, trying to grasp the lute that was attached to his back. With a huff, he marched to the elf and snatched his instrument away. Neer smiled.

Inside they found warmth and nearly two dozen villagers. Many of them wore golden pendants of the Broken Order Brotherhood sigil, and while Neer should've been comforted by their presence, she knew to keep herself guarded. Not every patron wore the pendant, and any suspicion of her identity could incite a battle she would rather not have to fight.

The aroma of fresh bread, roasted meat, and ale filled the tavern as they stepped further inside. Every table was full of men and women sharing stories and laughter. Some dealt cards while others played cribs, a strategy game known widely around Laeroth. As they walked past tables, Klaud sneakily apported a small number of coins lying around. It wasn't enough for anyone to notice, but by the time they reached the bar, he had a handful to sort through.

"My," the barkeep said as the trio approached, "you've been through hells, haven't ye?"

"Worse." Neer took a seat at the bar.

"Ye be needin' a room and a bath?"

"Just one room, and three of your finest ales."

The woman cleaned a glass with her apron while eyeing Neer with a hint of suspicion. "That'll be eight silver."

"Eight silv—" Neer stopped herself with a huff, playing the part of a wearied traveler. "Fine. Rob us blind, why don't you?" She counted out eight silver pieces from Klaud's pile and placed them on the counter.

"Your name?"

"Sheena." She gave an alias to better protect herself. Though Llyne was free from the restraints of the Order, it was widely known they had spies and mercenaries lurking around, still searching for the Child of Skye, and if anyone caught wind of her, she'd find herself in danger. It was always best to keep her eyes on the ground and her name unknown.

"Make sure this'n keeps out of trouble, yeah?" The barkeep said, eying Klaud. While his hood kept his face mostly hidden, it was still apparent that he wasn't human.

With a sigh, Neer remarked, "Trouble isn't what we're up to. Wouldn't have the energy for it either way."

The barkeep nodded. "Right, well, you're in luck. A healer with the rebels just wandered into town a few days back. I'll have someone gather him to patch up them wounds. Can't have you leaving a bloody mess around." She gathered the coin and then moved to the tap to fill their mugs.

Klaud started to speak, and Neer quietly cut him off. "Not here. No magic. No elvish."

He knitted his brows but silently obeyed. As the barkeep returned, she handed Neer the mugs and a brass room key stamped with the number 7. With a bow, Neer tipped her glass to the woman and then passed Klaud his drink. She turned to offer Loryk his mug, only to find he was no longer by her side.

"Loryk?" she called.

Looking through the crowd, she found him speaking to a performer across the room. The fellow bard was a beautiful girl with blonde hair and dazzling green eyes. Her ensemble matched that of a typical bard: colorful tights, a stunning doublet, and a feathered hat. The young woman stepped off the stage, and Loryk took her place. He tuned his lute before softly strumming the strings.

"Look!" a woman proclaimed. "It's Ebbard!"

A sudden hush fell upon the room, and low chatter rumbled quietly beneath the soft melodies of his instrument. Neer listened to his words as they softly flowed through the air. She remembered hearing this song in particular when she was younger. Dozens of parchments were used to scribble the verses until he got it right. It was a piece he lovingly titled *Vaeda*.

"... Beauty ever sweet, she caught me by surprise
One look upon her face, I'm lost in dazzling eyes.
She were but just a stranger, of which I never knew
Porcelain skin and hair of black, my love it surely grew.

Stunning was her voice, smooth as summer's wine
She turned and walked away from me, this maiden must be mine.
A manner which I take, just to hold her hand
If only she would look at me, she'd notice who I am..."

His voice slowly faded, and a heavy silence filled the room. Several women sniffed and wiped their eyes with handkerchiefs while their husbands sneered with jealousy. Applause slowly sounded throughout the inn, and coins clinked against the wooden floor as patrons asked him to sing another. Women flocked to the stage, begging him for a night of fun. With a look at Neer, Loryk winked with a smile, and played another tune.

Chapter Sixteen

The Depth of Rage

"Come rain, come shine, the Inn will sing. Bread and drinks and mugs to clink. We Brothers are broken beyond repair, so we raise our glass to the old despair!"

— Brotherhood tavern song

THE BUSY TAVERN SLOWLY EMPTIED into a handful of drunken or homeless patrons as the evening faded into night. Neer sat with Klaud by the hearth and basked in the warmth of its roaring flames. The orange light glistened against her blood-soaked hair and torn clothing.

"Excuse me." A man approached from behind, and Neer gasped at the familiar, unexpected voice.

"Coryn!" She laughed and turned around to greet her old friend with a light embrace.

Coryn was a member of the Brotherhood who joined several years after Neer was taken in. They were the same age, though he now stood a head taller and had a muscular build that better suited a warrior than an apothecary. "What are you doing way out here? I figure you'd be up north where the Order's making their stance."

"Heard there was trouble in the south," he said, before stealing a glance at Klaud. As his eyes returned to Neer, he stood straighter and broadened his shoulders. "Maybe we should take this somewhere private."

She nodded. "I have a room upstairs, but the elf comes too."

Coryn crossed his arms, eying Klaud. "He's with you?"

"He is."

"I don't trust them wild elves, Neer. They're dangerous. It's why I've been sent here. Word has it they're scouring this place. If you're caught with him, you're dead."

"Well, then, a private room upstairs sounds like it's just what we need." Her eyes bore into his, and he faltered beneath her gaze. It was unwise to challenge the daughter of their famed and fearless leader. And while Neer wanted to believe this respect came from her own skills in combat and her innate strength of magic, it was the fear of her adoptive father that kept most Brotherhood members from challenging her.

"Fine," he said curtly. "But if he starts anything—"

"He won't. Contrary to belief, not all 'woodland heathens' are out to get us."

Coryn snorted in disagreement. Neer waved Klaud forward as she led him and Coryn up the narrow wooden staircase to the second floor of the Moonshine and Inn. Loryk was left downstairs on the stage as his melodies filled the tavern and coin lined his pockets.

At the end of the hall, Neer found her room and unlocked the door. Everyone slipped inside, and she locked the door behind them. Moonlight brightened the room through a small window, allowing her to navigate through the darkness. She lit several candles and sconces throughout the small space.

Near the entrance, Coryn placed a small black box on the round wooden table. He opened several drawers and flipped open a hinged top to reveal dozens of potions, herbs, vials, and other medical supplies.

He shook a large bottle of clear liquid and then doused it onto a white linen cloth. "Take a seat," he said, motioning for Neer to sit in the chair opposite him. The wooden legs creaked as she got comfortable and extended her arm to him.

"Oh... this is bad." He lightly touched the deep, open wound with the damp rag, and Neer winced at the burning pain that came from its medicine. "What happened? It wasn't this one, was it?" He glanced at Klaud.

"No," she said through gritted teeth. "I told you, he's good."

"Yeah. I'll believe that when I see it." The rag turned red as he cleaned her skin and then tossed the soiled linen onto the table. Iron hooks clinked as he searched through a drawer and collected a small needle hook and gut. "So? What's the story?" He carefully stitched her injury. Neer curled her fist and clenched her jaw as pain fizzled through her arm. "Talk to me, Neer," Coryn said. "What's the story?"

Through a deep breath, she explained, "E-elves. They're attacking the lower settlements."

"God's body... so the rumors are true. What do they want?"

"I don't know." She winced. "I'm hoping Reiman may have some idea."

"Oh yeah. He is one of them after all." He didn't notice her sudden glare as he focused on her wound. "I've got to say, Neer, times are really changing. The Brotherhood is scattered, thanks to the Order coming in from every direction. Bandits, Blades, thieves and the likes are up in arms over this bounty for your head, and now elves are knocking at our back door. Just watch your back out there. If we weren't friends, I'd consider taking you in myself. One hundred gold pieces is life changing nowadays."

She turned away with a huff. "Everywhere I turn, someone's trying to kill me."

"Welcome to the land of luxury." He smiled. "You've got a powerful gift. That comes with a price."

"More like a curse."

He pulled the needle tight and tied off the gut before wrapping her arm in a thick white bandage. "Least your *curse* can save the world. Most of us get the shit end with nothing but a few coppers to our names. You've got something great, Neer. Don't let it go to waste."

"Thanks, Coryn."

He smiled before wiping her blood from his hands and quietly motioning for Klaud to take her place in the chair. The elf barely winced as his injuries were sutured and wrapped in bandages.

"Looks like that's it," Coryn said. "Make sure to clean those wounds twice a day with this." He passed Neer a vial of blue

CURSE OF THE FALLEN

liquid. "With a normal person, I'd say give it a fortnight before removing the stitching, but you've both healed so quickly already, I'd say you'd be good in half the time."

"Thank you."

She dug a few coins from her pocket, and Coryn quickly pushed her hand away. "Last thing I need is for word to get back to Reiman that I had you pay for life-saving treatment."

Neer lightheartedly glared and then dropped the silver into his medical kit. "Courtesy of the drunk and unaware Hillebough patrons."

He shook his head with a smile. "Still up to no good, I see."

"Old habits die hard," she remarked. "It was good to see you, Coryn. You can share a drink with us if you'd like."

"Thanks, but I should be carrying on. Plus, being seen with that one can put a target on my back."

"You've got the sigil," she said of the Brotherhood pendant pinned to his breast. "No one will think otherwise."

He gave her a disapproving glance before looking at Klaud. "Keep yourself safe, Neer. These elves are no joke. If he wanted to kill you, even with all your strength, he could do it. We're no match for them."

"Thanks, but I can take care of myself."

His lips pressed into a thin line as he nodded and then stepped to the door with his box of medicines and herbs. Neer unlocked the entry, and Coryn slipped out of the room.

With a huff, Neer looked at Klaud. "You hungry?" she asked.

He answered with a subtle nod, and they walked downstairs to order dinner from the barkeep. After paying for two bowls of stew, Neer turned and eyed the nearly empty tavern.

Firelight illuminated the walls and kept the room alight with dancing shadows and popping flames. Two other groups made up the crowd inside the once-busy inn. The barkeep scrubbed a dirty rag across the wooden bar while Mila, a songstress from Lidvik, played beautiful songs on her harp. Loryk was no longer at the stage, and Neer could only imagine the trouble he would get himself into with so many beautiful women pulling on his arms.

While leaning against the bar, Neer's gaze fell upon a wooden game box lying on an empty table. She pulled Klaud to the dingy surface and got comfortable on a wooden chair. Klaud sat beside her as she collected the box with a smile and poured out its contents. Several ivory dice, wooden spoons, and old cards put a smile on her face.

"Do you know what this is?" she asked.

Klaud examined the objects with a hint of surprise. "It's a game. *Riiaa.*"

"We call it cribs. Do you know how to play?"

"Is that cribs?" Loryk stepped behind Neer with three fresh mugs of ale.

"Where have you been, Ebbard?" She giggled before sipping her drink. "Up to no good I assume?"

"Well, o' course!" Loryk exclaimed with a guilty smile. "So, we playin' this'r what?" He grabbed the dice. "Come on, then, *elf*! Let's see if a 'uman can best you!"

Neer smacked his head, and Loryk yelped while rubbing his scalp. With a groan, he handed her the dice.

"You'll get your turn, doof!" she quipped while snatching the dice away.

He stuck his tongue out at her, and she laughed. Klaud gulped his drink and retched at the taste, causing Neer and Loryk to burst with laughter. Valde lived up to its reputation for having the best ale, though Neer wasn't surprised Klaud didn't have a taste for it. As Reiman once so proudly explained, the elves had a refined palette for the finer wines and cuisine.

"This was always my favorite game," she explained as she set up the pieces. "Loryk and I would play for hours."

"I can't read these symbols," Klaud explained.

Neer looked at the cards and realized they were scribbled with human numbers. With scrunched lips, she borrowed a quill and inkwell from Loryk, then sneakily etched elvish symbols along the cards. "There!"

They took turns strategizing and making their moves. Loryk had always bested her when they were younger since this was a game of strategy, which he was surprisingly good at, and she was frustrated when Klaud, too, beat her in every round.

"Weren't you trained to be good at this sort of thing?" Loryk

CURSE OF THE FALLEN

teased while taking Neer's seat. "You're losin' your wit there, Neery!"

The bard and elf played several rounds, and Neer snorted when Loryk lost every hand.

"Looks like this *elf* is better than you too," she teased.

Klaud laid down a card, and Loryk grunted angrily. With a huff, he tossed his cards on the table. "All right, you win! Congratulations!" Loryk raised his hand to high five, but Klaud sat motionless with a quizzical look in his eye. Several seconds passed, and things quickly grew awkward. "What's 'e doin'?"

Neer studied Klaud for a moment before explaining. "You slap it."

"Why?" Klaud asked.

"To acknowledge his defeat."

With furrowed brows, Klaud lightly tapped Loryk's palm with the tip of his fingers.

The bard looked wide-eyed at Neer. "Pathetic," he griped.

Loryk gathered the mugs and moved to the bar, while Neer shuffled cards and Klaud set up the spoons and die. The barkeep giggled while Loryk boasted about one of his many adventures. Neer smiled. No matter how outlandish and brave his stories seemed, the ladies always seemed to fall for it. Cards tapped against the table as Neer passed them between her and Klaud. When a familiar term caught her ear, she lifted her gaze and listened to the conversation behind her.

"You sar 'im?" a man said with a drunken slur to his voice. "A pale face? Here in Llyne?"

"Yeah. He wasn't like the others. No, this'n had a nasty look about him. Carson said he was lurkin' through the village all quiet like. Probably lookin' for some poor sap to prey on!"

The first man choked. "Why're we letting them demons in our country? Just look over there! That one's sitting with the likes of us as if he belongs!"

Neer tensed when Klaud's gaze shifted to the men as they turned to him.

"What are they saying?" he whispered to Neer.

She was quiet for a moment, before reluctantly explaining, "They mentioned another elf—erm, evae—roaming around.

Then they commented on you."

"Ask them about the other evae."

Her brows furrowed. "Klaud, that really isn't a good idea."

"Ask them."

With a backward glance, she looked at the men who hatefully glared at her companion. She exhaled to relieve the pressure of her emotions, then approached their table.

The two men, both with thinning brown hair and torn, dirt-stained clothes, turned to Neer as she approached. Their tankards were half-empty, and their breath reeked of cheap ale.

"What the 'ells d'ye want, bitch?" the man with a deep scar along his face asked.

Neer said, "The elf you were speaking of. Where did he go?"

"Fuck off, you stupid bael!*" the more sickly and pale man said, before he spat in her direction.

"Lest ye want us ter turn this sword up yer sweet little arse!"

Neer tensed with pursed lips as he smacked her bottom and laughed. He then placed a dagger atop the ale-stained table. The silent gesture would've threatened Neer had the cracked iron of his blade been properly cared for. From the looks of it, his weapon wouldn't cut through butter, let alone her skin.

"Tell me where he went," she continued with more aggression.

"I don't think I will. Old man Kingsmut's got a nice reward for bringin' in any pale faces we can find. Wouldn't want you snaggin' up all the coin now, would we?" the scarred man remarked.

"This may be Llyne, but we don't want no demon cock suckers infiltratin' our lands!" his sickly friend added.

"In fact..." The scarred man stood, and with his sword in hand, he stepped closer. "I say we make good of that'n, then give this little bitch a proper punishin'!"

She reached for her sword but quickly stopped herself.

"What's this?" the sickly man sneered. "Kitty's got claws, does

---

* A lewd term used by humans that means demon lover. It's spoken to those who are sympathetic toward other races, magic users, or are otherwise against the Order and Divines.

CURSE OF THE FALLEN

she?"

"You know the laws, bael," the scarred man growled. "Even in Llyne, women aren't ter carry weapons'r fight. Drawin' that sword on me'll be the last thing you ever do."

Seething, burning rage ignited within her. Daring eyes glared up at the man who could easily overpower her. Her knuckles turned white as she clutched the hilt of her sword. The other patrons stood and watched as the trio faced off. Klaud straightened in his seat and slowly reached for the spear on his back.

The scarred man pulled Neer close with a hard grip to her backside, and she removed her weapon from its sheath. As she swung to his chest, a harsh voice interrupted their feud. Sharp steel stopped along the man's breast as Neer halted her attack. The color washed from his face, and his eyes widened as she glared at him.

"Aye!" The barkeep called as she stepped past Klaud, who now stood behind Neer with his spear in hand. "Ye want trouble, best take it outside. I'll have none of that here!"

"Ye all sar it!" the scarred man protested. "A woman! Pullin' out a sword on a man!"

"Get home, Niall, 'fore that wife of yours hears of this!" The barkeep's tired voice hinted she had spoken this phrase far too many times before.

The man drunkenly grumbled, and with a step back, he downed the rest of his ale, then turned to Neer. "Stay out of our way, 'fore we turn this'n over as well." He pointed a thick, dirty finger at Klaud.

Hatred seeped from her eyes like poison as she glared at him. The men laughed at her anger, but she never faltered. This wasn't the first time her strength was underestimated, and she never lost sleep over the sound of laughter spilling into horrid screams as she cut down those who thought her weak.

As the barkeep shuffled them outside, Loryk politely thanked her for her time.

"Well that was... frightenin'," he stated as they stepped outside. "You all right, Neery? Neer?"

She scanned the dark, lonely streets and quickly turned when a light shuffle echoed from the alley nearby as the drunkards slipped into the darkness. Loryk called out as she strode over, leaving him and Klaud behind. The two men turned back as Neer approached them. Purple moonlight reflected off her sword and shined onto their dirty, drunken faces.

"Look at this, Niall," the sickly man laughed. "Stupid bitch thinks she can take us!"

"If she wants a fight, we'll give 'er one."

Shoddy weapons wriggled in their hands as they turned to face her. Clutching his dagger high above his head, the sickly man ran forward with a pathetic war cry.

Neer twisted her sword as she fell into a readied stance, when suddenly, Klaud appeared behind the man and swung his spear. Blood spilled from the sickly man's back as he fell to the ground, whimpering in agony. Niall stood in his place as his friend was cut down. Terror replaced his anger as he stepped away from Klaud, and he gasped as the elf appeared behind him, holding his shabby iron sword against his throat.

"What d'you want?" the man begged. "I'll give you anythin'!"

Klaud spoke and Neer translated, "Where did he go?"

"He?" the man cried.

"The elf you saw before," Neer asked without bothering to involve Klaud. She knew this was the information he needed. The tip of her sword touched the man's chest. He breathed quickly, spewing hot, nauseating breath in her direction. She didn't notice the stench as her anger raged. "Where. Did. He. Go?"

"I last sar 'im headin' north... t-to Galacia!"

"What did he look like?" Neer translated.

"'E looked like all you heathens! Dark eyes, light hair... w-was wearin' dark clothes, too! Like 'e was some kind of assassin crawlin' through the darkness!"

"Avelloch..." Klaud whispered.

Neer hadn't the mind to ask what he meant. Instead, she watched the man squirm pathetically in the arms of his captor.

"P-please," he begged, "let me go! I'll never do no harm to another elf! I swear it!"

Her lip twitched with rage at the sound of his pathetic cries, and she swiftly placed the tip of her sword to his chest. Only moments ago, he felt powerful enough to threaten her life, yet in the

CURSE OF THE FALLEN

face of danger, he whimpered like a child. She had seen this look all too many times: the brave men forcing the weak to do things they begged them not to. Would her cries have been ignored? Would he have stepped away at the sound of her begging?

No. Just like all the others, he would've done what he desired. Just like all the others, he would have had control. Looking into his frightened eyes, she pressed the tip of her sword hard against his chest.

"Yes. Beg...," she threatened.

He whimpered when fresh blood soaked through his clothes.

"Plead for your life... For your freedom."

He screamed louder when she pressed harder.

"Nerana!" Klaud said, but she didn't hear. Rage had consumed her.

"How does it feel?" Her bright eyes darkened. "To be at the mercy of someone greater than you?"

"Please!" the man cried.

Her eyes widened and lips pursed together. White knuckles held tight to the sword she pressed into his skin. For a moment, she was still and silent. Her eyes tightened with rage as she looked through the man who stood before her, and she saw red.

"Nerana!"

Klaud's voice cut through her thoughts, and she was pulled from her trance. Her now bright eyes fell to the sword in her hand and then to the man whimpering behind it. She stepped back, trembling with regret and confusion. Her gaze shifted to Klaud, and she was taken back by the deep concern lingering in his eyes.

Niall flinched when her sword dropped to the ground. The steel blade quivered as it bounced against the cobblestone and reflected wavering light across her back as she fled the alley.

Chapter Seventeen

Galacia

"A fish in the barrel keeps the hunger at bay. The stench on a line keeps travelers away."

– Sayings of Galacia

EARLY THE NEXT MORNING, NEER sat alone in a secluded pond. Waves rippled along the banks, while sunlight shone from a clear sky, sparkling atop the water. Her fingers moved in slow patterns along the water's edge, and she watched as waves trickled and bounced around her.

She looked at the sky and exhaled a slow breath. After her fight in the alley, the group hid themselves in a meadow far away from villages or roads.

Tears filled her eyes as she relived the moment she held her victim hostage and took pride in his suffering. She understood the pain of being constrained and abused, of feeling like there was no tomorrow and wishing for an end. To put another in that position, to be the captor, even if the victim wasn't innocent...

She looked at her palms and wondered how she came to hold her sword to his chest. It was a terrifying feeling to lose control and hold someone else's life in her grasp without realizing. When a bird chirped nearby, Neer blinked away her thoughts and brought her gaze to the beautiful Tree that grew on the ledge overlooking the water. Its wide branches held white flowers that

CURSE OF THE FALLEN

brightened and dimmed with her every breath. Nestled within the overgrown roots was a small stone Pillar of the Divines[°] with foreign symbols along the top. Clear veins ran along its sides, creating beautiful designs. The pillar was said to be a gift from Kirena, the Divine of purity, compassion, and health. Jewelry, coins, wilted flowers, and incense lay at the base of the relic, proving the loyalty of even the rebels. No one dared to speak their devotion aloud in Llyne, but they carried it all the same.

Stepping from the water, Neer slipped back into her clothes and returned to the campsite where Klaud sat studying the map. "We should head up to Galacia, then back west to Porsdur," he said with a finger on the old parchment. "If we take the High Road it will only add a few hours to our journey."

"No," Neer replied. "The Road is dangerous. Very dangerous. We have to travel out of sight." She examined the map. "We should follow the river to Porsdur, retrieve the glass eye, then travel to Galacia. From there, we can make our way east to Havsgard."

"We can't risk losing Avelloch."

"Who?"

"Avelloch. He's a friend. A... brother. If he's in Galacia, we must find him and—"

"Why?" Their eyes met. His look softened before falling away. "In the letter, Azae'l mentioned bringing someone home. Is he the 'someone' that she was referring to?"

"Yes. If it's truly Avelloch, we must find him. He's important... more so than I..." A hint of sadness clung to his voice before he straightened and regained his composure. "He's also a skilled fighter. One of the best. We can use him in the Trials."

"Fine," she huffed, "but if he isn't in Galacia, then we go to Porsdur. With or without you. I can't spend my time tracking down your friends."

With a nod, Klaud agreed, and they set off on their journey.

---

[*] A place of faith and sanctuary. The Pillars can be found all throughout the continent, with most being in the plains and woodlands of the human territories.

These pillars are revered by humans as holy places where one can commune with the Divines, pray, and seek guidance from their wisdom and gifts.

❊ ❊ ❊

Three days passed as they moved closer to their destination. Tired feet carried them through the trees. The High Road was in sight, but they stayed hidden in the thicket of grass and shrubs. A winding river bordered them to the right, while the Road sat to the left. Loryk trudged behind, complaining profusely of the blisters on his ankles and feet. Neer ignored him, as she had her own injuries to worry about.

People occasionally wandered along the High Road, carrying on their daily travels. Children made a game of tossing rocks and chasing after a cart of wares. A courier cursed the younglings as they pushed him aside and caused the contents of his large canvas sack to spill into the dirt.

As the strangers slipped out of sight, and far from earshot, Loryk said, "Remember our old courier, Arlen? Man was near death an' still carryin' them letters all across Llyne."

"He's probably still out there somewhere, crooked and old, hobbling about along the High Road."

"Best be gettin' ye mail, snappies!" Loryk cried, mocking the old man.

"These scrolls ain't gonna deliver themselves!" Neer croaked, and the pair giggled.

"Can you imagine what it were like before the 'igh Road? I 'ear they used doves'n pigeons'n such to fly your scrolls from place to place."

"You jest!" she scoffed. "How would it ever get to you?"

The bard shrugged.

Further along, they came to a fork in the road. Loryk squinted through the bushes as he struggled to read the weathered sign. "Looks like Galacia is that way. Just over the bridge." He pointed to the right, where the Road crossed over a river.

"We have a map, you know?" Neer teased.

Loryk playfully mocked her with his tongue out. They waited for the road to clear, which seemed like days to Neer, and one by one they sprinted across the long and narrow bridge. Once across the river, they ducked again into the overgrown shrubbery.

They followed the river as it ran alongside a small fishing

CURSE OF THE FALLEN

village, and Loryk gagged at the pungent odor of rotten fish and sweat. Wooden cabins and overgrown ferns lined the edge of the Road. Neer picked an apple from a low-hanging branch and took a large bite. The tart juice filled her mouth and hydrated her parched tongue.

Her attention moved to the nearby Road as children ran and played while women tended to their gardens. Men dressed in straw hats and soaking wet overalls spoke merrily to one another as they hung fish on a line to dry.

"Have you found the key to the docks yet, Lee?" a man teased as he hung another fish.

"Not yet. I'll bet my left boot them rascally boys done took off with it! Maybe threw it in the river!"

"You've got to control them boys, lest you want them to wind up in the barracks."

"I know... Once they come back from their ma's down in Egested, I'll have a talkin' with them. They're just growin' boys. I'm sure as sugar they'll outgrow this mischief."

"Should've had a girl. My Arabella is a right good angel."

Lee scoffed half-heartedly. "I'd never trade my boys for the world. They're a handful, but they're good lads. Wishin' they were born a few years apart instead of a couple of minutes, though," he chuckled. "Would've saved me a lot of headache these last eight years."

The men moved back to the docks. "Yeah, you might still have a nice head of hair too!"

"Divines," Loryk groaned, "'ow can they stand this smell?"

"It's a fishing village," Neer said. "What did you expect? Rose petals and daisies?"

"It wouldn't kill 'em to add some to their windowsills, would it?" he griped. "Should we just march in lookin' for 'im?" Loryk asked, referring to Klaud's friend.

Neer watched the villagers. The community was composed of no more than a dozen homes, making it hard to slip in and out undetected.

"No," she explained, "we shouldn't draw attention to ourselves. We'll wait until nightfall, then search the docks and mill."

"Right." With a look around, Loryk tucked himself into the

shrubs and collected a small leather sack of berries and nuts from his satchel.

Neer stayed her place as she peered through the trees, searching for this mysterious elf who plagued the night. Surely, if he were here, the villagers would have taken notice.

"Klaud," she said as he sat nearby, sharpening his spearhead. "What is your friend doing here? Is he with the others?"

"No," he started without looking away from his task. "Avelloch is after the Nasir—the evae leading the invasion into your lands."

"The elves haven't made it this far," she said, silently cursing herself for using the slang term yet again. With a deep breath, she pushed aside her disgruntlement and said, "Why would he be here?"

"We believe the Nasir is responsible for Azae'l's curse. After she fell ill, he went missing, and now his people are attacking Vleland and the human lands." He paused. "The Nasir isn't foolish. He'll be hiding. Searching for whatever it is he's looking for. Avelloch must have tracked him here."

"If there was an elf here, these people would know it."

Klaud glanced through the quiet wood and to Galacia. He watched the villagers for a moment and then turned his attention to Neer. "They don't know that *we* are here."

As the moons rose and the village settled into a restful slumber, Neer and the others darted into the street. The small tavern, which could hold no more than ten occupants, brightened the road with light shining from its two front windows. All other candles and hearths had been snuffed out, leaving smoke to billow from chimneys. Sneaking through the village, they passed a large message board just outside the inn. Aged parchment crackled in the soft breeze, and Neer stopped, noticing the familiar warning poster. Grief washed over her as she softly touched the large symbol of the Order scribbled over the portrait of a young girl's face. Below her image the message read:

Seeking of the highest decree: The Child of Skye. Born to the name Vaeda Vindagraav. Current age 24. Fair of skin, blonde of hair, and teal of eyes. She has received The Mark high upon her right arm and

CURSE OF THE FALLEN

must not be trusted. Any known whereabouts of such a demon shall be brought forth to the Order at once. Let no man fall heed to this devil's disguise. For the powers of Nizotl have drenched her soul, and she must be washed clean before entering the gates of Arcae. Reward for her capture has been increased to 100 gold pieces of any currency. Any harboring or unwillingness to bring forth her whereabouts will be met with the severest of punishments.

Go forth and carry in the Light.

Loryk came to her side and ripped the parchment from the board with a loud tear. "Come on, Neery," he said before gently pulling her away.

This wasn't the first she had seen of such a warning, though finding it so unexpectedly had her feeling vulnerable and defeated. At the very least, the Order still didn't know what she looked like, which was helpful in keeping herself hidden. Her only telling features were The Mark* branding on her arm and her uniquely colored eyes.

Shaking away the fear, she forced herself to refocus. She pulled up the hood of her cloak and followed behind as Klaud searched the shadows and streets. They snuck through the village before stepping onto a long bridge that crossed the river. The loud creak of aged wood was drowned out by the lapping of the quick moving water below. As they slowly crossed over the river toward the dock house, the stench of rotten fish burned their noses. With every step, the horrid odor strengthened, and Neer held her breath. Old wood rattled as she approached the dock house and pushed against the locked door.

She turned to Klaud and asked, "Can you teleport inside?"

"I can't move through things."

She huffed, remembering their conversation from long ago of his limited abilities.

---

* The Mark is a branded scar in the shape of the sigil of Order. It is placed upon those who have been deemed unworthy and unforgiven in the eyes of the Divines.

Only the most dangerous and unforgivable criminals are punished with such a marking, making them immediately recognizable as outcasts and blasphemers.

Her eyes returned to the door when a faint shuffling came from inside. "I heard something!" she hissed and then pushed against the doors, trying desperately to open them.

Loryk pulled her away and warned of the loud noise she was creating. They followed Klaud around the shack and found deep claw marks along the back wall. He knelt forward and touched the markings with a curious gaze.

"What is it?" Neer asked.

"These scratches... there are five claw marks on each."

"So what?"

He stepped away and looked into her eyes. "What animal do you know of that has five fingernails?"

Her jaw dropped, and she examined the markings further, wondering why anyone would scratch so deep into the back of a shed. More shuffling echoed from inside, and she leapt back with a frightened gasp. She clutched the hilt of her sword while Klaud apported his spear into his hand. The night was deadly silent as they stood in the darkness, waiting. Watching.

Neer's heart skipped as light whimpers and muffled cries broke through the silence.

"He's here!" Klaud said before vanishing from his place.

Neer stood with Loryk in a daze as they looked around, reeling from Klaud's sudden disappearance. Old hinges creaked as he reappeared and pushed hard against the doors. They raced to his side as the sound echoed loudly through the quiet village.

"Avelloch!" Klaud said with a hiss.

"What's 'e doin'?" Loryk asked in a panic. "'E's gonna alert the whole village!"

"We don't know if he's in there!" Neer pulled Klaud away. "Stop this! They'll hear you!"

"Azae'l is waiting!" Klaud called through the locked doors. His pale cheeks were flustered, and his naturally calm eyes were panicked.

"Neer," Loryk whined, "shut 'im up! If they see you, we're done for!"

"Klaud!" She pulled his arm, but he refused to budge.

"I'm not leaving without him!" He pushed harder against the door. "Avelloch!"

"Stop this! Please!" Neer begged.

CURSE OF THE FALLEN

They took half a step back when the lock clicked, and there was a sudden silence. Hinges whined when the doors slowly opened, and the stench of rotten flesh and fish filled the air in a cloud of reeking odor. Klaud stepped closer and held tight to his spear. Neer stiffened as she peered through the crack in the doorway, and Loryk held his lute above his shoulder, ready to strike anyone who dared exit and attack them.

Neer's heart raced as slow footsteps thudded closer, yet no one appeared through the darkness. Boots scraped against the old wooden floors as someone grunted and struggled... and then there was silence. Dead silence. It settled into her bones and made the air heavy. Neer breathed deeply, paralyzed with fear. Klaud pushed open the door, and a man stepped into the moonlight. His clothes were dark as night. A hood concealed his face with its shadow. In his hands were swords dripping with the blood of the two freshly murdered bodies lying at his feet.

Chapter Eighteen

Stranger in the Shadows

"They hunt in the night, feeding on our flesh. The devils of the wood, pale-faced and hungry, have no soul. They are as wicked as the night is dark and will rip your bones in two with a fiendish delight."

— Demons and Ghouls, a collection of ghost stories

THE STRANGER'S DEADLY EYES GLARED into Klaud's, and his shoulders rose and fell with every hard, angry breath. "Why have you come here?" he growled in elvish.

Klaud stiffened, and said, "I could ask the same of you. Coming into *lanathess* territory alone? Are you insane?"

"I have to find him! He must pay for what he's done!" He stepped closer. "You've caused me to kill the only people that can lead me to him! And for what? These *lanathess*?"

"For her!" Klaud said. "I do this for *her*."

The stranger scoffed and shook his head. He returned his weapons to their holsters on his back, creating an X across his shoulders. With a glance at Neer, his eyes widened and anger softened. He quickly turned away, and with a frustrated sigh, he removed the scarf covering his face. His dark hood fell to his shoulders, revealing his white hair and bright skin. Turning to Klaud, they shared a long gaze, before the stranger extended his hand, and they gripped forearms. Looking into his eyes, Klaud smiled. It was the first sign of happiness he had shown and put a

CURSE OF THE FALLEN

bit of attractiveness to his otherwise dull appearance. *"Brenavae."* Klaud pulled the stranger into a tight hug.

Loryk and Neer shared an uncomfortable, confused glance. "These elves..." Loryk muttered. "Strange lot, they are."

Neer inched closer, listening as the stranger spoke quietly to Klaud. She jumped back when he brought his sword to her throat. Dark blue eyes glared into hers, and she was stunned by the man before her.

"You...," she started. "You were in Vleland. We saved you!"

His eyes shifted to Klaud, and he asked, "You travel with these *meena'keen*?"

"She's a sorceress," Klaud responded. "We're to take on the Trials together."

"The Trials...," he scoffed. "You're more deluded than I thought if you believe those trials will do anything for her."

"It's our only hope."

"There is no hope!" He hissed with a hint of venom.

Klaud turned away with closed eyes. "She asked for you." His voice was sad and desperate as he carefully retrieved the letter from his cloak. The stranger holstered his weapon and snatched the parchment. He tightened his jaw and pursed his lips together, quickly reading the note.

"She believes in you," Klaud said.

The stranger scoffed, and with a hard sniff, he returned the note to its owner. "She hardly knows me. You were there for her, not me!"

"She's your blood, Avelloch... She loves you more than anything."

"What would you have me do? Abandon everything, rush to my death, and allow her to die in vain?"

"She will never die in vain." Klaud stepped closer, speaking with aggression and pain. "We have to save her!"

"Her fate was sealed the second she chose to leave!"

"You know what she must do, Avelloch. It wasn't our place to tell her what's right or wrong!"

Avelloch walked across the bridge, passing by Neer without a glance in her direction. Halfway across, he stumbled back as Klaud appeared before him, and they stood face-to-face with deadly eyes.

"Without her, we lose everything!" Klaud gripped his shoulders. "Help us... Help *her.*"

Avelloch turned away and stared at the river with distant eyes. Mid-length, blood-spotted hair hung across his shoulders, waving softly in the breeze. With a deep exhale, he nodded and finally agreed. "Every death he causes is on you, Klaud. The longer he's out there, the less time we have."

"And every second we waste is another second closer to death for Azae'l."

Avelloch scoffed. His eyes shifted to the dock house before he glanced at Neer. He shook his head and stepped past her. She was silent as he approached the dock house and slipped into the darkness of the doorway. As Neer peeked inside to investigate, Avelloch marched out with a leather bag. The grim look in his eyes struck her with fear. She'd never seen such darkness.

He looked at the ground, and regretfully admitted, "I couldn't save them."

Before she could ask, he stepped away without a backward glance. Fear gripped her as she peered into the dark shed. Moonlight illuminated the interior of the dock house through small cracks in the roof. The smell of blood was heavy in the air; its taste lingered on her tongue. She held her breath and stepped closer to the bodies lying near the door.

Two men lay together with sliced throats. Their clothes and skin were saturated with crimson. Blood dripped from their wounds, collecting in puddles beneath her boots. The tattoos covering their arms were reminiscent of the markings worn by the elvish warriors she fought in the villages not long ago. She wondered if these men were also elvish, though it was hard to tell through the dim moonlight and thick blood covering their faces.

She turned away as a strong odor caused her to choke. Covering her mouth, she coughed and gagged before noticing flies buzzing in a dark corner above two disheveled lumps. With a deep breath, she took a step closer and spotted moonlight reflecting in a clouded, bulging eye. Slow steps pulled her closer, though her mind was screaming for her to run. She had to know what happened. To know if this stranger was the cause of so much death, or if his words had been true and he wanted to help but

CURSE OF THE FALLEN

couldn't.

She held her breath, gripped the thick netting that was draped over two small bodies, and quickly uncovered them. Flies buzzed loudly when they dispersed, clouding the small shack. She turned away while tucking her face into her bent arm. Sickness filled her and made it hard to breathe. The loud noise was sure to alert the entire village as the insects swarmed before escaping into the night.

Slowly, the room fell silent. With her eyes closed tight, Neer gulped down her fear, and turned to the fully exposed, decomposing bodies. With a gasp, she stumbled back. Two bloated, maggot-infested boys were slumped together as if someone had thrown them aside like a bucket of waste.

Old blood stained their ripped clothing, while insects and flies feasted on their rotting flesh. Anger and fear rushed through her as she imagined the torment these children must've faced at the hands of their murderers.

As she turned back to the men, who still had warm blood dripping from their throats, a gurgled breath came from behind. The color drained from her face, and she slowly turned to the boys when a faint, wheezed breath shattered the silence. The more swollen of the two was silent and still, while the other inhaled a slow, partial breath.

She stared at him for far too long, contemplating her sanity. This boy was no more than rotten flesh. He couldn't be breathing. Unless... no. Only those born of dark magic could reanimate a corpse. Is that what these men were doing? Is this what the assassin was trying to prevent?

Her mind spun with adrenaline and fear. She wanted to run, but her body wouldn't allow it. Instead, she was stuck in a neverending gaze, staring at the rotten and pungent face of the lifeless child, when suddenly, his clouded eye turned and met with hers.

She fell back, splashing into the puddle of blood. Her fingers slid across the wet floor while her petrified gaze focused on his. The boy, whose twin lay still and decomposing beneath him, crawled to his feet. Skin sloughed from his left arm, landing in a thick, gooey pile along the floor. Patches of blond hair sat atop his maggot-ridden head. A deep growl vibrated from his rotten throat.

Trembling and terrified, Neer crawled backward. He walked slowly, moving through thin columns of moonlight that exposed the bones and decayed muscles covering his frail body. Every slow, thudding step brought him closer, but Neer couldn't move away. Her body wouldn't allow it. She could only watch as the reanimated corpse carefully made his way to her.

Shaky breaths escaped her tight throat as the young boy stood over her. She looked up at him, horrified that the legends of necromancy and undead were true—that dark magic existed and had come alive before her—when suddenly, a firm hand pulled her from behind and rescued her from the cabin.

Avelloch threw her out and locked the doors. Slow steps dragged across the floor, and then a heart-stopping jolt shook the wooden entry as the boy attempted to escape.

"What's 'appenin'?" Loryk cried. "Neer!"

She jumped at the sound of her name. Her eyes shifted to Avelloch as he watched the door with his weapons in hand. It wasn't anger that pulled his face, but sadness. Sadness born of sorrow and contempt, not of guilt or regret. She had no time to wonder if he truly attempted to save them before the door shook again, and another gurgled cry echoed from inside.

"You did this?" she asked while retrieving her sword. "You did this to them!"

"No." Intense despair clung to his eyes, though his expression was strong and hard. "The men were hiding the bodies when I found them."

"Did you reanimate them? How did this happen?"

They turned back when footsteps pounded along the creaking bridge, and firelight brightened the darkening world as villagers approached with torches. Loryk stood before Neer to shield her from the horde.

"Over here," a man called, "at the docks!"

Torchlight moved through the village as angry voices called out into the night.

"We must leave," Klaud said as he apported his spear. "If not, more innocent blood will be shed."

"We can't leave them with this!" Neer pointed to the shed.

"Should we save every village we come across?"

CURSE OF THE FALLEN

She marched to Klaud, fury seeping through her pores. Standing face-to-face, she dared him to challenge her.

"She's right," Avelloch said, "they won't stand a chance against a *haeth'r*."

"A what?" Neer asked.

Klaud explained, "A reanimated corpse."

The doors rattled when a vicious snarl vibrated through the air. A dozen men stood along the bridge, each of them trembling with rage. Firelight danced across their clammy foreheads as they glared at the strangers. They held dull axes and rusted iron maces tight in their hands. Arrows were loosed from beyond the river and struck near the group.

"Hold it right there," a man shouted. He stood before the others, dressed in a leather vest and cloth trousers. Greasy hair stuck to his balding head. "Just who are you?"

"Those are pale faces! They're with the demons!" a woman said.

"Look at 'er eyes," a man shouted.

"She's the Child!"

Loryk stepped forward, and with his arms opened wide, he attempted to reason with the people. "We found these two lingerin' about in the woods!" he lied. "'Eard Kingsmut's got a nice bounty on wild elves."

As he spoke of his desire to bring the elves in for a reward, the doors rattled behind, disrupting his moving speech. The villagers jumped back and gripped tighter to their weapons. Loryk closed his eyes in regret as his words, which had begun to persuade the villagers, fell suddenly on deaf ears.

"Who's in there?" the greasy-haired man snapped. "Move!"

The man pushed past with a shove, and Loryk stumbled aside. Neer caught him just before he fell into the river below. The man hit the lock with his axe, and the loud crack of snapping iron cut through the deep rumbling of the shaking door. With another jolt, the broken lock fell to the ground, and the door burst open. Putrid odor moved through the air, causing everyone to wretch and turn away. The boy stepped forward, displaying his marbled skin for all to see. The villagers gasped loudly. Women fainted, while men scrambled in fear.

"What is that!"
"It's a demon!"
"The Child did this!"
"Nizotl's come for us!"

They shouted over each other in a panic. Arrows struck the boy, but he never fell. Hard steps pounded along the bridge as a man pushed through the chaos of the crowd. He stood before the boy, and a sudden hush fell over the village. Tears welled in his eyes while his bearded chin curled, and he fell to his knees with a great thud.

"My boys!" he screamed. "My boys..."

The soft trickle of the river was loud against the deep, sudden silence. Firelight shined on the boy's face, showcasing his decomposed body like a morbid statue on display. His cloudy eyes moved from one thing to another, and his body quivered with every raspy breath.

"You'll pay for this!" the greasy-haired man shouted at Neer. "You'll pay for this, you demon!"

"Tell them to stay calm," Klaud whispered to Neer. "If we upset it, it'll attack."

"What's he saying?" the man said.

"Kill him!" a villager demanded.

"Burn the witch!" a woman snarled.

The crowd marched forward, shouting obscenities as they prepared to strike her down. Teeth fell from a rotten mouth when the boy belted a loud, screeching growl. His puffy feet pounded heavily across the dirt as he raced toward the villagers. Horrified, they tripped over each other and ran back across the bridge. The boy's arms flailed wildly, spewing loose skin and maggots, as he ran toward them. The crowd scrambled back, while his father remained still.

"Lee!" a man shouted.

As the boy inched closer, ready to attack his own father, a sword sliced through his neck. His head rolled into the river, and with a hard kick, Avelloch forced the body to follow. Floating away, it bulged and rumbled. Avelloch pulled Neer aside, ducking behind a barrel, and she flinched when the body burst open with a shuddering splat. The villagers screamed as acidic flesh and foam tore through their skin.

CURSE OF THE FALLEN

A burst of light, followed by a wave of heat, rolled over Neer when the dock house was set ablaze, and Klaud stepped through the doors before slamming them shut. He kicked over a heavy barrel, barricading the entry.

Neer gazed at the father who remained motionless on his knees. Firelight reflected in his distant, teary eyes. These were the rowdy twins who were supposed to be with their mother in Egestead... the twins who were senselessly murdered and hidden away.

Her gaze tore away from the father when Avelloch pulled her from their hiding place. They raced away with Loryk and Klaud, escaping Galacia as the distraught and furious villagers chased after them. Arrows plunged into the dirt and struck nearby trees. Two horses stomped and snorted in a stable at the edge of the village.

Klaud pulled Loryk to a horse. "You take Nerana!" he called while leaping onto the saddle.

Avelloch mounted and gripped the reins. "Come on, *meena'keen!*"

Neer settled in behind him and held tight to his waist as they raced down the High Road in the dead of night. The fear of being caught was outweighed by the dread of witnessing the boys and their father. How she wished she could do something—anything—to help them. She understood the pain of losing everything. Of losing family. No one should have to suffer such a fate.

Her thoughts broke at the sound of galloping hooves and the shouting of men following behind. Neer curled forward when arrows whizzed past her. Avelloch flinched and shook his head as blood dripped from the fresh cut along his ear. Neer turned around to find several men with large axes and iron maces chasing after them.

"Go ahead!" Klaud ordered as he intentionally fell behind.

Avelloch leaned forward, and the horse ran faster. Neer couldn't take her eyes off Loryk as she and Avelloch raced away. She wouldn't allow anything to happen to him and prepared to use her magic if necessary. Her eyes narrowed as Klaud pulled an object from a pouch on his belt. He followed Avelloch over a cobblestone bridge and then tossed the object to the ground. Black smoke and flashes of light startled the horses that followed.

The villagers coughed and wheezed as they ran into the smoke that billowed high above the trees.

Klaud sped up to match Avelloch and Neer. She exchanged a glance with Loryk, who nodded in response. The horses raced over the grass-filled road as they moved further from the villagers and onward to their destination.

Chapter Nineteen

Naik'avel

"When shadows snuff out the Light, the world will weep with pain."

— Evaesh prophecy

LATE INTO THE NIGHT, THE group found themselves hidden deep within the woods. Tall grass buzzed with colorful lightning bugs while bright red leaves fell from tall limbs. A shallow stream trickled nearby, flowing across rocks and pebbles.

Neer sat by a roaring fire with her knees to her chest. Her mind revolved around the boy who reanimated. His sawing growls and sloughing flesh flashed through her mind. She blinked the thoughts away, but they returned, and she was filled with fear and guilt. Something had brought him back, and she wondered if Avelloch had something to do with it, or if the elves with the Nasir were to blame.

Her eyes shifted to Avelloch as he stood nearby with Klaud. They spoke quietly to one another, and she found herself suspicious of their intentions. Now that he had an ally, Klaud was stronger than before. She shook her head and turned away, convincing herself he could be trusted. There was no reason to think otherwise.

With a sigh, she curled tighter into her knees and stared into the flames. Loryk sat across the campfire, scribbling quickly into his half-filled notebook. Embers popped as juices from a large venison dripped into the flames.

"That boy...," Loryk started as he finally closed the book. "'E was really undead, yeah?"

"You saw it the same as I," Neer answered.

"I thought them creatures were only legend..."

"They're real... I just don't know how."

"What d'you mean?"

"The undead are creatures of darkness, Loryk. I've learned about them during my studies with Reiman. Only necromancers with the Mythic Nine° have been known to reanimate, but there were no altars or runes set up in the dock house... I don't know how he was brought back without necromancy."

"You don't think—"

Their conversation was interrupted when the elves returned to the campfire. Avelloch sat close to Neer, and she averted her gaze to the fire. Klaud tended to the meat before retrieving his leather canteen. He took a large gulp before passing it to Avelloch.

He took a sniff and shook his head. *"M'yashk?"* he pressed. "We should keep our heads clear."

"M'yashk?" Neer asked, excited to hear of the familiar elven wine. Reiman always kept a beautiful decanter in his office, and they'd often share a drink after a long day of training or battles. It was the purest, smoothest wine she had ever tasted, and Reiman was sure to remind her that it was only the elves who crafted such a delicacy. Human ale and mead were nothing in comparison to the pristine drinks of the elven lands.

Avelloch passed Neer the canteen, and she eagerly took a large sip. Its flavor was different than what she was accustomed to, but it was delicious all the same.

"So," Neer started while passing Klaud the drink, "how was that boy reawakened?"

---

* The Mythic Nine are a shadowy cult known for performing dark spells and incantations, including necromancy, poison, energy draining enchantments, and energy blocking potions.
While many believe the Mythic Nine work against the Order of Saro, the Priests and shamans have been known to use their potions and magic.

CURSE OF THE FALLEN

Avelloch, who had a disgruntled sneer across his face since her mention of the m'yashk, asked, "How can you speak our language? When we met, you could barely say your own name."

"You've met?" Klaud asked.

Avelloch sighed with a slight growl and returned his attention to the fire. "In Vleland. We ran into each other in a destroyed village."

Neer argued, "You mean, when I saved you."

He cut her a menacing glare, and she matched his gaze with equal intimidation. Loryk stared between them with frightened eyes, while Klaud withheld a smile. Turning away, Klaud wiped his face to rid of his half-hidden grin and said, "It's her magic."

Avelloch's anger turned to suspicion as her identity was revealed. "You're magic?" he asked, and Neer turned away to hide her eyes. "How—"

"Why don't we focus on why you're in my land?" she snapped. "We're far from the border. Are you with the others? Did you do something to those boys?"

Their voices overlapped as they rose with anger and hostility. "Typical of a human to assume I'm a murderer because of my blood—"

"You *killed* two people—"

"Those men were with the others invading your land—"

"They were just alone? Halfway through Llyne, targeting innocent children?"

"I'm not the enemy here!"

"You are—"

"Enough!" Klaud called.

Neer turned away as his voice cut through her argument. She breathed heavily as anger clouded her clarity.

"I don't know how the boy was reanimated," he continued. "Avelloch, were the men performing rituals or magic as you arrived?"

Avelloch's intense eyes shifted away from Neer, and with a slow blink, he explained, "No. They killed them and then hid the bodies before planning to escape."

"How do you know that?" Neer asked.

His angry eyes returned to hers. "They told me."

"They just told you?"

"A person will spill many secrets with enough pain."

Her eyes widened. "You tortured them?"

"They're murderers, meena'keen. They deserve no mercy."

"So, it was justice, then? Torture them for information and leave them to die?"

"Is it wrong to inflict on them a fraction of the pain they've caused? To have them suffer at the hands of someone preventing the very thing they've created? There is no justice in this world!"

"There are prisons or banishment! How can you be so heartless as to torture another person?"

His eyes narrowed. "If you expect your idealistic view of justice to keep them from burning down another village or killing more innocent children, then you are mistaken. These people—the ones who are torturing and raping and pillaging—they don't fight with honor. They don't respond to prisons or banishment. An eye for an eye is the punishment they deserve. It's the only justice they'll receive."

The world was quiet as they glared into the other's eyes. If they were to fight, Neer would surely see her end, and rather quickly at that, but still she sat, daring him to make a move. When the fire popped, Neer flinched, and Avelloch made no movement, as if the sudden disturbance went completely unnoticed. Slowly, his face softened. He leaned back, and with a deep breath, his shoulders fell.

"I don't expect a lanathess like you to understand," he remarked. "You shroud your ignorance of the world with hatred and deceit. You speak of justice and honor, yet you kill by the thousands those who are different or misunderstood." His gaze shifted to hers. "Do not believe yourself to be better than me, meena'keen. Had you not been born with magic and outcast like the rest of us, you'd have just as easily killed me that day."

Neer snarled. "Don't be so quick to assume that of me, *elf*. I'm not as heartless as the rest of my people."

"No." His eyes pierced into hers. "But you're just as misguided."

Anger seethed deep inside her, turning her face an awful shade of red. She turned away as the heat of her fury brought

CURSE OF THE FALLEN

sweat to her brow. The conversation died, and the world was silent once again. Neer glanced at Loryk as his quill scribbled quickly across his pages. With his tongue out and eyes squinting, he didn't seem to notice the argument that had just taken place.

Neer glanced at Avelloch as he passed her a helping of venison. With a foul sneer, she snatched the meal, and he scoffed while shaking his head.

"The *haeth'r*," Klaud started, "you believe it reanimated on its own?"

Avelloch nodded and explained. "The men weren't *drimil* like you, and Elashor wasn't with them either. I don't think he would be part of this, anyway. The necromancer likes to keep himself hidden in the graveyards."

A troubled look crossed Klaud's face, and he stared at the ground with deep uncertainty.

"Klaud?" Neer pressed.

His eyes flashed to hers, and she was filled with dread.

"It's happening...," he remarked.

Avelloch shared an equally troubled gaze. Neither of them spoke as they looked at one another in horror.

"What? What's happening?" Neer asked.

"*Naik'avel*...," Klaud whispered, as if to himself. "The spindra, the wispers... They're creatures of darkness. It's the reason they fade to ash as they die—because they were never truly alive to begin with. They're conjurations of dark energy being manifested from the souls of the dead."

"What?" Neer gasped, which broke Loryk's trance and caused him to look up at the group. He asked Neer what was going on, but she ignored him. Fear encased her, making her stiff and vulnerable. "What do you mean they're manifested from the souls of the dead?" she asked.

"Just that," Klaud said. "Everyone is born with grey energy. It's neither dark nor light—but is always in between. When the light energy keeping the world in balance fades, the dark energy grows... It can send the world into chaos. It can manipulate the energy within us and conjure monsters that once never existed."

"So, these creatures... they're... people?"

"No. The people are gone... but their energy remains, and it's

173

that energy which can destroy everything."

Neer gulped down her fear. Of all she had been taught of the creatures of darkness, never did she know how they came to be. Reiman worked with the best scholars in Laeroth to help train her into the fierce and intimidating warrior she had become, but there were still things she didn't understand about this world. Magic, for instance, was never taught in its entirety. While she learned basic spells and incantations, the history and depth of magical energy was never explored. He would always say it was best to leave some mystery to the world and focus on what was ahead.

She turned her gaze to Avelloch when he sighed and leaned back against a log. "So... do you have a plan? Are we going straight to the caves?" he asked.

"No," Neer explained, thankful for the change of conversation, "we have to retrieve the glass eye from my home. It'll allow us to see past the illusion hiding the entrance of the cave. Once we get that, then we'll be on our way to Havsgard and enter the trials."

"*Glass eye?*" Avelloch asked, and Klaud translated to an elvish word he understood. With a nod, he turned away. "I assume Thallon made mention of these hidden caves?"

"Who else?" Klaud remarked, and Avelloch shook his head with a scoff. "You may have your disagreements, but he knows more about the First Blood than anyone."

With a deep scowl, Avelloch wiped his face and exhaled an angry breath. "So, where is this glass eye?" he asked.

Neer wanted to ask who they were speaking of but decided against it. She was determined to get these Trials over with as soon as possible. The arguments of these elves, who would most likely remain strangers to her once they made it through this journey, didn't concern her in the least.

"The eye is in Porsdur," she explained. "It's only a day from here, so we should arrive tomorrow... so long as Klaud doesn't have any other friends to chase down."

He shook his head. "It was just the one."

With a silent nod, Neer closed her eyes and took in a deep breath. In just a day's time, she'd be back home and one step closer to ending this journey... one step closer to freedom.

CURSE OF THE FALLEN

Her eyes shifted to Loryk as he scribbled once again in his notebook. "What are you writing?" she asked, as she had never seen him scrawling so vigorously.

The scribe paid her no mind as his hand moved hastily across the pages. With a lick of his finger, he turned the page.

"Loryk!"

He jumped nearly a foot in the air and quickly slapped his notebook shut before holding it securely in his arms. "Oh, Neery," he started nervously. "What was that? Hmm?"

"Let me see that."

"Oh this? It's nothin', Neer! J-just some pathetic sonnets!"

"Give me that notebook, Loryk." She reached for the book, and he quickly pulled it away. She knew he was remarking on their journey, as that was his purpose of following her around, and now that he wanted to keep it hidden, she knew something lucrative was written. They wrestled for a moment, but she easily overpowered him and snatched it away.

She scanned the last few pages and read aloud what he had written in such a short time, "The beautiful, raven-haired mistress fought valiantly against the bloodthirsty assassin... They fell into a light squabble which soon ended with his hands on her..." Her eyes widened. Blood rushed to her head. Though Avelloch couldn't understand her, she was mortified. "Strike through this!"

"What!" Loryk argued.

"Strike through this! Mark it out!" Loryk stumbled when she shoved the book into his arms. "I would never—and to think that—you're repulsive for even imagining such things!"

"It's just a story, Neer! This's what the people love!"

"Mark. It. Out."

While arguing, Neer didn't hear as Avelloch leaned close to Klaud and asked, "Are they going to do this all night?"

With a deep sigh, Klaud turned up his head and took a large gulp of wine.

CHAPTER TWENTY

THE LEGENDS OF WAR

"I've seen the ashes of war, and I know its sorrow and pain. Don't delud yourself. Even those who survive are forever changed, haunted by the ghosts of the men they've slain."

— Master Reiman

THE NEXT MORNING, NEER GATHERED her belongings and stood by the horses.

"Great mornin' we're 'avin," Loryk said as he approached her side. "Clear skies, warm breeze, two questionable elves, and Laeroth's most wanted ridin' 'orseback together."

Neer glanced at him with a playful glare as she secured her things in the saddlebags. "You forgot to mention the famous, noisy, *perverse* bard."

He stepped to the horse and rubbed its coat. "While you three are fightin' and buckin' up to one another, I'm focused on the beauty of this situation."

"The beauty?"

"That's right." He turned and leaned against the saddle. Neer smiled as they stood close. "Just picture it. The world's most feared and rejected sorceress, fallin' for a mysterious and dangerous elf. There's drama and tension and romance! It's the perfect

CURSE OF THE FALLEN

love story!" Neer rolled her eyes and shook her head. She returned to packing her things as Loryk continued, "It's why I'm 'ere, ain't it? To write stories and make the world see magic users as more than demons crawlin' through the night?"

"So, having me lay with the enemy will change their minds?"

"It's poetic, Neery. It'll give you both some 'umanity. Emotions. You know?"

"Uh-huh," she remarked with heavy sarcasm. With her finger to his chest, she slowly pushed him away. "If you write about me touching anyone else in that way again, I will take that quill and shove it up your—"

"Got it!" He quickly slipped away. "Come on, Klaud! The lady's gettin' antsy! Better get a move on, yeah?"

As Avelloch came to Neer's side, they shared an uncomfortable glance. She looked at the saddle and then shifted her eyes to Loryk and Klaud as they mounted their horse. "Any chance I could ride with Loryk?" she asked.

Avelloch stepped closer, tying off the saddlebags. "You can ride with Klaud, but your... *friend* would be walking."

"And why is that?"

"Because if he rides with me, I'll have to kill him."

"If you touch him, I'll—"

They glanced at Loryk as he spoke with boisterous enthusiasm while Klaud steered the horse. Avelloch turned back to Neer with annoyed, glowering eyes. With a huff, Neer was lost for an argument, as she understood his frustration with Loryk's constant speaking. Over the years, she had grown used to it, though in the beginning she shared in Avelloch's vexation.

"Well," she said, "it's no reason to kill him."

With a huff, Avelloch climbed onto the saddle and waited for Neer. Through gritted teeth, she climbed behind him and got comfortable in the saddle.

"We have to take the Road," she explained. "The hillsides are far too dangerous on horseback. We'll ride at a distance to not draw suspicion. It isn't the people of Porsdur that we should be wary of, but those traveling along the Road. If anyone suspects you're elves... evae... it could mean trouble."

"I thought evae were accepted here?" Klaud asked.

"Only those we know, and even then, you're treated as second class. Just stay on your guard. Follow the path and speak to no one. If you find anyone bearing odd symbols or cloaks of white and gold, avoid them at all costs."

They broke through the trees and set off on the long, miserable journey.

As the sun rose higher, Neer leaned forward with exhaustion. Her cheeks and arms were tinged with pink as they baked beneath the afternoon sun. The quick clop of horse hooves caught her attention, and she turned around to find two priests of the Order riding in her direction. Their golden trimmed white robes glowed beneath the autumn sun as they sat with excellent posture and proud eyes.

She pulled up her hood before doing the same to Avelloch.

"What are you—"

"Be quiet!" she hissed. "We need to leave the Road. Casually."

"What?"

"Just do it!"

With a hateful sneer, Avelloch gripped the reins and led them around a wide curve before veering onto an overgrown path. Loryk turned back as they left the road and then pointed in their direction, instructing Klaud to follow.

They slipped into the trees and watched silently as the priests rode by. Their narrowed, suspicious eyes were on the densely packed woods as they searched for the strangers they previously trailed behind.

Neer leaned over, watching them through the thicket of leaves and shrubs. Once the sound of their horses disappeared into the distance, she exhaled a deep breath and closed her eyes.

"That was close," Loryk said before dismounting and stretching his legs. "I think it's a good time to rest," he explained. "Those priests'll be waitin' up the road for us to pass 'em by, and I could use a break from the sun, any'ow."

The others dismounted and tied the horses to a tree. While Loryk sat on a log nearby, Neer stood by her horse and took a sip from her canteen. She eyed Avelloch as he came to her side and rummaged the saddlebags. He glanced at her with a disgusted snarl before quickly turning away. Feeling uncomfortable, she stepped to Loryk and sat next to him. He turned with a smile before passing her a helping of dry bread and jerky. She unwrapped the thin cloth and happily ate her meal.

"What're the Order doin' 'ere?" Loryk asked as he bit into his own snack.

Neer took a sip of water and swallowed her small bite of bread. "Scouting." She tore off another piece. "I'm sure my use of magic in Smedelund has brought them here."

"Oh yeah," he said with a sigh. "Fuckin' 'ells. This's *our* land! We've earned it! Took it right out from under their pompous little noses!"

"Yeah, well, apparently the elves feel that same way. Klaud says a man called Nasir is leading his people here because they want to reclaim their land."

Loryk scoffed. "That's different. The Great War 'appened centuries ago. It isn't our fault that we still live 'ere."

Neer glanced at Avelloch and Klaud as they approached the campsite. "What was that about *elves*?" Klaud asked.

Neer turned away with regret. "I was just telling Loryk this Nasir could be invading because he wants to reclaim Laeroth for the elv—uh, evae."

Avelloch grimaced. "And what do you know of the *Siik'Noraï*?"

"Of what?"

Klaud explained, "The final war between our people. The one that saw the evae cast from our land and into the forests."

Neer turned to Avelloch. "It doesn't matter what I know," she said. "What matters is that our people have been living separately since your defeat. Me, my parents, *their* parents...none of us were involved in the Great War. Why should we be punished for the crimes of our ancestors? Why should your people pillage and murder for a chance to reclaim what belonged to those long dead?"

His fierce eyes bore into hers. "Why should *yours*?"

Slowly, she turned away, and the argument ended. It was no surprise to Neer that Avelloch believed the humans were at fault for the Great War, as history had been told in favor of the race gifting its story. With her time and training in the Brotherhood, she was fortunate enough to have knowledge of both sides, given that her adoptive father and the leader of the rebellion was elvish. She understood that while the elves believed the humans invaded and cast them out for their own power and greed, the humans blamed the elves' racism and manipulation as cause for their exile.

While the others sat quietly, Neer couldn't shake the discomfort she felt from Avelloch. Unnerved by his anger and the constant tension, she said, "We don't have to like each other, but if you're going to be around you could try showing some kindness."

"Would you show kindness to the evae that murdered those innocent boys? Or to the ones who ravaged those villages and killed dozens of innocent lives?" He paused. "I have no reason to trust or be kind to your people, *lanathess*."

"But you do have reason to trust me."

"You think because you saved me that I owe you my trust?"

"You owe me your kindness. Is it really that hard for you?"

He stiffened. "My people have always shown kindness to yours, and always they've been betrayed."

"Klaud isn't as hostile as you. He trusts me pretty well."

"Klaud has not lived through what I have. He hasn't seen the dismembered bodies of innocent villagers lying in the forest. The women that were raped or children that were tortured. He hasn't seen the men that were skinned alive just for being evae. Klaud lives like most of my people, in a world of good intentions and forgiveness."

"And you don't?"

He fell silent and turned away. "I can't."

With a timid glance at Klaud, who shared in Neer's discomfort and sympathy, the conversation ceased, and the tension that had risen between them became unbearable. Their races had always had a hostile and distrustful relationship, but to know that humans had been actively invading and destroying elvish lands filled Neer with anger she never knew she had.

Time slowly passed as they waited in the woods before Neer stood and dusted herself off. "We should get moving," she said.

Loryk remarked, "We should wait just a bit longer, Neer. If the Order—"

"If they try to ambush us, we'll be ready. No one will question a couple of dead priests in Llyne, anyway."

She untied her horse and led it toward the overgrown path. The others soon followed, mounted their saddles, and then broke through the dense shrubbery and back onto the High Road.

They rode for an hour in silence. Neer wanted to speak, to make amends with Avelloch and explain her ignorance of the human invasion, but she was at a loss for words. She knew he wouldn't believe anything she said, so she remained quiet.

Further up the Road, past an old, faded signpost, they came to the edge of a wide valley, and Neer smiled at the familiar community of broken homes and smoldering storefronts far below. A towering stone wall surrounded the destroyed town, while working farms and mills bordered its outer territories.

"This is it," Neer said. "Porsdur."

"This is your home?" Klaud asked.

"Yes. It's hidden beneath the illusion of a destroyed village… It's actually quite beautiful inside."

"Why is it hidden?"

"Well, the most notorious Brotherhood in the country can't live out in the open, can we? The Order would be at our doorstep in a second."

Her eyes scanned the horizon as she soaked in the towering Everett mountains in the distance. A trickling river moved alongside the High Road, winding down the hillside and straight to the city.

Birch trees with red and yellow leaves brought a wealth of color and life to the valley below. Sunlight brightened the outlying settlements as farmers gathered crops and herded their cattle. Smoke billowed from the town's brewery, which was the largest in Llyne. Neer watched with a smile. Many years were spent in these fields, squashing freshly grown melons and shooting arrows at targets of all kinds. It was the home of the Brotherhood, though to the passerby, it was just another fallen village.

"Be mindful of the travelers," she explained as they followed the Road down the hillside and closer to the valley. "There will be more here now that we're coming to the Pass."

Avelloch purposefully hid his face as they passed by several wanderers along the way. A courier tipped his hat while walking by; a bodyguard for hire was dressed to the teeth in perfectly sculpted armor; a hunter with a long bow and bandaged leg hauled a sackful of meat. Neer clutched tighter to Avelloch's waist as she closed her eyes and laid her head on his back. Fear mounted deep within as she imagined the repercussions of being noticed. The recognition of her identity or the elves could send the wrong passerby into a panic that could end with the Order knocking at their door.

"What are you doing?" Avelloch hissed beneath his breath as they moved far from the nearest traveler.

"I can't be seen," she explained. "This is the best way to hide without looking suspicious."

With a disgruntled sneer, he repositioned himself and straightened his back.

Moving closer to the valley, the horses walked over an arched bridge and then arrived at the outskirts of the seemingly destroyed town of Porsdur. Nearly a dozen working farms, inns, and taverns lined the High Road just outside the city walls where the Pass˚ met the Road of Llyne. Beautiful stone pillars held tall iron gates that were locked together with a latch in the shape of the Order's sigil. Rugged footpaths wound through the woods along the roadside, connecting the gated footpath to the High Road.

Neer inhaled a deep breath as the fresh scent of wheat and wild strawberries filled the air. Children laughed and played in small creeks while dogs chased cats around fence posts. Past Whoreson Keep, they came to Milly's Pub and Brewery, which sat just beside the locked gates of the High Road Pass. The dingy musk of eastern ale seeped through the aged walls of the famed

---

˚ The unnamed footpath, often referred to as the High Road Pass, or Pass, is a dirt road that connects eastern and western Laeroth by way of the High Road in Styyr and Llyne.

Since the Brotherhood took control of Llyne, the eastern gates of the High Road Pass have been sealed. While this helped to prevent the exporting and importing of goods to and from the rebel state, many citizens have created alternate routes through the wooded roadside to ease their travels and enter the unlawful territory for private trade or visitation.

CURSE OF THE FALLEN

alehouse.

She instructed the others to remain outside as she dismounted the horse and stepped to the tavern alone. She looked around the large, familiar room with a subtle grin. Many of her nights had been spent at the bar, playing cribs with her friends or talking to the barkeep, Benjamin. He was only a few years older than her but had been working at the brewery since before she came to the Brotherhood nearly ten years past.

Her smile widened as she spotted Benjamin speaking to a trader at the bar. The barkeep politely declined the seller's offer, and she pushed more of her exotic valuables. Neer stepped to the counter and patiently waited for their conversation to end.

"Nerana!" Benjamin smiled as he stepped away from the still speaking trader. "Good to see you again. What's it been? Six... seven months now?"

"Has it? Feels like a lifetime."

"How've you been, you old git?"

"Seen better days, Benny."

"Awe, hells, haven't we all? You looking for a drink?"

"Actually, I'd like a key to the back room." Neer spoke a hidden message to her friend. While Milly's gave the impression of an ordinary tavern, it was actually an establishment of the Broken Order Brotherhood. Dating back to its creation decades ago, Milly's had been a frontline source of income and trade for the rebellion and over time became one of the few gatekeepers into the hidden city.

"Seeing yourself home, are you?" He leaned forward on folded arms. "What about the outsiders?"

"How did you—"

"I've got eyes and ears all over this place."

She turned to the door, where her friends waited just outside, and explained, "They're with me."

"I'm not sure the others will take kindly to their being in the city gates."

She gazed daringly into his eyes and held out her palm. "The key, please."

With a careful nod, he turned to the back wall where several keys hung in two rows above the counter. But he didn't bother with them, as it wasn't truly a key he searched for. From within a locked drawer, Benjamin collected a small potion, and with a quick look around, he slipped it into Neer's hand.

"Thank you, Ben."

"Good to have you back, Neer. See you around."

With a careful glance at the patrons, who hadn't noticed their exchange, Neer stepped outside and mounted the saddle behind Avelloch.

"We good?" Loryk asked.

"Got it." She revealed the potion.

At the stables nearby, they dismounted their steeds and collected their belongings. Klaud and Avelloch were silent as they followed Neer and Loryk to the crumbling outer wall of Porsdur, where two guards stood tall and proud at the gate. Their armor boasted the crest of the Broken Order Brotherhood, which was a cracked and broken replica of the Order's sigil. The weathered symbol was worn by all those who followed in the Brotherhood.

"Forrest. Raymond." Neer stifled a smile as she greeted the guards, who stood perfectly still with axes in hand.

With a glance at the Road, she waited until it was clear of any straggling wanderers and then splashed the contents of the potion on the enormous wooden door. The crumbled gate faded away to reveal the bustling village inside. Beautiful wildflowers and tall birch trees with leaves of orange, yellow, and red lined the cobblestone streets. As they stepped inside, the door became solid once again. Residents gathered by old man Dom's home as he smoked a pig and passed out fresh corn cobs. A young man gifted spotted flowers to his betrothed, and her fair cheeks were flushed with pink as she accepted them with a kiss.

Two crossed battleaxes hung above the door of the smithy. Iron hammers clinked against hot metal as weapons were forged. Pulled hide dried on racks by the roadside and gave off the strong scent of tanning leather. Everyone talked and laughed as they walked by.

"Nerana!" A familiar voice rang over the others, and she turned with a smile as Gil approached with his arms wide. She knelt to the ground and pulled him into a tight embrace. "How are you, child? Did the road treat you well?" He eyed the elves

CURSE OF THE FALLEN

standing behind and raised his eyebrows in suspicion.

She stood and crossed her arms. "Fairly. There is much to discuss, Gil. Shall we go inside?"

"Wouldn't have it any other way," he said before turning to Loryk. "You look like shite, boy! Get on home and wash up!"

Loryk gasped, clearly offended by the dreled's more callous welcome. "I'll 'ave you know, I've been through 'ells and back! We can't all turn into a raven and fly off into the sunset!"

"Stop with the whinin'! Now get on home before I turn into a giant beast and rip the skull from your neck!"

Loryk, appalled by such a threat, was unable to think of a clever rebuttal, and with a huff he stomped away, heading in the direction of his home. Neer turned to Gil with an ill-hidden smile.

"Gil...," she scolded.

He brushed off her reproach with a wave of his arms. "Boy'll grow a backbone one of these days. 'Til then, I'll see to it that he isn't a whimperin' milk drinker. Toutin' on about his adventures but can't toughen up to a man a fourth his size!"

"You'd be surprised, Gil. He's stood his ground plenty of times."

"Bah!" Gil argued.

As they wandered through the village, Neer breathed in the scent of juniper berries and freshly baked pies, eying the windowsill where they cooled beneath thin cloths. It wasn't so long ago that she and her old friend Gina snatched a blueberry tart from that very window. She received several lashings for the thievery but still claimed it was worth the beating, as the sweet taste of the famous tart still lingered on her tongue.

Past the bakery and several private homes, they came to a small house whose porch was shaded by a weeping willow. Glowing flowers clung to vines that wrapped the wooden posts. Neer dug beneath the edge of the porch and retrieved an iron key tethered to a rock painted with a sunflower. Removing the mud and filth from its notches, she unlocked the door and ushered everyone inside.

The home was bright with sunlight from its many windows. A small hearth with an old cauldron and hanging rack sat along the right-side wall. Two chairs and a table were to the left, along with a bookshelf filled with old tomes, scrolls, and trinkets.

Behind a half wall at the end of the room was a bed, dresser, and small bathing tub. Klaud and Avelloch remained at the entryway while Neer moved to the back of the home by the dresser and changed from her filthy clothes into something more comfortable.

Sitting atop the bed, she turned to Gil as he leaned against the wall with his arms crossed. "You want to tell me what you're doing with a couple of evae?" he pressed.

"The taller one with the spear is a magic user. He saved Loryk and me from spindra. We found the angry one later on in Galacia. They're setting off to the Trials too."

He grumbled. "Wait a second, there! You haven't completed the Trials?"

With a great sigh, she closed her eyes and explained, "No. The entrance was sealed."

"Sealed? How in the world could it be sealed?"

"Klaud believes it isn't the true entry. He thinks the ahn'clave only intended for those worthy enough for the Trials to know its true coordinates."

Gil sighed. "And you're saying these two are on their way to the Trials, too?"

She nodded.

"Seems rather convenient, don't you think?"

"Maybe it's fated. We saved Avelloch that day in Vleland, if you don't recall. You patched him up with travaran."

Gil turned to the elves, who sat at the table speaking quietly to one another. "Aye, I remember."

"What sort of odds would bring us together again? What else but fate would have Klaud save us, only to find he's also seeking the Trials?"

"Fate's a tricky thing, Neer. Many a people have deluded themselves into believin' a coincidence as fate, only to find themselves in a right bit of trouble."

"Was it not fate that brought me here to the Brotherhood? Would you call Loryk singing every night at the Sword and Sheath, a wretched place he only went to because he was traveling and needed the coin, a coincidence? Look at where it has brought us. This is fate, Gil. I know it."

He sighed. With another glance at the elves, he stepped forward. "Just... watch yourself, child."

"I know. If anything happens, I've still got my magic."

A disgruntled, worried look flashed across his eyes. "If you haven't stepped foot in the caves, then why have you returned home, and with these Divines-awful evae? They smell like me wife's chamber pot after a hot summer's day."

"They aren't that bad." She giggled.

"It isn't just them that's carryin' such a stench." He eyed Neer, and she withheld a smile.

"We just needed a rest," she said. "I wanted to check in on you and speak to Reiman."

"'Fraid you just missed him. Old lad's just headed north with the soldiers. Apparently, the Order's been bargin' into Llyne as of late. Already burned down Ragistead and Larpin. The rebellion's losin' hope."

"He's going to fight the Order?"

"That and help rebuild what's been lost. If they keep at it, they'll soon be at our gates. We'll be losin' followers left and right. If we aren't careful, Llyne will fall right back into their hands."

Neer nodded. "Seems we've all got our own jobs to do."

"That's right." He placed a hand on her knee. "But don't worry, child. He believes in you, just as I do."

She smiled half-heartedly, wanting desperately for his words to be true and regretting that the fate of the country rested on her shoulders and hers alone.

Chapter Twenty-One

Porsdur

"For the lost, the weary, the broken… you may call this place your home."

— Broken Order Brotherhood

Neer sat at the table in her small home and slurped her favorite chicken liver stew. She swallowed a spoonful and then caught notice of Avelloch's disgust as he sat across from her.

"What?" she said.

His face twisted as he muttered. "Repulsive creatures."

"I can understand you, you know?"

He cut her a sideways glare and then leaned forward with his hands together. Firelight danced across his face as he looked into the flames. While Neer and Avelloch sat in an uncomfortable silence, Klaud rested by the hearth on a stool. His black hair fell loose from its tie and hung across his shoulders as he read Azae'l's note, which he often did during his time alone.

"Who is Azae'l?" Neer asked Avelloch.

"How do you—"

"I've read the letter."

"Of course, you did…" He leaned back and crossed his arms. "She's my sister."

Her jaw dropped slightly. "Your… sister? You don't seem too involved in her rescue."

"There is no redemption in false hope. She's going to die. Going to Nhamashel won't make a difference."

"But stopping the Nasir will?"

"The Trials are dangerous. We will most likely die before reaching the cave, and even then, it's only a slim chance the potion will work... I'd rather spend my time tracking the person who killed her. It won't keep her alive, but it will keep others from dying."

"Do you not care about her at all?"

"Of course, I do! I may not cry over her letters each night, but that doesn't mean I don't carry pain."

"You'd rather hunt her killer than keep her alive?"

"I love her. But I know there is nothing I can do to save her."

"We're going through the Trials. You don't think that matters? You think she'll die regardless?"

"Yes."

"That's a bit harsh."

"It's truth. There is nothing anyone can do to change it. Klaud has deluded himself into believing this cure will change things... but her path was set long ago. Even if she's to be cured of this curse, she won't live another year. It's just the way it is. He knows it, but he won't accept it."

"If that's what you believe, then why are you joining us?"

He turned to his friend, who had become so lost in his misery he hadn't caught a word of their conversation. "We're *brenavas*. If it is my help he needs, then I will give it... I won't lose them both."

"Brenavas?" She had heard mention of the word numerous times yet hadn't a clue what it meant.

"Brothers. We do not share blood, but we are family."

She paused. "Having hope isn't a bad thing, Avelloch. Sometimes it's all that someone has."

"And what of those who don't?"

Their eyes met, and she was surprised to find that he was no longer angry or hostile. Something different lingered in his eyes. Something broken and hollow. She started to feel sad for him... pity, even. Her gaze shifted when Avelloch turned to Klaud, and they watched as his eyes closed and head bobbed as he dozed off.

H.C. NEWELL

It had been days since any of them had a full night's rest, and it showed in the deep circles beneath his eyes. Neer set her spoon aside and carefully led Klaud to her bed, where he sank into the feather mattress and quickly fell asleep.

She grabbed a coat from her dresser and walked through the home to the door. As she slipped into her boots, she glanced at Avelloch, and asked, "Would you care to walk with me?"

He gave her an inquisitive look before slowly standing and coming to her side. As they stepped outside, Neer breathed in the cool night air. Glowing lampposts kept the village alight while fireflies and glowing plants illuminated the trees and gardens.

"I've spent almost half my life here," she explained as they wandered the empty streets. "I came when I was fourteen. I don't remember much of my life before that, so this is the only home I've ever really known."

Avelloch didn't speak, though Neer didn't mind as she was lost in her memories. It had been several months since she had seen her home, and she was glad to be in a familiar, safe place. The cobble road led them up wide stairs that curved around a beautiful garden. Colorful glowing bugs hovered above the plants, and thistleweeds opened to allow their brightly lit bulbs to float through the air.

"Do you have places like this in Nyn'Dira?" she asked, referring to the forests where the elves resided.

Avelloch's chest puffed as he inhaled a deep breath and looked around. "No," he said, releasing the breath he took.

She glanced at him with a hidden smile. "You aren't one for talking, are you?"

"No."

She picked a glowing pink orchid and twisted it between her fingers. "I suppose I'm not used to the quiet anymore. Before I came here, I was alone like you. I didn't have a family or friends... Loryk saved me. He brought me here, and once I realized that not *all* people were as evil as I thought, I started to see the world much differently."

Neer glanced at Avelloch with a knowing look. Her eyes shifted to the path as she sniffed the flower and then followed the stairs to a large courtyard with wooden stalls of trinkets, wares,

CURSE OF THE FALLEN

and weapons. In the center of the open plaza stood an enormous Tree with glowing blue daffodils and thistleweed bulbs sparkling along the branches.

The two moons shined in the night sky, covering the world with a bright glow. Neer touched the tree and closed her eyes. Warm energy tingled her skin. With a smile, she knelt in the garden surrounding the tree trunk, and Avelloch quietly followed.

"This has always been my favorite place," she said. "After sunset, when the world was quiet, I would sneak out and find myself here. It's the only place I've ever found peace."

Avelloch was silent as he admired the gardens. His eyes followed a bulb as it floated past him and illuminated his face with its soft glow. He touched the plant, and it gently bounced away into the sky.

"Have you ever seen a tree like this before?" she asked.

"This is a *Ko'ehlaeu'at*. They're very sacred."

"Ko.. koko loo…" Her face twisted as she attempted to say the long and difficult elvish word, and she was surprised to find Avelloch softly smiling at her horrid mispronunciation. As they fell into a quiet laughter, she said, "Don't make fun of me!"

He hid his smile, though she could see the amusement in his eyes. She was glad to find he wasn't as angry or hostile as he led her to believe.

"Come on," she said while standing. "There's something I want you to see."

They walked quietly through the streets and into another district of town. She bundled into her coat as a breeze slipped through the trees and set a chill down her spine. Her eyes moved to the homes of her old friends, who had since grown and left the village. She led Avelloch down a passage between two small homes and to a large field of practice dummies and archery targets.

"I would train in this field," she said. "Reiman had me out here for hours. It was torture."

"Reiman?"

"My teacher. More like a father, really. He took me in and taught me everything: magic, history, language… He even taught me how to fight. He's from Nyn'Dira too. Said to have moved here about seventy-five years ago."

Avelloch was intensely quiet, and Neer turned to him curiously. He was tenser, with darkness that shielded his once-vulnerable eyes.

"Avelloch?"

He turned away, which broke his guard only slightly. "What does he look like?"

"What?"

"Does he have dark hair and a black marking on his face?"

"No. He has light hair and no markings that I'm aware of. Why?"

His head shook, though his anger seethed. "It's nothing."

She paused for a moment, contemplating his reaction. "You were thinking he's the man you're searching for?"

"It would've been too convenient, but I had to be sure."

"Sorry. I suppose I'd be suspicious of that, too, but Reiman has raised me almost half my life. He's a good person."

"The Nasir hates Ianathess more than anything. He'd never live among you. He's probably hiding in a cave or abandoned village somewhere."

"What's *Ianathess*?"

He stepped to a box of old sparring weapons and absently shuffled through them. "It's another word for human. Such as elf is to evae."

She was filled with shame as she suddenly realized how often she had used that word around him.

As their conversation ended, she set her gaze to the training ground and approached a hay bale target across the field. Hay rustled as she ripped several arrows from their places around the bullseye and then collected the child-sized bow lying on a bench nearby. Standing in position, she prepared to strike the target. It was awkward using a bow so small, but it wouldn't matter as she had always been less than coordinated with it, anyway.

Drawing back the arrow, she released it, watching as it flew several yards to the left of the target before striking into the dirt. With a frustrated exhale, her shoulders relaxed, and she looked at Avelloch. "I've always been shit with a bow," she admitted. "Reiman would make me stay in these wretched fields for hours until I hit the target."

Avelloch stepped closer and reached for the bow in her hands. She politely offered him the weapon and then stepped aside. He inspected it with a grimace, and Neer asked, "What is it?"

"Nothing."

As he lifted his shoulders and straightened his back, Neer said, "Tell me."

He glanced at her before drawing back the arrow and releasing it at the target. Hay shifted as it struck just above the bullseye. He passed her the bow. "It isn't surprising you had a hard time hitting the target with a weapon of such poor quality."

"What?" She examined the bow, which had signs of wear from heavy usage, but overall was a well-crafted and sturdy weapon. "This was made by our best bowyers."

His eyes glowered with condemnation. Neer ignored his silent ridicule and placed the bow back onto the bench. She then turned to the nearby home and placed her hands on her hips. Her eyes followed the vine covered trellis to the second story roof, and she smiled before climbing up.

Avelloch stood on the ground, watching her with a curious eye. She paid him no mind as she moved upward and then crawled onto the gabled roof. The home rested at the highest point of the village, allowing her to see far into the distance and beyond the stone walls guarding the city.

She pulled up her knees and admired the golden lit streets and soft moonlight. Nearly one hundred homes were spread throughout the tightly knit community, and she could see all of them from atop the old roof.

The trellis creaked as Avelloch climbed to the top and came to Neer's side. She smiled as he got comfortable and overlooked the town below.

"I used to come here at night," she said. "I'd just watch the people in their homes. Having dinner, playing with their families... being *normal*." Her smile faded as she imagined the life she never had. The one that kept her awake at night, wishing for a change. "I don't remember much of my family. It's been so long since they died... their faces are just a blur." She paused with sadness. "Sorry. I'm not trying to get personal."

He inhaled a deep breath and kept his eyes on the streets below.

Not wanting the conversation to end, Neer asked, "Why was Azae'l cursed?"

Avelloch was silent for a moment, and Neer had believed he wouldn't answer at all. As his eyes slowly moved from one home to the next, he said, "The Nasir is threatened by her. She's the last living descendant of the First Blood." Neer remembered First Blood to mean ahn'clave, who were the ancient race that vanished without a trace. "He's a man of power and vengeance. Killing her would give him a sense of pride and power among his people."

"His people?"

"He's of the Klaet'il clan. They value strength and power above all else. The First Blood are treated as royalty by non-humans, and with her being the last, she's extremely respected and honored."

"If she's your sister, aren't you First Blood too?"

"Yes, but it's... complicated."

"Well, whatever the case, we'll get through this and save her. In fact, that's why we're here." She gave him a sly look before climbing down the roof and stepping around the home to the front porch.

Beautiful plants and vines encased the entry. Neer breathed in their scent and was brought back to her time living in this very home. Digging through the garden, she found the lockpicks she hid years ago. Though Reiman had his doors open for her anytime she needed, she sometimes liked to sneak in when he was away and sleep in her old room.

Avelloch came to her side as she slid the picks into the lock. The iron handle rattled loudly in the stillness of night as she moved the pick around before hearing the satisfying clink of the unpinned latch.

"Come on." She hurried Avelloch inside and secured the door behind them. Using a flint, she ignited several sconces and brightened the spacious room. A large desk sat at the back with papers, books, and scrolls scattered across its surface, cabinets, and shelves.

She smiled while peering at her old home. The familiar scent of fresh ink lingered in the air, while old parchments lay scattered beneath the gentle dance of candlelight... It was comforting and safe. A stairway along the right-side wall led up to Reiman's large room, while two doors on the left led to the kitchen and her old bedroom.

"Don't touch anything!" she said as Avelloch retrieved a book from its place on a shelf. "He'll notice."

"How? This place is filthy."

"Trust me." She shuffled through the desk drawers, being careful to leave everything exactly as she found it. "It has got to be here!"

"What are we looking for?"

"The glass eye." Papers crinkled as she searched a cabinet of scrolls. "It's a small, clear rock encased in an iron pendant."

Wooden planks creaked beneath their feet as they scurried across the room, searching every crevice and box they could find.

"Found it!" Neer called with a smile. "It was on the desk the entire time." She looked across the room and found that she was alone. "Avelloch?"

Her gaze shifted to the soft stream of firelight flickering from her old bedroom door. Curious, she stepped inside and found Avelloch admiring a weapon on the wall.

"This is my old room," she explained. "I haven't been here in ages." Her fingers collected dust as they trailed along the top of the dresser. Old books, clothes, and wooden swords rested in their places on the shelves just as they always had.

Avelloch scanned the old furniture and weapons. He touched a small woven circle hanging on the wall before turning his gaze back to the weapons rack, which held a beautifully crafted longbow.

"That never saw much use, unfortunately," she admitted.

"It's evaesh," he said.

"Really?" She stepped closer to examine the weapon.

"So is the *tiaavan*."

She raised an eyebrow, and he pointed at the woven circle. The handcrafted piece was made of twisted sticks, bent iron, and small red stones that she foolishly believed to be jewels when she crafted it long ago. "Oh yeah," she took it from the wall and held it in her palm. Her eyes were set on the tiaavan, while his gaze was focused on her.

"Reiman always told me these bring peace to those who are lost. I always believed it would work too. I'd just lie in my room, staring at it, wishing for things to change. For peace to come... Then I'd wake the next morning, and things were still the same. I wanted to smash it to pieces, but I couldn't. Whatever hope I had for it to work overpowered the anger that knew it wouldn't."

His eyes drifted to the tiaavan in her hand. "My mother made one for me when I was young. I believed it would work too." He studied the poorly made object with sad eyes. "I guess the naivety of children is common among us all."

She stared longingly at the tiaavan and remembered the comfort it brought as she wished for a better tomorrow. Maybe it was naivety that made her believe things could get better. Even now, as she stood with this stranger, ready to take on the life-threatening journey of curing her curse, she was torn by the weight of knowing that this could all end badly. That everything she had been through could be for nothing. That the pain of being labeled a demon, of losing everything, of never being normal, may never leave her.

"A child's naivety," she quietly remarked while staring at the tiaavan. "Life is cruel and unfair. If you want peace, you have to fight for it. That's the lesson he should've taught me." With a deep breath, she tossed the tiaavan aside. Scanning the room, her eyes fell to a glass jar of clear and clouded crystal shards. "What the hells?"

She walked across the room and pulled the jar from the shelf.

"What is this?" he asked while taking a shard.

She carefully snatched it away. "These are *arnemaeus*. Memory shards. They're extremely rare. With the right incantation, you're able to put your memory into one. I don't know why they're being stored in my old room, though, or how Reiman came to have so many." She examined the clouded crystal in her hand. "I suppose viewing one couldn't hurt. It could be fun to see what he left behind."

"How do you use it?"

"There's no magic in viewing it, only in placing the memory." She curled the shard within their hands, closed her eyes, and waited as a memory appeared in their minds:

An iron door creaked opened to reveal a dark and cold room. Blood stained the walls and floor where a young girl lay strapped to a metal table. She wore dirty, blood-soaked rags as she screamed and fought. Long blonde hair hung over the edge of the table, dripping with blood that pooled across the stone floor. Scars, burns, and opened wounds covered her tiny body.

"Please!" the girl begged. "Help me!"

The orange metal of a hot iron brand glowed in the shadows, illuminating two gloved hands holding it tight as it was carried nearer. She screamed and thrashed against the restraints that tethered her ankles and wrists to the metal bed. Her frail voice echoed loudly against the stone walls as she pleaded to be released.

Strangers, wearing black hooded robes, stood around her. They looked down at her face, which was cut and bleeding, and she opened her eyes. Teal green orbs, glowing from the redness of her tears, pleaded for her captor to stop. The view fell from her face to the hot iron.

"*Aegrandir kronel vok'norei!*" a menacing voice hissed.

"Please!" she begged. "Please! Don't! No!"

Blackness overcame the vision, and the singe of burning flesh was followed by a horrific, agonizing scream.

The memory faded, but Neer's eyes were closed tight. Sweat covered her body as she relived the haunting moments of her past. Neither could she move or breathe as she clutched the shard.

Slowly, her eyes opened. She stared at her hands gripping the shard so tight she feared it may crack. Misty eyes looked at Avelloch. His anger was replaced by something worse, something she never wanted from anyone—pity. Through a bitter sigh, she wiped her eyes and concealed her grief. With a hard sniff, she rushed through the home and stepped into the cool autumn night.

Chapter Twenty-Two

Echoes of the Past

"Memories are windows into the past, meant to be locked and untouched. Do not be consumed by what once was or seek to lose all you have."

— Vethad, the Book of Time

NEER SAT IN THE SILENCE of her home and twisted the memory shard between her fingers. With a distant gaze, she looked through it, reliving the memory inside. How could Reiman have such a memory? Who was it that held the brand to her skin? She imagined every possibility, but none seemed to make sense. Reiman would never have tortured her. He would never be part of the horrors she endured, but how he came to retrieve such a memory, and why he would keep it locked away remained a mystery.

As she sat at the table, drowning in her thoughts, Klaud and Avelloch stood by the fire in quiet conversation.

"*Aegrandir?*" Klaud asked. "You're sure?"

"Yes… and the *triandal.*"

Klaud's face paled, and his eyes widened with fear.

They turned away from one another as the door burst open and Loryk stood cheerfully in the doorway with a basketful of fruit tarts.

CURSE OF THE FALLEN

"Mornin' everyone!" He smiled before bragging about how lovely the day was.

Gil followed behind and pushed Loryk aside to enter more quickly. "Get a move on, sprite! We haven't got all day!"

Loryk glared at the dreled before passing out breakfast to everyone. They absentmindedly accepted his gifts without so much as a nod in his direction.

"Rude creatures, you elves, I tell ya," he commented while passing an apple tart to Avelloch.

The assassin thrust forward, as if ready to attack him, and Loryk jumped back with a silent yelp. With a deep huff, Avelloch turned away, and Loryk scrambled across the room.

"Everything all right, child?" Gil touched Neer's arm, and she jumped from her trance. "Nerana?"

Without speaking, she placed the shard in Gil's hands and forced him to watch the dreadful memory. Once it was over, he stepped from the table and gripped his forehead. "Oh, Neer... why'd you go and watch such a thing?"

"Why does he have this? Did he do this to me?"

"That wasn't Reiman, child."

"Then who was it?"

His eyes moved to the men standing around, who all looked at Neer with sorrowful eyes. "Reiman... could tell you were troubled. From the moment you arrived, you were angry. Hostile. You hadn't eaten properly in years and had screaming fits every night."

"That never happened!"

"It did, child... It was awful. You'd lash out, do all sorts of nasty things with your magic."

"Why would I do that? I would remember if—"

"You were in a rage, child. Defiant. Reiman needed to know what happened to you. How to help you. So, he had the scholars take those memories and lock them away."

"But they aren't my memories, Gil! I'm seeing from another person's eyes!"

"The shards are a strange thing. It's a manifestation of your memory but isn't always seen from your own eye. It isn't always the same circumstances that truly happened, but merely the way you remember them."

"That doesn't make any sense! This is—"

"Magic, my dear, isn't always the best indicator of the truth. I was there when they extracted the memories. So long as the shards exist, so, too, will the memories live within you."

"So, I'll destroy them!" She stood, ready to toss the shard into the fire.

"You cannot!" Small arms pushed against her waist. "Listen to me, child! These shards are a matter of dark energy. Destroying them will not only leave you absent of the memories and their effect on you... it'll release dark energy into the world."

"What am I to do, Gil?" Her voice broke and throat tightened as she withheld her tears.

He led her to the chair and patted her hand. "You survive, Neer. You go on, and you survive, just like the rest of us. Use this pain to gain strength. We've all had trials and struggles. It's what makes us who we are."

A tear fell as she scoffed. "You sound like him."

"Bah! Don't go comparin' me to that blasted evae." Gil rubbed her hand as she smiled. "Come along, child. You've got work to do."

Neer was silent as he called Loryk over and passed her a fruit tart. The pastry was warm in her hands and filled the room with the scent of cinnamon and apples. With a sigh, she placed the food onto the table and crossed her arms.

"You all right?" Loryk asked, taking a seat across the table. "Eugenia made these fresh for you. She remembered 'ow much you loved 'er apple tarts."

Neer forced a smile and picked at her breakfast. With a glance at Loryk, who stared at her with concern, she forced away her sorrow and took a bite of her meal. He smiled and leaned back into his chair. "I see these two're still around."

She glanced at Avelloch and Klaud as they stood nearby and picked at their food. "Where else would they go?" she asked.

Loryk shrugged. "People're startin' to talk, though. Askin' what they're doin' 'ere. With *you.*"

Neer glared. "If Reiman can walk these streets, so can they."

"Reiman is a founder of the brother'ood. He's respected and

feared and trusted. These two're strangers. Can you blame 'em for bein' unsure when the elves're invadin' like this?"

"I suppose."

"We can't 'ave the people thinkin' Reiman's own kin is allowin' traitors inside our gates!"

"They aren't traitors!" she snapped. Her rush of anger caused the others to turn to her with confused glances. She, too, was taken back by her lashing out in their defense. Turning away, she tore off a piece of her tart and finished her meal in silence.

After breakfast, the group moved through the village and stopped at the Shared Wares, a shop that sold various styles of outfits and armor.

"Well, aren't you a fine-looking bunch!" Mari, the clerk, said with a smile. "Haven't seen many elves around here! Are you two with Reiman?"

"They're with me," Gil said as he stepped onto a stool by the counter. "Mornin' Mari. How're the little sprites?"

"Well, Coren got into the grapes again. Smashed 'em to bits with them rowdy boys from the west wing! Janie's sharp as ever—that wit of hers is going to get her into trouble someday!"

"Good to hear. Listen, I know it's short notice, but we're looking for a couple of getups for the lads and lass here. They're sure to find trouble walking around in such attire."

She eyed the elves, and then moved around the counter to examine Klaud's outfit. "Impressive," she said. "This stitch work is phenomenal. I'd no idea the pale faces had such an eye for garments. Figured they all looked like a hunter done threw some leather and hide together like a furry potato sack." She turned to Avelloch and gripped his chin. "My, he's quite handsome. Gives old Reiman a run for his money, aye?"

"They aren't that good lookin'," Loryk said while crossing his arms with his fists beneath his biceps to give them definition.

"What are you doing?" Neer chuckled.

"What d'you mean?"

"Are you flexing?"

"No!" His arms quickly fell to his sides. Her laughter turned his face a bright shade of pink, and he grumpily stomped out of the shop.

Mari and Gil spoke more of the elves' attire before she moved to the back of the shop and returned several minutes later with two bundles of leather armor. While handing Avelloch and Klaud their clothes, she politely escorted them to the dressing rooms.

"So, what are you thinkin'?" Gil asked.

Neer laughed. "I think they'll put up a nice fight."

"They can't be as stubborn as Reiman, can they?"

She turned to Gil with a knowing glance, and he shook his head with a chuckle. Klaud and Avelloch soon returned, and Neer burst into laughter at Avelloch's ill-fitted, much too tight armor. Gil smacked her legs, and she concealed her amusement. Avelloch stood awkwardly with his arms hanging away from his torso and his legs spread apart. Klaud turned to him with a smirk, and Avelloch's face twisted into an angry scowl. He reeled forward, ready to attack his friend, when his pants ripped from behind. His scowl deepened as Neer and Klaud fell into a fit of laughter.

"Oh dear, must be a size too small," Mari said while hurrying him to the back. He returned moments later wearing a more fitting outfit, and upon looking at Klaud, he swiftly punched his arm.

"All right, missy, step on back." Mari led Neer to the back, where she was fitted for a leather chest piece. The sigil of the Brotherhood was branded onto the top right corner. "How does it feel?"

She examined the armor and ran her finger over the sigil. With apologetic eyes, she explained, "I can't wear the sigil."

"Right." Mari kindly removed the armor and brought her a similar, fresher piece. "I haven't got around to branding this'n yet. See if it fits. There you go."

Neer remained still as Mari braided the sides together and pulled them tight. As she tied them off, Mari stepped around and looked at Neer with a smile. "Fiercest damned warrior I've ever seen. You'll knock them elves dead in a second."

The armor was smooth and strong beneath her fingers as Neer touched her sides and stomach. "It isn't the elves I'm after." She glanced at Mari. "Thanks, Mar. It's beautiful."

"Only the best for the best, aye?"

With her hand on Neer's shoulder, they walked back to the storefront and approached the others.

"What's the damage, Mar?" Gil asked.

Neer stepped to a shelf where Klaud examined a few gemstones. She stood beside him, admiring her armor, when she noticed Avelloch looking at her through the corner of his eye. He peered at her armor before slowly meeting her gaze. His eyes lost their hardness and anger as he looked at her with something different. Something... warm. Feeling uncomfortable about staring for so long, Neer averted her eyes, though the warmth of his gaze lingered.

Outside, they rejoined Loryk, who invited them to the Patched Shack tavern, a place he and Neer visited often. The streets were full as residents wandered from place to place in the warm autumn day. Humans and dreleds from all over Laeroth coexisted within the hidden city, and it was one of Neer's favorite things about Porsdur.

Though the Brotherhood was known for its tolerance of outsiders—a vow they all swore to follow upon joining the rebel faction—it didn't stop the villagers from peering at her companions as if they were wild beasts. A man spat at their feet when the elves stepped by, and a woman whispered of their unwelcome arrival.

Neer clutched her fists and bit her tongue. Now wasn't the time to make a scene. They wouldn't be in Porsdur for long, and once she completed the Trials and returned home, she didn't want any bad blood between her and the locals. It was already bad enough that the Child of Skye was a resident of their beloved town. She didn't want to create tension where it didn't have to be.

Loryk placed a hand on her shoulder and looked sympathetically into her eyes. She turned away, not wanting to be coddled or cared for. It was times such as these she wished to have a friend more understanding of her disgruntled view of the world, though she would never wish away the hapless doof that was Loryk.

A smile tugged at her lip as she thought of his affection and friendship, and he quickly took notice. With a bright grin, he wrapped his arm around her shoulders and squeezed tight.

The aroma of mead filled the streets when they approached the Patched Shack. The building was a wooden longhouse with an arched double doorway and wide courtyard. The soft beating of drums echoed from inside, becoming louder with every quick push of the door as patrons came and went.

Loryk opened the door, and everyone stepped inside. Neer led them to a round table by an open window while Loryk stepped to the bar to undoubtedly woo the attractive barkeep. The tavern was full of life and chatter. Many familiar faces sat around playing cards, telling stories, or having a casual drink. As Neer looked over the patrons, she overheard a conversation nearby and focused heavily on their words.

"Thorne," Michael, a man of forty who worked at the butcher shop, said, "I heard he's been seen out in Ravinshire."

"Divines...," Patricia, his wife, responded. "I thought the Hunters were only myth. Could they really be out there?"

"Who knows? The world's gone to shit. I'll just be happy once this war's over and the High Priest's head is on a pike."

Neer's eyes narrowed at the mention of Thorne, a famed bounty hunter with the Shadow Blades. She didn't know much about the Hunters, only that they were dangerous and not to be trifled with. Neer could only assume the Order hired Thorne, as the going rate for a bounty hunter of his prowess was too steep for the average citizen to afford.

"Fresh mead!" Loryk cheered as he set five tankards onto the table, and Neer fell from her intense thoughts.

The sweet-smelling drinks spilled over the edges of their cups and soaked into the wooden surface, matching the sticky and fragrant stains from previous occupants. Gil was the first to grab his drink, and he chugged the contents down before the others had a chance to take their first sip. With a satisfied sigh, he slammed the tankard onto the table and wiped his mouth.

"So," he started as Neer brought her lips to her cup, "where do these elves believe the Trials to be?"

Neer glanced at Avelloch and noticed the anger that flashed across his eyes. She hadn't realized until now how often the term *elf* had been used in his and Klaud's presence, and while it was commonplace for the humans to speak down to the outsiders of the forest, she was compelled to defend them, despite the backlash she was sure to face. "They're *evae*," she stated while looking at Gil. "And Klaud says the entrance is in Havsgard."

With another peek at Avelloch, she found his anger had faded into curiosity. It was hidden beneath the coldness of his eyes, but she could see it.

"Ah...," Gil started, "that's only a few days ride from here. What about the lad? You really think he's up for the task? I'd be right to ask the missus to join on your adventure before bringin' this milk drinker and his quiverin' nuggets along."

Loryk scoffed in offense, and Gil shook his head.

Neer wrapped her fingers gently around her large tankard as they argued. His was a thought that pressed heavily on her mind since her decision to embark upon the Trials. She knew taking Loryk was a risk, and now that she had companions better suited for the journey, she felt compelled to leave him behind.

With a gulp of her drink, she gently set the mug onto the table. "Loryk," she started, "he's right. With everything going on, I think it's best if you stayed behind."

"What?" he remarked. "You said I could come along! What's changed?"

"It's getting too dangerous to be around me. You're safer here with the Brotherhood."

"Was I safer with the brother'ood when I 'elped you escape that brothel? Or when we fought off those creatures that were threatenin' Geoffrey's keep? When I came up with the plan to get you that arun and nearly lost my 'ead?"

Neer glanced at Klaud, whose soft eyes had hardened at the mention of the arun. She composed herself, hoping her worried expression hadn't alarmed him further, and returned her attention to Loryk. "It's different now."

"It isn't. Now that you've got some flashy, 'andsome elves you think that I'm—"

"It isn't like that!"

Loryk huffed and pinched the bridge of his nose in frustration. It wasn't often that he grew flustered or agitated, and the weight of his anger was crushing. She knew he was right, that they had always been together during the most grueling of times, but this journey would test them beyond the measures of simple monsters or mercenaries.

"D'you remember that promise you 'ad me make years ago?" he asked. "It was the night we returned from that village the Order'd destroyed." He paused, waiting for a response she refused to give. "You said, 'I've never known evil like I know it with the Order. I don't care what it takes—I'm goin' to stop 'em.' Then you looked at me, and you said, 'You're the only family I've got left. Promise me that if I'm goin' to die, you'll be there with me at the end. I've been alone my entire life... I don't want to be alone in death too.'" He paused when she closed her eyes. "We're family. Always 'ave been. If this's the end, then I need to be there. I won't 'ave you dyin' in the arms of no elf."

"And if it's you who dies in the Trials? What am I supposed to do?"

"You think I'll be runnin' 'eadfirst into the fight? Not a chance!" He chuckled. "Not with you three doofs goin' in first. Whatever's in that cave better be ready, s'all I got to say about that. And once it's over, I'll be the greatest bard to 'ave ever lived. This's what bein' a poet's all about you know—adventure."

She looked into his soft eyes and found comfort where there was once anger and contempt. She knew she could never lose him, but she couldn't bring herself to force his decisions. Throughout her life, her parents, the Order, the Brotherhood... the world... they all forced her to do things she would've never chosen for herself. Had the roles been reversed, and Loryk were to enter the Trials to free himself from this curse, she would resent his decision to leave her behind.

With a reluctant sigh, she said, "Don't make me regret this."

He smiled and clutched her hand. "Not a chance."

She forced a smile while lifting her cup, and Loryk cheered happily. Mead splashed onto the table when their tankards clinked, and they made the silent oath to stick together. As Loryk took several gulps of his drink, Neer watched him with deep sadness as the thought of losing him weighed her mind with regret and fear.

As Klaud sat unperturbed by the recent argument, Avelloch leaned forward onto his closed fists. Neer caught a glimpse of his gaze before he averted his eyes. With crossed arms, he leaned back in his chair and brought his attention to the various patrons nearby.

    Neer didn't worry herself with him as she contemplated her decisions and wondered if this was truly the path they should take, or if fate was nothing more than a children's story. The thought was pinned to her mind as she looked at Loryk and vowed to see him through this journey, even if it cost her everything.

Chapter Twenty-Three

Kindness and Cruelty

"We're family. I'll always have your back, even if it takes me to my grave."

— Loryk to Nerana

As the sun rose the next morning, Neer sat in her home and laced up her boots. Avelloch secured his swords into their sheaths while Klaud extinguished the fire in the hearth.

"It's a few days to Havsgard from here," Neer explained as she stood and secured her armor piece over her clothes. "We can head east through the woods above Galacia and then follow the Road into the mountains."

"And you're sure this is where the Trials will be?" Avelloch asked. "Thallon's ego is bigger than his brain. He'd never admit to ignorance if he didn't truly know the way."

"I'm sure," Klaud responded.

Neer asked, "Who is Thallon?"

Avelloch huffed with irritation, though Neer could see it wasn't directed at her. "He's a scholar."

"You have scholars?" she asked.

Avelloch's eyes narrowed into a disgusted glare. "You really think we're that simpleminded?"

She turned away, feeling mortified for assuming they were anything less than intelligent. The Order had used the same rumors and insults for decades to keep their people from coexisting. Neer wasn't surprised to find the evae may also have these same beliefs of humans; that they're savage, ignorant heathens. Even with her attachment to Reiman, who explained the rumors to be untrue, Neer still believed the elves to be undisciplined and dangerous.

Before she could apologize, Loryk entered the home with a bright smile and freshly baked muffins. "Mornin'," he said. "I 'eard Gil's waitin' by the stables. You ready to go?"

Neer glanced at his leather chest piece. "Wearing armor, are you?"

"Figured it'd do me some good out there on the Road. Didn't need it much before now, did I?"

"Learning to use a sword is much more useful than wearing armor."

"We've got three of the greatest warriors this world 'as ever seen." He opened his arms and motioned to his companions. "I'm sure I'll learn to swing a sword in no time."

She smirked before snatching the muffin he offered. "Greatest warriors in the world?"

"You do the fightin', I'll do the writin'." As the rhyme slipped from his tongue, his eyes widened with pride, and Neer laughed as he quickly jotted it into his notebook.

"Let's go, Ebbard." She led everyone outside before locking her home and hiding the key in its place beneath the porch.

She took a final glance at Porsdur as they stepped across the narrow bridge to the gates. Every neighbor, tree, home, and crack in the road brought a new memory of her years spent within the hidden walls. The trials could test her far beyond her capabilities, and should she never see her home again, she wanted to remember every detail.

"You ready?" Loryk asked, placing a hand on her shoulder.

She straightened her back and gulped down her emotions. Turning away, she gave him a quiet nod and then stepped to the gates.

Outside of the city, they passed by two young men arguing

over who had lost the potion to the enchanted city gates. Neer smiled as their bickering reminded her of her younger days with Loryk. Focusing on the road ahead, she continued toward the stables, and her smile widened as Gil emerged from a stall. He stood with his arms crossed as he eyed Neer and her companions.

"Didn't think you'd be leavin' without sayin' goodbye, did ya?" he remarked.

"Of course not," she said. "We knew you'd be out here."

He nodded. "Be careful out there, you two. Especially with them evae you're luggin' around."

"We're careful, Gil."

His hands fell to his hips as he sighed. "I've been hearin' rumors. Whispers of the Order bein' seen all throughout Llyne. They're gettin' desperate."

"Haven't they always been?" Neer crossed her arms.

"Don't be foolish, child! Stay off the Road and don't go speakin' to no one! Let that one there do the talkin' if needed. I've sent word for the other dreleds to be on the lookout for ya. If you run into trouble, they'll be around." He stepped closer and motioned for Neer and Loryk to kneel. They did as they were told, and he touched their shoulders. "You two are the only ones that you can trust out there. Protect each other. Come back home safe, all right?"

Neer nodded with a smile and then pulled Gil into a tight hug. Loryk half-heartedly griped before patting Gil's back.

As they stood, Gil cleared his throat and stepped aside. "Now go on," he said. "Time's a wastin'."

With a sad glance at Gil, Neer leapt onto the saddle behind Avelloch while Loryk settled in behind Klaud. She couldn't take her eyes off of Gil as they traveled down the High Road, and he waved with a smile as they departed. She returned the gesture, though it was filled with sadness and finality.

With a stiff nod, Gil crossed his arms and watched as they made their way over the river and out of sight.

Neer wrapped her arms loosely around Avelloch's waist and set her gaze to Loryk, who rode several paces behind with Klaud. The bard's voice was a constant stream of words as he spoke softly to the evae holding the reins.

The journey was long and uncomfortable as they rode for miles beneath the dying light of another day. Neer hid her face from the villagers as they passed through a small farmstead sprawled across the plains.

"Why are you hiding?" Avelloch asked.

Neer refused to answer, as she feared that even her voice would alert the others of her presence. Once they had passed the village, she exhaled a relieved sigh and released her grip on Avelloch's waist. Gazing at the trees, she began to wonder how long this journey would be and if they'd run into any trouble along the way. She was always careful to keep herself concealed from prying eyes or seedy wanderers, but she knew fate wasn't always on her side. If anything, it often seemed to deny her of good fortune or happiness.

Her eyes shifted to the roadside as they rode past an overturned and ransacked wagon. A horse lay in a puddle of blood while an old man sat beside the cart. Blood dripped from a wound on his forehead, and he gripped his side with a groan.

"Help!" His voice was barely a whisper. "Please…"

As they quietly rode past, Neer turned back, guilt-ridden and sorrowful.

"Stop the horse," she said.

"What?" Avelloch argued. "We can't help him. It's too dangerous."

"He'll die without our help."

Avelloch groaned as Neer leapt from the saddle and rushed to the man's side. He reached out to her, thankful for her return. She dug through her satchel and retrieved a healing potion. Pulling the cork, she carefully applied it to the wound on his head, and he groaned as it sizzled and popped.

"That'll heal up in a few days," she said.

"Thank you… Oh, thank you…"

"Why are you out here without protection? The Road is far too dangerous for a farmer to travel alone."

"You're telling me." He gripped his side in agony.

She lifted his shirt to find a stab wound in his side. Using more of the potion, she was able to heal it enough to stop an infection from festering.

"Thank you... Divines... Times are tough with the Order trekking in. Nobody's wanting to trade. I have to bring my grain and produce up to Wilshire myself. Didn't think I'd be getting into trouble this far in the country."

"Go home. Keep off the main Road. Bandits and thieves like to hide in the woods and wait for men without guards to pass through."

"You wouldn't be strapped for coin would ya? I've got a bit left that the others hadn't found. Could really use the protection on the way back."

"Sorry. We're heading toward the mountains."

"Very well. Thanks for the help."

"Safe travels."

She mounted the horse and found the others giving her hard looks. She ignored their disapproving gazes and asked that they set off, and they did so without argument.

"Your kindness will get you killed," Avelloch stated flatly.

"It was my kindness that kept you alive, wasn't it?"

"You are naïve, lanathess."

"And you are heartless, elf."

He scoffed, though she couldn't tell if it was in amusement or agreement.

Further down the Road, Neer instructed Avelloch to veer onto an overgrown path. As they left the roadside, she turned back to be sure Klaud had followed and was surprised by his conversation with Loryk.

"*Drimil*," Klaud said. "Nerana. Klaud. *Drimil*."

"*Drimil*?" Loryk pondered for a moment. "Nerana and the clouds..."

Neer chuckled as Klaud closed his eyes in frustration.

"What is it?" Avelloch asked.

Her smile never faded as she explained. "I think Klaud is trying to teach him your language."

Avelloch scoffed.

"What?" she remarked. "It'll make things easier, and it keeps him from singing."

"He's wasting his time. Our people aren't meant to coexist."

"At least we're trying." She paused to subdue her anger. "If you're so against traveling with us, then why are you here? You don't strike me as the type to go along with something you don't believe in. If so, you'd have joined Klaud at the beginning instead of running off on some heroic journey that could have seen you killed, or worse."

He huffed with a slight growl. "Don't presume to understand me, *human*."

"I'm asking, *evae*."

The tension mounted as he glanced at her with anger.

"So," she said, "are you going to tell me, or do you enjoy making this trip as long and insufferable as possible?"

He was silent once again, this time for several minutes. Neer started to believe the conversation had ended, until he said, "I'm here... because you helped me."

She was taken back by his honesty, which was unnaturally personal, and she struggled to find a response. "Should I have let you die?"

"I've encountered many lanathess in my lifetime. None have shown any compassion or sympathy toward my kind." He paused. "You risked your life to save me... That kindness has stuck with me."

"I'd say that humans aren't all so cruel, but I have a hard time believing it myself most days." She sighed. "I understand your rage. It's easy to hate us for the bad things we've done... the unforgivable things..." She clutched the brand on her arm. "You said before that if I wasn't cast out like the others that I'd have left you to die that night. Maybe you were right. I'd like to think you weren't, but I don't know. I suppose, if there's some good that's come from my sad excuse of a life, it's that I didn't care that you were evaesh or dangerous or meant to be my enemy. I just saw someone that needed help."

He glanced back at her with a long, vulnerable gaze. "I could've been the cause of those attacks. I could've killed you."

She smiled. "I may not be an elvish assassin, but I'm stronger than you think."

His cheeks lifted with a subtle grin. He returned his attention to the trail, and they rode in comfortable silence.

As sunlight waned across the sky, they came to a small clearing and set up camp. While the others tended to their own matters, Neer gathered an armful of tinder and wood. Dry branches and dead leaves crunched underfoot as she wandered alone, thankful to have a moment to herself. Her eyes shifted to a small stream where animals perched along the bank for a drink. They scurried away as she stepped closer and knelt beside the water to refill her canteen.

She admired the colorful leaves and fresh air as she sat in the peacefulness of her solitude. But the tranquility didn't last as she imagined ghouls and bandits leaping from the bushes ready to attack. Her eyes darted from one place to the next, never settling on anything as she was filled with fear.

As birds took flight, the limbs above rustled, and Neer quickly unsheathed her sword while staring above. Feathers and leaves drifted from the heavens as the animals raced away. Finding that she was alone, she exhaled a deep breath and returned her weapon to its scabbard on her belt.

With the canteen full, she took a drink of water and then walked back to camp with her bundle of tinder and firewood. In the clearing stood Loryk, tending to the horses. Neer dropped her armful to the ground and then turned as soft voices echoed from nearby.

"It's them elves," Loryk remarked.

"What are they doing?" Neer asked as she collected the sticks into a pile.

Loryk shrugged and continued feeding his horse. Feeling a bit curious, Neer stepped through the trees to investigate. Within a small clearing, she found Avelloch and Klaud in what looked to be a heated battle.

With a hard grunt, Klaud swung the blunt end of his spear, and Avelloch flipped quickly beneath it. He jumped behind Klaud, ready to strike him with a large stick, but the magic user teleported away. With a quick spin, Avelloch slashed at him as he reappeared. The stick cut through empty air as Klaud disappeared once again. Avelloch flipped backward and landed beside Klaud just as he reappeared. Klaud teleported again, this time ten feet backward. Avelloch stood strong and determined. His fingers wriggled along his weapon.

Klaud smiled and disappeared again. Avelloch turned around just as Klaud appeared behind him and instantly pulled the mage into a headlock. Klaud struggled against him, then teleported back. They spun aside before coming to a stop as their weapons pressed against the other's throat.

Perfect teeth gleamed in a proud smile when Avelloch patted Klaud's shoulder and then stepped away.

"Impressive," Neer said as she made her presence known. "Where did you learn to fight like that? You were predicting his moves before he made them."

With a sly smile, Klaud stepped quietly through the trees and left the others behind.

"My father," Avelloch stated while scanning the ground. "Why is it you refuse to use your magic? If you are the great *drimil* you claim to be, why must you fight with your weapons?"

"Drimil? That's *magic user*, right?"

With a frustrated huff, he nodded.

She smiled and asked, "Why? Afraid I'll make an exception and use it on you?"

"You don't have the strength to kill me." He found a stick similar in size to a dagger and pressed it to her chest. "You're too kind, and it makes you weak."

Her eyes tightened before she snatched the stick and fell into a defensive stance. With a hidden smile, Avelloch twisted his own sparring weapon and matched her posture. Taking a step forward, she struck at his chest. He caught her arm and spun behind, pulling her close.

His weapon pressed against her throat and his breath tickled her ear as he said, "You've got to do better than that, meena'keen."

She pulled away and turned around. "What does that mean?" she asked, jabbing her weapon. As her stick moved to his throat, she cut down into a spin that aimed for his legs. He twisted aside and placed the end of his weapon to her spine.

"Meena'keen?" He pondered for a moment before explaining, "Outsider."

Her eyes narrowed and chest puffed at the insult. With a deep grunt, she slashed toward his arm. As he dodged her attack, she cut back and aimed for his chest. He ducked beneath her arm, hooked his leg beneath her foot, and flipped her to the ground. Kneeling over her, with their faces close, he pressed the stick to her chest. She drew her weapon to his side while falling but found her wrist firmly in his grasp, preventing it from touching his side. Her surprised, amazed eyes met with his as he leaned closer and playfully taunted her.

"Weak."

Unable to hide her smile, she took his hand, and he lifted her from the ground.

"I'll be stronger once I can use my magic freely," she explained.

"It isn't magic that will prevail, but your wit. You should be quick with a sword and adept with your mind."

"What are you now? A philosopher?"

There was an infectious warmth to his smile when he chuckled, and she couldn't stop herself from staring.

"The world has seen dark days if I'm the wisest person around," he said.

"You're a good fighter, Avelloch, but don't flatter yourself."

With a breathless laugh, he stepped aside, and she admired him while recounting their fight. Since her arrival to the Brotherhood, she was trained to fight and defend herself against many different warriors. With humans, she always prevailed, but she knew the evae were different. They were swift and nimble. Even when he wasn't trying, Avelloch was better than anyone she had ever fought against... including Reiman.

So many days were spent in the yards training and sparring with her adoptive father. At only fifteen, she was forced to fight until her fingers bled and her eyes were swollen shut. He didn't do this for the thrill but rather to keep her strong and resilient. He never went too far and always made sure she was taken care of. He trained her to be strong and fierce, and for that she was grateful.

Her thoughts were broken when Avelloch explained that he'd return to camp with more tinder and logs, and she watched with a tinge of sadness as he stepped away.

Moving through the darkening woods, she approached the

camp, where Loryk sat fiddling with his lute.

"Where've you been?" he asked.

"Sparring with Avelloch."

"Pfft!" Loryk shook his head. "He's too damned good, Neer. All them evae're better fighters than 'umans."

"Calling them evae now, are you?"

He tossed her a canteen, and she quickly drank the water inside.

"Might as well," he said. "I've been practicin' my evaesh too. Take a listen: Hello, my name was Loryk. How do you scrub?"

"Impressive." She smiled and corrected his mistakes. Bashful, he practiced the proper way of speaking, and after several attempts, he proudly got it right. "Is Klaud teaching you?"

"I learned mostly by listenin' to you all talkin', but Klaud is teachin' me. 'E's also been training me to use a weapon. I'm not near as good as you, but I can 'old my own."

"That's nice of him."

"It just passes the time on the road. He threatened to take out my tongue if I kept singin', so we settled our differences."

He moved back to his instrument, and she closed her eyes. The beautiful melodies were soon interrupted by the muffled tread of footsteps, and Neer turned around to find Klaud approaching from behind. His naturally sullen expression faded into annoyance when he glanced at the unburnt pile of wood.

"Why wasn't a fire started?" Klaud demanded while turning to Loryk, who stared back cluelessly. With a sigh, Klaud dropped the rabbits he planned to cook and said, "He needs to pull his weight!"

The others were silent as he stomped into the woods.

"What's with 'im?" Loryk asked.

"He expected you to start a fire," Neer explained with a light scolding.

"Oh, I see. So, while you're off playin' with Avel-cock, I'm supposed to start the fire, yeah?"

"Well, you do need to make yourself useful, Loryk. If we do all the fighting, you can at least start a fire."

Loryk sighed defeatedly. "Right, right, fine. I'll just get started on somethin' useful, I suppose!" He wiped his hands together and then dug through his satchel in search of a flint. As he stepped away to gather more tinder and wood, Neer eyed the rabbits at her feet. With great distaste, she skinned the first animal. It was a sloppy mess, as her untrained hands slipped and fumbled over the raw meat. A smile formed across her lips as she imagined Avelloch's grimace at her pathetic attempts.

While deep into her task, she heard the scuffle of footsteps echo from behind. For a moment, she was fear-stricken, and every slight breeze and rustling limb caught her attention. But the woods were empty, and being so far from civilization, she knew she was safe. They were far enough from any large settlements to ever be found, and if mercenaries came strolling about, she was confident she could take them.

But it wasn't mercenaries or thieves who worried her. It was the monsters that stalked the shadows, the undead and wispers that now plagued the land. Creatures so vile and unimaginable, they were only found in the most wicked of stories. A loud thump came from the east and she flinched, slicing deep into her palm.

"Seven hells!" she hissed, and then gripped her bleeding injury. The contents of her satchel spilled out as she hurriedly overturned her bag and searched for a healing potion. Upon finding the near empty vial, she dripped it over her injury and exhaled a deep breath as the pain was numbed.

Her relief was short-lived when sudden, quick footsteps approached from all around. Before she could turn, a thick sack was forced over her head. She fought and screamed as her sword was pulled from its sheath. Searing heat boiled her blood when a thick needle pierced her neck and liquid was injected into her veins. She unleashed a raw, vibrating scream and fell into the grass, paralyzed with agony. Every muscle contracted. Her heart skipped as the excruciating toxin fizzled through her.

Pinned to the ground by another, she was unable to fight as two strong hands held her wrists together, and with a swift strike to the back of her head, she fell silent and still.

Chapter Twenty-Four

Pursuit of the Order

"Neer..." a frail voice called to her from the void. It spoke from everywhere and nowhere at once. It was a voice from her childhood that brought her comfort and peace, though she couldn't place who it belonged to. "Please...," it whispered softly through the deafening silence.

Neer struggled, but her eyes never opened. She was stuck in an endless abyss of shadows and ice. Feeling weightless and alone, she could do nothing but wait.

Wait for life.

Wait for death.

Wait for an escape.

Soon, the waiting was interrupted when the deep emptiness filled with pain. Burning, inescapable pain. She was trapped in an endless void, forced to endure tortures she could only recollect through the memories that haunted her. A figure moved through the endless darkness. Its cloak was faded and torn. Angry eyes looked at her from beyond the shadow of a hood, and she was paralyzed by fear. A ragged, pained cry echoed all around, and she opened her eyes with a gasp. Through several hard blinks, her blurred vision slowly cleared, and she saw white-and-golden robes draped over the feet of the priest standing before her. She struggled to move, but her weakened arms and legs were bound to the legs of an old wooden chair. Through ragged breaths, she lifted her eyes to meet with the High Priest's gaze. A sadistic smile pulled his thin lips to the side, and his familiar green eyes were bright with pride. A manicured beard covered his chin and upper lip while dark hair hung across his shoulders. His youthful skin and slender cheeks gave him the appearance of an age much younger than his seventy-five years.

"So..." The voice that haunted her nightmares sent chills down her spine. "It seems our paths have crossed again... *Nerana*." His smile widened as he mocked her name. "I should've expected to find you here, in the arms of the Brotherhood meant to destroy me. To destroy everything the Divines have given for us to grow and prosper."

Neer struggled against the ropes that bound her wrists and ankles, but her muscles were weak. Her heavy eyes shifted from left to right as she scanned her surroundings. Flittering candlelight illuminated the musty and molded walls of an abandoned cabin.

A deep emptiness filled her chest as her body burned with exhaustion, and shallow breaths expanded her lungs to their capacity. She focused on her energy, hoping to use her magic to free herself, but the warmth never came. Nothing more than fatigue coursed through her aching bones and tired mind.

"Without your magic, you aren't so intimidating, are you?" His blade touched her cheek, and she winced as her skin was sliced open. "Brown hair... olive skin... a new identity ... all these changes... yet your eyes remain."

For a moment, she was the scared little girl clinging to life as he and his men performed their heinous experiments. She was reminded of the grueling nights she spent alone, crying, wondering if this was the end. She gasped as he lifted her sleeve to reveal the branding on her arm.

"You belong to the Order," he growled. "The Divines aren't through with you yet."

Looking into his eyes, she was filled with rage. "Fuck the Divines!" she growled. "Anyone that would see fit to make you rule isn't deserving of the dirt beneath my feet!" She spat in his face and breathed through flared nostrils. "You're nothing more than the cowards you preach about! Even Nizotl would be made speechless in the shadow of your wickedness!"

Iron suits clanked as his knights stepped forward. The large men towered over the tall Priest with weight that outmatched his twice over. The High Priest stiffened with a deep breath and casually lifted his arm, wordlessly commanding his soldiers to stand down. Staring curiously at Neer, he said, "Spoken like the true heir of Nizotl himself."

She glared at him as energy swirled within her. Her teeth clenched so hard she feared they might crack. His words were nothing more than lies spilling from his tongue. A manipulation meant to instill fear and uncertainty in those who were different... in those who were powerful.

"If that's true, then you should watch yourself, *priest*. You've said it yourself: even without magic, the heir of a Divine is the most vile and dangerous creature to walk the mortal plane."

With a nasty snarl, he stepped forward and smacked her cheek with the back of his hand. Blood filled her mouth as her head swung to the side "You will not threaten me, demon."

She spat blood on the floor. "It has taken you sixteen years to find me." The taste of metal lingered on her lips. "So, you tell me... whose Divines are really in charge here?"

Red-faced and trembling, he called the two guards forward and gruffly commanded, "Take watch outside!"

The enormous knights, dressed in heavy armor with thick golden scapulars that hung from their waists, marched outside. Neer glanced at the three other knights standing along the back wall behind the High Priest. Her gaze shifted as he stepped forward and looked menacingly into her eyes.

"Let's see whose Divines are in control."

With a sinister grin, he stepped aside to reveal a prisoner strapped to a chair across the room. Neer's fury vanished. There was nothing but pain and emptiness as she gazed at the curly auburn hair tangled with leaves and dirt. Tears welled in her eyes as she examined the thick blood dripping from his swollen nose and cut lip. The dark red pooled across his lap as his head hung forward. Broken and bruised fingers showed the torment he had endured. Her lip quivered as she stared at the broken man before her.

"Loryk…?"

She was hollow, empty. Devoid of anything but pain and guilt. He must've come after her when she was captured. She worried she couldn't save him, that the Priest would torture him to death before she had time to wriggle from her restraints. Without her magic, she was powerless and weak… Without her magic, she was hopeless to save him.

She gasped as he slowly lifted his head. Firelight reflected against the bruises and cuts that covered his face with blood. "Neer…," he groaned.

She choked at the sound of his frail voice, and glancing at the High Priest, her sorrow turned to rage. Redness brightened her face as she pulled against the restraints, and with a raw, raging scream, she said, "What have you done! Untie these binds, you coward!"

Loryk screamed as a blade slid down the length of his arm. Neer watched in horror, paralyzed with anger and guilt, as a line of exposed muscle and tissue stretched across his skin. With a growl, she tugged harder against her binds, causing her wrists to bleed.

"I will kill you!"

"You don't like this?" the High Priest taunted. "The sound of your friend…"

The crack of a snapping finger sent Loryk wailing, and Neer's throat burned as she screamed. Her chair tilted and shook as she fought to free herself. Fury from the depths of her soul made her hot and sweaty.

The High Priest pulled Loryk's hair back and pressed a dagger to his throat. Loryk was silent as he fell in and out of consciousness. "Let's see how powerful you truly are."

Her eyes widened as the blade moved slowly across his skin. The High Priest stared hungrily as Neer was overwhelmed with fear and rage. Every quick heartbeat quivered through her veins. Her wrists were bloody and raw as she fought against her restraints.

The Order had taken everything from her: her family, her childhood, her life. They wouldn't take his. She would burn this world alive if it would see an end to the Order. An end to the madness that had taken ahold of the living and warped their sense of morality. The High Priest wouldn't take another thing from her, not while she was still alive... Not while she could fight.

With a deep breath, she collected the fury deep within and unleashed all the rage that had brewed her entire life. In a single instant, the world stopped spinning. The wind no longer blew, and all noise was made silent as she gathered her energy and unleashed it all.

Chapter Twenty-Five

Final Breath

Raw, undisturbed energy that had been festering since her childhood erupted through in a powerful wave of magic and rage. The cabin shifted and moaned as the ground split beneath it. Trees snapped as cracks formed across hardened soil, becoming shallower as they traveled away from the crumbling shack.

The High Priest and his guards crashed to the floor. The sound of their clashing armor was silent against the heavy tremors of the world. Thin blue veins formed around Neer's darkened eyes. Her skin was pale, and her body was rigid as she awakened the power deep within. The arms of the chair cracked and splintered as she clenched her fists around them.

The release of such power lifted the weight inside her, and as the world slowly fell silent, she found herself growing weak and tired.

As her magic faded, and the world was still, she collapsed. Her head fell to the side, and her eyes returned to their bright teal. Heavy lungs struggled to take shallow breaths as she fought for consciousness. "Loryk...," she whined through parted lips. "Loryk..."

He moaned, but never spoke. A shallow nick on his throat was all that remained from the recent threat on his life. Neer closed her eyes at the sight of his breathing.

"Extraordinary...," the High Priest remarked as he stood in amazement. He called two knights forward and demanded, "Kill the bard. Retrieve the Child. We're going back to Skye to finish what we started."

Neer gasped at the sound of his threatening words, and she stared at the floor as the knights' heavy footsteps thudded closer. Her weak muscles were unable to fight against her binds. "Please…," she begged as they approached Loryk. "Don't…"

The High Priest shushed her and gently rubbed her head. "It'll all be over soon, Child."

Tears filled her eyes. Using all her strength, she was hardly able to lift her head. "I'll go with you," she cried. "Please, let him live."

Icy fingers gripped her chin as the High Priest lifted her face, and she was forced to watch as a knight stood behind Loryk and slowly raised his sword. The bard was motionless as the weapon came down. His tired, defeated eyes met with Neer's, and for a moment, the world was still.

Moonlight glistened against the blood smeared across his swollen face. The welts on his cheeks grew larger as the hint of a smile tugged his lip. "It's okay, Neery…," he croaked in a broken and unrecognizable voice.

A tear fell from her eye as the blade drew closer. She held his gaze as long as she could, until the sword fell with a loud clash. Neer glanced at the knight as he coughed and spewed drops of blood across Loryk's back and hair, and then collapsed to the ground. A steel sword cut through his armor and sank deep into his back. She examined the intricate details of the twisted hilt and quickly realized this was no human weapon.

Her heart skipped as she lifted her eyes, searching desperately for the evae who had come to their rescue. Iron suits clanged as the knights fled the cabin in search of the intruders. As she watched the knights slip out of the door, two cold hands tightly clutched her shoulders, and she shuddered as the High Priest leaned closer.

"They'll never save you," he whispered.

Fear trickled down her spine as his grip tightened. But it wasn't a motion of anger or power… He was afraid. Surely, he knew the elves had come to Llyne, and if not, he understood the Brotherhood had more powerful warriors than any other faction aside from his own. For a moment, he felt powerless, and Neer couldn't allow him to regain his strength.

Her thoughts were lifted as he released his hold and marched across the broken and disheveled cabin. The binds of her ankles loosened as she fought to free herself, and she looked down to find large rats nibbling at the leather. They climbed up the chair, and quickly ate away at the restraints of her wrists.

As the leather strips snapped, Neer lifted her hands and rubbed her wrists. Her eyes shifted to the rats as they scurried away and she was puzzled to find one who stayed behind for a moment longer. It gazed into her eyes and softly nodded before following the others. She watched the small animals and came to the sudden realization that they weren't ordinary rodents; they were dreleds.

The splintered wood creaked beneath Neer's feet as she carefully stood. Fueled by rage, she charged at the High Priest and ripped the sword from the fallen knight as she passed by him. With a heavy, exhausted grunt, she swung the weapon to his chest. He ducked beneath her pitiful attack, and she gasped at the sudden pain of a dagger plunging into her side.

Their faces were close as he peered into her eyes. "You think you can best me?"

A twisted smile pulled his lips as he swung his weapon. Neer slipped to the side while lifting her sword toward his chest. The High Priest's dagger turned in his hand and deflected the oncoming blade. With his spare hand, he smacked Neer, and she stumbled to the side with a vibrant handprint across her face.

"Not so powerful without your magic, are you, Child?" He thrust his dagger forward.

Neer stepped aside and the edge of the blade caught the tip of her nose. Pushing his arm away, she drew up her weapon, ready to slice his arm in two. He blocked the strike, and both were caught with their weapons held close to their faces. With a hard kick, she sent the High Priest stumbling back. She slashed at his stomach, and he stepped aside, a mere hair's breadth out of reach. Jabbing forward, his dagger slashed deep into her shoulder.

She leapt back to make space between them. Blood from the deep cut soaked through her clothes and left her arm throbbing in pain. Hunched over in agony, she looked into his eyes and trembled with fury. A loud, raw cry left her throat as she charged at him, ready to end this, ready to finally relieve the world and herself of the agony he inflicted. As she closed in, he stepped back, hooked his leg through the bottom of a chair and flipped it at her.

She fell aside as the chair crashed into her, and before she had time to regain her balance, he pinned her against the wall with his dagger to her throat. He brought his face inches from her own. "Magic is the purest form of darkness, and those born of its power"—he pressed his blade harder against her skin—"must be purged."

He watched her once intimidating look fade to horror. Too weak to fight his grasp, Neer remained still as she looked into his eyes. The fear turned to anger as he threatened her life. With every passing second, her fury grew.

She would no longer allow herself to be his prisoner, and with a vengeful snarl, she thrust him back and plunged her sword into his chest. His hard eyes widened as he inhaled a sudden, pained gasp. His trembling fingers moved to the blade that pierced directly through his heart. With a pained cry, Neer kicked him back and pulled the weapon from his flesh.

Blood spattered her face as he choked and then fell to his knees. She stared down at his body. The sword trembled in her grasp as she watched him, waiting for him to move. Waiting for him to breathe. As the seconds turned to minutes, he never made a sound. Not a slight shuffle or twitch to hint at a sign of life, and Neer stumbled back as the weight of his control, the weight of a lifetime of running and hiding, was suddenly lifted.

The High Priest was dead.

She was finally free.

As a shadow passed through the cabin, she lifted her eyes and was stunned by the sight of a familiar face.

"Avelloch?" she asked.

A scarf and hood covered his face and hair, leaving him nearly invisible in the shadows. Confusion overwhelmed her as she wondered why he was there and how he had managed to find her. The thoughts vanished when a knight burst into the cabin with his weapon drawn. Neer stumbled back as Avelloch pushed her aside and stole her sword. He raced across the room and leapt off a fallen beam. Moonlight danced across his crimson-covered blades before they plunged through the knight's thick armor and sank deep into his chest.

The knight came to a sudden halt as Avelloch held his weapons in place. With a deep grunt, the knight stepped forward on shaking legs and then crashed to the ground. Avelloch stood over his victim, watching as he choked for breath until falling silent. He closed his eyes with a deep breath and then turned back to Neer.

"Are you hurt?" he asked.

She looked at the devastation around them. Dead bodies lay in pools of thickening blood, and the High Priest, who had caused her so much grief and sorrow, was dead at her feet.

"Neer!" Avelloch whispered sharply.

"It's over…," she said. "I don't have to go to the Trials." She turned to Avelloch, whose fierce scowl had yet to fade. "I'm free."

His hard eyes softened before quickly falling away. With a heavy sigh, he stepped over a knight and retrieved a lit torch from the wall. All other torches had been snuffed from Neer's explosion of magic, and this one was nearing its end as the flames slowly died.

Neer stepped to Loryk's side and gently tapped his face. "Hey… come on, Loryk! Open your eyes!"

The bard was motionless and quiet in the chair. His binds had been chewed through by the dreleds, leaving his arms and legs free from their restraints. Neer leaned closer to investigate him, and she gasped when a light wheeze vibrated from his swollen throat.

"Avelloch," she called, "bring the light! Hurry!"

He came quickly to her side and held the torch close to Loryk's face. Neer carefully lifted his head and, with a frightful choke, nearly dropped it. Beneath the shallow cut on his neck was an enormous lump. Translucent skin surrounded the blistered incision, exposing thick blue veins just beneath the surface.

"What is that?" Neer asked. "What's happening to him?"

Avelloch glanced around the room before noticing a dagger

lying in the rubble. With hard eyes, he stepped over the debris and removed the weapon from its place beneath pieces of fallen wood. He gently wiped the edge of the blade to clear it of dust, and he was stricken by the sight of glowing blue veins gently pulsing along the blade.

"Neer," he said. "Were you cut with this blade?"

She didn't hear as she focused intently on Loryk, touching his wounds and checking him for signs of breath. Avelloch asked again, this time with more aggression. She flinched and slowly looked over her injuries, revealing the deep wounds on her side and shoulder. Orange firelight surrounded the wound as Avelloch leaned closer with the torch. She gritted her teeth in agony as he lightly touched around her injuries, examining the glowing veins and light swelling.

"We need to get you to a *nes'seil!*" he said.

"A what?" she cried and gripped her side with a deep groan.

"It's someone... a person who..." He waved his hands, struggling to translate the word. "*Kila!*" he exclaimed. "They can help you! They can fix this!"

"What is it? What's happening to us?"

Avelloch slung Loryk over his shoulder and commanded Neer to follow. As she stepped outside, her eyes shifted to the high ridges extending outward from the destroyed cabin and into the forest. Fallen trees with bright green leaves lay dormant atop the jagged ground.

Purple moonlight reflected against the blood-spattered armor of five knights lying motionless on the ground. Crimson puddles rested beneath their enormous bodies. She turned to Avelloch as he slung Loryk atop a large mare nearby and then mounted the saddle.

The thud of horse hooves beat against the ground as Avelloch rode toward her with another horse in tow. The brown mare blocked her vision of the knights and interrupted her thoughts. Glancing at Avelloch, who silently urged her to climb onto her saddle, she did as she was instructed and settled into her seat.

As the horses trotted carefully across the uneven terrain, a faint shuffling came from behind. Fear trickled from Neer's stomach down to her toes, and her wide eyes stared ahead at nothing as the haunting sound of a grunting man came from behind. Deep, quivering breaths escaped her tired lungs as she warily looked back at the cabin where a shadow emerged from the doorway. White robes were saturated in red where a blade was struck through his chest. With another pained moan, he slowly straightened his posture. Dark, angry eyes scanned the forest before slowly meeting with Neer's, and she was stricken with fear.

Locked in a menacing gaze, the High Priest watched with vengeance as she escaped into the night.

Chapter Twenty-Six

The Longest Ride

"In the land of the wicked seek faith in the Light and have everlasting life."

— Rotharion, the Book of Light

THE EVENING SUN CAST WARM rays of light across the empty woods as Neer rode along an overgrown trail with Avelloch by her side. Tall trees, devoid of their leaves as late autumn had stripped them bare, surrounded them at every turn. The Road had faded into a narrow trail as they wound through the foothills of the Everett Mountains. Wild animals roamed freely through the open country. Fallen logs, covered in moss and mushrooms, were scattered throughout the woodlands.

Neer leaned forward with a groan. Her body was sore, and her injuries made the ride close to unbearable. But it wasn't her wounds that troubled her as Loryk's wheezed breaths grew louder, and the swelling in this throat increased.

"We need to rest," Avelloch said.

"No," Neer argued. "He doesn't have time."

"The horses won't make it if we keep going like this. We'll take a break and keep moving."

Her eyes fell to Loryk, and guilt washed through her. With a sniff, she turned away and wiped her eyes. Glancing through the woods, she found a small area by the roadside where they could set up camp. Veering her horse off the road, she slid from the saddle and tied the reins to a tree.

Avelloch followed and carefully placed Loryk by a tree. Neer turned sharply as Loryk wheezed and whimpered. Digging through her bag, she collected several vials of potions and herbs. Misty-eyed and broken, she stared desperately at the handful of ointments, fearful they wouldn't work. Whatever poison the High Priest had used, it was powerful. She could feel it coursing through her, throbbing with every heartbeat and burning like smoldering embers through her veins.

Convinced there was no other option, she shoved the vials back into her bag and marched to Loryk's side. Avelloch quietly fed the horses and watched as Neer knelt beside Loryk, placing her hands to his chest. Closing her eyes tightly, she pushed her magic into him. Energy swirled inside, filling her with intense heat and searing pain as she transferred her health into him.

His broken fingers slowly snapped into place, and the deep bruising on his cheeks faded. But the swollen, pus-filled cut to his neck never receded. Its blue veins still glowed as Neer depleted herself of energy and strength. Her shallow cuts spilled with blood as they grew deeper and wider. Her skin paled and shriveled.

"Neer?" Avelloch called. "Neer!" He quickly pulled her away, and she fell into his arms with a deep, exhausted breath. Dark circles surrounded her half-opened eyes as she breathed in shallow, ragged breaths. Avelloch glanced at Loryk with wide eyes. "You healed him?" he asked.

Neer groaned as she slowly pushed herself from his arms and sat upright. Turning to Loryk, she was filled with grief. She calmly nodded and then reached for her canteen. Avelloch quickly passed it to her, and she took several small sips.

"It didn't work...," she said. "He's dying..." With her eyes closed, she leaned forward and exhaled a deep, sorrowful breath. "Maybe I *am* the spawn of Nizotl. Maybe this is my punishment for denouncing the Divines and fighting against their priests."

"Why were you taken?" he asked. "Who were those men?"

Neer wiped her nose with a sniff and turned away. "He's the High Priest. The leader of the Order of Saro." She wrapped her arms around her knees with another sniff. "I don't fight with my magic because of him. He has a way of tracking me. They'll probably find us out here since I used my energy to help Loryk."

Avelloch was silent for a moment. His eyes shifted to the blood stain on Neer's shirt. "Your injuries aren't worsening like his."

She glanced at her side. "It's my magic. I can't heal myself, but it slows the progression." With a sigh, she shook her head. "How did the High Priest survive that? I stabbed through his heart—I *felt* his muscles tearing—but he was standing there, watching as we left."

"It could be what reanimated those boys. There were no altars or magics performed. It was—"

"No. This was different. It felt different. I can't explain it... He's over seventy years old, yet he looks barely older than you. That isn't natural for humans." She paused with despair. "Maybe this is why I'm needed by the Brotherhood. Why my magic is so important to the cause. Whatever is protecting and keeping him alive can't be destroyed by conventional means. He'd have been taken care of long ago, if so."

"What are you saying? That he's magically enhanced? Immortal?"

With a shrug, she turned away. "I don't know. I don't care. I just want to end this. That's why I'm going to Nhamashel. To rid myself of the curse that binds me to the Order. Then maybe I'll have a chance at stopping them. My country and people can finally be free."

"What's stopping you now?"

"My magic is too weak. I'm not even sure what all I can do or how to even do it. Reiman taught me to protect myself with a sword until we're able to lift the curse, and I can train with my energy." She looked at her hands and imagined a life of freedom and belonging. One where the Order didn't reign over their lands, and the people were accepting of others who were different. As a soft breeze rustled through the branches, chills covered her arms, and she trembled with a shiver.

Avelloch shuffled through his belongings before passing Neer his cloak. She looked at him with confusion and accepted his gift.

Warmth eased her mind as she wrapped herself in the dark, filthy garment.

"Thanks," she said.

With a silent nod, he turned away, and they sat in deep silence. She gazed at the rugged hillsides and barren trees. Since beginning their travels hours before, they had yet to pass by a single village or settlement. Neer wasn't surprised by this. The Everett Mountains were a rugged and dangerous place covered in barren woodlands, and the foothills were inhabited mostly by loggers, hunters, and recluses. If the overgrown dirt roads and faded or missing signposts didn't take claim of the wandering outsider, the wild animals surely would.

Neer, however, wasn't bothered by the dangers or mystery of the Everett foothills. There was a calmness to being so deep in the woods. It was as if no one else existed, and for a while, she was safe.

"Avelloch," she started when a thought occurred to her. "How did you find us?"

"Dreleds. It seems the one you know from your hometown has friends in the right places. He told them to watch for you. But even with their help, it took me two days to find the cabin."

"Why did you do it?" She looked around. "And where is Klaud? Why haven't we met up with him by now?"

Avelloch's shoulders rose as he inhaled a deep breath. "He isn't here."

"What? What do you mean? Where is he?"

"He left." He paused. "We heard you screaming, but when we got there, you and your friend were gone. Klaud suggested we carry on. He said that Azae'l needs us more than you do."

Neer was shocked by this revelation. The sting of Klaud's betrayal weighed heavily on her. He would've left them to die... but could she blame him? The person he loved was dying, and he was the only one who could save her. It was his only goal, and he warned Neer from the beginning that he wouldn't stay behind if she fell.

"How did the Order find me?" she wondered aloud. "I've been so careful. I don't understand how they knew where we were."

Avelloch tensed, and with a deep breath, he explained, "It was the farmer."

"The who?"

"The one on the side of the road."

Her jaw dropped and a tremor of guilt passed through her. Tears welled up in her eyes as she realized her fateful mistake. "You told me not to do it," she said quietly. "I helped him, and he... he betrayed me! Why would he do that?" She wiped her eyes. "I should've listened to you. I should've let him die!"

"I was wrong," he said.

Neer turned to meet his gaze and was surprised to find sadness seeping through his expression.

"If there's a chance to help someone in need, then you should take it. Don't allow the darkness of this world to shroud your kindness. Just because he betrayed you doesn't mean everyone will."

She sniffed. "It isn't worth losing the people that I love. Loryk could die." She paused as her voice faded into a soft whimper. "I don't know what I'll do without him."

Avelloch ran his fingers down her arm and then carefully pulled her close. She sank into his embrace and cried on his shoulder. His jaw was tense as he stared into the forest with distant eyes. He whispered a phrase she didn't quite hear and then wrapped his arms tighter around her.

He held her for several long moments, until slowly releasing his grasp and backing away. His hands lingered on her arms as their gaze met, and she was comforted by the warmth in his eyes. There hadn't been much vulnerability or understanding in him, and she was glad to see through the darkness that kept him concealed. For a moment, she could sense the worry and despair he felt, as it was the same weight she carried throughout her life. Loneliness, pain, regret... hopelessness. She understood it all. And while it pained her to see such suffering in another, she found solace in knowing she wasn't alone.

With a slow blink, she turned away and was left cold and empty as their strong gaze was broken. Glancing through the darkness of the woods, she slowly stood and reached for Avelloch's hand. "We need to go," she said. "If Creatures of

Darkness are rising, then they're sure to find us out here. We can't be too far from a settlement."

As she helped pull Avelloch to his feet, Neer stumbled back and then leaned forward to catch her breath.

"Can you ride?" he asked. She felt her sunken face and then touched the wound on her side. Her body was weak, and she worried she wouldn't have the energy to carry on. As her eyes shifted to Loryk, she stood straighter and forced any doubt aside.

"I can do it," she said. "We aren't losing him."

"Neer," Avelloch touched her shoulder, and she released her forced bravery with a deep exhale. "Rest. I'll take watch."

"We can't—"

"Rest." He looked into her eyes. "We can't save him if we're too weak to save ourselves."

Slowly, she turned away and gave a reluctant nod. He collected his swords as Neer got comfortable against a tree and bundled into his cloak. She closed her eyes and allowed herself to relax. "Thank you, Avelloch," she said, her eyelids too heavy to hold open. Her voice slurred as she spoke to him in her native language, saying, "Don't leave, okay? We need you."

The next morning, Neer woke to find Avelloch leaned against a tree with his eyes closed. She sat up and twisted her neck to rid it of the stiffness and ache. Overnight, her coloring had returned, and she regained much of her strength, though her body was still wrought with pain and exhaustion.

She crawled to Loryk's side and examined the infected nodule on his throat. His skin had fallen paler throughout the night, and his wheezed breaths were hardly a whisper as he struggled to breathe.

Placing her hands on his chest, she exerted a small amount of energy, taking care to not deplete herself. As he slowly regained color, she backed away and wiped the sweat from her forehead.

After drinking the remains of what little was left in her canteen, she moved to Avelloch's side and gently tapped his shoulder. "Hey," she said. "Avelloch…"

He woke with a sleepy gasp. With several blinks, he calmed himself and sat up while rubbing his face.

"Some lookout you are," she said with a sly smile. "Come on, we'd best get going."

Together, they lifted Loryk onto the saddle, and Avelloch climbed on behind him. Neer mounted her horse, and they rode further down the uneven, overgrown trail. Neer groaned as the wound on her side sent waves of pain through her body. She stiffened and clutched her side as blood seeped through her clothes.

Nearing midday, they stopped to rest and feed the horses. As Avelloch slipped into the woods to hunt, Neer stayed with Loryk. She carefully placed a canteen to his lips and poured water into his mouth. "Come on, Lor," she begged. "Just hang on a little longer."

She placed the canteen aside and noticed the glowing veins from the High Priest's dagger illuminating from her bag. Carefully, she retrieved the beautifully crafted weapon and twisted it in her hands. It was unlike any she had ever seen, with swirled patterns of gold carved into the steel.

As leaves crunched in the woods nearby, Neer turned to investigate and was relieved to find Avelloch approaching with two squirrels and a rabbit in hand. He sat quietly next to her and began carving into the animals. Neer gathered dry tinder and twigs into a small pile, struck a flint, and kindled the flames. The fire popped and whirred as Avelloch held the skewered meat over the heat.

"Thanks. For hunting," she said, and he silently nodded in response. She withheld a groan and leaned back, gripping her throbbing side. "I hope we find a village soon. Even a homestead or shack would be better than nothing."

Avelloch remained silent, staring at the meat as it slowly cooked.

"Why are you helping us?" she asked.

He cast a sideways glance at her before returning his gaze to the flames. "Should I have let you die?"

She smiled. "Trying to be poetic? I didn't take you for the type."

He straightened his back with a sigh. "I was repaying a debt. Now, we're even."

"Is that so?"

Another silent nod.

"You know what I think?" She sat up with a silent hiss and ignored the burning in her side.

"I'm sure you'll tell me," he said with a hint of playfulness to his otherwise bleak tone.

She laughed through her nose and leaned closer, pressing a finger to his chest. "I think you *care*." Her smile grew as he scoffed and turned away. "Deny it all you want, but I can see through this deadly façade. You *care* about us. Two humans." He remained silent, and when his eyes veered to hers, she continued, "I suppose we *lan-this* aren't all so bad, are we?"

He smiled at her mispronunciation. "You *lanathess* are all the same. Always assuming everything is about you."

"Maybe," she said, "but why else would you be here?"

His eyes scanned her face and hair before connecting with hers and reminding her of the familiarity of his gaze. His breath warmed her face as his lips parted. She could feel his apprehension. He didn't want to accept what he knew was true, that her words were more than mere teasing. Without realizing they had moved, they were suddenly closer. Their gaze connected as they leaned inward, and the warmth of his body met with hers. As their lips softly touched, he froze, and Neer quickly opened her eyes. She swiftly backed away and wiped her mouth as the tension washed over them.

She breathed heavily, struggling to understand how they allowed themselves to become so intimate and close. Clutching her chest, she glanced at Avelloch and was saddened to find his vulnerable, soft eyes had been concealed once again with darkness and anger. His body was stiff as he stared into the flames, not daring to meet her gaze.

"Sorry," she said, her voice quiet with shame.

His jaw tightened as his brows pulled slightly together in confusion. She hadn't the time to read his emotions as he exhaled a deep breath and fell into a less rigid posture. He quietly removed a cooked squirrel from the fire and passed it to her. She accepted her meal and was relieved to find kindness where his anger would be.

They ate their meal in a comfortable silence before cleaning the campsite and continuing on their way down the long, desolate road.

Chapter Twenty-Seven

Strangers of Mange

"Deep in the mountains, far from the wandering eye, is a place like no other—a village on high. Flowers and mushrooms and kisses exchanged; you won't find a place that's stranger than Mange."

— 'Mange the Strange', Fjord of Jokulsa

SUNBEAMS STREAMED THROUGH THE TREES with orange light that sprayed across the hillsides. Dusk would soon approach, and Neer was fearful of spending another night in the woods.

Looking desperately through the brush, she caught sight of a faded signpost lost within overgrown weeds and grass. She pulled the reins to stop the horse and then leapt onto the roadside. Avelloch was silent as Neer fought through the vegetation and revealed a wooden sign that read *Mange*.

"Avelloch!" she said with a burst of laughter. "There's a village! Just north of here!" Caught in her excitement, she climbed onto the saddle and moved faster down the trail, eager to get off the Road and somewhere safe.

Traveling further north, Neer spotted a second Mange signpost that led them down a shallow, beaten path. Voices whispered through the air as they rode slowly through the darkening woods. Neer glanced around, battling her excitement and fear as she worried over the noises and who they could be.

The barren trees that covered the hillsides were replaced with lush grass and bright green leaves. Woven vines of flowers and windchimes were hung throughout the limbs. Footpaths overlapped through the thickening grasses, creating no discernable pattern as they wove between trees and across trickling streams.

Neer held her breath as shadows emerged from the darkness. The figures wandered through the trees with laughter as they followed along the footpaths sprawled across the ground. Riding closer to the village, Neer stared in wonder as people walked the trails in little to no clothing. Flowers were woven into their unkempt hair, men held hands with men, and women stopped to kiss. They laughed and sang while dancing through the flower-filled trees, and Neer was made suddenly aware of why the village was known throughout Llyne as *Mange the Strange*.

The homes were mere shacks spread throughout the meadow in no noticeable pattern, and a strong, woodsy odor Neer had never smelled before filled the air. She stopped her horse as a woman, whose bare breasts were covered by only a flower necklace, approached the group with a man by her side. They giggled, a little too hard, curiously touching Neer's horse.

"Oh," the woman cooed, "how beautiful! We don't see many horses around here!"

Avelloch recoiled as the woman approached him and brought her hand to his leg. As it slid up his thigh, Neer quickly intervened. "We need a healer!" she remarked, a bit too harshly. Her eyes were fixed on the woman's hand as she slowly removed it from Avelloch's leg.

"A healer?" the man asked. "Yes! We have one of those!"

"Yes! Yes!" The woman clapped happily. "Follow us! Come along!"

Neer turned back to Avelloch as the woman led her horse down the path.

She realized that he hadn't understood a word of the conversation, and quickly explained. "They have apothecaries and want us to follow them."

"*Apothecaries*?" he asked, though the word was obscure and broken.

She smiled faintly at his accented voice as he attempted to speak her language. "It's a person that patches you up when you're sick. They make you better."

He nodded and then looked around. "These people are—"

"Strange?" She chuckled. "This place is called 'Mange the strange' for a reason."

"Humans...," he griped.

She chuckled and turned back around.

The shacks grew denser, and more people wandered the woods as they approached the village center. A man with long ropes of hair hanging halfway down his back stepped to Neer's horse with his arms opened wide. He wore a wool poncho and walked barefoot atop the rocky dirt path. Smiling brightly, he greeted her horse before lovingly kissing its snout.

"Travelers!" the man said in a warm greeting. "What has brought you out here into the Everetts?"

Neer hurriedly explained, "My friend was poisoned. He needs an apothecary, as do I."

The man's smile never entirely faded, though his brows furrowed in worry. He curiously stepped to Loryk and examined his wounds before waving three men over. They carefully pulled him from the saddle, and Neer panicked as he was carried away.

"Where are you taking him?" she asked, climbing from her horse.

Avelloch leapt to the ground and came to her side as the roped-hair man stepped forward. He stood with his arm in front of her as the stranger said, "Do not worry, weary travelers. We can speak to the Divines here. This place... it will heal him, just as it has healed all of us!" He spread his arms and motioned to the village.

Avelloch stepped closer to Neer when the villagers cheered and sang at their mention. He then turned defensively to the man as he passed Neer a vial of clear liquid and curled her fingers around it.

"Not to fret, my dear friends. The Tears of Numera will heal your ailments. Just a drop on each of your wounds, and come morn, you will be good as new!"

Neer was silent as the man walked away with a bright smile.

She inspected the vial, which appeared to be nothing more than water, and began to feel a deep unrest as she worried for Loryk's safety.

"We shouldn't stay here," Avelloch warned. His eyes darted quickly from one place to another as the eccentric villagers began lighting torches throughout the woods.

"They're strange, but harmless," Neer said, mostly convincing herself as she knew they were out of options. She only hoped the odd villagers of Mange could truly cure their wounds as they had promised. "We should be fine here for the night."

Avelloch stepped to the roadside and tied the horses to a tree. He passed Neer her belongings before securing the saddlebags and stepping away from the curious villagers as they ogled the very average steeds.

"Come on," Neer said while taking Avelloch's hand before walking through the crowded paths. She silently groaned and clutched her side as blood dripped from her wound. Forcing herself down the road, she hoped to find an inn or, at the very least, a safe place to wait out the night.

Avelloch gently pulled her close as men and women wandered around, cheerfully passing flowers to one another. He came to a sudden halt when a woman wearing a flower halo and bare-feet stepped in front of him. Avelloch leaned back as she stepped closer to him. Her smile faded as her fingers moved down the length of his face. With wide, curious eyes, she leaned closer and pressed her lips to his.

He stiffened as the woman pulled him close. Her tongue touched his lips, and he carefully pushed her away. His wet lips were parted as he glared at the stranger. The woman bit her lip with a wide smile before turning to Neer. As she stepped closer, ready to pounce, Avelloch threw his arm up and blocked her advancement. The woman giggled innocently before skipping away. Speechless, Neer watched her disappear, and with a deep exhale, she turned to Avelloch. His hardened eyes locked on her, before he took her hand and guided her along the pathways.

"That was... *strange*," Neer remarked.

Avelloch's lips pursed as he sneered. A deep wrinkle formed between his brows as he pushed through the crowds and led Neer to a secluded area in the woods.

"Where are we going?" she asked.

"I don't trust these people."

"They aren't going to harm us." She giggled. "Does a little kiss frighten you so easily?"

He glared at her before dropping his bags and placing his hands to his hips. The glow of firelight from the village flickered in the distance as they stood in a grassy clearing far from prying eyes.

"Wait here," he started, "I'll gather firewood."

"You don't want to stay in the village?"

"No." Without another word, he stepped into the trees.

Neer leaned against a log with a subtle smile. Her eyes shifted to the village as people cheered when a bonfire was turned from orange to blue. Embers sprayed into the air each time someone tossed herbs into the flames, changing its color and creating beautiful sparks that lit up the night.

Avelloch soon returned and dropped a small pile of wood between them. He then struck a flint and lit the tinder. Neer exhaled a sigh of relief as the warmth of the growing flames lifted the chill in the cool autumn air.

As Avelloch got comfortable and ate his dinner of jerky and dry bread, Neer inspected the vial she was given. "Do you think it's safe?" she asked.

"No."

With a disgruntled glance at Avelloch, she returned her gaze to the vial. "He said it's a gift from Numera.[*] She's the Divine of elements and nature... I think it'll be okay."

"You shouldn't take anything these people give! They've lost their minds."

"I don't have another option. Maybe my magic is warding it off, but for how long? They said this will heal me... and that's

---

[*] One of the six Divines of the Circle of Six who are worshipped and revered by the followers of the Order of Saro.

Numera, known also as Aenwyn, is the Divine of nature and elements. Her temple rests at the base of the Whispering Mountains in the region of Ravinshire and is the most visited of any of the six working temples, with the newly constructed Temple of Kirena, also in Ravinshire, coming in close second.

what we've come for, right?"

He took a deep breath. "Can you heal yourself?"

"No. My energy transfers into those I heal. I can't transfer my own energy back into myself." Her eyes moved back to the vial. "I'm going to use it."

She set the vial aside and struggled to remove her armor. Avelloch watched in silence, before placing his meal to the side and coming to her aid. Quietly, he moved her fumbling hands aside and untied the braided straps securing her chest piece together.

As it loosened, Neer exhaled a deep breath and tossed it aside. She then lifted her tunic and pulled it over her head. Avelloch helped her remove it from her injured arm and placed it next to her armor piece. She winced while examining the deep, bulging wound in her abdomen. It had doubled in size and oozed with infection.

She collected the vial from the grass and popped the cork, when Avelloch suddenly wrapped his hands around hers.

"Are you sure you should this?" he asked.

She smiled. "I thought you didn't care?"

He glanced at her side with a worried gaze. "This could alter your mind. You could become one of them."

"Maybe you should take some, too, then," she teased.

"Neer—"

"I'm fine. I've heard of the Tears of Numera. If it's actually magically enhanced water, then I'll be fine."

"And if it isn't?"

Their eyes met, and she lightly smiled. "Then, I guess I'll be living blissfully in the woods like all the others."

His jaw tensed as he glanced from her side to her shoulder and then to her hands. He looked into her eyes before slowly backing away. Her hand trembled as she hovered the vial over her side. Taking several deep breaths, she prepared for the pain and then carefully dripped the potion into the wound.

She gasped in agony as it sizzled over her raw, blistered skin. With gritted teeth, she moved to the injury on her shoulder. Struggling to properly angle her hand, she nearly spilled the potion down her arm.

Avelloch carefully took the vial. His face lingered close to hers as he administered the elixir over her poisoned laceration. His eyes were hard with concentration, putting deep lines between his brows.

As the flames nearby brightened, his features illuminated, and she admired his filthy, strikingly handsome appearance. She touched the dry blood that freckled the bridge of his nose and was filled with the guilt of knowing he had killed for her. He risked his life and broke faith with Klaud to find her. She was grateful for his heroism, yet she was confused. Since their night in Porsdur, he had shown her kindness and understanding, and she was overwhelmed by the attraction that pulled them together. But their kiss still rattled her mind, and she was disappointed in his reluctance to accept that he could feel anything but hatred toward a human.

Still, she couldn't overlook his bravery, which was made greater by his lack of trust and empathy for her kind. She knew that he cared, and for her, that was enough.

"Thank you," she said as he tended to her wounds, which no longer ached as the potion numbed them of pain, "for coming back for me... for... everything."

His gaze shifted to hers, and she could sense the vulnerability in his usually hardened eyes. No longer was he the angry or distrustful person she met so long ago. The warmth of his skin caressed her as their faces drew nearer.

He touched her face and then leaned closer, softly kissing her lips. She sighed while pulling him closer. All doubt and uncertainty were made instantly clear as his body pressed against hers. She lay on the grass as he crawled over her and slid his tongue through her lips. Chills covered his skin as she lifted his shirt and felt the muscles and scars along his back. Her eyes opened as he pulled away and met her gaze. The anger and vengeance that once guarded him had vanished. She breathed heavily while staring into the eyes of someone just as broken and defeated as she had always been.

He closed his eyes and gulped down his emotions. "Is your mind clear?" he asked. "Has the potion affected you?"

She smiled with tear-filled eyes, knowing it had no affect

other than sealing her wounds and numbing the pain. Overwhelmed by his familiarity and warmth, she lifted up and met her lips with his once again. Rolling over, she lay on top of him, blanketed by security as his strong arms held her close. His hands trailed down the length of her sides as she sat up. Her skin tingled, and her heart raced as she straddled his lap. His body was solid and hard beneath hers as he looked into her eyes with a gaze she had never seen before. It wasn't one of hunger or lust as it had been with the others she had the misfortune to lay with in the past. His look was different, and for a moment she was whole. Staring into his eyes, she felt what she had needed for so long: acceptance and understanding.

She gently touched his face and looked into his eyes. "Never clearer."

He wrapped tightly around her as she brought their lips together and lost herself in his touch as they shared this night as one.

Chapter Twenty-Eight

Purpose and Pain

"The Tears of Numera shall cure any strife. Just a few drops will save your life."

— Sayings of Mange

THE NEXT MORNING, NEER SAT beneath a gentle waterfall. Her fingers swept over the freshly scarred injuries on her shoulder and side as she scrubbed herself clean. As she sat alone in the tranquility of the woods, she thought of her night with Avelloch, and how much it meant to her. Never had she felt as safe and whole as she did with him.

But the serenity soon faded to sorrow when the haunting realization of their journey plagued her mind. It wasn't likely that all of them would see the end of the Trials. She knew this before embarking upon the dangerous quest, but with each passing day, her guilt and uncertainty beckoned her to reconsider, and at times, she truly wanted to.

The fear of her future brought back the awful memories of her past. She thought of the long nights she spent curled on the floor of her cell, wishing for an end, and the emptiness she endured when her family was murdered.

She absently stroked the brand on her arm. Bearing such a vile symbol filled her with disgust. With a deep breath, she dipped her head beneath the trickling water and forced the memories aside. Feeling uneasy with her solitude, she quickly dressed and found herself at the village where Avelloch stood by the horses. He dug through the saddlebags while a curious man patted his mare's face.

"Oh, the wonders you must hold…," the man said while nuzzling the horse. "If only you could speak, then we'd know the true beauty of your kind."

Neer stepped past the stranger and approached Avelloch. She happily accepted the apple he offered and feasted on her breakfast. "What are you doing?" she asked.

"Making sure nothing was stolen," he explained while looking through his things.

"These people aren't out to get us, you know?"

"You can never be too careful."

Before she could argue, they were greeted by the man with roped hair.

"Good morning, my friend," he said with a smile, "pleasant day we're having, yes?"

"It's been lovely, I — " Neer fell silent as the man stepped past her to greet the horse.

"How was your night?" he asked the mare. "I do hope we didn't give you too much of a scare!"

Neer was relieved to find that Avelloch was just as perplexed as her. With her brows together, she spoke to the stranger. "Is there any word on Loryk?"

He turned to her with a bright smile. "Your friend is doing marvelously. I had Luna and Beck take him to the hot springs. You should join them! It's a wondrous time!"

He gently took her hand and led her through the village. She turned back to Avelloch, whose angry snarl faded when their gaze met. With a deep huff, he secured his things in the saddlebag, then stepped closer to the man still petting the mare.

"Touch my things, and you will lose a hand," he said with a menacing growl.

The man chuckled happily, unable to understand a word the evae spoke. "Silly elves…," he said.

With a deep breath, Avelloch marched to Neer's side. Through the densely populated village, they followed a narrow path that led deep into the woods. Neer glanced at the villagers as they wandered around without a stitch of clothing. Flowered ornaments covered the trees in a rainbow of colors and filled the woods with a calming floral scent. Butterflies floated through the air, drifting from one tree to the next.

Murmuring voices hummed through the air as they moved further down the path. Heavy mist broke through the leaves ahead, and Neer was stunned as they came over a hillside to find a beautiful log cabin. Strong wooden beams were sprawled throughout the open room, which had no front door or walls.

They brushed past several unclothed villagers as they ascended the steps to the entrance. A man placed a flower necklace over Neer's head and kissed her cheek with a smile. She watched him in astonishment as he quietly stepped away and followed the trails into the woods.

Her eyes shifted to the flowers as she admired her gift. The man who led them here greeted every resident with a humble good morning.

"How is this place so green?" Neer asked.

He turned with a beautiful smile. "We gift Aenwyn with our respect and admiration, and she gifts us with her beauty."

Neer was taken aback by their usage of the name Aenwyn, as it represented the Old Ways, which the Order of Saro repealed at the time of High Priest Beinon's inauguration. The rest of the country now referred to Aenwyn as Numera, which was a more appropriate name, given that it had no evaesh ties, unlike its predecessor.

They stepped into the large cabin to find several residents standing inside. In the center of the room was a marble statue of Numera, the Divine of nature and elements. Her gown flowed beautifully across her feet, while natural flowers and vines hung from her opened arms. Crowns of flowers had been placed atop her head. Statues of the Divines were a rarity in Llyne, as many had been abolished and destroyed during the reign of the Brotherhood. She stepped to the effigy and gently touched its hand. For a moment, she wondered if the figure was real, as its detailing was nearly perfect.

Staring up at the Divine, she questioned her own beliefs and the beliefs of the Order. Neer had never been a full believer in the Six, but she never entirely denied their existence either. She was somewhere in the middle, always questioning, always wondering if what the Order said was true. While her mind told her it was all a lie to keep the powerful on top, her heart told her otherwise. Looking up at the face of Numera, who had seemed to gift the oddities of Mange with an abundance of her beauty and health, it was hard to dispute the possibility of her existence.

"Come! Come!" The man pulled Neer away and stepped to the sliding door along the back wall. Outside, they came to a sprawling hot spring nestled within beautiful green foliage. Unlit torches stood proudly along the banks, while dozens of people relaxed in the water.

Neer leaned against the wooden railing, searching for Loryk as she admired the misting waters.

"Neer?"

Her heart skipped at the sound of his voice, and she spun around to find him standing behind her. His clean and blemish-free torso was exposed as he wore nothing but his filthy braies. With tear-filled eyes, she pulled him into her arms and held him tight. Her arms ached as she squeezed him, fearing to let him go and lose him again.

"Loryk!" she cried. "I'm so happy you're okay!"

"You too, Neery." He gently rubbed her back.

She pulled away and wiped her nose with a sniff. Her finger ran along his neck where the poisoned wound had disappeared completely. "How did they capture you? What happened?"

"I 'eard you screamin' and went runnin' back to 'elp. Then I saw the Order tyin' you up to a 'orse. I ran over to 'elp you, but they 'it me over the 'ead."

Neer smacked his arm. "How can you be so stupid, Loryk? Do you have a death wish?"

"I wasn't goin' to let them take you without a fight! I'd give my last breath to save you, and you know it!"

Tears stung her eyes. She pulled him back into her arms and held him close. "Don't do that again! I don't know what I'd do without you!"

He wrapped his arms lightly around her and rested his head

on her shoulder. "I love you, Neery. We're family... I won't let anythin' 'appen to you."

She held him for a moment longer before slowly stepping away.

Loryk rubbed her shoulders. "Are you all right? 'Ow'd you escape?"

"I'm fine. Avelloch came for us. He took out the Knights on his own."

"And the 'igh Priest?"

Neer turned away in shame. With her eyes closed, she shook her head. "I thought I killed him... but he's still alive."

"Seven 'ells... Well, at least we're alive, yeah? Live to fight another day!"

She gave him a scolding look before turning and wiping the tears from her eyes. While she focused on subduing her growing emotions, Loryk turned to Avelloch and extended an upward facing palm to him.

Avelloch glanced at Neer in confusion, and she said, "You slide your fingers across his hand. It's a sign of respect. He's saying thank you."

Avelloch performed the gesture just as he was told, and Loryk smiled proudly before stepping to the railing and looking over the waters below. "Gorgeous 'ere, isn't it?"

Neer wrapped around his arm and leaned onto his shoulder. "Yeah. I never knew Mange was like this."

"Me either. And the women're so..." His eyes followed two naked women as they walked by.

Neer chuckled. "You're a pig."

"I deserve somethin' nice for all my troubles! A nice 'ot stew, a good breakfast, and some of that good ole' mornin' delight should do the trick."

She smiled coyly. "I'll be sure to find a good kitchen wench for you in Porsdur."

"I like 'em blonde and aggressive."

She pushed his head with a laugh.

He repositioned his hair and smiled. "Come on, then. Don't got much further 'til 'Avsgard. Could use the distractions, yeah?"

Neer glanced at Avelloch and then followed Loryk down

through the gardens and to the edge of the pool. Vibrant plants and large rocks lined the water, and warm sunlight glistened against the streams flowing into the spring. Loryk and Avelloch followed close behind as Neer stepped further away from the cabin to find a secluded spot far from the others.

Loryk smiled at a group of women who were relaxing in the water. They giggled and blushed as he walked by and then set their gazes to Avelloch. Their eyes glistened as they spoke excitedly about the *exotic elf.* They ate from a bowl of mushrooms and herbs and bashfully waved as he glanced at them.

"Come join us!" a woman with red hair called. "The water's just lovely here."

Neer stiffened and exhaled a deep breath as they beckoned him closer. With a glance at Avelloch, she was happy to find he had no interest in entertaining the strangers as his eyes were focused on the trail ahead.

Further down the path, Neer stopped beneath a secluded willow tree. She turned to the water with her hands on her hips and searched for a place to rest.

"You sure you want to be so far from the others?" Loryk asked, his eyes glued to the women still beaming at Avelloch.

"Go wherever you like," she said, stripping down to her undergarments.

"What do you s'pose they're eatin'?" he asked. "Look like leaves."

With an uncaring shrug, Neer carefully stepped into the water and found a comfortable place to sit. She exhaled a deep breath as she sank beneath the surface and felt the tingle of magic radiating through the spring. Loryk dipped his toe into the water before carefully following her in.

He nestled into a spot nearby, and Neer set her gaze to Avelloch as he stood on the shore. Her eyes shifted to his body as he removed his shirt, and she was brought back to their night together. In the darkness, she hadn't noticed the scars that stretched across his stomach and chest.

"Yoohoo!"

Avelloch turned as a woman called to him from down the trail. The comfort and elation Neer felt fizzled as the women who had called out to him from the water followed him down the path.

Water glistened down their skin as they walked without a shred of clothing to cover their bodies. They touched his arms and face, and he angrily pulled away with a tight fist.

"What's goin' on?" Loryk asked with a great huff. "I don't see what's so great. Damned pale face looks just like all the others."

Releasing her discomfort with a sigh, Neer turned to Loryk and said, "Maybe with a couple more push-ups, they'll be flocking to you too." She playfully pinched his bicep, and he pushed her hand away. With a smile, Neer casually stepped from the spring.

A woman stood close to Avelloch and curled her finger through his hair. "You are quite handsome! Are you human?"

"He must be a Divine!" another woman giggled.

"Look at these ears!"

Avelloch snatched the woman's hand away as she reached for his pointed ears. He glared, and the women swooned with red cheeks and soft giggles. His grip tightened on her wrist as they continued touching him and giggling. His angry eyes flashed to Neer as she broke through the crowd, and the women excitedly asked where she found him. Neer chuckled before pulling Avelloch's hand away. "He's evae," she explained, and they gasped in amazement.

"How did you manage to snag an elf?" a woman asked.

"And one so handsome?" another said while running her hand down his arm. He quickly pulled away and she grinned.

"Come on," the woman with red hair said as she took Avelloch and Neer by the hand, "there is room for everyone."

Another woman added, "I've never been with an elf before. I hear it's just magical."

Neer placed her hand over his as he clutched his fist. "Not everything has to be resolved with violence," she warned in evaesh. "They mean no harm."

The women squealed. "What are you saying?"

"He's just so yummy!"

"Is he yours?"

Neer turned to Avelloch. "Want to spend the afternoon in the arms of three gorgeous women?" she asked mischievously, knowing he'd refuse.

His face twisted in disgust. "Make them go away," he demanded.

The women fawned and squealed at the sound of his angry, exotic voice.

"Have it your way, then." Neer shrugged and turned back to the women. "Sorry, ladies, he's wearied from travel. But my friend Ebbard, here, is a famous bard."

They turned to Loryk and eagerly slipped into the water. His eyes lit up as the women got comfortable around him.

"'Ey...," Loryk said with a nervous chuckle. They fed him dried mushrooms while rubbing his waist and thighs.

Finally alone with Avelloch, Neer asked, "Are you this popular back home?"

"No."

"Shame... all those looks and talent shouldn't go unnoticed."

Their gaze met briefly before she motioned for him to follow her down to the spring, where they found a comfortable spot beneath a cherry blossom tree. She closed her eyes and sank into the water. Avelloch leaned against the edge of the pool with his arms stretched out to the sides. His eyes moved to the beautiful woods as birds and small animals flittered through the gardens. Neer watched the water run along his scars and imagined the many battles he must have faced. He couldn't be more than thirty years old, yet he held more scars than even the most vetted soldier. Her eyes lifted to his as he turned to her, and she quickly looked away.

"I was just admiring your scars," she explained.

"What's to admire?"

"They show your strength and courage." She moved closer and traced a thin line along his chest. "I imagine you got this one by saving some damsel in distress. It seems to be your motive."

"I'm not as heroic as you think."

"Really? Taking out half a dozen knights without so much as a scratch is pretty damned heroic."

"I may have gotten a scratch... or two."

She blushed as he teased her about the light marks she left on his shoulders and back. "Lucky knights," she teased back.

He lightly chuckled while turning away. Gleaming teeth appeared beneath his wide smile, and she admired the look of happiness that broke his permanent scowl. Her gaze shifted to Loryk as he began singing, and the ladies around him sighed with adoration. Neer watched them with a grin, knowing her friend deserved more than just a night with these women.

"Why are you seeking the Trials?" Avelloch asked.

The question caught her off guard. She turned away and drifted her fingers through the water. "The High Priest cursed me as a child, and now I'm bound to him anytime I use my magic. I found an object that holds energy powerful enough to break the curse… but it's protected by its own enchantments. The waters of Nhamashel should be enough to dispel it and allow me to harness the energy inside."

"The Trials are forbidden because of their brutality and danger. Even the strongest drimil have fallen," he warned.

"I can't keep living this way…always watching over my shoulder… always with the pain of constraining my energy." She looked at her hands. "Magic is a curse. If I could take it away, I would."

He leaned back and watched as she became disturbed. "I think this is more than just releasing the curse or freeing your people… You want vengeance."

Her bright eyes quickly met with his, and she couldn't conceal the shock of his revelation.

"What if I do?" she asked. "What if I wish to harm someone? Would you oppose me? Call me evil or vile or a creature of darkness like the High Priest has made everyone believe?" She turned away as tears filled her eyes. "The Child of Skye. That's what they call me. They say that I'm the direct descendant of the vain and murderous Divine, Nizotl."

He was quiet for some time, but she never pressed him further. The silence gave her time to calm her raging emotions. Her thoughts were interrupted when he spoke, and she was surprised to find it wasn't in a voice of condemnation or reproach, but one of concern. "I allowed vengeance to control my actions, and it cost me everything. What I thought was emptiness, and what I knew was pain, are a comfort in comparison to the misery I have now… You still have kindness in you, Neer. Kindness that will cease once you truly lose everything."

"You're forgetting one thing, Avelloch. I have already lost everything. He's taken my family… my home… my freedom… Vengeance is the only thing that I have left." She sniffed her tears away. "The High Priest is vicious. He condemns magic yet uses it to protect himself from harm. If I'm ever to defeat him, I'll have to gain enough strength to break through his enchantments and curses… I don't care what it takes, I'm going to kill him… And once I release this curse, nothing can stop me."

Chapter Twenty-Nine

Aerón'dok'fan

"The Trees are a mystery to be revealed. Located all throughout Laeroth, they gift the world with glimpses of energy directly from the Six. Only the purest of heart and soul may seek upon its gifts and receive the blessing of the Makers."

— Sacred Trees; a human tome of the Trees

The next morning, Neer sat alone beneath an enormous Tree as autumn leaves fell through the crisp morning air. Mist rose from the grass and sunlight peeked through the shadows as a new day emerged upon the sleeping land. Sweat dotted her forehead as Neer pressed her fists firmly together, and the tingling warmth of magic flowed through her.

The meadow was quiet and peaceful as she fell into rhythm with the slow, soft beating of the world. Every vibration of the soil moved through her. She could feel its pulse and gained strength through its energy.

Braided flowers, woven symbols, and melted candles rested against the twisted roots, while thistleweed bulbs hovered above the ground. Colorful flowers blossomed as sunlight caressed their petals and brought them to life. Glowing plants slowly lost their light as the chill of night disappeared. Long shadows were cast through the misty forest as sunlight brightened the land.

The stillness of morning was interrupted when soft voices

echoed through the woods, and with a deep sigh, Neer fell from her meditations. Chills stood her hair on end as the warmth of the energy faded. Her eyes shifted to the enormous Tree, which was much bigger than any she had seen before. She touched the bark and relished in the energy surging through her.

As she pressed her palm on the trunk, a spark of energy ignited within her, like a flash of lightning, and darkness surrounded her in pain and frost. Death, sadness, regret, and fury coursed through her like a raging fire. A deep rumble shook the ground, and she fell back, clutching her aching chest.

The Tree's glowing flowers retracted, and its strong branches faded to black. Neer turned sharply as a woman stepped through the woods. Her skin was made of green leaves, and her eyes were as bright as the sun. Vines and roots wrapped around her body in elegant patterns.

"*Miörën, nek'valör.* A sorceress walks in our midst. Vákalá. Trembling. Fearful." The woman's voice echoed through Neer's mind, yet her lips never moved. Sunlight illuminated her face as she stepped closer, and energy pulled them together when their gazes met.

The woman opened her arms and looked at the sky. Her wooden teeth were exposed as she continued her chant in a soft, echoing voice. "A heart of gold turned to stone… A familiar embrace in arms unknown… Four trials you must take if energy you seek… Many years shall pass, but few will you need… Shadows fall upon a sleeping land… Stay close to the light…" Her voice was a whisper as their magic faded, and the woman slowly disappeared. "*Aerón'dok'fan.*"

As she vanished, the darkness that plagued Neer was lifted, and she inhaled a deep breath of fresh air. Sunlight brightened the once dark and grey world while the pattering sounds of animals and leaves rustled through the warm air. Neer breathed heavily, confused and afraid of what she had seen. For a moment, she wondered if it was real, or if the magic of the Tree had altered her reality.

She turned to the Tree, surprised to find its limbs and leaves were vibrant and strong. The flowers that had wilted were now glowing and alive. Neer gripped her head, trying to make sense of what had happened. She jumped as a man came forward, his voice crying out against the silence.

"It's her... Aenwyn!"

Startled by his sudden appearance, Neer backed away as he fell to his knees with his arms opened toward the sky. Sunlight glistened against the tears on his cheeks.

Feeling weak and slightly ill, Neer hurried from the tree and back to the village. She pushed past the residents as they wandered excitedly through the trails, speaking of the great Divine. Many carried ornaments of twisted sticks, feathers, and flowers.

Past the crowds, she came to a small hut and burst through the door. Inside, Avelloch sat at a table, wiping bright green dung from his boots. With a twisted snarl, he tossed another leaf out the window. Neer didn't notice him sitting there as she stepped across the room and sat atop the bed. Her face was ghostly white, and her eyes were wide with fear as she raked her fingers through her hair.

"Neer?" Avelloch asked as he moved to her side. "What is it?"

"I don't know..."

He glanced out the window as a wave of excited cheering came from the dancing villagers. With a closer look outside, he found nothing was out of the ordinary, at least, not out of the ordinary for the people of Mange, who danced and sang through the meadow.

"What's going on?" he asked, turning to Neer. She stared into the distance, whispering to herself. "Neer!"

She jumped from her trance and looked at him with confused, worried eyes. "I think... I just spoke to a Divine," she said.

"A what?"

"A Divine! She came to me in the woods. She... spoke to me."

"You aren't making sense."

Neer shook her head, not having the patience or care to properly explain herself. Instead, she quietly repeated the chant, hoping to find its meaning. "A heart of gold turned to stone. A familiar embrace in arms unknown. Four trials you must take if energy you seek. Many years shall pass, but few will you need. Shadows fall upon a sleeping land. Stay close to the light... Aerón'dok'fan." Her eyes flashed to his. "Do you understand any of that? Does it mean anything to you?" The words spilled from her tongue as she spoke with intensity.

Avelloch exhaled a deep breath and slowly turned away. His eyes shifted from one thing to the next as he pondered, and with a gentle shake of his head, he explained, "Four trials… it could mean the *drimil tre'lan*, the Realms of Magic."

"The Realms of Magic?"

"Yes. There are gateways to the Realms in our world, and each holds its own magical energy."

"Do you think I'm meant to go there? Could this be prophecy of some kind?"

"I don't know." He moved to the window and observed the dancing villagers. "I think it's best if we focus on one thing at a time. Klaud should be close to Havsgard by now. He could be in the Trials. We need to get there as soon as we can."

"You want to help him? After he left us?"

"I left him. His loyalty is to Ael… Azae'l."

She noticed his change in his choice of words but decided not to question it as his eyes grew distant and hard. She stepped to his side and looked out the window to find everyone celebrating throughout the woods. They fell to their knees beneath the beautifully glowing Tree and sang of Numera's praise.

Neer asked, "Do you think it was really a Divine that came to me? Or was it whatever is making these people so… strange?"

"I don't know… I'm not sure what a Divine is."

She smiled at his mispronunciation of the human word. Turing away, she thought for a moment longer, and with a deep breath she pushed the thoughts aside. Whatever had happened could be dealt with once she had time to speak with the scholars and figure out its meaning. For all she knew, it was magic that had created such an illusion, and if so, she'd never find the answers on her own.

"Come on," she said while grabbing her things, "we should move out while they're distracted. Get this journey over with."

They stepped from the hut and into the cool autumn air. Through the village, they spotted Loryk exiting a stranger's hut. With a great yawn, he sleepily rubbed his face, and Neer chuckled at his disheveled clothing and messy hair.

"Morning, you strumpet," she giggled. "You look terrible."

"I got no sleep. These Mange women... they've got the stamina of full-grown stallions. I can't feel my legs, Neery. I'm startin' to worry."

"That good, huh?"

"Better. I think I'll let you off the 'ook for that mornin' delight we agreed on."

"Thanks," she laughed, knowing it was never an arrangement they agreed to. "We should get moving. Havsgard is still days away. Find your trousers, Ebbard, and let's go."

He looked down to find he was wearing his braies and an unfastened doublet.

"Oi...," he groaned before stumbling back into the hut.

Neer leaned against a fence post while waiting for him to return. She watched the villagers eat various mushrooms and herbs while dancing half-naked around small fires. Colorful paint stained their skin, and flowers and twigs hung from their hair and bodies.

"Odd lot, wouldn't you say?" she asked as Avelloch leaned on the fence beside her.

"Humans are an odd lot."

"Humans, huh? Getting used to us now, are you?" she asked with a grin.

He turned away with a hidden smile. A sheath rattled along his belt as he unclipped it from his waist and offered it to her.

"My sword..." She admired the weapon she thought was lost during her capture. Her fingers slid across the freshly cleaned and sharpened steel. "Thank you."

He respectfully nodded.

They turned as Loryk bounded through the doorway. He asked if they were ready to go as he marched down the path, leaving them behind.

"Avelloch!" Neer took his arm as he stepped away, and he turned back with a curious gaze. Nerves swelled inside as she looked into his eyes. There was a certain comfort that came with his presence, a comfort she once thought to be nothing more than a foolish wish. In all her years, there had never been anyone who saw her the way he did. His brokenness and solitude were far too familiar, and she was glad to find trust in someone who understood.

Her hands twisted together nervously as she confessed, "I'm glad you're here. Once we leave, it'll be a short journey to the Trials, and..." Her eyes fell away before she hesitantly continued, "I'm not sure what our night together was for you, but... it meant a lot to me. I just needed you to know that."

He gently took her chin and looked deep into her eyes. With a soft smile, he leaned closer and placed his lips to hers. She melted into his touch as his strong arms pulled her close. The doubt and uncertainty that lingered inside vanished as she fell into his embrace. His touch was gentle and protective. She never wanted to let go.

Her heart raced as he slowly backed away. Hot breath warmed her face as their lips lingered and eyes were closed. He leaned his forehead onto hers, and she clutched his arms, wanting desperately to keep him close.

His soft voice filled the silence as he whispered, "It meant everything."

Chapter Thirty

Shadows of Darkness

"Shadows born of darkness shall rise with the moon, devouring the Light, revealing the truth of unbridled woe."

— Nizotl, the Book of Darkness

THE ROAD WOUND THROUGH ROUGH terrain as the group made their way to Havsgard. Steep hillsides, jagged rocks, and unstable cliffs were but a few of the dangers they faced as large bears, mountain lions, and bobcats roamed freely over the hillsides. Not a soul dared to trek along this part of the trail, which left them to journey it alone. Tall mountains cascaded around them, and deep valleys of rock and grass sunk far below the reaches of the trail.

"I've never seen anythin' so beautiful," Loryk beamed while hastily scribbling in his notebook. Wrinkled pages, ink stains, and worn leather made up the old and well-used journal. It was a wonder the thing had survived their journey thus far.

Moving down the hillside, they passed several dormant and abandoned villages. The old stone houses and stables were small in comparison to the rocky cliffs surrounding them. Large rats scurried from home to home, and Neer retched as the stench of death rose like a putrid mist, growing stronger as they traveled past the desolate homes.

Neer gripped tighter to the reins as she rode quietly through the empty trails. Loryk rested behind her, while Avelloch followed on his mare. Leaves rustled through the hillsides as they fell from the tree limbs, their bright colors sending patterns waving through the wood as they fluttered to the ground.

The serenity was shaken when a raspy voice echoed through Neer's mind, shouting, "Go!"

Her horse came to a sudden halt and reared its front legs with a frightened squeal. Neer fell to the ground, landing hard on her side, while Loryk rolled down the hillside, hitting rocks and roots that cut into his skin. Avelloch leapt to the ground and caught Loryk just before he fell into a thicket of briars. He pulled him to his feet, and Loryk groaned while gripping the bleeding cut across his forehead.

Neer sat up and gazed into the village where the voice had called to her. Her eyes were fixed on the empty, silent homes as the horses snorted and stomped before trotting away in a panic. Dust swept the narrow trail as they moved quickly out of sight. The village was nestled in an alcove at the base of a large cliff and was made up of a handful of small stone houses.

Leaves crunched beneath Avelloch's boots as he came to Neer's side and touched her shoulder. "Neer?" he asked.

She stared wide-eyed at the abandoned village. Her voice was as hollow as the wind. "Did you hear that?" she asked. "The voice that spooked the horses..."

"I heard a growl. There was no voice."

Slowly, she stood, yet her eyes never veered from the empty homes. She stepped closer, peering at the village with confusion and wonder. Something had called her here. It couldn't be coincidence that a voice so clear and angry would speak to her. She wondered for a moment if it was Numera, the Divine that spoke to her in Mange, who made such a rageful cry. But this village wasn't Havsgard, yet something pulled her closer. A gentle nudge she couldn't escape, beckoning her nearer.

She stepped closer.

"Neer?" Avelloch asked.

"I think this is it," she said.

"This isn't 'Avsgard," Loryk stated.

"I know... but I can feel it. Something's guided us here."

He scoffed. "Fate isn't real, Neer, and neither are the Divines. We aren't goin'—"

He fell silent as she stepped off the trail and into the empty village. The gentle pull of warmth and energy called her closer, like an endless breeze moving gently across her skin. A soft buzzing, like the sound of a hundred flies, grew stronger as she walked to the stables. The sickening odor of decay burned her nose and caused her eyes to water as she looked into the stalls. Her body was frozen with fear and disgust as she stared down at the pile of larvae-infested bodies. Clouds of flies, black as night, swirled through the air as they moved from corpse to corpse.

She covered her mouth as sickness twisted her stomach. Rotten, bloated bodies, some without skin and others who had just begun to decay, were laid together in a mound of blood and sloughing flesh.

She couldn't turn away as the terror had made her immobile. The thought of running eluded her as she stared at the sunken, eyeless faces, and feared they, too, may come back to life. Her eyes glanced from one person to the next, watching them and waiting.

"Neer." Loryk touched her shoulder, and she leapt with a heart-stopping gasp. She trembled as he carefully pulled her away. "Look." They stepped around the stable to a collection of human body parts that were placed on the grass in the pattern of the sigil of the Order.

The sickness that turned her stomach suddenly rose to the surface, and she collapsed to her knees, expelling what little she had eaten that day. Tears filled her eyes as she stared at the ground, wondering how this came to be. Her fingers curled into the grass, and she shook her head in disbelief. As much as she wanted to believe it, she couldn't entirely place the blame on the Order for this. In all their horrific punishments and wicked sense of justice, they'd never perform such sacrilege. Mutilation after death was considered an abomination, as was leaving a body unburied and without a proper sending to the afterlife of Arcae. The Order was vile and ruthless, but they were also strict in their code of morality. They would never dishonor the Divines in a way such as this.

She stared at the lifeless faces of the innocent villagers lying in the dirt. Every open wound and drop of blood staining their beaten and torn flesh caused her blood to boil. When her gaze fell to a child, no older than ten, she was consumed with madness and rage.

No, this wasn't the Order. It was someone else. Someone who hated humans. Someone who wished them all dead.

Slowly, she turned to Avelloch. He stood nearby examining the bodies when he caught sight of her staring and then met her gaze. More tears fell from her eyes as she stood and charged at him with her dagger drawn.

"Neer!" Loryk exclaimed.

As she lifted her weapon, Avelloch grabbed her wrist and twisted her arm behind her back. "What are you doing?" he asked.

"Who did this?" Her voice was raw with fury and sorrow. "Was it Klaud? Was it your people? Did you lead them here? Did you betray us?"

"Why would I do that?" he said. "I saved you! I'm on your side!"

"Who else would do this? No one would've come all this way to massacre an innocent village!"

Her voice fell silent as Loryk called for her. He stood by a home, staring at the ground with wide eyes. "It wasn't Klaud…," he said.

Avelloch and Neer rushed to Loryk's side. Lying on the grass, covered in fresh blood, were eight fallen evaesh warriors. Deep lacerations and stab wounds marked their skin in clean, precise lines across their necks, eyes, and chests.

"Who are they?" Neer asked. "Are they with the others who are invading?"

Avelloch's jaw tensed as he glared at the bodies. "The Nasir," he said with a growl.

Neer shook her head. "How did they find this place?"

Avelloch didn't respond as he turned away. Scanning the village, he marched to a nearby home, and shouted, "Klaud!" His desperate, angry voice echoed loudly through the empty alcove, fading to silence as it rolled through the quiet woods.

"Oh shite...," Loryk said. "You don't think... 'E couldn't've..."

Neer looked at the evae lying at her feet. She couldn't imagine the cruelty that brought them to perform such a heinous and unthinkable act. To have butchered and slain a village and then displayed their bodies in such a way... her mind spun at the implications of such darkness. The world had truly fallen if people like this existed. Those who could so callously murder men, women, and children without a shred of humanity or guilt.

Her intense and troubling thoughts were broken when Loryk carefully nudged her shoulder as Avelloch returned.

"He isn't here...," said Avelloch.

Neer asked, "Did he do this? He killed the evae?"

Avelloch paused for a moment to examine the deep wounds along their flesh. With a subtle nod, he looked away. "Yes," he said. "These markings are too precise for these villagers to have made them. If he isn't here, then he must've entered the Trials after wiping out the klaet'il." He placed his hands on his hips as he peered through the village and then stepped to the stable to retrieve an unlit torch from the wall.

"What are you doing?" Neer asked.

"If we don't burn them, they could reanimate." Avelloch lit the torch and placed the flame to a body in the pattern. He then stepped to the stable and tossed the torch on top of the pile of corpses. As it touched their bloated, marbled skin, a wave of flames and smoke rolled through the air. Avelloch jumped back as the explosion engulfed the stable. Black ash drifted into the sky as the bodies bubbled and burned. Neer wondered if they had been doused with oil, though there had been no signs of it on their bodies.

Her ears twitched as soft voices overlapped in her mind, whispering of terrible things.

Death...

Darkness...

Regret...

Anguish...

She could feel it all as their souls tore away from this plane. With every lap of the flames and singe of burning flesh, the soft whispers grew into agonizing shrieks of horror and pain. She gripped her ears and fell to her knees, trying desperately to quell the voices that clawed at her from within. Her fingernails scratched into her scalp as she fought against a sudden wave of grief and agony.

Loryk and Avelloch shook her and called her name, but she couldn't hear as the raging voices consumed her thoughts and took hold of her emotions. Twisting and churning, she was filled with the dread and agony of the deceased. Her throat was raw as she screamed and begged for the pain to end. For the voices to stop.

Through the noise came a ragged grunt, and Neer shuddered as a flash of pain coursed through her. She leaned forward and gripped her chest as the raw voice triumphed over the others, begging, "Help us!"

Avelloch and Loryk grabbed their weapons while Neer remained motionless, unable to move from the agony that had afflicted her. Struggling to lift her eyes, she watched as a shadow emerged from a home. Its stone-covered body contorted and twisted as it hobbled into the sunlight and closer to the group. Its crooked arms hovered in front of its chest, and long fingers stretched down to its knees. Black eyes rested unevenly on top of its head. A large mouth was filled with razor-sharp teeth.

"It's a fench!" Avelloch warned. At the sound of its name, the fench released a pained shriek with the sound of several voices. Neer leaned back, horror-stricken by the creature that stalked closer.

"Help us...," it begged in a ragged, hollow voice. Its right back leg dragged behind as it moved closer.

Avelloch stood ready with his swords in hand, while Loryk whimpered and nervously held a dagger.

"Neer," Avelloch warned, "we have to go!"

"Please...," the creature begged. It stepped forward, closing the space between them, and Avelloch raised his arms to attack.

"Stop!" Neer jumped to her feet and pulled him back. He turned to her with a sharp glare, but her gaze was fixed on the fench standing before them. Its body quivered as it breathed in slow, wheezed breaths. "Can't you hear it?" she asked.

"Hear it?" he said with a hiss. "It's a creature of darkness, Neer! It cannot speak!"

"Help us...," it begged.

Avelloch jumped back as the fench growled and moaned with vibrating tones of falsetto and bass.

"Who are you?" Neer asked the fench. "What happened?"

It stepped forward, and Avelloch pulled Neer back.

"We are weak... We are tired..."

"What is your name?" she demanded.

The creature trembled. Its beady eyes closed. "We... do not... know... anymore..."

"Does this place hold the entrance to the Trials of Blood?"

"They came... They sought..." Its voice faded into choked growls.

Neer pointed at the burning bodies. "Was this the elves? Did they do this?"

"We do not... know... anymore..."

"Where is the entrance?" She stepped forward, demanding the creature speak.

It gargled and choked on deep growls. "Do not go..."

"Tell us!" She raised her palm to the creature, daring to use her magic against it.

Through deep, desperate growls, it revealed, "Along the surface... The ore's unmined... *Do not go!*" It choked as it growled.

Avelloch clutched Neer's wrist as she stepped forward, and she turned to him with calm, knowing eyes. He looked from her to the fench and reluctantly released his grip. She stepped to the creature and placed her hands to its shoulders. It growled and convulsed as it begged for help. A wave of pain took her breath away as she looked into its eyes. The voices that consumed her had returned, screaming for mercy. Begging for an end. She winced as the deep pull of emptiness and sorrow burned in her chest.

Looking into its eyes, she pushed through the agony and thrust her sword into its body. The growling ceased, and the voices that raged within were silenced. Nothing but the calming sound of a deep, grateful sigh lingered in her mind as the creature faded to ash.

Silence swept across the hillside. Fires burned quietly within the stables and atop the grass. Leaves floated through the wind as the sun dipped beyond the horizon and painted the world in a hue of orange and pink. Neer sheathed her weapon and turned to her friends.

"Are you all right?" Loryk asked while hesitantly reaching out to her.

She stared at the ground, where the ashes of the fench slowly lifted into the air as a breeze swept them away. "I think so," she said. The ache and whispers were still present, drifting away like a feather in the wind.

"What the 'ells just 'appened?" Loryk asked. "You were speakin' to that thing?"

"You didn't hear it?" she asked with a sudden rush of confusion and fear. Turning to the others, she was surprised by the deep puzzlement in their eyes.

"All we 'eard were growls, Neer. What's gotten into you?"

"It was begging for help."

"Right, and I'm just about good to sprout wings and fly us to this cave."

"It spoke! It said the entrance is along the surface where the ore's unmined."

"I think you need some rest, Neer. We've been travelin' for days with little sleep and no food."

Frustrated at his disbelief, she angrily turned away. Looking across the village, she spotted evaesh symbols etched into the wall of a nearby home. She stepped closer and ran her fingers down the word.

"'Here'," she read the symbols aloud. "Do you think this was Klaud?"

Avelloch inspected the symbols and then quickly looked around. "It was him," he explained. "The entrance is here."

With a nod, Neer exhaled a deep breath. "We have to keep moving," she said. "Whatever is going on can wait. We'll figure it out after the Trials."

Loryk groaned before he and Neer searched the home for other clues while Avelloch scoured the village. She overturned a table and checked every drawer.

"The eye must be here," Neer said, referring to the glass eye needed to view the entrance. "He wouldn't leave a note on this house if it wasn't. Search everything. We have to find it."

Loryk tossed dirty miner's aprons aside as he pulled items from a wooden shelf. "Was it really them elves?" he asked as he flipped through a dusty book. "They killed these people?"

"Yeah. I think so."

"And they weren't with Klaud?"

Fear and uncertainty fell through her as she considered his suspicion. They'd been through too much to lose faith now. Whatever had happened, she chose to believe in Klaud and Avelloch. Since their meeting several weeks past, they had proven themselves loyal and trustworthy. "No," she said.

He tossed the book aside and dug through an end table. "What was with that creature? Were you really speakin' to it?"

"I don't know, Loryk!" she snapped. He fell silent as she turned to him with desperate, pleading eyes. "Can we please just focus? I have no idea what the hells is going on, and I'm just ready to get home. Please."

With a quiet nod, he returned to his search and then explained he'd check outside. As he stepped through the door, she was left alone, and the solitude gave her a chance to breathe. She leaned forward with her fists against a table and closed her eyes. "What is happening?" she whispered. "Why is this happening?"

"Neer!" Loryk called, and she lifted her eyes with a quiet gasp. Racing outside, she found him kneeling in the dirt and was thankful to find him safe. "I found it!" he said. "The glass eye!"

"Loryk!" she said with a slight smile. "You're incredible!"

"Yeah, well... remember that when we get back 'ome, yeah?"

She gave him a playful glare before stepping to the village center and meeting with Avelloch. "The ore is this way," he said before leading them to the cliffside behind the homes. The rocky edges towering above the homes were sharp and uneven. Dirty pickaxes and chisels lay on a wooden table nearby, along with buckets of iron ore.

Neer carefully touched the cliff and examined its surface. "You think this is it?"

Avelloch said, "Only one way to find out."

She inhaled a deep, nervous breath. Once they entered the Trials, there was no turning back. All doubt that had followed her became real as she was suddenly made aware of her fate. Should they enter, they may not return, and everything they worked toward would be for nothing. Avelloch and Loryk had no other reason to enter such a dangerous place than to help guide her through. The pressing weight of such guilt compressed her lungs.

She stepped away from the cliff and leaned onto her knees. Trembling choked breaths were all she could muster as she stood at the face of her destination.

"Neer?" Loryk asked as he placed a hand on her shoulder.

Shaking her head, she looked into his eyes and was stricken by the possibility of losing him. "Is this a mistake?" she asked. "Should we have waited for the scholars or Reiman? Are we really meant to enter these ancient trials?"

He was quiet as he considered a response and then said, "I don't know. Maybe we aren't supposed be 'ere. Maybe we are. But I do know one thing, and it's that we can't just wait and see. Strange things're 'appenin', Neer. Bad things. You've fought and trained your entire life to protect our country from people like the 'Igh Priest… You think a silly little Trial is goin' to stop you?"

"I'm not worried about my own fate, Loryk… I'm worried about yours. You two don't have to do this. I can't have you go through these Trials just to wind up dead."

He smiled. "Who're you, a Divine? You can't control nobody's fate. Now me and this Avel-cock're goin' in there, with or without you. We're lifting this God's-damned curse and puttin' you at the 'ead of this fight! The Order will get what's comin' to 'em, and I'll be singin' of our glory the whole way through!"

"Are you sure you want to do this?"

"Positive." He pulled her into his arms, and she held him close. "Now come on. Time's wastin'."

With another look into his eyes, she nodded and stepped away to survey the cliffside.

With great doubt, she peeked through the glass eye, and her jaw fell open as an enormous, elegantly carved entryway appeared through the clear stone. Several columns rose from the base of the cliff to its height and framed a beautifully engraved double door.

"What is it?" Loryk asked.

"This is it...," she explained before passing him the item.

Loryk held the glass eye to his face and gasped in amazement. Without the eye, the stone cliff was as natural as a mountain should be.

"How do we get in?" she asked.

Avelloch dug through his bag and offered her a vial of orange liquid.

"Where did you get this?" she asked, realizing this potion was also used to reveal the hidden gates of Porsdur.

"Klaud snatched it from two men before they entered your village. He gave me half when I left to find you so that we could enter without him."

She smiled. "I had him stealing coin before we met you. He must've had a taste for it."

Avelloch's touch lingered on her hand when he placed the vial in her grasp. She looked into his eyes and could almost laugh at the irony of finally finding someone who understood her on a journey such as this.

"Don't die in there," she said. Avelloch stepped closer and tucked her hair behind her ear. She closed her eyes when more tears threatened to fall.

"Vas neemo see'nah," he whispered and gently placed his lips to hers. As he slowly backed away, he looked into her eyes and wiped the tear from her cheek.

With a subtle nod, she sniffed and turned to the cliff. Nerves fluttered in her stomach as she eyed the entrance of the Trials of Blood.

Loryk moved to her side and placed a hand on her shoulder. "Ready?"

She gripped his hand. "You?"

"They'll be singin' of my glory one way'r the other. May as well make good on those savin' your arse bits."

Tears filled her eyes at mention of his death. "We protect each other, yeah? This won't be our end."

With a smile, he kissed her head. "Not a chance, Neery."

The trio stood together, staring at the solid rock wall. With a deep breath, Neer uncorked the vial and forcefully splashed the potion onto the stone. As the vial ran dry, she dropped it to the dirt and then watched as the once hidden entrance came into view. Holding tight their hands, Neer inhaled a deep, nervous breath, and they stepped inside.

Chapter Thirty-One

The Trials of Blood

"Our time has passed, let the legends remain. Hidden deep underground are powers untamed. Darkness and terrors lie in your wake, take heed of this warning and face your fate."

— First Blood prophecy

A COLD MIST DAMPENED THEIR skin as they walked through the doorway and into darkness. Neer released her grip on their hands and looked around. The pale blue glow of hanging moss illuminated the chamber as the door behind them closed with the low grind of scraping stone. Glimmering crystal shards towered together in clusters around large mushrooms and rocks. The trickle of water lapped over the stone, resounding against the walls with a soft hum that gave life to the damp, frigid space.

"What do we do?" Loryk whispered, and everyone gazed through the cave in wonderment as his quiet voice repeated through the air, never fading. "Neer?" Loryk pressed, his quiet word mixing with the others.

Neer crossed her arms and peered through the darkness, searching for any sign or clue that could lead her down the right path. But she knew nothing of the Trials or their tests. Moving through them without Klaud was an enormous risk, and her breath caught in her throat as she worried about what was to come.

"Avelloch," she started, suddenly irritated as her voice was added to the constant chime of Loryk's unfaded words. Closing her eyes, she exhaled a deep breath. "Where do we go?"

His brows pulled together as he looked around, and the gentle patterns of light that were cast from the glowing waters danced across his face. He touched Neer's shoulder and pointed to a yellow glowing symbol etched into the wall across the cave.

She followed his lead as he stepped over the streams and through a dense pocket of mushrooms. As their boots scraped against the fungi, clouds of white spores drifted into the air at their feet. Loryk was close behind as they came to the wall and shielded their eyes from the brightly glowing rune.

Avelloch's eyes widened as he gazed at the foreign symbol. Neer carefully touched his shoulder, and he flinched.

"Avelloch?" she asked. "What is this?"

He gulped the lump in his throat and returned his gaze to the rune. Slowly, he reached toward it, and through a trembling voice, he explained, *"Zy'mashik...* A rune of the First Blood. It says—"

His fingers grazed across the rune, and the light reflecting against his face passed through empty air as he vanished. Neer stepped forward and reached out for him. "Avelloch?" she whispered urgently. "Loryk, we have to—" She turned around and was stunned to find emptiness where Loryk once stood.

The voices that once echoed through the air had ceased, leaving her in a deep, disorienting silence. She turned quickly from left to right, finding nothing but solitude and darkness. Her heart sank as she stared at the places they once stood, and the dread of her loneliness sank deep into her gut.

As her thoughts wavered between fleeing and continuing on, footsteps echoed from the left, and she turned sharply with a gasp. Her eyes followed as the sound moved toward a doorway at the far side of the cave and then faded into the blackness of its entry.

Paralyzed with fear, she was hardly able to take a breath. The large room felt small as she stood alone, waiting in the silence for the others to return. She gazed at the stone door of the cave

CURSE OF THE FALLEN

entrance and wondered if Loryk and Avelloch would seek its exit. If so, she could reunite with them and form a new strategy of survival.

As she stepped toward the door, a harrowing thought stayed her feet, and she released a deep sigh of regret. Should they exit the cave, there would be no re-entry as she had used every drop of the potion to reveal the hidden entrance.

Staring through the cave, her eyes fixed on the door, the thought of escape loomed in her mind. She couldn't do this alone, yet she couldn't leave. If Avelloch and Loryk hadn't left the cave, they would still be in the Trials, and without magic, they wouldn't survive for long.

Her mind wavered between all the possibilities, and before she could come to a clear decision, her eyes shifted to the walls as a gentle glow formed along the stone. Broken of her thoughts, she watched a trail of yellow crystals illuminate around the cavern walls, leading to the unlit doorway where the footsteps had descended.

As light caressed the room, Neer looked around and spotted a figure lying in the center of the chamber, whimpering in pain.

"Hello?" Neer called, her voice trembling as she called out to the crying stranger. She wearily stepped closer and squinted her eyes to make out the silhouette of a woman lying alone in the darkness. Neer gazed upon the stranger for a moment, wondering how she came to be there.

A ball formed in her throat as she pulled her sword from its sheath and inched closer. The pale light of the crystals shimmered against the woman's singed hair and dress. Large blisters exposing raw, pink skin covered her face and arms. The woman struggled to push herself up into a sitting position and then collapsed onto her bent arms as she coughed and wheezed.

"Vaeda..." Her soft cries echoed through the silence, crashing hard against Neer's mind as she spoke with a familiar voice.

All color drained from Neer's face as she stared at the woman who only existed in her memories. A person she never thought she would see again, and one who filled her with pain.

"Mother?" her voice was trembled and broken.

The woman leaned forward onto burnt and blackened hands.

She coughed again, and Neer inhaled a shallow gasp. "Mother?" she cried.

"Vaeda…" Her mother said. "Don't let them change you…"

Neer shook with guilt and sorrow. Her face twisted in pain as she relived the horror of her mother's final moments.

"I love you…" Her mother took one final breath and collapsed.

Neer's breathing trembled as she looked at her mother's lifeless body. It was an image that had been ingrained in her mind since the moment it happened sixteen years prior. The night her village was massacred by the Order of Saro and her parents were slain.

Neer gasped as her mother began to vanish. She dropped her sword and hurriedly knelt to her side, ready to take her mother into her arms, when she fell through her and landed hard against the stone. Curled into the ground, Neer tightened into the fetal position. Tears fell from her eyes as she shook with grief. Every breath trembled as she clenched her hands into tight fists.

"Come back…," she wailed. "Please. Don't leave me again…"

Lying alone, trapped in her misery, she was reminded of all that had been taken from her. Of the life that was nothing more than distant, blurred memories. But she knew that giving in to the pain wouldn't keep her alive. It wouldn't bring her mother back.

Slowly, she forced herself up and sat on her knees. With a sniff, she wiped her nose with her sleeve and glanced through the cave. "Loryk…!" she screamed. "Avelloch…!"

She choked on her breath as more tears fell down her cheeks. While shaking her head, she wiped her eyes, and the sudden pluck of a lute string caught her attention.

Her heart skipped as she listened to the sound as it faded to silence. She held her breath, waiting for another sound. Waiting for *anything*.

Another note echoed from the empty doorway.

She quickly turned around. "Loryk?" she called.

The string sounded again, and she was jolted with a spark of energy. Jumping to her feet, she snatched her sword from the ground and rushed to the doorway. As she approached its entry, she stopped and peeked into the blackness.

"Loryk?" she called. The loud echo of her voice softened as it moved down a long hall. Another pluck vanished her fear, and she raced into the darkness.

Her lonesome footsteps echoed through the empty halls as she chased the sound that had dwindled into silence. The soft glow from the doorway slowly faded as she moved farther from the entrance, and the air was heavy with moisture as she traveled deeper underground.

Neer slowed her pace as she trekked into undisturbed darkness. When a deep rumble trembled through the walls she came to a sudden halt. Her mouth was dry as she breathed in quick, gasped breaths. Every heartbeat thrashed in her ears as she turned from left to right, unable to see anything but blackness.

The sound of footsteps pattered from down the hall. She held her sword outward, defensively. Swallowing through the dryness in her throat, she took several deep breaths before gaining the courage to call out, "Loryk? Avelloch!"

The silence was deafening as she waited for a response that never came. Her eyes glanced from one place to the next as she searched desperately for any sign of light. Though she had only just stepped into the hall, it felt as if hours had passed, and she wondered if there would ever be an end.

Klaud had warned her of the dangers of the Trials, and she knew that whatever lay ahead wouldn't be easy. These caves were created by the ahn'clave, or First Blood, who were rumored to be the most powerful and devious magic users to have ever existed.

Neer believed herself a fool for thinking she could survive any test or trial given by a race so powerful and mysterious, and even more foolish to bring two non-magic users along with her. Wherever they were, she had no reason to believe they would survive without magical energy, as this test was meant for the most gifted of mages. Only those strong enough to survive could make it to Nhamashel, a cave that held the mystical waters that would dispel the call of the marq guarding the arun and allow Neer to lift her curse with the energy inside it.

Noises thumped against the cave walls and interrupted her

thoughts. She lifted her sword and pressed herself harder against the wall as the sound of footsteps echoed from every direction. Peering through the darkness, searching for whoever could be lurking in the distance, her eyes fixed on two glowing orbs that hovered in the tunnel ahead. Her breath caught in her throat as she gazed at them, watching as they slowly grew larger. She turned around, hoping for an escape, and was stricken by the sight of several more glowing orbs floating in the distance.

Every breath was loud as she gasped for air. Her mind spun as she glanced between the collection of white specks. A light scratching sound broke through the silence and dragged loudly against the stone walls, moving closer toward her. She backed further into the wall, her hands aching from the tight grip on her sword. The orbs followed the noise of her step, becoming larger and brighter. Neer trembled with a light whimper as the grinding creak of bones and the clicking of tongues echoed from the mysterious creatures.

Though the air was frigid, sweat dripped down her face. She stood against the wall, paralyzed with fear, as the orbs grew brighter, and she could see that they resembled eyes.

Dozens of pairs of eyes... staring directly at her.

The snarling, clicking creatures scratched against the walls as they stalked closer.

Neer jumped when a loud shriek pierced through the silence, and the resounding echo of growls quickly followed. Unable to see anything but the glowing eyes, she watched as they charged forward, and when she felt the rush of a stranger drawing closer, she swung her weapon. The sword met resistance as she slashed into her victim. A loud screech pierced her ears before the thump of a body hit the floor. Another screech echoed from behind. She turned and thrust her weapon forward. Thick, cold liquid drained across her hands as she stabbed through the now unmoving creature. She kicked it aside and stepped back.

A deep quake shifted the stone and the walls trembled. The glowing orbs disappeared like lightning bugs in the fog when the creatures scurried away. The sound of grinding rock moved throughout the hall before a thunderous crash shook the corridor, and everything fell silent.

Dust and pebbles sprinkled from the ceiling as Neer stood alone, too frightened to move. Through several deep breaths, she pushed through the fear and walked in the direction she hoped she was meant to go.

Moisture covered her fingers as she trailed her hand along the wall to keep her on the path. When another quake shifted the cave, she pressed into the wall and closed her eyes. A final crash, identical to the one before, brought an end to the tremors, and she forced herself forward on shaky legs.

Two steps ahead, the tunnel came to a sudden dead end. Following to the left, she came to another wall and then another, until she had moved in a full circle back to where she started. Her heart sank as she realized she was trapped. The heavy jolts and shifting rock must have been the corridors changing.

Sweat beaded across her forehead. She felt as if the world was closing in on her. Unable to see mere inches away, she clung desperately to the wall, feeling every lump and crevice as she searched for a way out.

Running her hands quickly along the course surface, she felt a slight shift in the rocks as a pebble moved out of place. Clawing at the loose fragments, the wall began to chip away, and a stream of light peeked through the small crack forming beneath her fingers.

A loud, shocked laughed escaped her throat as she gazed at the bright luminance that touched her cheek. She leaned closer and placed her eye to the wall but could only see white as it burned into her cornea. Stumbling back, she closed her eyes with a wince.

Anxious to be out of this dark hell, she tore at the wall, ripping her fingernails as she fought to dig her way through. But the crack in the stone never grew larger as she scratched and clawed. Her muscles ached and skin was hot as she leaned against the wall with her eyes closed. Furious and desperate for an end, she unleashed a raw scream that vibrated through the air.

She considered another walk around the walls that confined her. There could be another outlet or doorway she missed before. But the thoughts were quickly pushed aside as the fear of losing her only way out kept her in place. Should she step away, the wall could reseal itself or reopen and allow the glowing-eyed creatures to attack again.

She clenched her jaw as she waited for another shift in the stone. But she knew it wouldn't come. This path led her here, and it was her magic that would free her.

Magic that she had little knowledge and control of.

With heavy doubt, she placed her hands on the wall and conjured her energy into a raging vortex of heat and pain. Raw, untrained magic tore through her, like acid fizzling through her veins. She screamed as it strengthened inside her, creating pressure and heat that cracked the stone beneath her touch. The cave moaned as fissures grew across its length like bolts of lightning.

Her teeth clenched and jaw ached as she forced her magic outward in a powerful explosion. The heat from her energy evaporated the chill in the air, and she was flung back before smacking against the wall. Her body ached as she crashed to the ground. Blood seeped from the cuts along her face and arms.

Every movement was crushing as she struggled to roll onto her side. Slow, shallow breaths entered her lungs, and her eyes struggled to adjust to the bright beam of light shining from across the hall. Neer gripped her forehead as she crawled to her knees. With a wince, she pulled her arm back as her palm burned with intense heat.

She lifted her hands into the light and slowly blinked her eyes into focus. As her vision cleared, she examined her palms to find no trace of burns or blisters, though they felt as if her flesh had been seared. Bringing her attention to the light, she found a narrow tunnel.

As she crawled forward, she gasped at the pain in her hands. Closing her eyes tight, she ignored the burning of her palms and forced herself closer. At the entrance of the narrow passage, she pulled herself inside and squeezed through its shallow, uneven path.

Warm light became hotter as she reached the end of the tunnel and came to an adjoining cavern. The small room was covered in glowing vines that trailed across the walls and ceiling, connecting only at the base of the Tree that stood in the center of the room. Its wide branches created a glowing canopy that filled the room with light. Thick roots twisted through the dirt covered ground, becoming thinner as they grew closer to the walls.

Climbing from the passage, she approached the Tree and touched a flower. Magic tingled in the air, soothing her fear and doubt. Scanning the vine-covered walls, she found there was no doorway or exit. Her gaze returned to the Tree and she realized she was meant to meditate beneath its branches. She slowly knelt on top of the roots, curled her hands into fists, and then pressed them together. Her eyes were closed as she focused on the energy flowing through her, like waves upon the sand.

She had meditated beneath the Tree of Porsdur many times before, yet this time was different. The magic was stronger. Raw. Powerful. Every pulse filled her with strength and life. The bleeding cuts and flowering bruises across her skin slowly vanished as she sat beneath the Tree, embraced by the warmth of its energy.

The glow of the flowers and vines pulsed with her every breath, just as they did in the cave of Vleland, just as they did at the Tree in Porsdur.

The serenity that cradled her with warmth and light was suddenly stripped away. Within an instant, she was cold and alone. Nothing else existed, yet she could feel the energy of the world swirling around her, encasing her in pain. She wanted to break free of its hold, but it had her tethered to its will. She couldn't escape. Couldn't surrender.

Her body wriggled as soft whimpers escaped her throat. Her eyes remained closed as she was pulled further into the darkness, forced to endure its fury as dark images flashed through her mind:

Shadows dashing across the ocean floor.

A glowing Tree standing tall amidst stone.

An underground city abandoned and forgotten.

Enormous monsters screaming with rage.

And blood. A lot of blood. Staining the walls, covering swords, and dripping from hands.

The visions faded, and she was pulled further into a world of shadows and solitude. While her body remained beneath the Tree, she opened her eyes and found herself standing in complete darkness. She gazed at the emptiness around her, wondering if it was real. The air was heavy, artificial. All feeling and life had been removed from her being. She was as empty as this plane was dark.

Hollow. Void.

Nonexistent.

Standing in a realm far beyond her own, she felt like an illusion herself. Nothing was real. Life held no meaning. Nor did death. She simply... was. But she knew it was a vision, though she was present, standing in the blackness of whatever illusion the Tree had manifested.

She looked around in a daze, shallow water trickling beneath her feet. As she turned around, searching for anything, a large stone door appeared in the distance. Surrounded by black, it stood alone, hovering in the nothingness that surrounded them. Slowly, she approached, and was hesitant to open it before she found there was no knob. Stepping back to get a better view, her eyes fell to the ground as foreign symbols appeared beneath her feet in a circular pattern.

The glowing light illuminated her face as she knelt to the ground and placed her hands to the surface. Energy swirled within her and she used her magic to decipher the language. As it faded, the symbols hadn't changed, yet she could now read them with perfect clarity:

Enter the Trials with great feat; the waters wait for those who seek. Darkness is blinding for those with sin; waters are haunted by creatures within.
Shackles and streets guide the way; pale moonlight leads into the fray.
Enter this chamber if energy you seek; blood of the First holds the key.

A rush of icy wind struck through her chest, and she was flung back to the ground. Her eyes opened, and she found herself back in the cave. The glowing Tree sat before her, just as warm and bright as before. The air was light and pure, and she breathed a sigh of relief. She was no longer in the illusion that imprisoned her.

Gazing at the branches, she noticed a soft yellow glow radiating from behind. Curious, she stepped around the room, and her heart jolted at the sight of another rune etched into the wall. Its symbol was different, but she knew it was just as dangerous.

A hard knot formed in her throat as she struggled over what to do. Touching this rune could be her only escape from this room. It could bring back Loryk and Avelloch, or it could cast her into another vision of darkness and misery. She didn't understand the magic of the ahn'clave well enough to anticipate what could happen, and a cold sweat formed across her brow at the harrowing possibility of torture and sorrow.

Hoping for another way out, she glanced through the room and saw that the tunnel she crawled through had disappeared, leaving behind a solid stone wall in its place. Desperate and depleted, she returned her gaze to the rune. Its glowing light burned into her eyes as she contemplated her fate and the fate of the others. She considered waiting for them here, but they'd never be able to enter this chamber without magical energy. They may not be able to survive at all without it.

Nerves dragged her stomach into her feet at the thought of losing them. Whatever tests this trial had waiting, she would see them through, if for nothing else than to find the others and bring them to safety. They couldn't survive without her, and she wouldn't allow them to perish in these ruins alone.

Swallowing the lump in her throat, she held her breath and raised her palm to the rune. Her trembling fingers hovered above its gentle glow, and fighting through the fear and uncertainty, she pressed her hand on its surface.

Chapter Thirty-Two

Creatures of the Deep

The warm, tingling air turned cold as the wall beneath her touch vanished and she found herself in another area of the caves. A pool of water reflected light against stalactites cascading down the stone walls. She stepped closer to the water and saw a narrow tunnel leading beneath its surface.

A faint shuffle twitched her ears, and she turned with her weapon drawn. Her eyes widened as they met with another's, and she was overcome with relief. Standing behind her, covered in dirt and blood, was Avelloch. She dropped her weapon and wrapped her arms tightly around his neck.

"Avelloch…" Tears filled her eyes as she held him close, fearful of losing him again if she let go. The comfort of companionship replaced the dread of loneliness and sorrow. She wouldn't have to endure these trials alone, and neither would he.

He slowly pulled away and looked at her face. She clutched his arms and noticed the razor-thin cuts that crawled across his skin.

"What happened?" she asked. "Where were you?"

"I was in the cave. You two disappeared."

"Loryk!" She quickly looked around, her mind spinning as she fumbled over her thoughts. "He isn't with you?"

"No. I was alone."

The world stopped as her pulse increased. Her hands tingled as she gazed hurriedly through the cave, desperate to find him.

Staring at a dark exit, which led into the hollows of a dark tunnel, she knew he had to be there. Avelloch reached out for her, grazing her arm as she grabbed her sword and fled down the hall.

"Loryk!" Her voice echoed loudly through the corridor. "Loryk!"

Light from the cave opening dwindled as she ran further. Uncaring of her fate, unaware of how far she had gone, she found herself in the silence and desolation of the cave. Standing alone, with nothing but the sound of her panting breaths, she glanced from left to right.

"Loryk…!" she called.

Tears welled in her eyes as she leaned forward onto her knees.

"No…," she whimpered. "No! Loryk!" Her face was hot and throat was raw as she stood alone, shouting for a man she might never see again.

She stood quietly for a moment, preparing to head deeper into the void, when a distant voice echoed through the air. It slipped through her ears like a feather in the wind. With a spark of hope, she straightened and turned quickly toward the noise.

"Loryk?" she called.

"Neer…," his voice whispered from far away.

She gasped and stumbled back. Her quivering voice broke as she said, "I'm here! Follow my voice!" She continued shouting while walking backward in the direction she came. "This way!"

Footsteps pattered nearer, and she halted. Her breathing was deep as the noise moved closer, and a sudden rush of cold wind pushed her back. She stumbled before catching herself and peered through the darkness as the quick steps continued down the hall.

Fearful of losing their sound, she ran behind them, keeping in rhythm until reaching the glowing doorway and crashing into Avelloch. He wrapped tight around her to keep her from falling, while a shadow nearby tumbled to the ground.

"Loryk?" she wailed before pushing Avelloch away and rushing to the figure nearby. As she came to his side, she was relieved to see his curly hair and bulging, terrified eyes. With a trembled gasp, she pulled him into a tight embrace and held him close. Hot tears streamed down her face as she squeezed his shoulders.

"N-neer?" he asked.

She released her grip and then held his face, like a mother cradling their child. "You're alive. Thank the Gods, you're alive!"

"What 'appened?" His voice trembled with fear and confusion.

"We got separated. Are you okay?"

"I-I don't..." He touched his chest and stomach. With a gasp, he ripped away from her hands and glanced around the cave, scanning the walls and dark corners with terror-stricken eyes.

"What is it?" Neer asked. "What's wrong?"

"Spiders!" he cried. "They were everywhere!"

A hard, breathless laugh escaped her throat, though it was more from relief than humor, as she watched him tremble and shake. "It's okay. They're gone."

"Is it over?" He leaned forward onto his knees. "Is this the end?"

She lowered her head as her shoulders dropped. With a depleted sigh, she said, "No... I think it's far from over."

He growled. "Fuck...! Fuck it all to the deepest pit of the seventh 'ell!"

While Neer focused on Loryk, Avelloch knelt by the water. He touched its surface and then rubbed his fingers together. Scanning the ground, he noticed a vial nestled within a crack in the rocks. Etched into the stone beside it were the white markings of evaesh symbols. Turning back to the others, he said, "I've found something."

Neer rubbed Loryk's shoulder before moving to Avelloch's side. The bard stayed motionless in his place, glancing at the corners with watchful eyes.

Neer knelt beside Avelloch and peered at the markings. "'This way'?" she asked, reading the evaesh symbols.

"It's Klaud," Avelloch explained before revealing the jar of blue capsules. "He left this behind. It'll allow us to hold our breath indefinitely."

Her eyes shifted to the water. "Are you sure they'll work?"

"Yes. I've used them before."

With a huff, she backed away from the water's edge and sat against the cave wall. She leaned back and buried her face in her hands. "This is such a nightmare... We're never going to survive this place."

Her arms dropped to her sides as Avelloch sat beside her. She examined the thin red lines across his cheeks. "What happened to you? How did you survive without magic?"

He lifted his arms and slowly twisted them, inspecting the bruises and cuts. "When I touched the rune, you two disappeared. I was still in the cave, but it was different. There were people everywhere."

"People? Who?"

"I don't know. I couldn't understand them, but they seemed real. They could see and speak to me. When they realized that I couldn't understand them, they attacked. I had to fight my way out, ran down a hall, and found myself here."

She turned away in deep thought. "I thought you needed magic to survive here."

"You do. I don't know how he survived"—his eyes flashed to Loryk—"but I barely made it. If Klaud hadn't left this, then we wouldn't have the means to continue. Not without magic." He displayed the vial between his fingers.

"We probably still don't." She pulled her knees to her chest and wrapped her arms around them. Staring at the pool of water, she began to wonder just how far the tunnel beneath would go. How long would they be forced to endure the Trials, and if it was too late to turn back. The hall that led both Avelloch and Loryk to this spot was just behind them. They could follow it back to the main chamber and leave together. She could find another way to lift her curse without putting herself or her friends in danger.

"Gods...," she groaned while raking her fingers through her hair. "This was such a mistake. We should've never come here."

Avelloch exhaled a deep breath. "It's too late to turn back. Klaud's here, and I won't leave him. We need to catch up to him. He could be in danger."

She nodded. "Yeah... Do you think he's still alive?"

"I don't know. These trials aren't meant for the weak."

Her eyes shifted to Loryk as he came to their sides and passed her a canteen of water. She thankfully accepted it before taking a drink. As she wiped her lips, she handed the leather pouch to

Avelloch and then stood. "You good, Lor?" she asked.

"Y-yeah. Sure."

She squeezed his shoulder and pressed her lips into a tight line. "We'll see this through. Hope you've got a few good lines out of all this."

He produced a sound that was half-scoff, half-laughter as he looked around. They turned to Avelloch as he stood next to them and passed them each a blue capsule. "Swallow this and then take a deep breath," he said. "It'll last until you exhale and need to take another breath, so keep yourself calm."

Loryk trembled. "So, we're goin' down there?" He looked at the tunnel beneath the water.

"Yeah," Neer said, her eyes glued to the underpass. "You two ready?" She glanced at the others, and they gave her approving nods. With a deep breath, Neer stepped closer to the pool. Its lights reflected like waves against her face. "Let's get this over with." She slipped a capsule through her lips, inhaled a deep breath, and then dove into the mysterious depths below.

She swam at a steady pace, listening as the water broke when Avelloch and Loryk jumped in behind her. Glowing algae clung to the walls and filled the pool with soft light. The others came to her side as they reached the edge of the tunnel and stared into blackness.

Terror stricken, Neer closed her eyes to calm the hard beating of her heart. Her chest ached from the growing pressure of her emotions. She needed desperately to breathe and release the fear festering deep inside. Her eyes flashed to the surface of the pool, and she had to stop herself from swimming to the top.

Avelloch placed his hand on her arm, and she flinched. He quickly covered her mouth as she nearly gasped. Their eyes met, and she timidly nodded, assuring him that she was fine. As he removed his hand, she shared a glance with Loryk and then returned her gaze to the tunnel.

Clenching her hands into tight fists, she pushed through the terror and swam into the darkness. The water was calm as they moved further from the light until it had faded, and they were made blind by its absence. Desperate for an end, Neer continued on, keeping her right hand on the wall to follow its path.

The emptiness of the water was replaced by a gentle nudge as something pressed against Neer's leg when she swam by. It was soft, like a wool pillow that gently floated away as soon as it touched her limb. She pushed the harrowed thoughts of what it could be from her mind. Now wasn't the time to be consumed with fear.

She felt the same soft, dense nudge, and then another, followed by a quiet rattle, like the sound of chains. Neer stopped. She carefully felt around, before touching a warm face. The panic that rose within her was relieved when a kind hand touched her arm, and she knew it was Avelloch that hovered next to her.

She gripped his arm and moved around him to feel for Loryk. When her hand tangled in his curly mane, she tightened her fist and carefully pulled him closer. He began to thrash, and she calmly touched his chest to calm him.

Avelloch lightly tugged Neer's arm, and she felt the rush of water swirling around as he swam down the path. Neer held tight to Loryk's hand as they swam together through the unlit passage, following after Avelloch.

Traveling deeper into the cave they were surrounded by the soft, nudging objects that floated in the water. Neer gently pushed them aside as she swam through a thick cluster, listening to the rattle of chains that followed every light shove. The touch of soft linen pressed against her hand as she guided them away.

In the distance came a soft glow emanating from the wall. They swam faster, hoping for an exit, and came to a stop at the edge of the wall. It wasn't an exit, but another rune illuminating against the stone and shining against their faces.

Avelloch glanced at Neer and caught a glimpse of her troubled expression. Their eyes met, and she gave him a forced nod. Her grip tightened on Loryk's hand as Avelloch hovered his fingers over the stone and then carefully touched the symbol.

Light slowly filled the tunnel as glowing stones brightened in a line along the walls. Neer turned around, examining the once dark corridor, when her eyes fell to the cloud of dark figures floating throughout the tunnel, and she was paralyzed with terror. Tethered to the ground by thick, moss-covered chains were the shadows of shrouded bodies.

Hundreds of bodies.

Avelloch waved Neer and Loryk forward as he swam further down the crowded hall. They followed close behind, carefully guiding the bodies aside. Low voices whispered through Neer's mind, penetrating her thoughts with sorrow and death. She shook her head in an attempt to rid it of the foreign anguish, and fear pulled at her chest. As the voices grew louder, she stopped. The pain set deeper. Strangers cried and shouted. They clawed at her mind, begging for mercy and forgiveness.

Her eyes moved to the body of a child as he whimpered and cried for his mother. His confusion and fear weighed deep in her soul as she stared at the shrouded figure, unable to escape his hold. Something dark pulled her closer. It was cold and unending, drawing her nearer with its icy touch.

She slowly reached out to touch him. His voice was loud in her mind. His fear stung her soul. The dark linen of his shroud was soft beneath her fingers as she stroked his head.

When a low growl vibrated through the water, her trance was broken. The sound wasn't like the cries and screams that flittered through her mind, hollow and broken.

He was breathing. Growling and moving.

She stared at the body, wondering if this was a test given by the Trials. Hoping that this was in her mind, as Loryk and Avelloch didn't seem to notice his sound as they continued through the tunnel. Her eyes shifted to the chain that rattled beneath the boy's feet, and the color drained from her face.

He was reanimating.

She quickly backed away and held in a gasp as she bumped into several more bodies. Terror-stricken, she could only watch as they began to move and wriggle within the constraints of their tightly wrapped shrouds. Suddenly, the voices in her mind were overpowered by angry growls as the bodies all came to life.

Avelloch turned around in a panic as the shrouds unwrapped to reveal the bloated and skeletonized faces of the dead. A hand, stripped of its skin, swiped at his face. He kicked the body back, retrieved his sword, and sliced through the corpse's wrist. The undead released a loud shriek as its severed hand sank into the shadows below.

Neer slashed across the chest of an undead as it reached for her shoulder, and she was pulled back into the arms of another. Sharp, boney fingers pierced through her armor and struck her chest as the creature shrieked with fury. She fought to release herself as the sting of her injury burned her skin. Her face was hot as she withheld a scream.

A loud, bubbling shriek came from her captor as it ripped away from her chest and struck her again, this time in the side. Skin sloughed from the undead's arms as Neer fought to pull from its strong grasp.

The thrashing corpse was suddenly still, and the pressure of its arms released as it was pulled away. Loryk retrieved his dagger from its skull and then grabbed Neer's wrist as he swam through the angry, growling corpses. As they approached Avelloch, he struck through the head of a corpse that reached for Loryk.

Slashing through the horde, they escaped through a narrow opening at the end of the tunnel. The glowing stones that clung to the walls slowly faded as the group slipped into a larger area of the cave. Neer turned back, watching as darkness overtook the now quiet, lifeless corridor.

Soft blue light from glowing stones and algae that clung to the walls allowed her to see the faces of her companions. Loryk leaned forward, clutching his aching chest as he struggled to hold his breath. Blood clouded the water around his left leg where three scratch marks drew across his skin. Avelloch was nearby, staring intently at the cave that surrounded them.

Neer touched Loryk's shoulder, and he flinched. As their eyes met, she gave him a thumbs up. He turned away with a nod and then returned the gesture. She glanced at Avelloch with a concerned, questioning look that asked if he was all right. He stiffly nodded and set his gaze back to the cave.

Neer turned her attention to Loryk's leg as blood painted the water in a mist of light red. She dug through her satchel and retrieved a rolled bandage. Moving to his leg, she carefully cut off the bottom of his trousers and then tightly wrapped his injury. The cloth turned pink as she tied it off.

His face was red as he clenched his eyes in agony. She patted his arm before looking around. The rocks opened to the left, leading through large corridors lit with glowing plants. Feeling restless and desperate for an end, Neer swam past the others, moving deeper through the empty cavern. Colorful plants, tall seaweed, and glowing algae lined the walls, becoming thicker the further they traveled. Slowly, bright blue light emerged from the distance, casting upward from a hole in the ground.

They swam through and entered an underwater city. Cobbled streets, uneven and covered with barnacles, stretched across the rocky surface of a large, open cave. Tall buildings, with five rows of windows, bordered the empty road. An arched hall above the street connected the two buildings.

Swimming beneath the arch, the group came to the center of the large city. Several streets led to buildings of many different shapes and sizes. Columns of enormous stalagmites, covered in glowing fungi and plants, extended from the base of the cave to the top.

Neer tugged Loryk's arm and pointed at the merpeople° who swam in the distance. Their eyes were wide as they watched the mythical beings swam casually from place to place. Neer looked at Loryk as he stared in wonder at the sights around them. She could only imagine the stories he would write when they finally made it out of this place. She could almost hear his thoughts as she knew his voice would be a constant stream of noise if he could speak.

She gently touched his shoulder, and he turned to her with a wide smile. Avelloch watched as a merperson swam freely through several archways before disappearing into the depths far beneath the reaches of the city. His eyes fell to a large platform nearby, and he waved the others forward as he swam closer to investigate.

Following Avelloch, they approached the platform. Neer's

---

* Living only in children's tales, the mer were said to be vicious and cold-hearted, striking through the hearts of any that would dare trek into their aquatic lands.

Many believe the delvine, a race of semi-aquatic humanoids that live along the northwestern shores of Laeroth, are descendants of the mer, but Neer always thought this to be a rumor devised by the Order to create segregation and fear of their kind.

CURSE OF THE FALLEN

eyes fixed on a bright glow emanating from its surface. Another rune was etched into the stone. They hovered above it and looked timidly at one another. Loryk quickly shook his head in opposition while Avelloch met Neer's gaze. She could sense the urgency within him. He stiffly nodded while Loryk continued to protest. Her eyes moved to the rune, and she knew it was the only way.

She gave an apologetic glance at Loryk before turning to the rune, closing her eyes, and gently touching the stone.

The symbol brightened and burned their eyes with its luminance. Loud, echoing squeals came from all around as the merpeople raced toward them. The curled tentacles atop their heads became long as they extended around their fish-like faces. They bore sharp fangs and hissed at the group through lipless mouths.

Neer pointed behind Avelloch with wide eyes as a merperson appeared at his back, mouth open wide, prepared to sink its teeth into his neck. Avelloch turned around and struck his swords across the chest of his attacker. His long, platinum hair was caught in the grasp of another creature as it swam up from the shadows and pulled him into its arms.

Neer swam over and swiped her sword. A thin red line drew across its cheek as it backed away to evade her attack. It's tentacles and fins extended outward as it hissed at her. Avelloch swung his arm back and sank his sword into his captive's face. Green liquid spilled from its body as its grip released. Neer kicked it back and yanked Avelloch away. More hissing echoed from all around as the merpeople scurried away.

Neer and Avelloch were motionless as the mer fled from the platform and disappeared into the shadows of the ancient city. Light grunting came from behind, and Neer turned to find Loryk fighting a merperson with his dagger. As she moved closer, ready to help, a cloud of bubbles rose from the depths behind him.

Neer backed away as an enormous shadow appeared. Large, spiked arms struck against the platform, creating a deep jolt that shook the water. Loryk turned back and his eyes widened as the creature hovered overhead. Its body was covered by a thick exoskeleton, black as tar. Two glowing white eyes stared down at him.

The merperson Loryk had been fighting attempted to flee, racing quickly from the creature that lurked above. With a quick snap of its long arms, the menacing shadow grabbed the merperson and pulled them back. As it sank beneath the water, it reached forward and snatched Loryk from the ledge, dragging him into the depths below.

Neer reached out for him in a panic and was quickly pulled into Avelloch's arms. He covered her lips, preventing her from taking a fatal breath as she prepared to scream.

She pushed him away and swam quickly into the depths, not caring to wait or see if he had followed. The world darkened as she moved beneath the city and into empty waters. A flash of light illuminated the darkness below and exposed the silhouette of a devilish creature. Six tentacles extended from its trunk, while four arms held sharp-clawed fingers.

Neer squinted her eyes as she peered through the darkness, and she slumped forward when she spotted Loryk struggling in the creature's clutches. He pushed hard against its locked grip, unable to break free from its hold.

The creature lifted the merperson as it struggled and clawed for freedom. Lifted close to the creature's face, the mer's tentacles straightened as it hissed at its captor. Glowing white eyes fixed on the mer as the creature raised its empty left arm, clutched the mer by its waist, and then twisted their body in opposite directions.

Neer was frozen as the snapping of bones vibrated through the water. Blood and entrails obscured her view of the creature as the mer was torn in two. Its body drifted through the water as the creature released its hold and focused its eyes on Loryk.

In a panic, Neer lifted her arms and sent a blast of energy forward. A rush of energy spun through the water before crashing into the creature. It flipped backward, holding tightly to Loryk as it was hurled out of view. Neer swam closer in search of her enemy when something touched her arm. She turned back and drew her sword, when her eyes met with Avelloch's, and she stopped herself from attacking.

They turned back toward the creature as slow currents drifted through the water, becoming stronger as it spun in place.

A whirlpool quickly formed, and its current swept her and Avelloch away.

Neer covered her mouth and nose as she flipped weightlessly through the water. As she came to a slow stop, she closed her eyes and gripped her head. Resting near the surface of the water, she looked around to find the creature was floating far beneath her. Loryk glanced around in a panic before meeting Neer's face. He was alive, and that, for now, was enough.

The creature shrieked in anger as it peered through the water, searching for its prey. Neer closed her eyes and focused intently on her magic. As energy swelled within her, stinging her skin, and expanding in her aching, exhausted chest, she looked at the creature and then vanished. She reappeared instantly in front of it and struck her sword at its chest. The steel blade cracked as it met with the hard exoskeleton. As water rushed her from behind, Neer spun aside to dodge the deadly swipe of its claws. She teleported behind the creature and sank her weapon deep into the exposed flesh of its back.

An angry cry vibrated the water, piercing her ears and causing her mind to spin. Six long tentacles and four thick arms spread out wide as it shrieked in pain. Neer watched as Loryk fell from its grasp and quickly fled to safer water. With little time to waste, Neer lifted her sword and readied for another attack, noticing several lacerations on the creature's arms and tentacles. Marks she didn't make. Focused on the injuries, she came to the haunting realization that Klaud had fought this monster, and she wondered if he was still alive.

In her distraction, she didn't notice when a tentacle rose from behind, and with a quick jab, it stung her back. She exhaled a deep, pained gasp as heat burned through her skin. Her body was rigid, and her eyes were wide as scorching heat coursed through her, sizzling her veins and contracting her muscles. A thick claw wrapped tight around her body and pulled her toward its large open mouth.

Her throat burned and lungs were heavy with water as the potion had worn off. She thrashed as her chest convulsed, fighting for breath that would never come. Her fingers and toes tingled, and she was soon wrapped in a comfortable, secure warmth as her body grew numb. Visions passed through her mind of all she had been through in her life. Her childhood when her parents would read her bedtime stories, her days spent alone in the woods enjoying the solitude, her introduction to the Brotherhood.

The warmth she felt was a comfort against the agony she faced throughout her lifetime. An escape was all she wanted, and now that it came, it was hard to refuse. Her body fell limp as she drifted between life and death. With her eyes closed, she didn't see as Avelloch's shadow appeared behind the creature and struck deep into its spine. It released a loud shriek that broke through the tranquility of Neer's thoughts, but she wasn't afraid. The sounds drifted through her mind like leaves in the wind, carrying into the darkness until fading to silence.

The pressure of the claw released as the creature released its grip, and Neer floated lifelessly through the depths.

Chapter Thirty-Three

The Futility of Fate

Avelloch snatched Neer and swam away from the creature as it drifted through the water, motionless. Loryk was behind them, staring at Neer with wide, terrified eyes. His face had lost its color the moment she screamed. Her eyes were opened, unblinking, and her lips were parted as she laid completely still in Avelloch's grasp.

They followed the cave back into the city where they were forced through a labyrinth of twisting streets and roadblocks. Finding their way out of the sunken city, they came to a large cavern full of glowing plants. Avelloch moved faster as light reflected against a calm surface, and he broke through the water's edge while exhaling a deep breath. Loryk did the same, and then instantly he turned his attention to Neer.

"Is she alive?" he asked, his voice echoing loudly through the dimly-lit chamber. "Neer! Answer me, please!" He urgently tapped her face and felt her neck for a pulse. His trembling hands fumbled across her skin, never finding the gentle thud of life that would thump in her veins. "Come on...," he cried.

Avelloch pulled her close, being sure to keep her head above water as he swam to the edge of the lake. He dragged himself onto the smooth stone ground before pulling Neer onto a flat area of the rocks. Loryk followed behind, his voice never fading as he barraged Avelloch with a constant string of questions. Avelloch paid him no mind as he pressed two fingers to Neer's neck and waited for a pulse that never came. He tilted her head back, pinched her nose, and breathed two breaths into her mouth.

Sitting straighter, he placed his hands over her chest and began compressions. His face was tight as he focused on her survival.

"Do somethin'!" Loryk cried. "She isn't wakin' up! You're doin' it wrong!"

Loryk began pushing him away and Avelloch shoved him aside. Unbothered by his outburst, Avelloch breathed into Neer's mouth and continued his compressions. His jaw clenched as he watched her face. A light twitch pulled her lip before she began choking. Loryk fell silent as Avelloch turned her onto her side and water spilled from her lips.

"Thank the Divines!" Loryk gasped. "Oh Gods... Fuck the Gods... Fuck these trials..." He gripped his head and stood before pacing around. "She's alive... She's breathin'..."

Avelloch turned Neer onto her back as she fell quiet and still. He felt her neck and exhaled a deep breath at the faint thump of a weak pulse. With an exhausted breath, he slumped back onto his knees and closed his eyes. Wet hair clung to his face as he sat motionless and tired.

The cave was dark, with large rocks and thick stalagmites creating walls that closed them in. To the left, perched atop the solid stone, was a small Tree with brightly glowing flowers. Thick roots twisted through the rocks, weaving outward and becoming thinner as they traveled further from the trunk.

Through several exhausted breaths, Avelloch lifted Neer into his arms and carried her to the Tree. Loryk followed behind, keeping his eye on Neer as she was placed beneath the branches.

Avelloch glanced across the cave, peering at the dark corners and shadows that loomed all around. The water created a deep pool that broke into a narrow stream and circled behind the Tree. He reached into his pack and retrieved a flint and a vial of brown liquid. A flame appeared above the stone as he struck the flint, and shimmering magic formed into a dome-shaped barrier as he dripped the potion over its artificial heat.

Flowered branches cascaded over the invisible barrier, casting soft light into their shelter. Orange firelight flickered within the enclosure, creating warmth that eased the discomfort in their tired, aching muscles.

Avelloch sat on his knees and tenderly wrapped his fingers around Neer's arm. With his other hand clutching the twisting roots, he closed his eyes and meditated. The Tree brightened and filled the air with the warm sting of magic. Loryk leaned forward, mystified. His eyes were fixed on the glowing branches and pulsing lights that moved through the roots like currents in a river.

His eyes drifted to Neer, and he asked, "Will she make it?"

Avelloch remained silent in his meditations, and Loryk decided to give him space. Surely, Avelloch wouldn't do anything to compromise her life after saving her. Pulling his gaze away from Neer, Loryk leaned against the barrier and closed his eyes.

The warmth of the flames never died as they sat in a despairing silence. Loryk rested across the fire from Avelloch with his knees pulled to his chest. His curly hair no longer dripped as time had dried the moisture that once weighed him down. With a soft sigh, he turned to Neer. The bandage they had wrapped around her chest and waist was bloody where the two clusters of small puncture wounds oozed. He watched with hopeful eyes as she breathed through parted lips. Each breath illuminated and darkened the vibrance of the Tree. Blue veins, which were now covered by the bandages, extended from the sting mark on her back and curled around her sides and shoulders, and with her every inhalation they glowed brighter.

Neer stirred in her sleep while the others sat quietly across the flames. Her chest rose and fell with every quick, deep breath. Sweat dripped from her temples and her eyes shifted quickly under her closed lids.

"Neer?" Loryk crawled to her side as she began to twitch and moan. "Neer!"

She woke from her nightmare with a loud gasp. Sitting up, she clutched her chest and caught her breath.

"You're okay, Neer," Loryk said while rubbing her shoulder. "It's all right..."

She fell into a fit of coughing, and Loryk handed her a canteen. She drank the contents and then tossed the empty container aside. Her fingers tangled in her messy hair as she leaned forward. "Where are we?" she asked in a raspy, tired voice. "What happened?"

"We were underwater, fightin' that thing... I thought you were dead, Neer." Tears filled his puffy eyes. "We thought you drowned down there..."

She gripped her forehead with a sigh. "How am I alive? We were nowhere close to the surface."

"I don't know... Avelloch stabbed that creature through the back, and then we grabbed you and fled. Took us a long time to find this cave and get out of the water... Avelloch got you breathin' again, and he was able to do somethin' with the energy of the Tree... I guess it kept you alive."

She turned to Avelloch, who stared at her with sad eyes. Neer crawled to his side and touched a deep cut across his cheek.

"Are you hurt anywhere else?" she asked.

"I'm fine," he said.

She closed her eyes, harnessed her energy, which was stronger as she sat beneath the pulsing Tree, and healed his injury. Slowly, she reopened her eyes and ran her finger across his soft, blemish free skin.

"I'm glad you're okay...," she said and then turned to Loryk. "Both of you."

Loryk wiped his nose. "You too, Neery," he said.

"How's your leg?"

He stretched his injured leg to reveal the red-stained bandages. "'Urts like no other."

She crawled to his side and carefully unwrapped the linen to reveal his deep lacerations. He winced as she clutched his calf and healed his wounds. Hot magic radiated from her palms into his skin as the cuts fused, leaving behind faint white scars. She released her grip and backed away with a depleted sigh.

Sweat had formed across her forehead, and she wiped it away while asking, "Do you still have the arun, Lor?"

He pulled the small box from his fastened pocket. It was wrapped tight with cloth and twine to keep the lid secure. "'Ow much longer d'you think we'll be in 'ere?" he asked while securing the arun back in his pocket.

"I don't know...," Neer replied. "When I was alone, I received a vision. Did either of you see it too?" She translated to evaesh, and they shook their heads. She pondered for a moment, and then recited the message:

"Enter the trials with great feat; the waters wait for those who seek.
Darkness is blinding for those with sin; waters are haunted by creatures within.
Shackles and streets guide the way; pale moonlight leads into the fray.
Enter this chamber if energy you seek; blood of the First holds the key."

"What does that mean?" Loryk asked.

Neer sighed. "I don't know... The waters could be the test we just took."

"We shouldn't focus on prophecies," Avelloch interjected. "The Trials will—"

A panicked scream interrupted his words as it echoed from deep within the cave. The group fell quiet and still. Avelloch unsheathed his sword and peered at their surroundings. Another pained cry broke the silence, and he was made more alert.

Neer listened carefully. Nerves fluttered in her stomach and down into her toes. She swallowed her fear as she looked deep into the caverns.

"Help!" the voice called in evaesh, and Neer's heart stopped. It was Klaud.

With a gasp, Avelloch stood and shattered the barrier with his sword. Without a second glance, he raced into the darkness.

"Avelloch!" Neer called as she and Loryk followed behind. "Wait!"

The glowing limbs of the Tree quickly vanished as they ran further into the cave and toward the now faded voice.

"Avelloch..." Neer started, finally catching up with him. He stood at the edge of a deep drop off, and she took a measured step back, carefully pulling Avelloch with her. "Was that him?" she asked.

His eyes fixed on a narrow ledge that led around the chasm to another area of the cave. "I don't know," he explained. "It may be a trick. Something could have lured us here." His eyes shifted down into the canyon, and Neer could see the uncertainty in his eyes. It was the same look that she carried as she worried about Klaud's fate and wondered if he had fallen into the depths of the dark, endless gorge.

Panic and relief overshadowed her fear as his voice called out again, this time louder and closer. Avelloch sheathed his dual swords and then carefully walked along the footpath. He pressed his back against the uneven rock wall as he slowly moved across.

"We aren't goin' on that!" Loryk trembled

"Come on," Neer said while following behind Avelloch. "Klaud could be in danger."

Loryk noisily whimpered and stepped onto the ledge. His breaths were shaky and loud as he forced himself across, moving painfully slow and falling far behind the others.

Neer gagged and then held her breath when pungent odor of rotten flesh and excrement filled the air. Loryk stared at the canyon, too wrapped in his fear to notice the horrid smells, while Avelloch moved to a wider area of the footpath that met with the opening of a large, empty cavern.

"Help…"

They rushed into the cavern as a voice that wasn't Klaud's called from the darkness. Searching the empty cave, their eyes grew wide as they gazed at the narrow prison cells carved into the walls. Rusted iron bars held captive the bones and putrid remains of half-eaten corpses. Leather miner's aprons and broken axes laid beneath the piles of rotting entrails and flesh.

Avelloch lifted his sword as a frail voice whispered, "Help me…"

He and Neer stepped closer and peered into a nearby cell where a human man lay inside on his stomach. He crawled forward with bloody fingers and reached out for them. "Please…," he begged. Blood and torn flesh trailed behind his half-eaten legs.

Neer leaned against the bars, staring at the stranger with sorrowful eyes. "We have to help him!" She began pulling against the bars and searching for a lever to open the cell. She extended her arm through the bars to pull him closer, hoping to heal him with her magic. Cold iron stung her skin as she fought desperately to touch his hand while he struggled to crawl closer and take her grasp.

"Come on!" she grunted while pushing herself into the bars. His bloody fingertips slid against hers as he trembled and shook. She stepped back with a huff and glanced around the cell, searching for another way inside. But there was only solid stone. She closed her eyes and took several deep breaths, focusing on her energy.

"What are you doing?" Avelloch asked. "Neer!" He grabbed her shoulder and pulled her from her trance. She glared as their eyes met. "The prison cells in Anaemiril are known for their magical wards. Once inside, you won't be able to use it. You'll be stuck."

"We can't leave him like this! We have to get him out of there!"

"And do what?! If we help him escape, we'll have to carry him through these trials. It's suicide!"

"I won't leave him to die like this!"

Neer moved back to the bars, struggling once again to reach for the prisoner until the faint sound of hisses and growls came from the darkness of the cave.

Avelloch pulled Neer away and tucked into the shadows as the noises grew louder. Loryk, who had just stepped from the ledge, looked around in a panic before spotting his companions and darting to their sides.

The prisoner began screaming, and Neer fought against Avelloch's hard grip.

"No!" the man wailed. "Please! Help me! I beg you... Please!"

"What can we do?" Loryk whispered. "We can't leave 'im like this!"

Neer glanced through the room as glowing white eyes emerged from the darkness. The creatures moved closer, scratching and clawing, until reaching the cell and slipping their frail bodies through the thin bars. The man screamed as the creatures, with white skin that stretched tight over their boney limbs, bit into his legs. The sound of their teeth sinking into his flesh filled the air and mixed with echoing shrieks as the man begged for mercy.

Neer pushed Avelloch aside and ran to the bars. As the man clawed his way to her, a creature sank its nails deep into his back and forced him to the ground.

Staring at the man, who lay just out of reach, Neer realized there was nothing she could do. She stared at the tears and blood dripping down his face as he was slowly eaten alive.

She lifted her arms to the bars and concentrated on her energy. Her eyes were focused on the man as she wove her magic through the air and took hold of his and the creature's necks. A tear fell from her eye as she clenched her fists and crushed their throats. They released wheezed gasps before falling lifelessly to the floor. Fresh blood dripped from their lips as their pupils overtook the color of their eyes.

Neer crumbled to the ground as the weight of her grief sank to her knees. Avelloch knelt by her side and wiped the tears from her eyes. "Come on," he started with a strong, directive voice, "we have to move."

"I can't...," she sobbed.

"You showed him mercy. Let's not make his sacrifice be in vain."

She sniffed and took several deep breaths. Her eyes shifted to the cell, and she fell silent as she stared at the place he once lay. Not a speck of blood or white scratch blemished the stone. They had vanished without a trace.

"What...," she remarked, unsure of what she was seeing. "How?"

Loryk stepped closer and peeked into the cell. His face twisted with anger as he released a furious growl and smacked hard against an iron bar. "It were an illusion!" he remarked. "A trick! These damned caves won't give us a damned break!"

"It wasn't real..." Neer sniffed while wiping her nose. "What kind of test was that? Why would it force me to kill someone like that?"

Avelloch said, "Those creatures, the centry, are real. They've been known to capture people living near the entrances of Anaemiril." His gaze shifted to the empty cell. "This must've been a vision from the past. A way to drive you mad."

Neer wiped her eyes and glanced at Loryk as he stared wide-eyed into the distance. "Loryk?" she asked before following his gaze. Her shoulders slumped and jaw dropped at the sight of another brightly glowing rune etched into the wall ahead. Numbness trickled through her chest and into her fingers and toes.

"No…" She shook her head. "I don't want to touch those fucking things anymore! I just want to get out of here! No more fucking mind games!"

"Neer!" Avelloch called as she marched forward.

"I'm done with this place! Let's just get Klaud and go back home!"

As she marched past the rune, intense pain struck her chest. She fell to her knees, struggling to breathe. Avelloch and Loryk rushed to her side, unable to help as she fell back with a sudden, inhuman shriek. Haunting images of death and darkness flashed through her mind. The agony built with every broken face and bloody corpse she saw. Ashes and smoke overtook the visions and faded them to black. Darkness clutched her soul with a painful, scalding grip.

Lying on the ground, writhing in agony, her back arched and bones creaked. Her eyes rolled back and skin turned white as she screeched in various tones of voice. Loryk fell back and clutched his ears while Avelloch remained at her side, grunting from the pain of her piercing scream. Baritone and falsetto voices escaped her throat as she spoke an ancient and forgotten language.

"What's 'appenin'?" Loryk shouted. "Do somethin'!" He gripped her shoulders and called her name, but she didn't acknowledge him. Only the constant stream of foreign words slipped from her tongue.

Avelloch breathed heavily and looked around before his gaze fell on the rune. Glancing between Neer and the magical etching, he released a desperate cry and smacked the rune with the side of his fist. The chaos of her dual voices ceased, and she exhaled a long, deep breath. Her arched back relaxed and head nodded to the side.

Loryk placed his ear to her chest and sighed with relief. "Divines…," he cried. "She's still alive."

Avelloch was still for a moment, then pushed himself up and looked around. He scanned the darkness that surrounded them before gathering Neer in his arms.

"Oi!" Loryk jumped to his feet shoved Avelloch aside. "What the 'ells are you doin'?"

Avelloch grimaced as Loryk shouted at him in a language he didn't understand. As the evae glanced at Neer, Loryk shoved him back again.

"Come," Avelloch said in evaesh, "not safe."

"No bacon?" the bard asked angrily, clearly misunderstanding his words. "What the 'ells are you goin' on about?"

Avelloch huffed angrily and stepped past Loryk. He ignored the bard's shouting as he moved farther into the cave and away from the symbol that glowed softly against the wall.

Several hours into their journey left them quiet and exhausted. Avelloch looked at Neer, who remained unconscious in his arms, while Loryk trailed behind.

"Oi…" Loryk tapped his arm and pointed to the pale blue light shining through a large opening in the wall ahead. Carefully approaching the light, they came to the edge of an immaculate underground city. Large streams of glowing water carved through the ground, while square homes covered in stalactites, moss, and mud were left quiet and abandoned. Stairways led to several levels of the city that were built deep into the walls of the cave.

Avelloch stepped through the mysterious city with purpose and haste while Loryk stared in awe at his surroundings. The evae soon came to a nearby home with an open door and placed Neer on a stone bed. Loryk quickly followed, and the two closed themselves in before barricading the door with a stone dresser. The heavy furniture grinded noisily against the rock floor as they struggled to move it into place.

"What're we doin' this for?" Loryk asked in his native language, his voice strained as he pushed against the dresser. "We're all alone down 'ere."

He released a loud huff when they pushed it into position. The air was moist and cold, though his skin was hot from exertion.

Avelloch dragged a tall, empty shelf across the room and placed it in front of the window. As the room darkened, glowing crystals shined across the ceiling in beautiful patterns that cast a soft glow, illuminating the shadows.

He knelt close to Neer and dug through his pack. With a few drops of potion, Avelloch created a fire and barrier around them. With the warmth easing the tension in his bones, Loryk removed his shoes with a great sigh and leaned against the wall. Digging through his pockets, he retrieved a small bag of dried meat.

"Avel-cock," he called before tossing him a few strips. "You did good out there." His eyes shifted to Neer as he chewed his meal. "She's somethin' else, yeah?" Loryk spoke in his native language. "Don't know where I'd be without 'er... Feels like a lifetime ago we met. Would've never imagined that tiny, helpless kitchen wench would turn out to be so strong and brave."

Avelloch's eyes moved to Neer, who lay quietly on the bed next to him.

"You really like 'er, don't ya?" Loryk asked, though the evae couldn't understand him. They fell silent, and Loryk closed his eyes. His head bobbed as soft melodies seeped from his half-closed lips.

Avelloch repositioned himself to get more comfortable and interrupted the song. Platinum hair fell in dirty tangles across his shoulders. Scars crisscrossed his arms, and Loryk noticed a barely visible, yet familiar, brand that marked his skin.

"Oi," Loryk started, "that's the mark of the Order, isn't it? There, on your 'and?"

Avelloch's face twisted in confusion. Loryk pointed at the scar. He tensed before covering the scar and turning away.

"'Ow'd you get that? Why're the elves leavin' it around after they burn down our villages?"

The evae was quiet. His eyes set on Neer, whose own brand was exposed on her arm. Her blemish was just as faded as his scar.

"She got that as a kid," Loryk explained in human language. "'Ad it before we met. She don't remember much of it, thankfully, though she used to 'ave these nightmares. Said people in dark cloaks were after 'er. Reiman put a stop to it, but I think she still carries it." His eyes grew distant as he looked at the friend he had known almost half his life... a friend he could never live without.

"Avelloch," Loryk struggled to pronounce the evaesh words correctly, "thanks."

Avelloch nodded respectfully.

"I like no evae. Heard you were all... rubber."

Avelloch raised his eyebrow at the misused word.

Loryk didn't seem to notice as he continued, "Neer is eggs. Best friend I ever 'ad."

Avelloch turned to Neer, scanning her face with worried eyes.

"You're a right good evae, Avelloch." Their eyes met, and Loryk spoke his native language as he grimly warned, "Don't fuck it up."

Chapter Thirty-Four

Reflections of Betrayal

Neer shuffled in her sleep, dreaming of the same haunting, dark visions she had always seen. Flashes of pain and fire ripped through her as voices cried out, desperate for an end and for the agony to cease.

Avelloch slowly woke as Neer tossed noisily in her sleep. She moaned and twitched before sitting up with a gasp. Struggling to keep her eyes open, she looked around in a daze.

"Where are we?" she asked while examining the small, dimly lit room. Loryk snored softly across the fire, while Avelloch looked at her with relief. "Avelloch?"

He exhaled a deep breath and turned away. "Something happened to you when you stepped past the rune. We weren't able to move on without touching it."

She gripped her forehead as she realized they were still in the caves... still in the Trials. "It's never going to end, is it? We're going to die down here."

"We can make it. I'm sure the end isn't too far."

Their eyes met, and a slight smile pulled the edge of her lip. "It must be dark times if you're keeping me positive."

He smiled and turned to the fire. Orange light flickered against his skin as his look grew distant. She studied his eyes and noticed the vulnerability that had replaced the hardness and anger. He was afraid, and it terrified her. But she wouldn't allow him to see it.

She shifted her gaze to the fire and began to wonder what was to come. While she struggled to make sense of all she had been through, another thought pressed against her mind, muting all other notions of fear and pain as she contemplated her life, should she survive.

The chances of them seeing each other outside of this tomb were close to none. Humans and evae were forbidden from coexisting, both in Nyn'Dira and Laeroth. She crossed her arms as the thoughts made her sick. In the weeks that they had known each other, they'd been through enough for her to know that she needed him, even if only as friends.

"Avelloch," Neer started nervously, fearful of voicing her thoughts, "do you think once this is over… if we survive, that is… will we ever see each other again?"

His jaw stiffened, and his eyes fell away. He was quiet for a moment, and the sickness within her grew stronger. She was afraid to meet his gaze, afraid of the truth she didn't want to face. There hadn't been many people in her life who she knew she could trust, who she knew could understand her, and she didn't want to lose it now that it had come.

Avelloch closed his eyes before admitting with heart-wrenching honesty, "No. I'll go back to Nyn'Dira, and you'll leave for your journey."

She closed her eyes with a nod. "Our paths have crossed twice before. What's to say it won't happen again?"

"A person only has so much luck before it runs out."

"We'll just have to make our own luck, then." Her eyes gazed into his. He turned away and closed his eyes. "If my journey takes me to the forest, I'll find you," she said.

"Nyn'Dira is no place for your kind. If they find you there… they will kill you."

"Good thing I've got you to keep me safe, then. Saving damsels in distress is your motive, yeah?"

He laughed without a smile. Before he could speak, a furious snarl echoed from outside the home and brought their conversation to a sudden end. Avelloch straightened and grabbed his sword, while Neer listened to the footsteps that pattered against the empty streets outside.

"What is that?" she whispered

A hard thud rattled the door before a creature growled and clicked its tongue. The sound of fingernails scratching against the walls grated their ears, and creaking bones popped as it searched for a way inside.

Its footsteps and noises faded as it walked away, and Avelloch released a deep exhale. "We call them centry," he whispered, his eyes still fixed on the door. "They're evae that were sent here long ago as prisoners before the First Blood disappeared. They use their hearing and smell to see, so the barrier must be fading. We need to leave."

"What?" she whispered harshly. "We can't leave while they're out there!"

"We have no choice! If they find us here, we'll be trapped."

While he quickly gathered his things, Neer crawled across the fire and gently tapped Loryk's cheek. He woke with a loud yawn, and she quickly covered his mouth.

He pushed her away in shock. "What're you—"

Avelloch pulled Neer away and pressed his hand firmly against Loryk's mouth. The bard quivered beneath his bone-chilling glare.

Avelloch shifted his gaze to the wall behind Loryk as the sound of angry snarls and quick footsteps overlapped from outside.

"*Kila!*" Avelloch hissed. "They're coming! Do you have any defensive magic? Anything that can ward them off?"

Thoughts raced through Neer's mind as she struggled to remember even her name under such pressure. "An energy pulse," she said. "I can push them back."

"Get ready."

The growling intensified when overlapping footsteps thudded against the ground, becoming louder as they closed in on the home. Loryk jumped back with a yelp as hard fists pounded against the walls. Fingernails scratched and clawed against the heavy stone door, causing it to rattle and shift.

With every hard thud, the dresser that was acting as a barricade slid backward with a loud screech. Avelloch stared unblinking at the door. His knuckles were white as he gripped his swords tight in his fists.

Loryk whimpered, shakily holding his dagger as white boney arms clawed their way inside. Deep scratches were drawn into the wall as the centry fought to enter the home. Neer trembled as the overlapping sounds filled her mind. Still weak and wearied from all she'd been through, she struggled to conjure even a spark of energy. Faint magic swirled inside her, but she could never grasp it, as with every snarl and thump her focus shifted back to the centry.

"Neer!" Loryk called before shoving a vile of thick green liquid into her hands. He turned around with a gasp as a creature pulled itself inside.

Its head and right arm squeezed through the doorway, and Avelloch quickly slashed his blades into its skull. He yanked the swords from the centry's flesh and slung thick, slimy blood across the room. Several centry climbed over their fallen comrade as they fought to get inside, and the dresser shifted with a squeal when the horde spilled into the room like an avalanche of bones.

Neer drank the elixir and dropped the vial to her feet. Her blood turned cold as ice, and her body felt strong as steel. Energy swirled within her like a raging vortex. She inhaled a deep breath and gathered her strength, and with a push forward, the energy expanded from her open palms. The shockwave blasted the creatures into the wall. Their bones snapped before they fell lifelessly to the floor. Cracks filled the walls where they collided against the stone.

She turned to the doorway and raised her hands toward the mountain of snarling centry. Avelloch sank his swords into the throats and chests of several creatures as they clawed at him with vicious screams. Loryk tucked himself into a corner, slashing at a centry as it crept closer.

Energy burned inside her as Neer took hold of their necks. Avelloch and Loryk leapt back when the centry began convulsing and clawing at their own throats. Neer's eyes were dark and glaring. She slowly curled her hands into tight fists.

The sound of snapping bones and crushed windpipes filled the air and the centry fell to the ground, unmoving. Neer marched over their twitching corpses and through the doorway.

Outside, she lifted her palm and pushed back the horde with another powerful blast. The centry hissed while flipping across the ground. Raising her arms outward toward the creatures that filled the streets, she opened her palms wide and allowed the magic to twist and burn deep inside her. Her teeth clenched and skin burned.

She peered at the snarling creatures as they scrambled to their feet and raced forward in a wave of glowing eyes and sharp teeth. The ground trembled beneath their hurried steps. Neer's face twisted as the boiling energy tore through her, and with a scream, she clutched her shaking hands into tight fists before swinging her opened palms outward, away from her body. The cave trembled and creaked as a powerful shockwave ripped through the village, cracking the homes and creating a loud rumble that echoed through the open corridors.

The centry became still, and the cave, for an instant, was deathly silent. Not a second had passed, when suddenly, the creatures' upper bodies sloughed off from the waist. Blood splashed and organs slopped as they spilled to the ground.

Neer fell to her knees. Her lungs ached, and her muscles were weak as the elixir wore off and she was depleted of energy. Avelloch rushed to her side while Loryk stared in disbelief. Dozens of centry, all cut close to the waistline, lay in piles around them.

"Come on," Avelloch said as he pulled Neer to her feet, "we have to move."

Loryk stumbled forward, his wide eyes still set on the massacre Neer created. "You killed 'em all in one go? Just like that?"

Neer was silent as Avelloch gripped her waist and slung her arm around his shoulders. They walked carefully through the piles of bodies and made their way further into the cave.

Glowing crystals along the walls created a trail the group followed through desolate, rugged caves. The scent of must and stone filled the air, and the constant darkness left them disoriented. Neer had slowly regained her strength as they walked for what felt like days, though it had only been several hours. She hoped they were moving in the right direction and that the cave wasn't leading them in an endless circle.

She turned back as Loryk trailed behind, walking at a much slower pace as the fatigue and exhaustion weighed his feet. Neer slowed to match his stride and walked alongside him. "You all right, Ebbard?" she asked, teasing him with his stage name and hoping to lighten the mood.

He nodded shakily. "Just ready to get 'ome."

"I think you're the only bard to explore the forbidden ruins."

"Yeah? Think it'll get me more women than Fjord?" he asked, referring to his famed rival, Fjord of Jokulsa.[*]

"I don't know." She chuckled while wrapping her arm around his. "He does have the look of a Divine."

"'E can 'ave all the women 'e wants. I 'ad the best of 'em all."

"Yeah? Who's that?"

Their eyes met and he smiled. "Vaeda. Kitchen wench could break a man's 'eart with a smile."

"I seem to recall her scoffing at your ballads."

"She was a bitter little thing! The only one out of all the girls that couldn't stand to listen to my singin'!"

"Maybe she was playing hard to get?"

"I got 'er in the end for a while. O' course, now, she's a friend. More like a brother, really." Neer pushed his head, and he laughed. "My most famous ballad is written about 'er. Most of 'em are."

"Porcelain skin and *hair of black*?" She quoted the famous ballad, which referred to her naturally pale skin and current dark hair.

"Well, I've 'ad to change the lyrics over the years. Keep the song fresh, you know?"

"Mhmm." She eyed him with a suspicious smile. "I bet she replays your ballads in her head every night before falling asleep."

"Really?"

---

[*] Fjord is an infamous songster known for his unique musical style and dashing good looks. Born in the human continent of Aeshan, Fjord came to Laeroth during his musical studies and was believed by many to be the direct descendant of Rothar, the overseer of the Divines and immortal plane. Though the minstrel has never confirmed nor denied these claims, this popular belief has led to his overwhelming success and admiration.

She smiled with a nod. "Of course, those dreadful tunes just get stuck in her head. Bit annoying, actually."

Loryk chuckled with a large smile.

They fell silent as they moved further into the cave, and orange light slowly filled the dark tunnels. Each step brought them closer to its luminance. Soon, the cave opened and brought them to a room with a ceiling so high it couldn't be seen. A maze of stone half-walls led them to a pointed pillar, tall as a man. Bright red veins glowed throughout its length, while a vibrant rune rested near the top.

"Neer," Loryk started, "this's a shrine to the Divines. What's it doin' down 'ere with that rune on it?"

Neer's face glowed as she stepped closer to the stone. The rune was ancient and powerful. Its energy warmed her skin.

"We can't move past it, right?" she asked without looking away.

Avelloch stepped beside her and gently took her hand. As Loryk gripped her free hand, she turned to him, nervous and afraid.

Loryk smiled and said, "We're in this together, yeah?"

She squeezed his hand. With tear-filled eyes, she turned to Avelloch. His strong gaze was enough to give her confidence and strength. Turning to the pillar, she carefully lifted her palm, and with a deep breath, she placed it over the glowing rune.

Bright light surrounded them in warmth. Their clasped hands tightened when a deep groan shook the world, and they fell to the ground. The brightness slowly faded, and Neer crawled forward, aching from the impact of her fall. She looked around in a daze, horrified to find herself sitting on a dirt road. Fields of grass, a bright blue sky, and wooden cabins surrounded her. But the air still smelled of rock and must. The sun hovered overhead, yet there was a chill in the air, one that followed her through the caves.

"What is this?" Loryk asked as he stood and dusted himself off. "Neer? Avelloch?"

Neer crawled to her feet and stepped to his side. She reached out to touch his shoulder and her hand went through him. "What?" she remarked. "What's happening?"

Loryk called out for his companions while Neer stood in front of him, confused and panicked. "Loryk!" she cried. Her fingers moved through his shoulders as she tried desperately to get his attention.

"Stop." Avelloch pulled her back. His eyes were set on the bard, who looked around in fear. "He can't see us."

"Why not? What's going on? Where are we?"

"I don't know…" He scanned their surroundings with a furrowed brow. The rattle of an incoming cart caught their attention, and he quickly retrieved his weapons.

"Oh shite…," Loryk gasped. "This can't be 'appenin'! Not again…"

"Loryk?" Neer asked, but he never met her gaze.

Loryk tripped as he staggered back and fell into a shallow ditch. As the cart moved closer, Avelloch pulled Neer aside. Two horses trotted past before coming to a slow stop. The barred carriage they pulled had shackles and a large padlock on the back door. Two Knights of the Order, with their silver-plated armor and golden scapulars, stepped from the bench. While one knight unlocked the carriage, the other stepped to Loryk, who quickly crawled back in fear.

"Please," he stuttered, "don't do this!"

The knight picked him up and tossed him into the cart. He rolled to the back before crashing against the iron bars. The knight secured the padlock before climbing back onto the bench with his companion and commanding the horses forward.

Loryk tripped as he leapt to the cage door and fumbled with the lock, trying desperately to open the door. "Neer," he shouted through a cracked voice, "they're goin' to kill me! Please! Neer!"

She grabbed a rock from the roadside and raced after the carriage. The cart shifted and whined with every lurch. Neer caught up to the slow-moving wagon and struck against the padlock with the rock. But her hand and weapon went straight through, and she stumbled forward, tripping over her feet. Loryk choked on his cries as he tried unsuccessfully to free himself. He leaned against the bars with his eyes closed.

"This's the end…," he whimpered. "I won't survive this again…"

A sudden flash caught Neer's eyes as Avelloch's swords flipped quickly through the air toward the knights. She held her breath as the weapons moved through their backs and landed in a field ahead. Her eyes fell to the ground in despair while Avelloch grimaced with anger.

"This is a memory," Neer stated shakily. "Loryk told me about it long ago… It happened when he was taken by the Order for singing ballads that denounced the Divines…"

"What happened in the memory?" Avelloch asked.

Her face paled as the harrowing realization entered her mind. She gazed at Loryk with wide eyes, the reality of his fate sinking in.

"They're going to behead him."

Chapter Thirty-Five

Reflections of Pain

Neer and Avelloch followed the cart into the village of Rhys, a mining town in the foothills of the Whispering Mountains and the home of Loryk's family. Shabby cabins lined the pitiful, rocky road. Villagers, with large waistlines and auburn hair, threw rocks and shouted obscenities at him. As the cart came to a stop, Loryk fell over. He didn't fight as he was pulled from the carriage and dragged through the street. Blood spilled from his many cuts and gashes as he was pelted by the angry villagers.

"Traitor!"

"Blasphemer!"

"Blood of Nizotl!"

He kept his head down as he was knelt in front of a chopping block. Priest Ealdir, of Ravinshire, stood over him with undisturbed smugness in his eyes.

"Children of the Six...," the young priest started as he turned to the crowd, "we are here under the great mercy of the Divines to bring forth this traitor for his blasphemous and arrogant ways!"

Loryk kept his head down as the people shouted and hissed at him. His shoulders shook as tears slid down his face and dripped off his chin. A large man broke through the angry crowd, bounding closer until standing over the weeping bard. Loryk never lifted his eyes. The stranger's wavy hair bounced across his shoulders, as did his large stomach over his belt. He glared down at Loryk with condemning eyes. Red-faced and furious, a deep hock rumbled in his throat before he spat on Loryk's face.

Neer leapt forward with a great cry. Her fist swung through the man's face yet never touched his skin.

The man pointed a chubby finger through Neer at the bard. "You're no son of mine!" he said with a growl.

Neer's expression fell as she turned to Loryk. His nose was red, and his eyes were swollen from heavy tears.

The priest lifted his arms while praising the Divines, and the villagers watched with merciless conviction as Loryk was shoved forward and pressed against the cutting block. His chin shook as tears slid down his face. An executioner stepped forward and placed the sharp end of his axe on Loryk's neck.

"I remember this...," Neer said as Avelloch came to her side. Her eyes darted from one place to the next. "The Brotherhood comes... They save him..."

The priest shouted a prayer, and the villagers bowed on their knees. He spoke with great authority, asking the Divines to forgive this *poor man's soul*. Loryk shuddered and shook. Drool seeped from his quivering lips as he stared at the ground, whimpering.

"They'll save him...," Neer whispered. Her throat was tight, and her palms were moist with sweat. "They have to..." She peered through the village, staring at the homes and trees, hoping for their arrival.

A shadow moved over Loryk when the executioner raised his axe high into the air. His arms were thick, and his weapon held dark blood stains from his previous victims. Neer's heart throbbed in her chest. She couldn't touch him. He would need magic to defend himself, yet he had none. She turned her head, searching desperately for the Brotherhood who was meant to arrive. But they never came. Not a shadow or whisper approached from beyond the furious crowd that stood, waiting for Loryk's execution. Her heart stopped as she realized this memory was different. The fresh cuts and scrapes on his body were proof that this, for him, was real.

He was going to die.

She held her breath when sunlight reflected off the axe, and it swung for his neck.

Like a wave crashing against her, taking over her mind and willing her forward, she released a shriek and teleported forward. The axe struck downward, inching closer to Loryk's skin, when Neer grabbed him from behind and tackled him aside.

His body was warm against her skin as they rolled across the ground. She tightened her arms, fearful of letting him go. The axe sank into the block with a deep thud, and the village was deathly silent.

"What 'appened," Loryk cried as he pulled away from Neer's arms. "Where'd you go?"

Neer looked around in a panic as the world faded away in a puff of smoke.

"Neer!" Loryk remarked. "What's 'appenin'?"

Her lip quivered, and hot tears filled her eyes. She touched his face before pulling him into her arms. "We were here the entire time!" she explained through heavy tears. "You couldn't see us... I thought you were dead!"

Avelloch came to their side and touched her shoulder. "Everything is disappearing. We need to move," he said.

Neer wiped her eyes as she backed away. Her fingers grazed Loryk's cheek as she scanned his face. "Why didn't they come for you?" she asked. "They were supposed to save you."

"They did," he remarked. "When it really 'appened."

"The trials must know that you aren't magic," Neer said. "I have to use mine to save you." She gulped down her fear as she realized how close he had come to death. Worried over the remaining tests, she wondered if she had the strength to make it through what was to come.

As the smoke faded to nothingness, and they were surrounded by black, Neer held tighter to Loryk's hand, fearful of what's to come. The musty scent of the cave lingered in the air as they sat alone in pure darkness.

Seconds later, light filled the void as a dirt road, outlined in tall trees, was revealed through the void. The image stretched beneath them before coming to a sudden halt.

Neer touched the loose pebbles and dust. "It feels real," she said while swirling the dirt beneath her finger and thumb.

"What the 'ells is this place?" Loryk asked, his voice dripping with desperation and fear.

Avelloch took several timid steps in the direction of the path. "I think we need to follow it."

Neer said, "Maybe if we stay here, it'll—"

"We can't trick the trials," he interrupted. "Unless you have magic that can get us out of this, we *have* to finish."

Their eyes met, and she was stricken by the terror in his eyes. He didn't want to be there any more than she did. Neer slowly stood and gazed around at the emptiness surrounding the path. "Do you think we'll all have to experience memories like that?"

His jaw flexed, and his eyes hardened. With a stiff nod, he gave a silent answer. "Come on," he said. "Klaud shouldn't be too far ahead."

Neer wrapped her arm around Loryk's and followed Avelloch as he walked down the desolate path. Dust swirled beneath their feet as they traveled in silence.

"That was your father?" Neer asked. She had heard every story of Loryk's childhood and home. Some were happy. Most weren't. She had never met his family, and he vowed she never would, as he refused to return home after their betrayal.

Loryk nodded. "You know, 'e never liked me bein' no bard. Always said I was a disgrace from the start." He paused. "I always suspected it was 'im that called the Order."

"And the Brotherhood? How did they know to save you?"

"I was talkin' to Wallace one night. You know 'im—the big one who's always leadin' the charge against the Order."

Neer nodded. She knew of Wallace, though she had never spoken to him.

"Anyway," Loryk continued, "'e talked to me about joinin' the Brother'ood, and later that day, I was captured by the Order, just as you saw. 'E must've followed and 'ad 'is men rescue me."

Sadness weighed heavily on her heart now that she witnessed one of the most painful parts of his life. A realization struck her, and she inhaled sharply, her eyes widening with fear. The others turned to her, shocked by her sudden outburst. Before she could speak and explain to the others that these tests were meant to make them relive their most terrorizing memories, the world began to change.

The dirt road and blackness faded into a lush, thriving forest. Enormous trees, thick roots, and glowing plants surrounded them. The scent of wet leaves and fresh bark painted over the odor of damp rock. Avelloch glanced around before his eyes met with Neer's, and his jaw dropped in horror.

"No!" Neer gasped and reached for his hand. Her fingers swiped through his palm, and she stumbled forward through his body.

"*Kila...*," he sneered with anger. "This is Nyn'Dira," he said, speaking to Neer though he could no longer see her. He scanned the trees with suspicion. "I think—"

As he looked around, a dart shot him in the neck, and he fell to the ground with a gasp. Neer rushed to his side, trying desperately to yank the weapon from his skin. Avelloch's back arched, and his arms twitched as he struggled to move.

"What's goin' on?" Loryk asked. "Why's your 'and goin' through 'im like that?"

Avelloch sank into the grass, and his head fell aside as he stopped moving. Neer breathed heavily as she scanned over his body, overwhelmed with fear. "Shit!" she exclaimed. "I don't know what to do..." Her gaze shifted to his eyes before falling away. "Klaud can make things appear instantly in his hands... Maybe I can too!"

"No!" Loryk argued. "You can't go tryin' new things like that! Not 'ere!"

"I have to—"

Her attention moved to several figures who emerged from the trees. Loryk leapt back as half a dozen evae, with dark tattoos and bone necklaces, stepped through Neer and knelt beside Avelloch.

"No!" Neer cried while attempting to push them away. The strangers spoke a harsh and intimidating foreign language. "What are you doing?" she shouted. "Don't touch him!"

Loryk pulled her away as the strangers carried Avelloch through the forest. Neer fought Loryk away and stepped forward with her hands together. With a scream, she released a blast of energy that sent the strangers to their knees and caused them to drop Avelloch to the ground. She raced over, ready to help, but found her hands still moved through him.

"No!" she screamed. "Magic's supposed to work! It's supposed to help him!"

The strangers looked around in a daze until a man spoke authoritatively to them, and they quickly gathered Avelloch and marched away. As they moved quickly through the forest, Neer shook with anger and fear. She took another step forward and sent a second blast toward them. Trees were stripped of their leaves as powerful energy tore through the forest. The strangers flipped and rolled as they were hit.

"Neer!" Loryk pulled her back. "You're goin' to kill 'im!"

"They can't take him!"

"We've got to find another way!"

Four of the six strangers crawled to their feet, while the other two lay bleeding and injured. With angry snarls, they wiped the blood from their fresh wounds and stalked close with their weapons drawn. Neer was stiff as they approached her, their eyes still scanning the forest in confusion and fury. She held her breath as they stepped through her before sheathing their weapons and quickly carrying Avelloch away.

Neer and Loryk followed closely behind as they walked deeper into the forest. Long shadows swayed in the trees, and she timidly lifted her eyes to find dozens of bodies hanging above. Symbols were painted across their skin in blood and feces. Loryk quivered and gagged while Neer refocused on Avelloch, who remained limp in the arms of his captors.

Large flames danced atop torches, creating a pathway that led them to a clearing. Neer set her eyes to the four bodies that hung from large posts around the perimeter. Their arms were spread, and their ankles were bound. Dry blood streamed from their empty eye sockets and painted their opened backs where their ribs had been cut and pulled outward.

"What the 'ells is this?" Loryk remarked. "I've never seen anythin' so vicious."

Neer turned her attention to Avelloch as he was laid on his stomach against a large, slanted stone. His captors pulled his arms and shackled his wrists in chains that were embedded in the ground. Neer moved to his side as the others stepped away. Her fingers moved through his flesh, and she glanced at the mutilated bodies above. "Why are they doing this to you?" she asked. Turning to Avelloch, she fell back in horror at the sight of his fearful, open eyes.

He was conscious...

He was awake.

The captors backed away as a man stepped forward. He walked with great resolve as if he owned the world. Long dark hair hung to his mid-back, opposite the half-shaven heads of his companions. In fact, Neer realized he looked much different from them. His skin was much lighter, his bone structure wasn't as sharp, and he didn't hold the deep scowl that was permanently etched onto each of their angry, prideful faces. Their only resemblance, other than their primal clothing, were the black markings that covered their skin and faces. While his comrades were cloaked in dark symbols and drawings, this man had a single design along his left-side temple.

The man approached Avelloch from behind. Torchlight reflected against the sharp knife in his grasp. Avelloch's eyes closed tight as the blade sliced deep into his back, following the path of a thick scar along his spine. Blood drained across his back and covered the stone with a new layer of crimson.

"What do I do?" Neer cried while leaning closer to Avelloch. "Help me... please!" she begged, although he couldn't hear.

His face twisted as his skin was slowly carved from nape to waist. She turned to the man standing over him. His devilish grin sent waves of fury through her. Blood dripped down the handle of the knife as he passed it to his nearest companion and was given an axe.

She stood and lifted her arms toward the man who raised the axe above Avelloch's exposed spine. Her face was red with fury. The grass crunched beneath her feet as she stepped forward, and the man's eyes widened as her magic gripped his throat.

He lifted his gaze, and his bloodshot eyes stared at her in wonder. Fury coursed through her like a firestorm as they locked eyes. His resolve was unbreakable. Even in the face of death, he was unmoved. Unbothered by the magic crushing his throat.

Instead, the slightest hint of a smile tugged the edge of his lip. Neer's face twisted with rage. She unleashed a hellish scream and clenched her fists.

The man collapsed to the ground, unmoving. Blood streamed from his parted lips. Neer stared at him, her shoulders rising and falling with every hard breath. His body faded to smoke, and Neer turned as the others soon followed.

Stepping back, she looked at the four eyeless faces staring down at her. Their bodies were mutilated and covered in filth. To know Avelloch could have received the same fate, to know that he had truly been through this hell, sent her to her knees.

Avelloch grunted, and his deep laceration drained with thick blood. Neer scurried to his side and rubbed his face. His skin was warm beneath her touch. "Oh, Gods…," she cried. "You're okay…"

"Neer…," Loryk said, and she didn't have to look at him to know he urged her to heal Avelloch's back. She crawled to his side, and he flinched with a groan as she gently pressed her hands to his skin. Weak energy swirled through her, like dust wisping in the wind. She struggled to grasp at the threads of her magic as they pulled away, growing weaker with every desperate reach.

As the heat of her energy grew, she closed her eyes and forced her magic into him. Pain ripped through her as the fragmented energy tore and burned. She winced and groaned in agony as his deep injury fused beneath her grip.

"Neer!" Loryk ran to her side in a panic and pulled her away.

Sunken cheeks and pale skin replaced her once healthy appearance. Her breaths were shallow as she fought to keep her eyes open.

Avelloch slowly pushed himself from the stone. Blood stained his back where a thick, healing scar trailed along his spine. He sat on his knees, staring up at the hanging bodies as they turned to smoke. His hardened eyes fell away, and for a moment, he was still, gazing at the ground with a distant look.

Slowly, the forest vanished, and they were surrounded once again by complete darkness. "Divines…," Loryk whined. "When will this end?"

Avelloch inhaled a deep breath and winced at the pain in his back. He turned to Neer, watching as she fell limp in Loryk's arms. Sitting on his knees, he raked his fingers through his hair and peered through the darkness.

His eyes settled on a flickering light in the distance. Its waving pattern resembled a flame. He tapped Loryk's shoulder before pointing to the disturbance ahead.

Loryk huffed. "Let's just stay 'ere. Give 'er a bit of rest before we go runnin' into more trouble."

He gently laid her next to him and then dug through his bag. Searching through the contents of his stolen satchel, he collected a half-empty vial of potion and two helpings of bread and jerky. The stale bread crunched as he tore it in half and passed a piece to Avelloch. Before biting into his meal, he popped the cork of the potion and carefully poured it through Neer's lips.

With an exhausted huff, he sat next to her. His shoulders slumped forward as he ate his tasteless food.

"*Grenör toveii?*" Avelloch asked. Loryk gazed at him with curious eyes, and Avelloch pointed at Neer before turning his hand upward at his lips as if drinking.

"*Oh*," Loryk said, happy to understand his question. "Potion... erm..." He struggled to find the proper evaesh word and settled with one he could remember. "Strong. Good," he said before explaining in his common tongue, "Only got a bit left in another vial, but this should do 'er fine."

Avelloch nodded. "Will she *spira'veil?*" At Loryk's confusion, he explained. "Life. Live."

"Yeah. She lives."

Their conversation fell silent, and they turned away from one another. As Loryk took another bite of bread, his face twisted in disgust. "Food," he said in evaesh, before gagging.

Avelloch chuckled with a light smile. "I've had worse."

"Not I," Loryk stated.

Avelloch tore another piece of bread. "Your evaesh *ean'tretaas.*"

"What?"

He laughed. "Good. Better."

"Oh, yeah, um... biscuits?"

Avelloch shook his head. "*Tyluear*," he explained. "*Tyluaa* is food."

Loryk laughed. "Right. Well, *thanks*," he said, pronouncing the word correctly. "What're we goin' to do?" he asked in his native language. "I can't take much more of this. If Neer keeps fightin' this 'ard, we won't make it."

Noticing his distress, Avelloch glanced at Neer and said, "One left."

Loryk sighed with a nod. "Yeah. I 'ope she's up for it... She's been through a lot in 'er life. No tellin' what she'll have to relive." He paused with thought and then asked in evaesh, "You... cut... back?"

Avelloch pondered for a moment before touching his back and turning away. With a deep exhale, he closed his eyes and absent-mindedly rubbed the scar on his hand. "*Élet'atla*," he said, though Loryk couldn't understand every word. "It's a klaet'il death ritual to cleanse the soul. Only those who they feel have brought unredeemable shame to our people are condemned to such a fate..." He fell into a state of despair before scoffing and slightly shaking his head. Pulling his hand away from his scar, he sat straighter and stared at the orange glow in the distance. His voice was barely a whisper as he said, "If they only knew..."

Loryk finished his meal and smacked his hands clean. "We best see if she's feelin' better. She'll need some food before runnin' into hell." He reached for Neer's shoulder, and his breath caught in his throat as his fingers moved through her body.

He glanced at Avelloch with fearful, pleading eyes. His voice trembled as he explained, "She's already there."

Chapter Thirty-Six

Reflections of Regret

Neer slowly opened her eyes and was met with darkness. Cold, empty darkness. Fear jolted her awake, and she sat up to look around, scanning the void that surrounded her.

"Loryk?" she called. "Avelloch?"

Her heart pounded in her chest as she realized she was alone, and she worried if they had touched another rune while she slept, or if the trials had taken her someplace else. The moldy smell of the cave entered her nose, and she was reminded of the grueling tests they had to endure. Between each memory, the world would fade to black before transitioning into the next.

She swallowed the dry lump in her throat as she gazed through the emptiness, searching for anything that could lead her back to the others. Her eyes widened at the sight of an orange glow flickering in the distance. She stared at it for a while, paralyzed with fear. It was a memory she never wanted to relive. One that still haunted her dreams and filled her with dread.

"No...," she whimpered. "Please... anything but this..."

Hot tears swelled in her eyes as she stared at the fiery dome. She focused on her breathing, forcing herself to stay calm. There had to be another way out. A way to remove herself from the visions and escape to the caves. But with her limited abilities, she was afraid she couldn't do so.

"Loryk... Avelloch... if you're there... please don't leave me." She sniffed and exhaled a pained breath. "Don't let me die alone."

She closed her eyes and exhaled a deep breath, becoming lost in her misery. But there was no use in crying. No use in dwelling on the pain. It wouldn't keep her alive. That was the lesson Reiman had always taught her, to feed your emotions once you've survived.

Pushing herself to her feet, she wiped her eyes and gazed at the orange glow. The fear crept back in, and she forced it away. She wouldn't be stricken with terror and guilt. She had to survive, if for nothing else than to keep her friends alive. Her throat was tight as she stepped toward the glow.

Firelight and the odor of smoke filled the air as she approached her childhood village. Flames rose high into the air as they burned over cottages made of wood and stone. Bodies with scorched faces Neer could no longer recognize lay on the streets, blackened with burns. Horses screamed and kicked within burning stalls, adding to the chaos. The clash of weapons rang loud as people fought for their homes. Iron armor rattled and shifted as knights marched forward with greatswords and thick shields.

Podrick, the town baker, clipped a knight's chest piece with his shoddy iron axe. The knight swiftly kicked him in the stomach, and Podrick rolled across the street. As he lay on the ground, clutching his bleeding forehead, the knight stood over him with his sword drawn.

"What do you want?" Podrick cried. "What have we done to deserve this?"

Neer gasped as the sword was plunged into Podrick's chest with a loud crunch. Everything she had witnessed as a child was coming to life. Podrick's death, the destruction of her home, the steel swords spraying blood into the air like a cloud of red mist. She remembered every painful, heart-wrenching detail.

As the knight stepped away, Podrick lay on the ground. Firelight glistened against the blood pooling from his chest.

Neer dropped to her knees, unable to withstand the weight of what she caused. Staring at the bodies that lined the streets, she was incapacitated by grief. Tears carved trails down her soot-covered cheeks. She curled forward and clutched her head, wishing to be anywhere else.

"It isn't real…," she cried. "It's just an illusion… It isn't real…" Her face twisted when a woman cried out for her fallen child. "Please…," Neer sobbed. "I can't…"

"Vaeda…!" A woman's desperate scream broke through the barrage of noises, and Neer's breath caught in her throat. She lifted her head and glanced around, searching for the woman calling out to her.

"Unhand me, you bastard!" the woman demanded.

"Mother?" Neer crawled forward, scanning the streets from left to right. "Mother!"

Realizing her home was on the opposite side of town, Neer leapt to her feet and ran to her mother. Jetting down one familiar street after another, she came to the ashen porch of her childhood home. Her jaw dropped as she stared at the flames that danced along fallen beams and singed walls. Memories of her old life, a life she wished desperately could return, came flooding back. So many wonderful nights were spent cooking with her mother in the kitchen and reading by the hearth with her father.

She envisioned her younger self racing up the steps, giggling as her friends chased her. Her lip quivered as she became lost in the echoes of her past. Distant eyes peered at her crumbling home, and a faint smile tugged her lip as she pictured her old life.

When the walls shifted and spewed embers into the air, Neer blinked, and the visions disappeared. Her smile faded, and she examined her surroundings, realizing that she had been caught in a daydream of memories from a life that could never return. Her fate, and the fate of all those who were lost that day, was sealed. No amount of wishing or praying or fighting would ever bring them back.

Her eyes shifted to the home as it whined with another creak, and she gasped as the door opened, revealing a man lying inside. Burn marks covered his body and singed clothes.

"Father…," she said, her voice hollow with pain.

Two knights approached Neer from behind and grabbed her arms. She didn't fight as they pulled her to the High Priest. He lifted her chin and forced their gazes to meet. Looking into her eyes brought a sinister smile to his face. He nodded to his knights, and they escorted her away.

It was just as it had been when she was a child. When she was taken after the destruction of her home. The Order had ambushed the village in her pursuit. She was only eight years old at the time of her capture.

Only eight years old when she lost everything.

"Vaeda…" Her mother's voice reeled her back to reality, and Neer turned to her as she lay on the ground, crying. "Vaeda… don't let them change you…"

Neer was breathless as her mother clutched her bleeding stomach and then collapsed into the dirt. Her mother's eyes, which were once so full of joy and life, became forever closed. It was a sight Neer had never forgotten. Witnessing again the horrific extermination of her home left her devoid of emotion. Any thought of escape fizzled from her mind. She was empty, shredded. Although she was a child, she blamed herself for all that had happened, and she couldn't live with what she brought upon them. She couldn't forgive herself for allowing her family to be murdered.

"Take her to Skye," the High Priest instructed, just as he had done sixteen years prior. "We'll snuff out this demon and all that she's defiled."

As the knights dragged her away, Neer shifted her eyes to her mother when flames caught her dress, and the emotions that had left her suddenly returned in a vortex of madness and rage. She wouldn't be taken again. The Order wouldn't get away with what they've done.

She would kill them.

She would kill the High Priest.

She would end it all.

With a deep breath, she emitted a pulse of energy that flung her captors through the air. Nearby homes collapsed from the weight of her magic as the shockwave tore through the village.

The High Priest turned to her with hardened eyes. This wasn't how it played out before. Back then, she was a child, a mere bystander forced to suffer at the hands of their strength. Now, she stood face-to-face with the man responsible for all the sorrow that followed her throughout her life. All the aggression and guilt she carried came alive as she looked into his angry eyes.

"You did this!" Her voice cracked as she screamed, and the

fires burned hotter. "You caused all of this!"

Her fingers curled into tight fists as magic boiled inside her. As her anger festered, the energy escaped. The High Priest stumbled back as the ground began to crack. Nearby homes shifted and fell, spraying embers through the air. The High Priest regained his footing, and marched forward across the tremoring ground. He slashed his sword at her side. As it inched closer, she vanished and reappeared behind him with his sword in hand.

Her eyes were dark as she thrust the weapon through his back. He released a gurgled gasp as the weapon penetrated his chest. His body quivered before falling limp, and he faded into a puff of smoke.

As the weapon faded from her grip, Neer let out a raw, desperate scream and fell to her knees.

Ash drifted through the air as the familiar homes continued to burn. Her fingers curled into the soot-covered road as she leaned forward with sickness and sorrow. Tears spilled from her eyes, and her shoulders shook as she wept.

She glanced at her mother's body that lay on the side of the street nearby, blackened and burned. Neer choked back a sob and closed her eyes. "Help me...," she begged. "Someone please... find me..."

The heat of the flames vanished as the village faded into smoke, and the world darkened once again. Neer gasped when someone fell to her side, and she was pulled into their arms.

"It's okay, Neery," Loryk said with a sniff. "It's over... It's over..."

"Loryk...," she sobbed and wrapped her arms around his neck.

"You're all right, Neer." He rubbed her back before pulling away and passing her a canteen. "Drink this. Go on."

She took a sip of water before guzzling its contents. As it ran dry, she wiped her lips, smearing ash and soot across her face, and handed Loryk his canteen. Her gaze shifted to Avelloch as he knelt beside her.

"Are you okay?" he asked.

She nodded. "Yeah. That was my home. The Order came when I was a child... My parents... everyone I knew... they're all gone because of me. Because of who I am."

Avelloch sighed with despair. He opened his lips to speak and was interrupted by rain that slowly dripped from above. The smell of grass and trees filled the air as a lush forest appeared around them. Avelloch looked around in a daze as he examined their surroundings.

"What?" Neer asked, fear rising in her throat as they were thrown into another vision.

Loryk groaned. "Not again!"

Avelloch stood and stepped forward. His eyes narrowed as he peered through the dark forest. "This is Navarre…," he said. "It's my home."

Loryk wiped the rain from his eyes and looked at the glowing plants, large shrubs, and wide trees that surrounded them. "What're we doin' 'ere? You've already passed your test…"

Avelloch paid him no attention, unable to comprehend Loryk's spoken language. He stepped through the beautiful forest, forcing the others to follow. Walking carefully through the thick brush, firelight appeared through a window ahead. The small cottage was within a clearing surrounded by wildflowers and gardens. A wooden bridge with railings rested over a wide, slow-moving stream. To the left of the clearing was a covered well, and to the right was a round stone platform surrounded by flowers.

The bridge creaked as they passed over the stream and approached the quiet home. Through the window were several people huddled together, speaking softly to one another. Avelloch's face went pale, and he took a step back.

"Avelloch?" Loryk asked, but he was silent as he stared wide-eyed into the home. "What is this? Where are we?"

Evaesh whispers came from inside the home. They spoke of the woman lying asleep on the bed.

"Will she make it?" a man asked.

Another sighed. "No… the curse is irreversible. There is nothing we can do…"

"What're they sayin'?" Loryk carefully asked.

Avelloch turned when Neer took his arm. Their gazes met, and he quickly looked away.

"This is your sister?" she asked. With closed eyes, Avelloch nodded. "Why are we here? What kind of test can this be?"

Avelloch's face tightened, and with a quick sniff, he composed himself. Stepping closer to the home, he looked at the faces surrounding the sleeping woman. The hardness of his eyes faded as his jaw dropped, and he turned around, looking quickly through the forest.

"What is it?" Neer asked, panicked by his outburst.

"This isn't my memory…," he started while peering through the trees. "It's Klaud's."

Chapter Thirty-Seven

Reflections of Misery

Neer stood behind Avelloch, watching as he raked his fingers through his hair. "This is Klaud's memory?" she asked. "How do you know?"

"We're forced to survive the worst moments of our lives. First was Loryk, when he was sentenced to death... then my execution... and your home being burned." Their eyes met. "This was the night we were told she wouldn't survive... the night we all thought everything was lost."

Her heart dropped as she realized what was happening. Returning her attention to the home, she gazed at the woman on the bed. The people inside wept as they spoke of her loss, calling it a *great tragedy*.

Avelloch seethed. His arms hardened, and his fists were tight as he peered through the trees. "Klaud has to be nearby," he said. "We have to find him."

Neer glanced around, worried they might never track him down without a trail or trace of his whereabouts. "All of our memories had some kind of fight or altercation. Did he go somewhere that night?"

Neer and Loryk were silent as Avelloch stiffened. "I don't know," he said while staring at the ground. "I wasn't there."

Neer's jaw dropped. She ignored Loryk as he asked her to translate and instead stepped to Avelloch's side. He was motionless in his grief. Redness overtook his eyes as tears threatened to fall. When she touched his shoulder, he sniffed and turned away. He quickly rubbed his eyes and shook his head.

"Hey," Neer started, but Avelloch raised his hand to stop her.

"Come on," he said with forced resolve. "We need to find him."

She regretfully turned away and looked through the forest. "You know this place?"

"Yes. His home isn't far from here."

"Do you think that's where he'll be?"

He was silent for a moment, contemplating where Klaud could be, and then shook his head. "No."

Without further explanation, Avelloch turned to the left and raced into the forest. Neer and Loryk followed close behind, struggling to keep up with his fast pace.

"D'you think we'll find 'im?" Loryk asked as he ran alongside Neer.

"I don't know."

"'E must've been 'ere for a while. 'E's days ahead of us, yeah? What's 'e still doin' in these caves?"

Her eyes flashed to Avelloch as fear sank in her chest and tied her stomach in knots.

"Klaud…!" Avelloch's voice was loud as he shouted with desperation.

The dense forest became sparse and covered in moss. They leapt over fallen logs and winding streams.

"Avelloch!" Neer called. "Wait!"

He climbed skillfully over the moist timber and further up a tall hillside, leaving the others behind. As he reached the top, he stood alone and placed his hands on his hips. The rumbling sound of a waterfall grew louder as Neer and Loryk came to his side at the edge of a small lake. A light breeze rose from the narrow waterfall cascading down jagged rocks and crashing into the water below.

Neer panted with exhaustion. "What is this place?" she asked, wiping the sweat from her brow.

The forest was empty and calm, with not a trace of civilization in sight. Avelloch looked around and followed an overgrown trail around the edge of the water. The others quietly trailed behind as he came to the rocky hillside holding the falls.

With another glance around, his eyes widened, and he sprang forward. "Klaud!" he exclaimed.

He rushed to the hillside and crouched beside a figure slouched against the wall. His hands moved through Klaud when he attempted to shake his shoulders. "Klaud!" he shouted in a raw and desperate voice. "Klaud!"

Neer stepped closer, unable to believe they had found him. His lips were parted, and his open eyes held no life. In his hand was a vial with the remnants of a black potion inside. Neer attempted to grab it, but her hands moved through it with no resistance. She knelt and closed her eyes. Breathing deeply, she focused on her energy and raised her hand toward Klaud. Tingling magic pricked through her as energy swelled inside. Her skin was flustered with heat and glistened with sweat as she concentrated on the empty vial.

Her lungs ached as raw energy scorched through her. With a wince, she pushed through the agony. Tendrils of unseen magic wove through the air, connecting with the vial and entwining their energies. She felt the coolness of its glass and could sense the potion's moisture on her skin, when suddenly, it was in her grasp.

She gasped when smooth glass rested beneath her fingers. Through tired lungs, she took several deep breaths and passed the vial to Avelloch.

"What is this?" she asked, though Avelloch didn't hear as his fingers clutched the bottle. His bloodshot eyes fixed on Klaud. "Avelloch!"

As a tear fell from his open eyes, he dropped the vial to the ground and covered his face. His shoulders shook as he struggled to contain his emotions.

"What is this?" she cried. "Avelloch!"

He didn't respond, losing himself in his misery. Neer focused on Klaud and noticed his parted lips were dripping with the same potion in the vial. She placed her hands on his chest. Her fingers dipped through him as magic swirled around her palms. Energy gathered in her chest. It burned and ached as it moved through her arms and into her hands. She grunted and wheezed as she gave her life force to save him.

"Come… on…," she grunted before pushing more energy into him. Color slowly washed from her sinking and cracked skin. Light extended from her palms and grew like branches throughout his body, reaching from his chest into his fingers, toes, and head. His chest puffed as he took a slow breath, and his eyes slowly fluttered open. Avelloch yanked Neer back as her body shriveled and shook.

"Neer…," he called.

Loryk pulled her into his arms and shoved the end of a vial into her mouth. As it ran dry, he tossed it aside. "Come on, Neery. That's all we've got left."

She lightly nodded, and Loryk released a relieved sigh. "Divines… this better be over soon. All this for a damned cave?"

His attention moved to Klaud as he shuffled before pulling himself into a sitting position. He leaned forward and gripped his forehead with a groan.

"Avelloch?" Klaud asked weakly.

With heavy breaths, Avelloch clutched Klaud's shoulder and then pulled him into a tight embrace. His strong arms kept them close as he struggled to contain himself. He sniffed before backing away and tapping Klaud's shoulder. Klaud nodded with a half-hearted smile, and said, "It's about time you showed up."

Avelloch scoffed out a laugh and then turned away. His eyes shifted to Neer as she lay in Loryk's arms, motionless. Her eyes were hardly open as Klaud carefully took her hand and looked deep into her eyes. "Thank you," he said.

She weakly nodded and closed her eyes before collapsing into Loryk's arms. The others shared a glance and then turned as the forest slowly faded back into a dark, forbidding cave. Enormous stone walls created a labyrinth around them. Pale blue light lingered above and faded into bright orange as it drifted into the distance.

"Where are we?" Avelloch asked as he stood. He clutched his weapons, the purple veins on his swords glowing brightly against the darkness.

Klaud touched the cold stone wall. "Back in the cave."

"What can we do? She won't survive another attack."

Loryk carefully laid Neer onto the ground and stepped away. He treaded carefully to the end of the hall, focused on the pale glow above. Turning from side to side, he studied the transition of its color and then waved the others over. He pointed above and struggled to speak their language. "Prophecy!" he said in his native tongue. *"Pale moonlight leads into the fray.* We 'ave to make it to the orange light!"

Avelloch and Klaud shared a perplexed glance. Frustrated, Loryk stomped to Neer's side and struggled to lift her into his arms. Avelloch casually approached his side and touched his shoulder. "Carry," Avelloch said in evaesh.

Loryk nodded before stepping aside. "Blue light," he said in broken evaesh. "Bad."

Avelloch lifted Neer from the ground and looked at Loryk in confusion. Loryk turned away with a disgruntled huff.

"Trust me," he said. Their eyes met, and Avelloch subtly nodded in agreement. Loryk took one last glance at Neer before marching to the end of the hall and leading them in the direction of the orange light.

The orange glow lingered in the distance as they trekked endlessly toward its luminance. Their bodies ached after walking for hours through the shadows of the enormous maze. Skeletons lay scattered through the many halls, their ancient armor and weapons rotting alongside them. The group came to a stop as Loryk stood at the intersection of three halls. He gazed above and was disheartened to find the light was still pale blue.

"We've been walkin' for hours," he griped. "'Ow aren't we any closer?"

Avelloch sighed before stepping into a shadow at the base of a wall and setting Neer onto the floor. She lay motionless with her eyes closed, though her coloring had slowly returned.

"Come," Klaud said to Loryk. "We'll rest here."

Loryk started to argue, but as his eyes fixed on Neer, he decided against it. He moved to her side and then touched her face. "She's gettin' better," he said. Realizing he'd spoken in his native language, he turned to Avelloch and explained, "Good. Better."

Avelloch nodded in response before leaning against the

opposite wall and closing his eyes. Klaud knelt in the center of the group and created a barrier with his last bit of potion.

He then got comfortable beside Avelloch and smacked his hands clean.

"I needed you," Klaud said. "We could have made it through this together."

Avelloch snarled with disgust. "We weren't together because of *your* actions, not mine. She would've died saving you—even after you left her behind. We nearly died countless times because you weren't there."

Klaud's hardened look faded to one of sadness. "You're right… I never meant to forgo my morality, but you know how much we need Azae'l. If she dies, this world will fall to ruins." He paused. "Arguing over it is futile. We're together now. The end should be near."

Avelloch scoffed. "Was that your philosophy when *Azae'l* decided to throw her life away? You were there when she took the vow! You could've talked her out of it!"

"You don't think I tried?"

"No," Avelloch hissed with a vicious growl. His dark eyes glared into Klaud's. "I think your devotion to her has clouded your judgment. It's made you cynical and heartless."

"And yours hasn't? You chose a *human* over me. Over your own sister!"

Avelloch scoffed. "I've *never* turned my back on those who needed me. *You* were the one who ran—not me."

"Because Azae'l needs us more than she does! Don't you understand that?"

"I understand that you'd just as easily turn your back on *me* if it meant fulfilling what you believe is fate."

Klaud stiffened, though not with anger, but remorse. Slowly, he turned away, staring at the ground in his sorrow. "I'm this way because I *have* to be. *Someone* has to be. You can play the vigilante and take revenge on those who have already caused harm, or you can sacrifice your honor and stop it from happening in the first place." His eyes met with Avelloch's as he said, "I choose to stop it."

Avelloch turned away with a growl. He rubbed the back of

CURSE OF THE FALLEN

his neck in frustration. His jaw flexed, and his eyes were hard as he asked, "That memory. Was it true? Did you really try to... Were you going to end your life?"

Klaud turned away. "It was the night they told us she wouldn't make it... I went out to be alone. You know what will happen if we lose her, Avelloch. There is no hope. There is nothing without her. It's the reason I am the way that I am now. It isn't my devotion or clouded judgment... It's truth. We *need* her. The world *needs* her."

Avelloch pinched the bridge of his nose. "So, you decided to opt out? Just end it without a word to me or anyone else?"

"No. I just thought..." His words faded as he struggled to speak. "The pain of losing her was too much. I spent my life protecting her. Loving her. I couldn't watch her die... but I never went through with it. I couldn't. This place... it wouldn't allow me to stop myself. It forced me to."

Avelloch turned away bitterly. Disgust and anger pulled his face into a scowl. He stared upward, fighting against his tears.

"I'm sorry, brenavae," Klaud stated.

He exhaled a pained breath. "I've always regretted not being there. Had I the choice, you know I would've been by her side." He paused and wiped his face onto his dirty sleeve. "I can't lose you both. When this is over, just remember that."

Klaud nodded. "This place... It's far worse than I imagined."

"There are worse things than illusions and monsters."

Klaud's eyes grew distant, "You're right. This is only the beginning."

Avelloch nodded.

Klaud stammered on his words and shuffled before asking, "You don't think *she* has anything to do with this, do you?"

Avelloch turned to him with wide, furious eyes. He glanced at Neer before turning away. Klaud studied his expression, noticing that his anger was disturbed with confusion and guilt.

Avelloch never answered, and as the conversation ended, silence filled the lonesome corridors. As the others slowly fell into a restless sleep, Avelloch remained awake, staring deep into the darkness that surrounded them. His eyes fixed on Neer, who lay unconscious across from him. Time had replenished her strength, and she looked healthier now that the fullness of her face had returned.

His face twisted with sadness as he considered what Klaud asked. Firelight danced across his skin as his gaze shifted to the flames.

The sound of creaking bones and clicking tongues broke the silence, and he carefully gripped his swords as his eyes darted throughout the cave, searching for the intruder.

The distant noise soon became clearer and was accompanied by loud echoes of quick moving footsteps. Avelloch smacked Klaud's leg before standing with his swords in hand. Klaud, slightly disoriented from sleep, quickly retrieved his weapon and stood by Avelloch's side.

"They're everywhere!" Avelloch whispered harshly as the hissing and scratches overlapped throughout the corridors.

"We can't sit here and wait for an ambush," Klaud warned. "We need to move."

They turned around when a thunderous quake shook the walls. Loryk was jolted from his slumber, while Neer lay motionless on the floor. He looked around in a panic before shaking her shoulders.

"Neer!" he quietly hissed.

She struggled to open her eyes, and with an exhausted sigh, she pushed herself up on weak arms.

"Come on, Neer!" Loryk shoved her sword into her hands.

"What's happening?" she asked groggily. "Where are we?"

"We're still in the caves! Somethin's comin'!"

"What?"

Another powerful jolt caused Loryk to tumble aside. He crawled to his feet, while Neer struggled to stay alert.

The overlapping footsteps grew louder as they closed in. Loryk stepped back and tripped over a pile of old bones, causing a loud clack that echoed through the corridors. He froze as the cave fell deathly still, and not a footstep or click moved through the cold, dark air.

Klaud gripped his weapon while Avelloch stood before Neer. Chills moved down their arm, and they were paralyzed with fear.

Suddenly, chaos erupted when hundreds of footsteps raced

through the labyrinth. Overlapping growls and the sound of clawed feet came from every direction at once. Loryk stepped back when several dozen glowing-eyed centry rushed through the hall.

Klaud spun his weapon and plunged it through the barrier. Cold air crept over them as the transparent shelter disappeared, and Klaud teleported through the horde. Several creatures fell as he moved invisibly through the centry. He reappeared several yards from the group, and with a hard grunt, he struck his spear through the stomach of an oncoming centry and then threw it at a creature racing toward him. As it sank into its victim, the weapon vanished and reappeared back in Klaud's grasp. Without missing a stride, he swung it through the stomach of another centry. Intestines tore from its body as blood rained over its companions.

As Klaud focused on a creature ahead, another leapt at him from behind. Its long fingers reached for his back before a dagger was thrown in its direction and sank deep into its spine. The creature fell with a shriek, and Avelloch rushed to Klaud's side. They stood with their backs together. With his eyes ahead, Avelloch reached back and collected the dagger that Klaud silently apported from the centry at their feet.

"Kila!" Avelloch hissed. "There are too many."

"Don't tell me the great *Zaeril* can't handle a few centry," Klaud quipped.

Avelloch huffed in disapproval, and Klaud shook with a breathless laugh. As more centry approached, the duo fought them off back-to-back. Avelloch slashed his swords through several centry, then quickly ducked as Klaud spun his staff in a wide circle.

Neer stood and hugged the wall with Loryk. While he jabbed his dagger through the stomach of a nearby centry, Neer gathered what little energy she had and released a pulse. The creatures growled and hissed as they flipped backward across the ground. Loryk quickly caught Neer when she stumbled back from exhaustion.

"Oi!" he shouted to the evae. Klaud glanced at them, and his eyes set on Neer, who was struggling to remain conscious.

A thunderous footstep quaked the ground behind, and Loryk turned to face a giant beast that stood at the end of the hall. The large creature, with razor-sharp talons, a short beak, and scrawny, winged arms, stared down at him with solid black eyes. Matted feathers grew outward from its face and across his boney, slouched body. Its limbs resembled more of a man than bird as it stalked forward on all fours. Loryk leapt back as the creature turned upward and released a powerful, metallic-sounding scream.

Klaud and Avelloch held their positions as the centry fled back into the labyrinth, retreating in fear from the monster ahead. When the large creature lifted its arm high into the air and swung at Neer, Avelloch rushed forward. She was slouched over, unable to react as its razor-sharp talons swiped closer. Avelloch tackled her aside, and the creature slashed through the empty air as they rolled across the ground, evading the fatal attack.

Klaud appeared in front of the creature and struck his spear through its chest. Black blood, like tar, spilled from its body. The cave vibrated as it reeled back with a booming shriek. Klaud teleported onto its back and lifted his spear, ready to strike through the back of its neck, when it grabbed his leg and tossed him aside.

He was flung through the air before landing hard atop the ground and rolling down the hall. Avelloch leapt forward, and the giant creature slammed its fist into the ground before him. He fell back as the stone cracked beneath the powerful hit. With a vicious snarl, Avelloch ran up its arm, swung himself around its back, and slashed its eyes. As the creature shook and fought, Avelloch dropped one of his swords and clutched the creature's feathers to steady himself.

A shadow moved overhead, and Avelloch turned while slashing his blade. His sword sliced deep into the beast's winged arm, and it thrashed in anger, attempting to fling him aside. Blood poured from its body as it stomped its feet, creating tremors that shook the cave. Avelloch dropped his sword as he clutched the creature with both hands, fighting to stay upright as his body was swung from side to side.

Neer glanced through the cave, unable to find Loryk in the shadows, and noticed that Klaud was still laying on the ground nearby.

She turned to the screaming beast as it fought to remove Avelloch from its back. Her eyes shifted to the ground where purple light emanated from his sword. Racing forward, she ducked beneath the angry swipe of its talons, grabbed the sword, and teleported above the beast's head.

She fell from the air and struck the sword downward through the base of its skull. The ear-shattering screams and thunderous stomps fell silent as the creature collapsed to the ground. Dust plumed into the air when the cave rattled and quaked.

Avelloch released his grip and tumbled to the ground with a groan. He crawled onto his knees and gripped his ribs. Neer climbed down and peered through the corridors, panicking as her fear set in. She stumbled forward, still weak from using her magic.

"Where is Loryk?" she asked. Avelloch exhaled several hard breaths before glancing around. His eyes set on a slumped figure across the hall, and Neer fearfully followed his gaze. A breathless gasp escaped her tired lungs when she spotted Loryk lying against the wall. A trail of blood dripped from his head and trailed down the stone. "No!" she exclaimed.

She rushed to his side and touched his face. Her heart stopped when she noticed blood dripping from his ears.

"Loryk?" Her hollow voice soon filled with panic. "Loryk!"

She tapped his face and called his name, pleading for him to wake. "Loryk!" Her cries echoed loudly through the dark halls. With her hands on his chest, she pushed magic into his body. She could feel his life slipping as his energy faded. "Come on! Come on!"

Though her lungs struggled to expand, and her heart shriveled, she continued fighting.

"Neer!" Avelloch pulled her back.

Her cheeks were sunken, and her eyes were ringed in dark circles. Her body had become frail, and her hair had lost its sheen as she pushed her life into him.

"We can't leave him!" she cried weakly. "He's all that I have…"

Avelloch looked at Loryk, who lay motionless against the

wall. They turned when a light scuffle echoed nearby. Avelloch stiffened as a shadow slowly rose from the ground, and Klaud's silhouette staggered forward.

Avelloch's shoulders fell as he released a deep sigh. Blood dripped across Klaud's face from a deep cut that sliced his forehead. He leaned against the wall with a groan and clutched his head.

"Come on," Avelloch said while standing and helping Neer to her feet. "Help her." He guided Neer to Klaud's side and draped her arm around his shoulders. "I've got Loryk. We need to go."

"Where?" Klaud asked, his voice raw with exhaustion and pain.

Avelloch carefully lifted Loryk from the ground. Curly hair painted his arm in red. "Nhamashel," he explained.

Neer stepped forward and stumbled to her knees with Klaud. He winced while pushing against the wall to lift them to their feet. As they regained their stance, he held tighter to her waist and followed closely behind Avelloch as they walked through the silent halls.

Chapter Thirty-Eight

Blood of the First

Klaud marked their path, allowing them to better navigate the long and desolate hallways. He scratched an X into the wall before exhaling a deep breath and regaining his strength. Neer's weight grew heavier around his shoulders as she struggled to stay conscious.

Orange light filtered through the halls the further they trekked, bringing with it a warmth that soothed their cold, damp skin. Avelloch turned to Neer, who walked slowly beside him, clinging to Klaud's shoulders. Her eyes, which were once so full of life and hope, had become listless and dull. Paleness blanketed her color and exposed the dark circles beneath her eyes. She hadn't spoken since their attack, and her sad eyes remained on Loryk as he lay unmoving in Avelloch's arms.

As they turned a corner, the orange light grew brighter, and the warm air tingled with magic. Avelloch squinted as he peered through the glow and then slowly stopped. He scanned the area to find several corridors were opened in a half-circle at the courtyard where they stood. Straight ahead was a curved wall with a towering doorway, glowing with swirled light that traveled its length.

"This is it," Klaud remarked. "Nhamashel."

Avelloch glanced at Neer and found her eyes were fixed on Loryk. He set his gaze on the bard before returning his attention to the door. "How do we get inside?"

"I don't know." Klaud released a pained groan. "I need to sit."

He walked with Neer to the wall, and together, they sat beneath the warm glow. Avelloch followed and placed Loryk on the ground next to Neer. She checked his pulse and pushed magic into his chest. Her energy was weak, and her body was frail, but she would do whatever it took to save him.

Avelloch pushed hard against the door and then stepped away. "It won't open," he explained while approaching Klaud's side. He stood with his hands on his hips and stared at the door.

"It could be an illusion," Klaud suggested.

Avelloch dug the glass eye from his pocket and examined his surroundings. The doorway and walls were unchanged, but the floor held glowing red symbols in the center of the courtyard. He stepped closer, still peering through the glass eye, and knelt on the ground. "Here," he remarked, "on the floor."

"What is it?" Klaud asked before pushing himself up with a grunt. He limped to Avelloch's side and took the glass eye. Staring at the ground, Klaud knelt and touched the ancient runes. "Can you read it?" he asked.

"No. This is ancient First Blood text. I don't understand many of these symbols."

Their eyes met, and they sadly turned to Neer, who was tapping Loryk's cheek. Her soft whimpers filled the silence as she begged him to wake.

Avelloch watched her sorrowfully before approaching her side and asking, "Neer? We could use your help."

A tear slid down her cheek as she touched Loryk's face. "He isn't going to make it...," she said.

Avelloch sighed with despair and pain. He touched her shoulder and passed the glass eye. "Maybe he will."

With a sniff, Neer took the glass eye and turned to the door, recognizing it instantly. "This was part of my vision in the cave...," she said in a dull and lifeless voice. Scanning the room, her eyes fell to the glowing inscription on the ground. Avelloch helped her stand, and she stepped to the ancient markings. He held her arm to keep her steady as she read the inscription aloud, "Enter this chamber if energy you seek... blood of the First holds the key."

She looked at Avelloch and then passed him the glass eye. He carefully took it and watched as she hobbled back to Loryk's side. Kneeling over him, she placed her hands on his chest, forcing what little energy she had into him, hoping to keep him alive.

"Blood of the First," Klaud said, pulling Avelloch's attention away from Neer and back to the inscription. "It could be literal."

"First blood... you think I can open the door?"

"Your blood opens the *ilitran*. It wouldn't hurt to try."

Avelloch released an exhausted huff. "You're saying that after all of this, a First Blood was needed to open the doors all along?"

"This *is* a First Blood test. It would make sense that they wouldn't allow others to enter their sacred chambers."

With a slight nod, Avelloch knelt above the rune and unsheathed his dagger. He cupped his hand around the blade and then slid the sharp steel across his skin. His face curled as he squeezed blood onto the stone, and the once invisible inscription glowed brightly beneath him. Rocks shifted along the wall behind, and he turned with his weapon drawn. The cave rumbled and creaked as the door slowly opened, surrounding them with purple moonlight.

Klaud stepped cautiously to the door and peeked inside. His shoulders relaxed as he gazed into the mysterious cavern. Turning back, he nodded to Avelloch and then stepped inside.

The soft glow brightened Avelloch's bruised and filthy skin as he gazed through the door with wide eyes. He turned around and stepped to Neer's side. Reaching for her hand, he pulled her to her feet before gathering Loryk in his arms. "Come on," he said.

Neer followed close behind as he stepped through the doorway and into the hidden chambers of Nhamashel.

She was surprised by the smell of fresh air and the glow of natural moonlight that greeted them inside. Tears swelled in her eyes as she stepped out of the harrowing tunnels and into the safety of the mystical cave. Narrow paths led through giant trees and thick brush. Colorful flowers and lush grass replaced the cold, grey stone.

Ducking beneath branches and teetering over logs, they followed the trail before coming to a lake. They stood at its bank and stared over the clear water glowing with the streams of light. A

Tree, illuminated with flowers, was perched on a small island in the center of the lake.

While Avelloch stared in wonder at the beauty around them, Neer's attention was set on Loryk as she lovingly tucked a curl behind his ear. "Come on, Lor…," she begged.

Grass crunched as Avelloch stepped away from the water and carefully sat Loryk against a tree. Neer was quick to his side, pushing her energy into his chest. Avelloch slowly stepped away and stood at the water's edge with Klaud.

"This is it…," Klaud said. "The last ingredient needed for Azae'l's potion is on that island."

Avelloch asked, "Do you think the legends are true? Can this place really heal them?"

Klaud tensed for a moment. His head dropped slightly before his gaze met with Avelloch's. "It has to."

Avelloch glanced back to Neer as she spoke softly to Loryk.

"He won't make it," Avelloch whispered. "It's been hours since the attack, and he hasn't opened his eyes."

Klaud said, "The water should heal him. We need to get him to the island."

Avelloch agreed, and together, they moved to Neer's side. She didn't notice their approach as she touched Loryk's face.

"Loryk," she whispered, and his eyes opened slightly. "Hey!" A tear fell from her eye.

"Neer…"

"Hey… look at me. I'll help you, all right? We're going home."

His head fell to the side, and his eyes closed once more. With her hands on his chest, she forced her energy into him.

"Neer." Avelloch touched her arm. "You aren't strong enough."

Her skin was pale, and her cheeks were sunken. Tears spilled down her face as she looked at Loryk. She carefully touched his cheek and closed her eyes.

"Come on," Avelloch spoke softly, "we can help him."

Her chin curled and her face twisted as she fought to withhold her grief. "Avelloch…," she whimpered, begging for someone, anyone, to take away her pain. She couldn't lose him. He was good. Too good to deserve such a fate. She should've told him to stay behind. She should've told him not to enter these trials, but she allowed it anyway, and now he could die. The only person in the world she loved could be taken from her. The last piece of her home and family. Her heart was empty, and her soul was torn.

She couldn't lose him.

Avelloch's expression fell as she cried, and he carefully pulled her into his arms.

"Let's get him across the lake," he said. "The water may have the energy to heal him."

"It's my fault...," she cried. "I let him come here. I knew it was too dangerous... I'll never forgive myself."

He pulled away and tenderly wiped a tear from her cheek. "Let's just get him across the lake. The waters could save him."

She sniffed and turned to Loryk. Her fingers slid down his face as she imagined a life without him. In all the hell she had endured, he was always there to help her. To give her a reason to keep going. He gave her a family and purpose when she had none. He saved her from a life of damnation and cruelty.

"Come on, Neer." Avelloch's voice was kind as he gently took Loryk in his arms and brought him to the shore. Klaud touched Avelloch's shoulder and then vanished. He reappeared in the water and then vanished once again. The soft ripples flowed across its crest as he appeared beneath the Tree and began working on his potion.

Avelloch stepped into the lake with Neer. The tingling water turned black as they moved further into the depths. Bleeding wounds fused across their skin as the blood and dirt slowly washed from their bodies.

"It's healing us." Excitement rang in Neer's broken voice. She glanced at Loryk, and her heart dropped. The bleeding cuts and dark bruises across his skin weren't healing. The water around him didn't turn black. "It isn't working! Why isn't it working?"

Avelloch dipped him further into the water, leaving just his face above the surface. Still, there was no blackness in the water. His wounds did not heal.

His eyes never opened.

Neer sputtered and shook as tears fell from her eyes. She forced herself to swim, though she had no care to do so. Nothing mattered. She was hollow, empty. Everything she had was taken. She was now entirely alone.

As they approached the island, Avelloch crawled onto the shore and walked across the grass. Water dripped from his clothes and skin as he made his way onto the island and placed Loryk beneath the Tree. Klaud paid them no mind as he focused his attention on mixing ingredients in a mortar. Moonlight shone from large cracks in the ceiling and sparkled across the beautiful, grassy island.

"This is a Tree…," Neer said while touching its bark. "It can heal him…"

"No," Avelloch said through a pained, forced voice, "his injuries are too severe…"

Neer touched Loryk's face, which had grown paler. Slow, shallow breaths entered his lungs. She carefully dug the arun from the fastened pocket on his tunic. Her fingers ran across the cloth-wrapped box as tears filled her eyes. "I should've just lived without my magic…," she sobbed. "I should've stopped him from coming along. I knew it was too dangerous. This is my fault. I don't want this anymore." She dropped the arun, and it tumbled into the grass as she wept into her hands.

Avelloch placed the arun back into her hands and curled her fingers around it. "He wants this for you."

"No, he doesn't. He tried talking me out of it!"

"He wants you to have peace." Their eyes met. "You have a chance to make a difference."

Her eyes moved to Loryk, who was motionless and quiet beneath the tree. It wasn't like him to be so quiet. She shook her head, and carefully gripped his hand. "I'm going to save you," she promised. "Don't die on me, okay? Please… I can't do this without you." Her voice faded into quiet sobs. "I love you, Loryk. Please… just hold on a little longer."

Through uneven breaths, she leaned forward and softly kissed his forehead. He didn't react to her touch. Her lips lingered on his skin before she slowly backed away.

With a sniff, she looked around and set her gaze on a white glowing stream. The water moved from beneath the tree and emptied into the lake. Klaud was nearby at the water's edge, focused on his task. Neer clutched the arun tight in her hands, forced herself to stand, and then stepped to the stream. She knelt by the water and dipped the arun beneath its surface. Closing her eyes, she focused on her energy as it swirled through her.

If she was to use the energy of the arun for anything, it would be to save him. She could live with the curse. She could live with running and hiding. But she couldn't live without him. He was the only person who had shown her the true meaning of family and love.

As she concentrated on her energy, she felt comfort in knowing his ailments would soon be healed. With the magic of the arun coursing through her, she would be able to heal him back to perfect health.

Moonlight brightened around her as she recited the incantation inscribed along the arun. A tear slid down her cheek as she opened the box. Avelloch stood behind her, and Klaud was broken of his concentration as bright light emerged from the arun and a ball of energy lifted from inside. Neer's eyes were focused on the orb as it rose into the air and then gravitated to her chest. Warm, tingling energy swirled like a vortex within her. Sweat blanketed her skin with its damp embrace as her magic melded with the energy of the arun. She closed her eyes, feeling its stinging warmth move closer, filling her strength and power.

As it floated closer, just inches from her skin, the warmth was suddenly stripped away. A cold hand pushed her aside, and she rolled into the stream with a great splash. Bitter cold filled her body, and the unexpected detachment from such strong energy left her weak and immobile. As Avelloch rushed to pull her from the water, Klaud quickly concealed the energy back into the arun and shoved the box into his pocket.

"What are you doing?" Avelloch hissed.

"We don't know if the potion will save her." Klaud tossed the vial to Neer as she was pulled from the water. He clutched the arun. "But this will."

Avelloch's mouth fell open, and rage clouded his eyes. "We can't take this from her!"

"The potion will rid her curse!"

"We don't know that!"

"It will, brenavae! They will both have what they need!"

Avelloch became still. His fists hardened, and his face grew stiff with anger and doubt.

Klaud said, "I know this is wrong. I know I shouldn't take this from her. But if we lose Azae'l, we lose everything!" He took Avelloch's shoulders. "You must understand. This is the only way."

While Avelloch seethed with confliction, Neer crawled to Loryk's side. As she approached, he opened his eyes with a slight gasp. He panicked, just for a moment, until their eyes met. She smiled at him. "Loryk?"

He looked around, breathing quickly. "Where are they? I can't find 'em!"

"Loryk?" she cried.

"I don't want to go!"

"You aren't going anywhere! Loryk?"

"No! I'm not ready... I can't..." His voice faded. A slow breath left his parted lips, and his eyes dulled. Neer touched his face. She grabbed his shoulders, screaming, shouting at him to wake. Tears fell from her eyes as she begged him to listen. Her hands pressed hard against his chest, and energy she didn't have was forced from her body. The magic was cold. Bitterly cold. Avelloch pulled her away as she grew frail and lifeless.

"You can't!" he warned. "You'll die!"

She weakly pushed him away. Staring at Loryk's body, wishing for him to take a breath, she was shrouded in grief. Her body trembled, and water shook atop the moistened grass. Thick veins swelled in her neck as her fingers dug into the soil. Her olive complexion flushed as heat radiated from deep within. Every breath was another reminder of all she had lost. All the pain, all the suffering. Fuck fate. Fuck the Divines. Fuck everything. She didn't need it. Years of torture had led to this moment. The lies and deceit, the anguish and resentment. The loss and loneliness. It would never fade.

Staring at Loryk, she was consumed with misery. A deep hell from which she could never return.

She had lost everything.

Her back straightened, and her head turned to the sky as a

shockwave of energy erupted from her body. Solid black eyes stared into the abyss. Winds swirled around her, wisping her hair and pulling the grass. Avelloch rolled across the ground. Klaud knelt to the dirt and clutched his spear as powerful magic pushed him back.

As Neer's magic strengthened, the cave tremored. Wet tears lifted from her cheeks. Water that once dripped from the ceiling was suspended in the air. Deep breaths entered her lungs while grass slowly died at her knees, replaced with ash and dry, cracked dirt. The stream dried up, and large rocks fell from above. Waves of grey energy pulled from the flora and funneled into her.

Klaud pulled a black crystal from his pocket and recited a chant, while Avelloch fought against the magic and crawled to Neer. Dark grey energy was pulled from his body and circled with the patterns that moved around her. He called out to her, but the deep tremors shaking the cave silenced his voice.

His skin shriveled, and his fingers turned black as he reached out to her. He was inches away, ready to take her hand and end her rage when Klaud grabbed him from behind, and they disappeared.

Consumed in fury and defeat, Neer pulled the life from everything. Water, air, and energy moved around her. Brown hair whipped across her face as her dark eyes stared above. She watched as rocks fell from cracked stone and crashed around her. Slowly, her gaze moved to Loryk. She looked into his lifeless eyes, and the madness faded. Water fell around her like rain. Hovering rocks crumbled and crashed into the lake. She touched his face and gently closed his eyes.

Her gaze moved to Klaud's vial at her knees. Water, swirling with light, rested inside. A tear slid down her cheek. She wanted to destroy it, to forget everything and end it all here. But she couldn't. Turning to Loryk, she was reminded of all that was taken from her: the family, comfort, safety, and home that had been destroyed. She couldn't turn back now. She must do this... for everyone she had lost. They wouldn't die in vain.

The Order would be destroyed. Those who had betrayed her would suffer.

She opened the vial and drank the potion. Her back straightened, and her arms fell aside as light was emitted from her eyes and mouth. In her trance, she was no longer present. The potion swirled within her, pulling the curse which bound her to the Order. Black particles rose from her lips as the curse was expelled from her body. As the last bit of magic left, the light instantly faded. She fell to her side, free from the restraints that held her soul. Free from the curse that haunted her every move. Pushing herself up, she observed her surroundings and found that Avelloch was gone. He left her here alone. No one was there to comfort her. No one was there to care.

The sorrow faded. Rage boiled deep inside, burning and festering within. Slowly, her eyes opened, and for a moment, black replaced the teal, consuming them in darkness.

the Forbidden Realms

Book two of the *Fallen Light* series
chapter preview

*May also be read as an epilogue

Chapter One

Blood and Steel

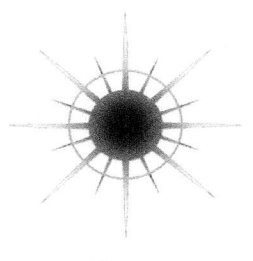

Nerana

Her life ended that day.

Six months passed, when she embarked upon the dangerous and forbidden Trials of Blood. Now, she walked alone, tired and hungry, as she made her way to the village of Rhys deep within the heart of Ravinshire. Clutched tightly in her arms was a worn leather notebook, the pages filled with scribbled stories and songs written by the friend she'd never see again.

Wolves howled in the distance, and the moons shone in the dark sky. Neer wrapped her arms tighter around the notebook, vowing to protect it before herself should trouble find her. Dried blood, blackened with age, stained the edges of the crinkled pages.

After Loryk's death, she spent weeks in the crypts beneath Porsdur. The old sconces were hardly enough to keep the moist hollows illuminated, but still she sat, speaking to his grave, and reading every word of his lengthy journal. Now, she walked through his home of Ravinshire, where she planned to gift his family, though undeserving, with his final thoughts and poems.

Neer didn't do this for them. She needed closure, a way to move past such a deep and dreadful end to what was once the most valuable friendship she ever had. She couldn't carry his writings forever, and she knew, despite their differences and beliefs, Loryk loved his family. For that, they should know the truth of his fate.

Dirt shuffled beneath her boots as she carried on down the desolate High Road. Tall yellow grass covered the empty fields surrounding the road in every direction. Heavy trails from wagons and carts rutted the packed dirt, though the sprawling road of Ravinshire didn't see much use. Each village was at least a day's walk from another, and since her entry into the region two weeks ago, she'd only passed by a handful of merchants, couriers, and bandits—none of which noticed the teal of her eyes as they walked by with pleasant smiles or attempted to steal her coin. She was lucky, for the Child of Skye was forbidden in all of Laeroth, and in a place such as Ravinshire, the Order would've been contacted immediately upon her recognition. So, she kept her eyes on the dust and pebbles at her feet as she walked through the night.

Hours passed before orange light slithered through the peaks of the Whispering Mountains and broke the heavy darkness. The endless wheat fields and creaking windmills faded into dense woods as Neer moved closer to the logging district.

She passed by a faded signpost, and the faint whine of rusted hinges caught her attention. Sun and rain had washed most of the chiseled letters away, but she could make them out enough to read Morinth. With a heavy, relieved sigh, she headed toward the small village.

Each step took her closer to civilization, and she breathed in the scent of fresh cut pine. A river, flowing through the foothills of the Whispering Mountains, carved through the thinning trees, its water lapping against the banks.

Tanning racks were set out along the streets, quickly changing the scent from fresh pine to hot leather. Doors creaked as residents ventured out of their homes. Their red hair and round waistlines were typical of Ravinshire natives. Deep wrinkles laid cracks across the faces of men far too young for such aging, their tired eyes and calloused hands proof of the hard labor they daily provided.

Neer focused on the road and wandered through the street as the villagers whispered of a stranger's arrival. Morinth was three weeks from the border of Llyne, far enough into Ravinshire territory that the possibility of a straggler walking through was near impossible. Whoever would come this far into the southern hold had reason, and the villagers weren't eager to welcome strangers.

"Six blessin's!*" a man greeted Neer with reserved disposition. Being from the South, where a man's hide is as thick as it is strong, it was clear he wasn't looking to extend an invitation. "Where's yer pa, girl?"

"He's ill," she lied. It was known that in Ravinshire women were lesser than men, and the residents had no trouble enforcing such beliefs. Had Neer explained she was traveling alone of her own volition, she would have been accused of sacrilege and publicly lashed. Even her clothes, which were tight trousers and a long-sleeve top, were considered too masculine of attire for the women of Ravinshire. Luckily, they didn't invoke such strict rules upon travelers, but she kept herself guarded all the same. "I'm to bring him wares from Dorthe.†"

"Dorthe, aye? Let's see what ya got there."

She sighed and turned to the sky. With a wince, she slung the bag from her shoulder and opened it for the man to see. He peered nosily into the white canvas, finding clothing, a small coin purse, and medicine. The man eyed her for a quick second and then backed away. His attention moved quickly to the weapon on her side, and he tensed.

"Women shouldn't be carryin' weapons. That an elvish blade you got? You know them're forbidden in Laeroth."

She stepped back, keeping her eyes on the ground to avoid him recognizing their color. "Yes. My father bought it off a merchant during first winter when he fell ill. Spent most of our coin on it, but he said it'd do me better than a human weapon if I'm to find myself in trouble on the road."

He eyed her suspiciously. "Well, you don't look like much

---

* A common greeting among the devout, though to Neer it's more a warning than welcome. The phrase refers to the six divines of the Order of Saro. Anyone faithful enough to speak such a harmless phrase is viewed as an enemy to our heroine, as they'd see nothing more than to put her head on a spike.

† A village in Ravinshire. Neer chose one at random. She had never been, and hoped it was still a working civilization to better suit her lie.

trouble. Keep that thing hidden, 'less ya want to be findin' yourself in the temple dungeons."

She nodded. "I'll keep that in mind."

The man grumbled while crossing his arms. "Well, the Mansker Inn is just up the road an' to the left. Be sure to ask Mariah for a bath. You could use one."

"Thank you." Her voice was unenthused. It had become her natural tone since she returned from Nhamashel. She performed the usual bow with her hands cupped together in front of her chest.[*] The man returned the gesture and then stepped aside.

The village had come to life within the minutes Neer had spoken to him. Chickens squawked and cows lowed while farmers tended to their daily chores. She kept her head down and made her way past the residents that walked the streets.

Upon entering the inn, she was greeted with the smell of freshly baked bread and strong mead. Her eyes averted to a man sitting by the hearth. The soft melodies of his drum mixed with the quiet conversations of the patrons. Mist filled her eyes, and she quickly wiped it away.

A young girl swept nearby, paying no mind to Neer as she carried out her duties.

The tinkling of chimes brightened the dull noises of the inn as a woman dressed in nothing but a thin skirt adorned with tiny silver bells sat across a man's lap. The innkeeper, with fiery hair and a red face to match, angrily swatted their table.

"Knock that off! This 'ere's a family place!" She nodded to the girl sweeping across the room.

The patron slowly stood and slipped into her top.

The innkeeper eyed Neer suspiciously while scrubbing a tankard with her dirty apron. "Need a room?"

Neer nodded silently, purposefully averting her eyes to better hide her identity. "And a bath."

The innkeeper turned to the sweeping girl. "Enid! Show our

---

[*] A common gesture of prayer, thanks, greeting, or goodbye used among the richly devout, though it seemed reserved for those of Ravinshire or anyone in the presence of a Priest. Neer never found herself using such a gesture as it was forbidden in her rebel hold of Llyne.

guest to the downstairs rooms."

The young girl went happily to Neer's side and took her hand, leading her down a narrow staircase behind the bar. They entered a small basement where deep wooden tubs sat behind long curtains. Barrels along the left wall dripped with liquid that left the place reeking of southern ale.

"You can stay 'ere." The girl opened the door to a small room. Inside was nothing but a bed and dresser. "Why're you so filthy?"

Neer glanced at her dirty garments. With a huff, she stepped into the room and sat on the flat feather mattress. "I like dirt," she said while removing her worn boots.

The girl stepped closer and touched the hilt of Neer's sword. Its glowing veins, which were hidden within the scabbard, had become dull and translucent since its time with Avelloch. "Where'd you get this?" Enid asked. "Looks real different."

"A friend."

"Women aren't supposed to be carryin' such weapons. You can get in big trouble, should the Order find out!"

Neer scoffed in offense, and then watched as the girl inspected the frayed hilt. "What's your name?"

"Enid."

"I used to be a kitchen wench too. When I was about your age."

"Really? Did you like it?"

"No. Not really."

Enid shook her head. "Me either. I want to be an adventurer, like you. I'll bet you've seen all kinds of stuff." She sat on the bed and twirled her fingers. "Ma says I'm not meant for such things. Said I'd best get used to cleanin' the inn."

Neer was silent as she fell into her memories—the long nights waiting tables and cleaning the grimy, sweat-stained sheets at the Sword and Sheath. How she wished she could go back and tell herself to take another path. To find a home and never let go of those she loved.

Her thoughts broke when Enid slowly stepped to the door, and Neer, though desperate to help her, was at a loss for words.

"I'll fetch you some hot water for that bath, Miss. For three bronze, we can clean your clothes."

"No thanks," Neer said.

The girl stood silently for a moment and then skipped away.

Neer closed the door and leaned onto the mattress. The road would've been comfier, and it was free, but she couldn't complain. At least the inn was safe, so long as no one suspected her of being the sorceress she was.

She sat atop the bed and pulled a weathered note from her boot, where she'd safely hidden it. It had been enchanted to withstand the elements and time, never to be destroyed or lost. Lying back, she unfolded the page. It was from Loryk's full adventure book. Of all the stories, poems, and ballads, this was the only journal entry. One she couldn't part with.

We're still in this bloody cave. Neer's unconscious from the rune, and I'm stuck in this house with ~~Avlock~~ ~~Evalork~~ ~~Avvahl~~ the blond one. He's okay enough. Seems to really care about Neer. He won't stop looking at her and making sure she's okay. I hope she's all right. Never been to no place like this…We may not make it out. If anyone's holding them back, it's me. I should've just stayed back home. I'm no fighter. I'm nothing, really. This place has been hell.

I don't know why I'm writing this. Feels foolish. But I guess I can feel it coming. The end, that is. We aren't all going to make it out of here, and if it's me that falls, I just hope that my stories can live on. I never had much in life, but I did have a family. The Brotherhood was always good to me, and I'll always be grateful.

Neer, if you're reading this and I'm gone, just know that I love you. Always have. You're my best friend. My family. You can do this, and you aren't alone. That evae over there cares about you. I can see it in his eyes. He's good, Neer. Plenty of people are. Don't go getting all cynical and crazy like before. Whatever happens, we'll always be together. You'll never be alone.

Go send the High Priest and all those blasted people of the Order to the farthest reaches of the deepest hell. I'll be waiting for them.

Guess this is it. I'm getting sleepy anyhow. Not sure how to end this thing right.

Farewell.

She wiped away her tears and scanned the page multiple times, though she didn't need to. The words were engraved in her mind. She had spent days in Nhamashel, waiting for her energy to strengthen enough for her to teleport back home with his body. After a reunion with Reiman and Gil, and a beautiful ceremony for Loryk where he was laid to rest in the crypts beneath the Tree of Porsdur, she set off on her journey to Ravinshire.

Her thoughts lifted when Enid lightly tapped the door with her knuckle and announced, "Your bath's ready, Miss."

Neer placed the folded note into her boot, undressed, and stepped out of the room. Chills covered her cold, aching body as she stepped into the tub, turning the water murky from her filth. She exhaled a deep breath, and her muscles relaxed.

Her eye quickly reopened when hard footsteps raced across the ceiling.

"Mariah!" a man exclaimed. "Have you heard?"

"What is it?" the innkeeper asked, seemingly unenthused by his outburst.

"Priest Ealdir[*] is here!"

"Truly?" She was more alert. "What could he want with a place like Morinth? We're naught but a logging village."

"Word has it, they've found a sorcerer nearby."

Neer's stomach dropped. She lifted from the water to listen closer.

"Sorcerer?" Mariah asked. "There ain't no sorcerer here."

"They got word of one living around here. Said a neighbor saw them creepin' around in the night, using their magic."

"That's enough, Roger. Fetch some water and clean the glasses. There'll be no more speak of such blasphemy."

Footsteps echoed away and then disappeared behind the creak of a heavy door. Neer slipped quickly into her clothes and gathered her things. Upstairs, she handed the innkeeper a silver coin.

The woman raised her brow. "You ain't stayin'?"

"Change of plans."

The innkeeper shoved the coin in her pocket, which Neer then apported back into her palm. She pulled up her hood and headed to the door. Outside, hundreds of soldiers sat atop their horses. They slowly stopped as residents gathered along the streets.

The innkeeper stepped outside with a mug still in hand. When

---

[*] Not to be mistaken for the High Priest, who is Neer's most formidable foe. Priest Ealdir is one of many Priests that reign over Laeroth..

the horses parted, a priest rode through the crowd. His silver cloak and golden robes revealed his position as a Priest of the Order.

Dark hair hung across his shoulders, and tan skin revealed his nationality of Llyne, where years ago he was forced out of his home when the Brotherhood took siege of the land. The people of Ravinshire, hearing of the treachery inflicted by the rebels, came together to construct him a new temple in their territory, where he now resided.

Neer watched him with a careful eye while everyone bowed on their knees. Dust swirled beneath his robes when he leapt from his steed. He walked down the street, and two knights, wearing thick plated armor with golden scapulars, followed close behind.

"Simon," the priest said in a smooth accent.

The smith stood and bowed. "Your Grace."

"I've received word that your village is harboring a sorcerer."

"I'm sorry, Priest Ealdir, but if there was such a person here, we would never—"

"I understand." Ealdir placed a hand on Simon's shoulder. The smith's large stature shifted under the priest's touch, and Ealdir turned with a subtle nod.

The knights unsheathed their weapons, and harsh light reflected off the newly-forged steel. It glinted in Neer's face, and she covered her eyes.

The smith faltered. "These're good people. We follow the teachin's and do naught a thing out of line!"

"Simon, friend, we aren't looking to shed the blood of the innocent. A demon walks among you. Do you want your children to be influenced by a sorcerer? One with a soul so twisted and foul that only the Divine Nizotl* himself could have created it?"

---

* Nizotl, the Divine of trickery and deceit, is one of the six Divines of the Circle of Six: a collective name given to the six divines of the Order of Saro.

Since the reign of High Priest Karlo, the predecessor of the current High Priest, Beinon, the Divine Nizotl has been viewed as the giver of magic and darkness. Any human born of magical blood is considered a demon of his creation and is therefore sentenced immediately to death.

There are many beliefs as to why Nizotl would gift a human with magical blood, the most widely accepted being his own desire for power and chaos.

Simon shook his head. Ealdir nodded in approval while his men scoured the town. Neer stepped back as they walked into the inn. The stillness of morning was quickly broken by the throwing of furniture and frightened screams.

"That's 'er!" a patron shouted. "It's the innkeeper!"

Knights rushed to the porch with their weapons drawn.

"What? No! You're mistaken!" she cried.

The butcher and smith rushed to her aid, but three knights quickly blocked their path.

"Please!" the smith begged. Tears carved clean trails down his red cheeks. "It isn't true! You've got the wrong person!"

"Simon!" the innkeeper called to the smith.

"This demon is your wife!" Ealdir said. "You know the penalty for such treason!"

Enid whimpered as she was dragged to their sides. The family cried and begged while the villagers stood by mutely. Some wept and covered their faces, while others wore satisfied expressions.

Ealdir stood before the smith and his family. "Six Divines of unity and peace," the priest started, "protect these souls as they're transferred into your realm from this life. Clean their spirits so they may once again be free."

Ealdir bowed to the family, who sniffled and begged at his feet. He drew back his weapon and struck at the smith's chest.

Neer ripped her sword from its scabbard and transported instantly behind the priest, sinking her weapon deep into his back and through his chest. Blood spurted from the wound and painted the family in red. The priest gasped as she twisted the sword, feeling the rip of his organs.

Neer pulled his head back. Solid black overtook the prominent teal of her eyes. An angry, satisfied whisper left her lips as she warned, "Send the Divines my regards."

She pulled her sword from his body, and the knights charged. Her gaze moved to the family, who stared at her in horror and rage. She was crushed by their anger. The heavy clank of metal armor filled the silence as the knights drew nearer.

Neer took one last look at the family who cast hateful glares at her, and then she closed her eyes and disappeared.

EXCITED FOR MORE?

The Forbidden Realms, the second installment in this six-part epic fantasy adventure, is available now!

As many of you know, self-publishing can be *very* hard! I do *everything* on my own, and while I have some help along the way, the most successful authors are those who have a loyal fanbase and lots of reviews on GoodReads and Amazon!

If you would, please take a moment to leave a review or rating. It helps more than you know.

Sign up for the email newsletter and be the first to know about special projects, new releases, events, and giveaways!

Be sure to follow H.C. Newell on
Facebook and Instagram!

hcnewell.com

About the Author

H.C. Newell is a Nashville-based epic fantasy author. She started writing screenplays as a child, and that passion for creating stories grew into a love of fiction. In 2014 she started her novel series and quickly realized that the adventures and lore of an epic fantasy world was her calling. It was then that she devoted all her time, passion, and love to create the world and characters of Fallen Light.

When not writing, H.C. enjoys hiking, photography, playing video games, and spending time with her niece and nephews.

H.C. has a little sister, Heather, who holds the namesake of the undead after she refused to read any of the early drafts. Don't mess with authors, kids. They can – and will – name the zombies after you.

For more information about H.C. Newell
and the Fallen Light series, please visit:
www.hcnewell.com

Acknowledgements

I would like to thank my husband, who has always encouraged me to keep going even when I wanted to give up, has read through every draft (there were at least seven of the first book alone), and supported me when I spent hours every day writing my story.

I love you more than words can say.

To my cousin Nikki and friend Keith. You have both made this series possible. A big thank you to my parents for always encouraging me to follow my dreams and to never give up. To my sister for providing me with an evaesh word for my zombies, and for helping me with some editing.

Author S.L. Barrie was a major help in reading my novel before publication and giving me incredible feedback.

A huge thank you to artist Thea Magerand for creating the exact cover I had in mind, and for being such an incredible person.

To everyone that has been part of this journey and helped me make this dream come true:

From the bottom of my heart,
Thank you.

This glossary is meant to be read after *the completion of the novel. It contains all characters, references, and places visited throughout the novel.*

Aenwyn...............	See *Numera*
Ahn'Clave............	Ancient race of evae that disappeared centuries ago; previous inhabitants of Anaemiril
Anaemiril.............	Ancient cave system that spans the reaches of Laeroth
Arnemaeus............	See memory shards
Arun..................	A rare magical receptacle holding powerful energy
Avelloch Líadrindel...	Evaesh assassin; Ahn'clave lineage
Azae'l.................	Unknown person who Klaud and Avelloch seek to save from a deadly curse
Bael	Slang term for demon lover
The Blades...........	See *Shadow Blades*
Brenavae..............	Evaesh term meaning brother
Broken Order Brotherhood	An organization meant to dismantle the Order of Saro; also known as The Brotherhood
Centry	Devolved evae that were once imprisoned by the ancient ahn'clave
Child of Skye.........	Label used by the Order of Saro in regard to Vaeda Vindagraav
Circle of Six	Collective name for the six Divines of the Order of Saro
Creatures of Darkness..............	Manifestations of dark energy from the deceased
Delvine...............	Semi-aquatic humanoids that live in the waters surrounding the island nation of Erasin
Dreled.................	Therianthrophy halflings
Dren...................	Feline creatures of darkness
Drimil.................	Evaesh term meaning magic user
Ebbard.................	Stage name of Loryk Vaughan
Elf	Human slang for evae

GLOSSARY

Erolith..............	The world of which Laeroth resides
Evae.................	Official race name of the elves
Everett Mountains...	Mountain range along the coast of Llyne
Fench................	Stone covered creature of darkness
First Blood...........	See *Ahn'Clave*
Fjord of Jokulsa......	Rival bard to Ebbard
Galacia..............	Small fishing village within Llyne
Gilbrich Willby.......	High ranking member of the Broken Order Brotherhood; friend to Nerana
Glass eye.............	A magical item meant to reveal hidden illusions
Havsgard.............	Mining village in the Everett Mountains
High Road............	A single road that connects through each human territory of Laeroth; also known as The Road
Kila..................	Evaesh curse for irritation
Klaet'il...............	Evaesh forest clan
Klaud Alwinör	Magic bearing evae; devoted friend to Azae'l
Knights of the Order.................	Men who were given to the Order as infants and tortured into becoming fierce warriors
Ko'ehlaeu'at	See *Tree*
Laeroth	Continent containing human and non-human territories; collective name of the human territories
Lanathess............	Evaesh slang for human
Llyne.................	Hold within the human-led territory of Laeroth; home of the Broken Order Brotherhood
Loryk Vaughan......	Famous bard; best friend to Nerana
Mange................	Hidden village in the Everett Mountains; known as Mange the Strange

GLOSSARY

Marq................	Enchantment used for protection of mystical objects or places
Meena'keen...........	Evaesh term meaning outsider
Memory Shards......	Magical stones meant to absorb or completely destroy one's memories
M'Yashk..............	Evaesh wine
The Nasir.............	Evaesh leader of the Klaet'il
Nerana Leithor........	Magic bearing human; heroine of our journey
Nhamashel............	A magical cave hidden deep within Anaemiril
Nizotl.................	God of Darkness; Divine of the Circle of Six
Numera...............	Goddess of Elements; Divine of the Circle of Six
Nyn'Dira..............	Evaesh territory; inhabited primarily by Evae
Nyx	Race of evae who hunt and feed on the living
Order of Saro.........	Religious faction that oversees the human-led territories of Laeroth; also known as The Order
Pale face..............	Derogatory slang for evae
Porsdur...............	Village within the hold of Llyne; central hub of the Broken Order Brotherhood
Ravinshire............	Hold within the human-led territory of Laeroth
Reiman Leithor......	Founding member of the Broken Order Brotherhood; adoptive father to Nerana
Revalor...............	See *glass eye*
Rhyl	Evaesh forest clan
Ria Vindagraav......	Vaeda's mother
Shadow Blades.......	Human mercenary group
Shared Wares.........	An armory within Porsdur
Smedlelund...........	Small lumber village in the hold of Llyne

GLOSSARY

Spectro-magnificator	A rare tool meant to manipulate light into a key for runes or other various enchanted items.
Spindra	Arachnid creatures of darkness
Styyr	Hold within the human-led territory of Laeroth
Sword and Sheath	A famed brothel
Tiaaven	Small evaesh wreath meant to attract peace
Thorne	A notorious bounty hunter with the Shadow Blades
Travaran	A magical potion meant for healing
Tree	Mystical trees which hold magical energy
Trials of Blood	A magical test meant to protect the cave of Nhamashel
Vaeda Vindagraav	Birth name of Nerana Leithor
Valde	A village within the hold of Llyne
Vleland	Evaesh territory; home of the nyx
Whispering Mountains	Mountain range dividing Ravinshire from Nyn'Dira
Wispers	Unknown creatures of darkness
Z'falendel	Evaesh book of runes
Zeke Vindagraav	Vaeda's father
Zy'mashik	Evaesh term for the ancient runes

Printed in Great Britain
by Amazon